THE
DARK
THAT
DWELLS

MATT DIGMAN   **RYAN RODDY**

Copyediting by Lisa Gilliam: Reedsy.com

Custom text ornaments by David Moratto:
www.DavidMoratto.com

Cover, interior, eBook design by The Book Cover Whisperer:
ProfessionalBookCoverDesign.com

Library of Congress Control Number: 2020901130

ISBN: 978-1-7342614-1-7 Paperback
ISBN: 978-1-7342614-2-4 Hardcover
ISBN: 978-1-7342614-0-0 eBook

Printed in the United States of America

FIRST EDITION

MATT

To my dad, thanks for all the stories.
Especially the ones that weren't
exactly true.

RYAN

For my parents, who continue to
support my many endeavors, and for
my dogs, who have faithfully
listened to this story read aloud more
times than any human ever will.

CONTENTS

PROLOGUE

SIDNA LET THE FIRE FADE FROM her fingers, and the light's reach retreated, leaving her cloaked in darkness.

Breathless, she fell back against the temple's rough, sandstone wall and cried out, her voice little more than a whisper. "Ronin?" She waited, but only the pounding of her heart replied, beating faster with each moment of silence.

Where is he?

She wiped the sweat from her forehead, sweeping aside a fallen strand of her loosely braided dark-brown hair, then pulled up the sleeve of her brown leather jacket. The faint green light from her wrist-mounted display resolved into a small two-dimensional map of the tunnels nearby. As the pathfinding software worked, multiple routes branched away from her, each seemingly identical.

She hesitated, unsure of her choice. "Pick one. Just pick one."

Ceramic pottery shattered in the distance, and her heart nearly burst from her chest. Terrified, she threw herself against the wall again, eyes closed tightly, waiting to die.

But she lived.

Ronin!

She pushed off and sprinted down the hall, knowing the Guardian would never be so subtle.

The end of the tunnel opened into a large chamber. Across the room, a bright white light disappeared through a doorway and around the corner, swallowed by a dark gullet.

Wait!

She made her way through the debris-filled chamber then rushed through the exit, slamming into the solid wall on the other side. She grabbed her shoulder and looked back, expecting to see the Guardian's crimson light, but there was only darkness.

On she ran, chasing after the wildly dancing light, always ahead of her but just out of reach. She flew through ancient rooms and long-forgotten halls, steadying the holstered pistol at her side. As she rounded the next corner, she stopped just in time to keep from crashing into the man ahead.

He held out his hand, palm down. "Hold up." He was out of breath, stifling a cough. "If we aren't more careful, we'll run face-first into that bastard."

Sidna struggled to catch her breath too; her vision blurred, and the world spun. She stared at the dusty stone floor beneath her boots and put her shaking hands on her knees for support. After several shallow, rapid breaths, she forced herself to breathe deeply, willing her heart rate to slow and her lungs to fill completely.

She looked up at Ronin.

His dark leather boots, green left-shoulder cape, and well-used white-and-green light armor marked him as an Aeturnian Ranger. There was an eagle painted on the armor of his left shoulder, diving downward, and a short, scoped rifle hung from his back by an old, worn strap.

Long years of travel were etched upon his face, and his black hair betrayed a hint of gray. Yet, in spite of the difference in their ages, it took him far less time to recover.

He peeked around the corner. When he turned back to her, he nodded grimly in reassurance. The bright white light from before shone from his forearm, and he swept the beam back down the opposite end of the corridor.

Sidna tensed. For a moment, she thought she'd seen the Guardian.
Just a shadow.

Somehow, she knew she'd always see it when she looked into the darkness, even if she did manage to escape it.

It was a living nightmare, relentless and unyielding, hide thick with plated armor. It was tall too, nearly half a meter more than Ronin. Black fog, pungent and sulfurous, emanated from the broiling heat within, adding to its already dreadful appearance. It had grasping, armored gauntlets full of hot plasma, and pulsating red light spilled out from between its plates, surging with each unnatural breath.

It was by far the most terrifying thing she'd ever seen.

"Okay." Satisfied they weren't followed, Ronin bent down to look into Sidna's eyes. He gently put his hand on her shoulder, smiled, and tilted his head toward the other end of the corridor. "There's another side chamber that way. Let's get inside and catch some air."

She nodded and stood. "Yeah. Air is good."

They jogged into the chamber. It appeared to be some sort of office or reading room, judging from the decayed scraps on the floor, scattered shelves, and rotted tables. Across the room, on the opposite wall from the entrance, an exit led further into the unknown.

She looked back. Unfortunately, there wasn't a door to close behind them.

Ronin looked around and seemed to settle on an empty shelf. With a few dull, wooden thuds, he moved it to cover the entrance. After a few more pushes and pulls, he backed away and walked across the room.

"Now." He dusted his hands together. "Let's get outta here."

She walked past him and looked up into his eyes defiantly. "You can't be serious. I'm not leaving until—"

He raised his hand. "We're leaving. We didn't plan on that . . . thing."

"If we go now, we came for nothing."

"We can always come back."

She put her hands on her hips. "The way back will have moved by then. Do you have any idea how much this cost?"

He stepped forward. "More than our lives? You can't come back if you're dead."

She sighed and looked down. "Fine. But you're paying half next time."

"Gladly." He opened a small panel on his armlet and tapped a few keys.

The device's speaker sounded a pleasant, two-note tone that lingered in the air. In front of him, the soft blue light resolved into a flat square map. The temple's network of tunnels and chambers spread out, and a small, flashing red dot marked Ronin's current location.

Sidna moved to his right side and went to one knee. One of her boots was untied, and her gray, tight-fitting flight pants were riding up her leg.

As she adjusted her clothing, Ronin reached under his left arm and grabbed the edge of his cape. He pulled it forward to obscure some of the light from the hologram. "Okay. That's us there." He nodded toward the dot with his head. "Hmmm. I think this corridor leads to the last intersection on this floor. Past that, if we make our way to—"

He was cut short as a huge black mass tore through the wall where the entrance used to be. Blood-red light flared under its impossibly dark armor, spreading throughout the room.

The Guardian bellowed a strange, otherworldly chorus in its deep, resonating voice.

Sidna shook herself from her paralyzing fear and ran as fast as she could for the exit. She could feel the creature's grasp at her back; she knew its fingers were about to take her.

Instead, she felt Ronin's palm through her jacket, shoving her into the passageway. She stumbled, and when she was back on her feet, they ran.

A deafening wave of sound came from behind as the Guardian burst into the hall. Billowing smoke flowed into the space before it, red glow pouring through.

Ronin spun around and planted his right knee on the stone floor, scoped rifle suddenly in his hands. Staccato muzzle flashes lit the corridor brilliant white, and the barking sounds of the rifle echoed down the hall. Eight shots later, the last casing ejected from the rifle, hit the wall, and bounced to the stone floor with a hollow, metallic sound.

Sidna watched in horror as the monster strode through the smoke unharmed. The armored plates on its arm stood up like hair on an angry animal, and the light spilling through grew more intense. Raging fire formed in its rising hand.

Ronin grabbed Sidna's shoulder and threw her to the floor. Searing heat followed a bright flash as the small flare of energy flew overhead. The end of the corridor exploded, showering them with rubble. Through her blurred vision, she saw Ronin calling out to her, though she could barely hear him over the ringing in her ears. When she could breathe again, the scents of ozone and burning hair filled her nose.

She took one last look at the monster then hurriedly spun to her belly. With help from Ronin, she scrambled to her feet then ran away from the Guardian toward the hole in the wall. They leapt over the pile of rubble and, surprisingly, landed in a new passageway.

Ronin stopped and pulled a smooth, silver disk from a pouch on his belt. After a few quick twists of its outer surface, the disk produced a low, intermittent *beep*. He tossed it back through the hole, and they ran to the right, down the corridor they had just discovered. After a few seconds, Sidna felt the shockwave, and small pieces of stone rained down from the ceiling.

Ronin shined his light back down the hall, revealing the pile of broken stone that had collapsed into the opening. He tapped her shoulder. "Come on!"

They turned and ran again, weaving through the winding passages until Ronin signaled for her to wait. Completely drained of energy, she stopped, crossed her forearms against the nearest wall, and pushed her forehead against them. She wanted to fall down but somehow managed to stand.

Pulled again by a tug on her jacket, she reluctantly jogged to a nearby room. Once they were inside, Ronin turned off his light and quietly edged along the wall toward the opposite end of the room.

Sidna saw it too. "Is that sunlight?"

Ronin looked back. "Yeah. And maybe a way out."

They moved around the wall and through the next room, where they found a massive cathedral.

Wide stone columns ran through the center in two rows, going on as far as she could see. A wide, faded red carpet ran down the length between the columns, with matching tapestries on the walls. They bore the image of a robed corpse with a white, skeletal face. It held a curved rod with a long, crescent-shaped blade in its bony hands.

Stone benches sat in evenly spaced rows. Along the tops of the stone walls, there were high rectangular fenestrations, letting in just enough sunlight to see.

It was morning on Veridian.

We made it!

They jogged to the area of the columns and took cover behind one of them. Sidna reached up to her arm. When her fingers came away, they were wet with blood.

"Let me help." Ronin pulled his cape up from behind him then unsheathed his tech-knife from the scabbard on his chest. With the humming blade, he cut away a thin strip of the green cloth then motioned toward her injury.

She removed her jacket and tossed it to the floor, noticing its collar was matted with blood.

Ronin tied the cloth around the upper part of her arm. She winced and sucked in hard. With a start, she realized that underneath the blood, the iridescent metallic patterns of her implanted *viae* were visible.

She turned to hide the markings, but Ronin grasped her arm. He looked up into her eyes and gave her a knowing grin.

He knew the whole time.

She smiled back.

And he doesn't care.

Ronin suddenly pushed past her. "Wait here." He pulled his rifle and put his back to the nearest column, edging around the surface.

She turned. "What is it?"

"I'm not sure. For a second, I thought—" He gasped and spun away from the column. He tried to raise his rifle but wasn't fast enough.

Sidna screamed, watching helplessly as he rose from the floor, lifted by the black hand around his neck.

Even in the glow of dawn, the Guardian was no less terrifying; its smoke and night-black armor seemed to devour the morning's light.

It stared into Ronin's eyes dispassionately as the Ranger struggled to wrench free of its grip, boots kicking wildly above the floor. As he fought, the beast's other hand grabbed him near his midsection, rotating him horizontally.

Sidna ran forward. "No!"

In the bloody blur of movement that followed, Ronin died horribly, one half of him flung to the left and the other to the right.

She tried to scream again, but she couldn't make a sound. Her hands trembled, gripping her pistol as the hulking mass turned toward her, red light flaring from its empty eyes. Terror took her as the monster started to lumber forward with its slow, steady gait. She stumbled backward and fell, and the pistol skipped away on the stone floor beside her.

Past the gun, she saw her fallen protector, his face mercifully turned away.

Ronin . . .

She turned back to the creature as it extended its arm toward her. Ronin's reassuring smile flashed in her mind's eye.

Alone again . . .

Cold anger replaced her fear.

Always alone.

The monster's smoke flowed forward, but before the substance could reach her, it swirled away, shooting back toward its source. The metallic lines and symbols of Sidna's *viae* surged with blue light as she raised her arms before her.

The Guardian seemed confused, curiously watching the churning fog, no longer under its control. Roaring wind swept the gas around violently, and the air crackled with electric intensity.

"*Die.*"

Sidna's furious storm buffeted the beast, and as the cathedral's stone walls and columns collapsed around her, she fueled the tempest with all her rage.

CROSSROADS

BLOWING WIND TROUBLED THE COURTYARD'S shallow standing water as Fall moved through it, studying its surface.

I know it's here.

Heavy raindrops spattered against his light metal armor as he walked. Multiple forks of lightning streaked across the cloud-filled sky. Booming thunder followed the display, deep rumblings loud enough to suppress the sounds of footfalls behind him.

Without warning, an arm, cold and wet, shot around his neck. He choked as the vice tightened, pressure building inside his skull.

This one's strong.

He vied for leverage, slowly sliding his boot back until it lodged against the other man's shoe.

There.

Fall lifted and drove his boot down on top of the man's foot. As the grip loosened, he twisted his torso then jammed his armored elbow into the attacker's ribs, feeling the satisfying crunch of fracturing bone. He seized the arm and flipped the man over his shoulder, slamming him into the solid stone below.

To Fall's surprise, a hidden blade sprang from the man's wrist. He quickly pushed the arm away, and the weapon's deadly edge careened along the silvered metal of his breastplate. He retreated, flowing into a defensive stance as the attacker rolled and rose from the water. Though it seemed to pain him, the injury hadn't left the man as hobbled as it should have.

Fall breathed deeply, taking his surroundings in and settling himself within them.

Be mindful. Be where you are.

The smell of the surrounding forest, verdant, rode along a short gust of wind. Beautiful, high-pitched tones resonated from the hanging chimes nearby, and the wooden fortress creaked and moaned.

In the early hours after midnight, the shrouded moons barely revealed the other man's features. He shifted to Fall's left. Fall side-stepped to the right. They closed the circle as they maneuvered, sloshing through the ankle-deep water.

The man pivoted and rushed forward, dropping into a crouch as he spun low in a sweep. Fall tried to hop over the leg, but it caught the bottom of his boot. He stumbled and fell, managing to push away just as the other man's heel crashed down into the water.

They both came to their feet, and the man lunged forward. Fall deflected the incoming blow then pulled the wrist forward as he delivered a swift backfist to the vulnerable armpit.

The man reached for his twice-punished thorax. Fall took the advantage and pushed him away then quick-drew the sword from behind his lower back. Before his opponent could recover, he plunged the blade between two ribs, piercing the man's heart.

He dislodged the bloody sword, and the dying man fell away without a sound.

Be faster.

Fall sheathed his sword and walked a few paces beyond the body. The water level had risen. The intensity of the rainfall had increased during the fight, enough that it was becoming difficult to see.

He opened a leather pouch on his belt and retrieved his hunter-green bandana. Pulling it around his brow, he tied it into a knot behind his head, leaving the two ends to hang down over his upper back. The cloth was already soaked, but it served to keep his damp, dark-brown hair out of his face.

He heard splashing. Two men approached from the darkness ahead.

They wore loose black robes, and one of them had his hair up in a knot. He wore a curved steel sword at his side. The other had a shaved head, holding a similar sword up high, point facing forward.

Fall tapped his left middle and ring fingers onto the palm of his glove twice then held pressure. The long holster on his left leg split into two halves with the smooth sounds of well-oiled machinery. A firm leather grip rotated into place horizontally between the two halves.

He reached down, took hold of the grip, and pulled straight up. With a jerk of his arm and the whir of servos, his charcoal-gray mechanized bow unfolded to a length of one-and-a-half meters. On either side of the grip, two small cams rapidly spun, and the loose bowstring snapped taught.

"Killer." The casing on his back opened in response to his verbal command.

An arrow shifted up from the quiver. He reached up and took it then nocked it to the bowstring. He drew back, took aim, and released.

The arrow flew, embedding into the right eye of the man with the shaved head. Its spinning head drilled deep, dropping him before he could scream.

Enraged, the other swordsman rushed forward. Fall placed the bow over the holster and pushed down. It retracted and folded automatically while the mechanism closed upon itself, back into its original configuration.

His right hand was already on the grip of his sword, and as the bow holster closed, he drew the blade.

The man's steel sword shot upward. He swung again and again as Fall parried the blows in a rapidly shifting dance.

Frustrated, the man pressed forward to meet blades. They both pushed, staring each other in the eyes.

Without warning, a blade sprouted from the man's wrist, darting for Fall's throat. He tumbled backward, and the unbalanced warrior flew over him. They both spun, returned to their feet, and backed away.

Nice try, but I've seen that trick before.

Moonlight caught on their blades with a flash as the clouds parted. Fall ran his palm over the fuller of his blade, pulling the sword into a ready position. He squeezed the grip, feeling the letters of its ancient engravings.

Now it ends.

The man attacked. Fall moved to the right as the opposing sword swung down. When the blade rapidly shifted back upward, he met it with his own and pushed it away. The sword slashed at his stomach, but he spun away, untouched.

As he recovered, the man came again, swinging his blade from low to high. Fall planted his feet and brought his own blade down to intercept it.

Got you.

He pulled up, riding along the blade, and slashed at the man's neck.

Blood and water spread in an arc through the air, and the man's hand went to his open wound. A moment later, the curved sword fell to the water, soon followed by the one who'd dropped it.

Fall took a few deep breaths, sheathed his sword, and resumed the search.

Now where's that figurine?

He took a step then paused in disorientation. The sky went completely white, then the horizon, then the trees, all moving toward him, accelerating.

He looked up and spun around, hands spread wide. "Oh come on. I was almost done."

The rest of the setting vanished then went completely black.

The pseudarus unit opened with a hiss. Fall removed the bulky, wired helmet from his head and held it in his lap.

I can still smell the trees.

He climbed out and took a few easy, controlled steps. Before long, the dark, musty room began to feel more real than the simulation.

He stretched then walked to the small locker in the corner and opened it. His gear, identical to the virtual substitute, waited inside.

First, he donned the polymer-fiber, charcoal-gray combat suit then stepped into his leather boots, armored in the front with leather straps that flared out behind.

He fixed the silver, segmented armor over his suit—chest, shoulders, elbows, and knees. On each pauldron, a burnt-orange fox sat on a diamond-shaped field of hunter-green with a contrasting gray outline, thick tail curled around it.

He tied his forearm guards snugly into place. They were made of the same metal, but hunter-green in color, continuing up just past his elbows where they faded to orange. The backs of his gray fingerless gloves were armored with the green metal as well, padded and flexible.

His gray belt came together with a central silver clasp and held a few formed leather pouches. They contained supplies for repairs and survival as well as materials for his arrows.

He attached the mechanized bow holster, green with two orange stripes near the top, to the belt and fastened its other strap around his left thigh. He slung the high-tech quiver, painted just like the bow holster, over his back and secured it. After it all felt right, he knelt down and picked up his sword and scabbard.

The sword's straight, flattened cross guard was silvered like the blade, and a small matching metal ring was attached to the base of the pommel. He stood up and held it behind his lower back as he fastened it to his belt. Two lock-points engaged, affixing the scabbard.

He grasped the hilt and pushed forward with his palm, ensuring the lock-point tethers would extend. Once the scabbard lay parallel to his body, he released the sword, and the tethers retracted, returning the weapon to its original position behind his back.

Lastly, he tied his thin hunter-green scarf around his neck, the furthest part of it transitioning to burnt-orange.

He moved, testing his mobility, reaching for each weapon and tool to make sure the fit was right. Satisfied, he left the small room through its automatic hatch.

The pseudareum was a collection of suites. Each contained a locker, changing area, equipment rack, and the pseudarus unit itself.

The machines resembled large black eggs, standing in the rear of each small suite. Through manipulation of the mind and senses, the pseudarus allowed a user to experience simulations as if they were almost entirely real.

The area between the suites was a dimly lit corridor with holographic advertisements for new programs. Everything from starfighter cockpits to partially censored sex scenes played through their demos. Customers clustered around each display, eager to find new thrills and experiences.

Fall activated the wall-mounted display next to his suite. He selected his session and looked through the data.

"Insufficient virtua." He sighed as the screen returned to its home status.

If this job doesn't work out ...

From somewhere nearby, a woman called his name. "Mister Arden! Is Fall Arden here?"

He could barely see past the other patrons, so he leaned this way and that as people shuffled past him. He stepped over bundled cables on the floor that ran through the hall, trying not to bump anyone with his scabbard.

"Fall Arden?"

He was getting closer. He kept weaving and finally broke through, dodging one final person who crossed his path.

An attractive woman with long, almost-brown blonde hair gathered neatly above her neck turned toward him. She was tall and fit, probably in her mid- to late twenties.

She wore a uniform, a form-fitting jumpsuit made of blue-gray cloth, padded on the shoulders and zipped up the center. There was a white mortar-and-pestle with black outlines sewn onto the left shoulder, and her last name was embroidered on a patch near her left upper chest.

Hansen.

He looked up into her sea-green eyes and held out his right hand. "Fall Arden."

"Oh, good." She smiled, shoulders relaxing as she took his hand. "Commander Hansen." Her accent had the slight hint of a Runian drawl, one he hadn't heard in a long time.

"Is something wrong?" Fall asked.

"No, everything's fine. I was in the area, so the captain asked me to get you."

"Get me?"

"The departure time's been moved up. We have to go now." Her eyes went from his face, to his armor, and then back up again. She smiled. "That is, if you're done playing your game."

He smiled back, though somewhat less friendly. "*Training.*"

Hansen looked past him, and he followed her eyes to the image. A woman lay out on a sandy beach, arching her back as the surf rolled in over her thighs.

Commander Hansen nodded sarcastically. "Intense regimen."

Fall looked down then smiled again. "Hey, never know what I'll run into out here. Best to always be prepared."

She turned, smiling over her shoulder as she led the way to the pseudareum's exit. "And here I thought the Frontier was this *big bad* place."

Fall followed her, adjusting a strap on his left forearm. "Only if you go out alone."

She walked up to the exit hatch, and it opened. She held out her hand, motioning for him to go first. "Well then. I guess it's good you have *me.*"

Crossroads Station's promenade was crowded, busy as always. And though Fall hadn't been there in over a year, nothing had changed. It was still a strange mix of juxtaposed cultures, most of them civilized. Yet even with their differences, almost everyone behaved, unwilling to lose the privilege to come aboard. The station was the last stop coming or going, located right on the wavering line between Fathom and Frontier.

Along each side of the wide, angular path, a multitude of open-faced shops comprised a bazaar. Neon signs and bright lights enticed customers, while flamboyant entrepreneurs and dancing holograms called potential customers to see the wares. There was a constant drone of noise from conversation, advertisements, and intricate musical jingles.

Off to one side near a particularly busy shop, a lanky man in flowing, tattered robes peddled to one of the shortest men Fall had ever seen. That short man's children pulled at his shirt, bouncing up and down while he tried his best to move on.

The tall man handed his shiny black cube to the short man's son, and it morphed into a flittering butterfly; the little boy smiled broadly as he looked up.

His sister snatched it away, and it transformed into a snarling dragon with black, fiery breath; she smiled triumphantly in contrast with the little boy's disappointment.

Realizing his children were enthralled, the short man scowled and tapped the device on his wrist.

The tall man looked down to his own device and nodded with a knowing smile. He turned to the next customer, already moving on as the short man hurried his children along.

The predator and his unhappy prey.

"Wow." Commander Hansen looked around in wonder. "So many different people."

Fall nodded. "There's a lot of them, that's for sure."

She raised her eyebrows. "Not your thing?"

He shrugged. "Let's just say I won't be sad to go."

She seemed to mull that over. "I bet you've seen a lot. Must be hard to impress you."

"No, I'm surprised by things I see every day. I just prefer to be a little farther out from all of this."

She looked back ahead. "Yeah, I read your profile."

"I have a profile?"

She looked without turning her head. "It's part of my job to know who's coming on board."

"Anything interesting?"

She lifted the corner of her mouth. "Eh, pretty incomplete, actually. I know you're from somewhere on Valen. No criminal record. No real health issues. You just up and left the Fathom and haven't been back since."

"That pretty much covers it."

"Nothing big since then?" she asked.

He smiled wryly. "Criminal record needs updating."

She narrowed her eyes with a smile. "I'm serious."

He looked down as they walked. "I don't usually get so many questions on this type of job."

"Well, I've never met a real Aeturnian Ranger before. I've read about them, or seen the vids, but no one really knows anything about you guys."

Fall nodded. "We keep to ourselves. The job attracts a certain kind of person."

"Yeah, I could see that." She walked in silence for a few moments. "Maybe later, if you wanted to, you could tell me more."

Fall looked up, down the path. "Maybe . . ."

A domesticated strahg drew his attention, lumbering ahead of its master with enough mass on its back to attract a small moon.

The dark-green animal moved on all six legs in a slow, smooth rhythm that never jostled its burden. Its long neck swayed back and forth as it walked, and its rounded shoulders went up and down like sluggish pistons.

The garishly dressed lady walking beside its undulating tail seemed more than satisfied with herself and her luggage. She saw Fall staring and turned up her nose as she passed by.

What a nice lady . . .

As he and the commander continued, he let his view shift outside.

The wall of the promenade facing the exterior allowed a view outside. Ships moved to and from multiple docking ports along the hull. Small stars seemed to fly in as they grew larger and resolved into transports or luxury liners. Other ships pulled away and became tiny points of light before disappearing in a flash.

An annoyingly harsh voice rose to his left as he walked.

The proselytizing man wore a long, hooded white robe with a violet flame stitched onto the breast and waved his arms about flamboyantly. A small crowd had gathered to hear him.

The Elcosian priest claimed that his god, Elcos, would protect their souls from the gathering darkness. Elcos would bring the nations of the Fathom back into balance, and the arcanist witches, wherever they might be hiding, would be hunted and punished no matter how deep they fled into the Aeturnian Frontier.

The crowd nodded and affirmed the message overtly. Fall wondered if they really did agree or if they simply had to keep up appearances.

No one wants an Elcosian priest's attention. Who could blame them?

Fall and Commander Hansen passed into the food courts. The aromas of any number of foods mixed together. In particular, the smell of spicy kaba meat wafted by, and Fall remembered he hadn't eaten yet.

I wonder if she's hungry too. We might have time to . . .

"Olivia."

Fall shook himself from his thoughts. "I'm sorry?"

"Olivia Hansen. That's my name."

"Oh, Sorry. I was thinking about food. Nice to meet you . . . again."

"Didn't get a chance to eat today?"

"I had leftovers in my room." Fall stopped and looked up. "Which reminds me. Will I have time to get my stuff? I still need to pack." He frowned a little as he walked again. "I thought we were shipping out tomorrow morning."

She put her hands behind her back and shook her head. "We already moved your things. The captain didn't want any delays."

He watched his boots walk in rhythm on the multicolored panels of the Star-Walk. He looked up to her. "In your cargo bay?"

"In your new quarters." She smiled reassuringly. "Don't worry. You'll have plenty of time to get settled. The captain just wants to get going. You'll find out he's kind of . . . impatient."

"Hmmm. As long as your people got everything."

He stopped. "Um . . . " He caught up and walked backward ahead of her. "I don't suppose you found an animal with my things? A snake or maybe a tyk?"

She tilted her head. "No one mentioned any animals. Why do you ask?"

"No reason." He reached up and rubbed the back of his neck as he turned. "No reason at all."

Docking area 72-B was relatively empty.

Crews from a few ships went about their duties, checking and loading supplies near their docking ports. A few of the groups were in uniform, but none of them represented any major official military organization.

Military ships rarely entered the Frontier due to the Accord. Specifically, the Principality of Alidia and the Republic of Rune stayed clear. They'd fought some serious skirmishes near the border just over ten years before, and tensions remained high, but both nations knew any overt presence around Crossroads did more harm than good.

Rune. Alidia. Elcosians. Troubles I don't need.

He looked out through the docking ring's wall as they neared the ship.

The *Morning Rain* was a beautiful ship, elongated with gently flowing curves and a bow that formed a rounded nose. It wasn't large, with only five decks, but Fall realized it must be fast. Each of the four rounded corners of the stern housed a powerful engine.

Its profile was dotted with relatively small humps along the belly and back. It was technically a science vessel, without any real weapons. It had smooth dorsal and ventral fin-like projections that made it look like some kind of sea creature, and with its blue-gray coloring, it would have been right at home in an ocean. Its name was inscribed on the side along with the stylized comet of the Vaughan-Heighas Expeditions Corporation.

Not bad . . .

Fall and the commander passed through the station's inner and outer docking hatches, onto the ship's second deck, walking until they reached the first intersection. In cross section, the passages were like circles, flattened on top and bottom, curving gently. The lighting was soft and dim, emitters scattered along the walls and floors.

"Any chance I might stop by my quarters before I meet the captain?" Fall asked.

"Sure. I could show you the way."

"That's okay, I bet I can find it."

She shrugged. "Suit yourself. Your quarters are on deck three. Just ask the computer if you get lost. Room three-oh-eight." She pointed ahead. "Here's the lift."

They entered and rode up to the third deck together. As the doors opened, he turned toward her and smiled. "Thanks for the help, Commander."

She returned the smile. "No problem. After you get cleaned up, go to security for clearance. Then, head to the sick bay for your screening. After that, report to the bridge." She reached out and touched his arm near the elbow. "And one more thing. It's *Olivia*." She smiled as the lift doors closed, leaving him to stand alone in the corridor.

Huh ...

He looked both directions, but there weren't any hatches along the curved hallway. Blue lines went down each wall with a large number 3 spaced every few meters.

He looked up. "Computer?"

A pleasant, disembodied female voice responded from nowhere in particular. "Yes, Mister Arden. How may I assist you?"

"Can you help me get to room three-oh-eight?"

"Certainly, Mister Arden. Please follow the floor lighting to your destination."

Blue lights flashed along the center of the hallway floor in short pulses. He followed them around the curve, passing rooms 306 and 307, finally reaching 308.

The computer spoke as he stepped up to the hatch. "Welcome home, Mister Arden."

He thought about that for a moment.

I guess it is home, for now.

The hatch opened, and he stepped inside. To his surprise, all of his things were laid out neatly, better than he could have done himself.

He walked to the bed and picked up the nearest holophoto from the small nightstand. Above it, the three-dimensional images of him and his mentor, Thane, shook hands just after their final mission together.

He put the emitter back then stripped down and placed his combat suit into the automated cleaner near the bathroom. By the time he was out of the shower, it was clean, dry, and ready to wear.

It'd be easy to get spoiled on a ship like this.

Once he'd geared up again, he checked himself in the mirror. He didn't look half bad, though a full night's sleep might help with the dark circles forming under his eyes. There hadn't been much time for rest with all the travel.

He froze.

Hermes. How could I forget?

He walked back into the main part of his quarters.

"Hermes? Hermes, you better be in here."

He wasn't.

I'll kill him if he messes this up.

Fall took one last look around then left.

He wandered the third deck without any real plan. "Computer?"

Hermes liked to go where he pleased—that in itself wasn't an issue. The problem was, he also liked to *do* what he pleased.

Normally, Fall wouldn't mind, but this job was set to pay pretty well.

He wandered the third deck without any real plan. "Computer?"

"Yes, Mister Arden."

"I'm looking for someone. Well, *some thing*. A little of both, really."

"Could you rephrase the question, Mister Arden?"

"Not really." He sighed. "Has anyone on the ship reported anything strange? An animal or someone that doesn't belong?"

"Yes."

"Which one?"

"There is a request for assistance in the sick bay. The on-duty nurse has reported a loose animal."

"Great. Thanks."

"Of course, Mister Arden."

Fall took off jogging to the nearby lift. He used the panel inside to set the lift for deck two. When he arrived, he followed the markings that led to the sick bay.

The entrance was comprised of two large hatch doors, currently wide open. Inside, beds with medical displays and equipment lined the smoothly angled walls. There was a small operating suite to the rear and an office to the left.

On one of the stretchers, a woman hugged her knees to her chest, wide eyes rapidly scanning the ceiling. In the middle of the room, a man crouched low, staring up suspiciously, wielding some kind of pole in his hands. He looked ready to use it.

Fall stepped inside. "Hey."

They both started in surprise, and the woman almost fell from the table.

Fall looked up as he heard a crash and saw some cables rustle above. "There!" The woman pointed.

The man ducked down even farther and uttered a curse as some sort of small gray thing flew out from the cables and into the office. The man edged slowly toward the office with the trembling pole, ready to strike.

Fall raised his palms toward him and smiled. "Easy, I'll get it."

He walked to the office, stopping short as Olivia came out, almost bumping into him.

"Oh. Hey. Did you just see . . . well, anything?" he asked.

She looked back into the office then shook her head.

Her hair was down, drawn into a ponytail. She'd changed into casual clothing too—a T-shirt and short shorts. She walked past Fall, looking down and scratching her head as she slipped out the exit.

The man with the pole stood up slowly. "Doctor Hansen?"

Olivia didn't look back.

Fall leaned around the corner into her office. On the table, there was an active holophoto, showing Olivia and another woman smiling after a sporting event. In the picture, Olivia wore the exact same shirt and shorts.

Hermes . . .

Fall walked back into the sick bay. "Well, sorry, guys. Couldn't find it. Just sit tight. I'm sure help is on the way."

He walked out and looked around then cupped his hand to his mouth as he whispered loudly. "Hermes? Hermes!"

Olivia leaned around the corner toward the lift. She motioned for him to follow.

He looked to see if anyone else had seen, then went after her onto the lift.

When the doors closed, he crossed his arms. "You know, they might not like you busting up their sick bay."

She shrugged with a smile.

"Can't you behave this *one* time? Just for a few days?" Fall asked, frustrated.

The lift opened, and she turned toward his quarters. Fall followed her, walking inside his room as she entered.

She strolled over to the couch and lay down with her hands behind her head, a grin spreading on her face. Her form distorted and shifted, shrinking to the size of a house cat. In its place, a small, furry red imp appeared.

The devious creature's ears swept out behind him, long and pointy. He had wide and hyper eyes, a broad sharp-toothed grin, and a little protruding potbelly. "I totally had you."

Fall sat down on the bed. "No way. I knew it was you."

Hermes sat up. "So those were *my* legs you were staring at?" He made a kissing motion. "I'm flattered."

"You wish." Fall stood up. "Listen, you can't do this right now. We need this job."

Hermes rolled his eyes. "Yeah, we're broke, blah blah blah." He sat back against the cushion. "Tell you what. I'll behave on one condition."

"What's that?"

"Set me up with this doctor babe. She's smokin' hot."

Fall launched a pillow at him.

He dodged it. "Okay, okay. I'm just messin' with you. Relax."

Fall looked back to the hatch. "How'd you get in here, anyway? The computer should have stopped you."

"Please. That glorified calculator? Remember who you're talking to."

Fall scowled. "Don't mess with their systems, Hermes. They'll find you."

He looked off to the side and mumbled, "No promises."

Fall opened a pouch on his belt. "That's it. You're coming with me."

Hermes pleaded. "Aw come on, I'll be good, I promise."

Fall pointed to the pouch. "Inside."

"Fine." His image wavered again, and in its place appeared a silver cylinder, small enough to fit in the palm of Fall's hand. It floated across the room and settled into the pouch.

Fall closed it. "All right. Now stay in there until I say so."

His belt moved twice.

"Good." Fall walked out into the hall, shaking his head. "We have work to do."

SINS IN THE DARK

THE ALIDIAN DROPSHIP FELL TOWARD NIX, the winter moon. Engines screaming, it broke through the outer atmosphere, plunging into a deadly storm of gusting wind and freezing sleet.

Ban squeezed his chest straps, jaw muscles tightening as a thousand angry collisions assaulted the moaning hull. As he often did, he repeated the ancient Doanian Knight's Creed, hoping its words might suppress the growing tension in his mind.

Through dread den and lost land, hope endures. When kingdom crumbles and turns to dust, wisdom keeps. And in the darkest night of faith long forsaken, the light will forever shine.

Hope. Wisdom. Light.

"Hey, boss."

Ban opened his eyes. "Richards."

Richards sat up across from Ban and smiled. "You . . . look a little pale."

Ban swallowed, voice hoarse. "It's nothing."

"You sure? If you're nauseated . . . "

"I said I'm fine."

Becks leaned forward. "Rowan." Her smoky voice was quiet, yet firm. "Not now."

Ban turned his head slightly to see her.

Saira.

Like the rest of the squad, she was dressed in royal-blue, medium-grade powered armor. He could see the full curves of her lips, but her long, straight black hair hid her piercing brown eyes. Ruddy lighting from red lamps along the ceiling's edge darkened her already coffee-colored skin.

Ban looked back ahead.

Richards, the squad's rifleman and tech expert, was a lanky man with sharp, angular features. He was fair-skinned, with light blonde hair that swept back behind his ears. His nose was crooked from some fight in his youth.

His big mouth had gotten him into a lot of trouble in the past. Of course, it had probably gotten him out of just as much.

Richards sighed. "You'd think this was a funeral." He grinned and looked to his right at Tyr. "Am I right?"

Tyr, the squad's explosives expert, was a bulky, tall man. He had dark-brown skin and a smooth, shaved head. A rather nasty scar ran from his left eyebrow to his right bottom lip. He was fearsome in appearance, and Ban knew he could be when the need arose.

He held a small metal rod attached to a chain around his neck, shaped as if someone had taken both ends and twisted them in opposite directions. He squeezed it firmly and looked down with reverence.

Richards put his hands together. "Say a prayer for me?"

Tyr didn't respond but nodded, silent as always.

Becks leaned forward, elbow on her knee, looking up. "*Please*. There isn't a god out there who'd have you."

Richards leaned back, hands behind his head. "Lucky you. What'd Wolf be without *me*?"

Ban closed his eyes with the slightest of smiles. "For starters, we'd be focused."

"And bored . . . " Richards trailed off, picking at one of his armored gauntlets with the other.

They all went quiet then, sounds of ice, metal, and fire replacing conversation. After a few moments, the hatch near the fore of the dropship opened, and Lieutenant Garret entered, wearing his billed blue cap and earpiece. He was older than Ban by about twenty years, hair short and gray at the temples. His green, calculating eyes spoke of experience.

He took hold of a metal bar to steady himself. "We're approaching the drop site, Bond-Sergeant. Assemble your squad."

"Yes, sir. Wolf Squad, prepare for battle." Ban's straps retracted into the wall, seat folding away as he stood.

He checked the readiness of his chest plate, pauldrons, and upper limb armoring. The sharply angled, royal-blue, metal armor looked almost purple in the red light. His durable under-dressing was solid black, visible at the neck and joints. The armor of his legs and boots checked out as well.

He readied his light machine gun. The weapon was black, with royal-blue plating, about one meter long. It had a short stock, continuous with the trigger guard, an elongated narrow body with a short scope, and a thin barrel projecting out past the body. On the underside, a cylindrical canister fed the weapon its ammo.

Becks, Richards, and Tyr went through the same exercise, finishing around the same time.

Ban turned to his bond-corporal. "Becks?"

She looked at Richards and Tyr then nodded. "Solid."

He ran his free hand through his short black hair then looked into his helmet's reflective visor. His gray eyes were tired, his face almost as pale as Richards's.

I need more sleep.

He placed the helmet over his head. It sealed tight with a snap, and after a short boot sequence, the heads-up display appeared.

He cycled through the various modes with movements of his eyes and changes in his depth of focus. The vital signs of his squad, armor condition, power levels, a map, and mission objectives scrolled on and off of the HUD. He looked over the squad one last time as identifying information seemed to hover in the air next to them.

Becks inspected her sniper rifle, checking the moving parts and the magazine. Tyr gave one last kiss to the small, twisted metal pendant and tucked it away before picking up his rocket launcher. Richards looked up as he readjusted the material at his crotch.

He shrugged when he made eye contact with Ban. "What?"

Garret cleared his throat. "You've studied the briefing, so I won't waste time on the particulars. However, Lieutenant Holland has asked that I reinforce the mission *parameters*. Wolf Squad is to support Griffin Squad as they infiltrate the base. You are to provide an adequate distraction and cover, never interfering with Griffin's movements."

Ban looked up. "Holland can have all the glory he wants."

Garret shifted in place. "And he'll get it. He won't hesitate to step on anyone who stands in his way."

"Understood, sir. I know my place."

"He knows it too, Bond-Sergeant." Garret looked them over and nodded. "It's time."

The marines moved against the walls where their seats had been. Ban took his light machine gun from the rack near his seat, glad to have his suit's help with the weight. When the squad was in place, he hit the deployment button with his fist.

Cables fed down from openings above, and yellow strobe lights flashed. He reached up for his cable and grabbed it with his armored left hand, and a strip of lighting glowed yellow in a hexagon on the floor around him. The other marines were in position, so he hit the button again, and the hexagon began flashing on and off.

Garret reached up to his earpiece and looked down. He nodded once and looked back up. "Marines! Drop zone!"

Richards hurriedly pulled his helmet into place. "For Alidia!"

The lights shone green, and the hatches beneath them rapidly receded. Ban held on to his cable tightly as he fell into the blinding white below.

Hope. Wisdom. Light.

"Move!" Ban sprinted for the tree line.

Snow fell, and the powder whispered under his boots as he ran. He bounded toward a short snowbank.

He looked up as the dropship retracted the cables. The ship had segmented blue heavy armor with swept-back wings, twin engines, and a narrow, blunt nose. The engines flared as it sped away just above the treetops, bending the trunks forcefully as it did, snow swirling away into the air.

Garret radioed in. "Wolf, move to waypoint alpha and set up. Holland and his boys are expecting you."

"We shouldn't disappoint his royal highness," Becks said as she hopped a fallen snow-covered tree.

Richards jumped after her. "He might tell his cousin."

Tyr remained silent.

Ban followed after them. "Forget about him. Keep it tight, and let's get this done."

Before Holland gets someone killed.

Wolf Squad jogged for a little over a kilometer, moving relatively slowly. Some areas between the trees were deep, sometimes over a meter, and without terrain warnings from their suits, they might have fallen right in.

After they cleared the forest, the listening post came into view. Its walls were camouflaged with a broken-up design of white and gray, making it difficult to see from a distance. Thick snow blanketed the edges of the base, and frost covered the faces of the walls, further obscuring its outline.

Richards spoke after a few moments of silence. "Think they saw us?"

A hail of gunfire from atop the compound's nearest wall was the answer. Snow and splinters of wood flew up in bursts nearby.

Ban keyed the comm. "Spread out and return fire. Keep the attention on us."

Becks was already sprinting away, deeper into the forest. "Roger that."

Ban knew she was used to thinking independently. Her days as a mercenary marksman had taught her to move fast and worry about details later.

He checked his map on the heads-up display as he knelt behind a large stone. The topographical data suggested a ridge in the direction Becks was headed. He placed a waypoint there.

She responded. "Already on it, but it's sweet of you to hold my hand."

He smiled as he added additional markers. "Richards, go here. Tyr, there. I'll cover."

Ban recalled the briefing he'd received before the mission. The enemy compound was shaped like a pyramid with a flat top, having a square base with flattened vertices. The walls were about ten meters high but could vary in height in a few places. Guard posts were located along the structure at the vertices, and there were sensor dishes and radio equipment near the highest point. The interior contained multiple bays, offices, and labs.

Wolf Squad was approaching from the southeast side. The main base entrance was on the north side. A vehicle bay was located near the southeast corner on the south wall, and a well-plowed road led away from the bay and into the forest. There was a fortified hatch near the corner of the south and east walls that led inside.

The base was disguised as an outpost, but in reality it was a clandestine Runian science station, illegally located just inside the Frontier.

He watched as Becks's map marker indicated she was moving into position.

She radioed in. "Ban, you have one enemy eyeball on you."

A red, diamond-shaped marker appeared on the map where an enemy sniper was located.

"Go ahead, Becks."

There was a momentary pause before the report from her sniper rifle echoed throughout the forest. The red diamond disappeared.

"Down. Relocating." Her radar marker was already moving away from her firing position.

Ban ordered the rest of the squad in. "Now!"

Richards and Tyr moved fast and low as Ban came around the stone with his light machine gun. He unleashed a steady barrage along the top of the nearest wall. When he stopped, the wall was pocked with holes, and there wasn't a man left standing that he could see.

He brought the gun down and knelt back behind the stone. A quick look at the map showed that Richards and Tyr were near their waypoints.

Becks reported. "In position. Marking targets."

New markers appeared on Ban's map. Red chevrons marked the combatants, but there were fewer than he'd anticipated.

Where are the rest?

Two quick bursts of static on the radio let Ban know Tyr was in position.

"Richards here. No sign of enemy movement on the right flank."

Ban watched carefully. Someone moved inside the fortified guard tower at the nearest vertex.

He placed a target marker on the tower. "Tyr, let him have it."

Tyr rose up with his rocket launcher and prepared to fire, but before he could, there was a massive explosion on the other side of the base.

Richards chuckled. "Um, Tyr. I think you missed by *just* a bit."

Not good.

Ban slammed his fist down on the stone. "Lieutenant."

Garret responded. "I saw it. Stay on the line, Bond-Sergeant. I'll raise the *Talon*."

The explosion was an ominous sign. If Griffin Squad's approach had been noticed, Lieutenant Holland would be furious.

Tyr fired upon the guard tower, and it bloomed in a shower of metal and glass.

"ARN *Talon*, this is Garret. A large explosion has been detected away from Wolf Squad's area of fire. Please advise."

A young female officer responded dispassionately. "Lieutenant Garret, Griffin Squad is under heavy enemy fire. The diversion was unsuccessful. Mission objectives have been modified. Wolf is to proceed to the nearest point of entrance, infiltrate the base, and secure the target."

Garret sighed. "Understood, *Talon*. Proceeding with new objectives."

Ban pulled up his map. Tyr was about thirty meters from the wall.

Garret's voice was tense. "Bond-Sergeant, fix this. *Now*."

"Yes, sir." He looked back to the map. "Tyr, you're on this entrance." He placed a marker. "Richards, watch the right flank. Becks, bring down anyone stupid enough to raise his head. I'll move to the left flank and advance. It's too quiet on this side. Keep your eyes open."

Ban scanned for movement along the flank as he moved.

The forest was completely silent except for distant, muted sounds of gunfire. Nothing moved, except for a short gust of wind that swirled some snow around a clear spot under a tall tree.

The limbs fanned out in two rows as they spiraled up the tree. Along each branch, pointed indigo leaves bristled in the wind. His eyes were drawn further up.

Above the treetops, the red desert world of Horvis dominated the sky. It was a xeric, waterless world with no redeeming features except for its moon, Nix.

A drop of blood, hanging over my head.

His thoughts drifted for a moment as he stared off into the forest around him.

Blood and acid . . .

He came to his senses and shook his head; he didn't have time for regret. He resumed his slow sweep and, satisfied that the left flank was clear, moved to the base's wall.

Richards had also made it to the wall, and Tyr was already setting up the mole on the fortified entrance. Once he had it attached, he backed away.

Ban searched the tree line. "Becks, how are we looking?"

"All clear, Ban." Her voice was calm and measured.

He motioned to the entrance. "Do it."

The mole device began to spin rapidly with a scraping sound. The hot, molten locking mechanism fell from the rear of the device, and Tyr moved to the entrance. He placed a magnetic grip on the hatch then tossed another to Richards, who did the same.

Ban nodded, and they pulled in opposite directions, causing the hatch to split down the central seam. Ban moved up and tossed in a small sphere, which rolled and came to a stop on the other side.

Small-arms fire erupted from inside. He checked his map and signaled to Tyr. Tyr pulled up his launcher, leaned, and fired a rocket through the entrance.

Ban followed behind the rocket and unleashed a heavy barrage of fire from his light machine gun. Tyr and Richards moved in, flanking him and firing—Richards with his assault rifle and Tyr with his heavy pistol.

Ban moved to the nearest outcropping of a wall in the hallway and waited for the smoke and dust to settle. He checked the map; no targets remained.

He moved to retrieve the device. A hologram had been projected from the sphere, taking the appearance of an armored marine running down the hall, cycling over and over. It had the added benefit of a sensor device that relayed target positions to his heads-up display.

They advanced as a squad, and after moving further into the room, Ban saw the results of their work. The room was set up as a transition area between the inner base and the snow outside.

A table and a set of lockers had been turned over and used for cover. Debris from a partially ruined wall littered the rough floor, and a few small fires burned. Behind the makeshift cover, soldiers in winter gear lay dead on the floor.

Tyr moved to the next hatch and once again set up the mole. After breaking through, he forced the hatch with his armored hands.

There was a small hangar on the other side. The lower level had vehicles—an armored transport of some kind and a few small, all-terrain types. The second level had a command room.

The squad slowly made their way to a set of stairs that led up. After climbing the stairs, they entered the enclosed room. Computer displays flashed on the desk inside, and nearby sat a steaming cup of brown liquid.

Ban moved into the room toward the desk, noticing an arm lying out to the side. He edged around the desk and saw a dead man, his eyes wide with surprise.

A pool of blood had spread along the floor, and a wound on the man's neck seemed to be the source. The blood wasn't yet dry.

This happened right before we arrived. The man had just sat down to his drink.

Richards peeked over Ban's shoulder. "Wow. Don't drink the coffee."

Ban shook his head. "Keep moving."

They continued to move through the second level toward another hatch that led farther into the base. That hatch was unlocked and stood open, and there was a bloody streak on the hatch's frame.

Ban moved through the hatch into the next corridor. Emergency lights rotated in the hallway, but otherwise it was dark. He switched to low-light mode, and his screen adjusted for the flashing lights.

The squad moved through the corridor slowly while checking each side hatch. Most were sealed, and one appeared to be an unremarkable storage closet filled with cleaning supplies. Every two meters, the hall had partitions that jutted out.

Ban took deliberate steps as he moved forward. He peeked around the next partition. It was clear. He moved ahead to the next and leaned out slightly to see around.

A small blur ran out along the floor, and Richards jumped back. Ban almost shot it before he recognized it—a tyk, the stupid rodents ubiquitous on most settled worlds. Harmless or not, the thing still had Ban's heart pounding after it squeezed through one of the slightly opened hatches.

Becks radioed in. "Ban. There's a squad of six combatants setting up outside your entrance hatch. Should I open fire?"

He keyed the comm in response. "Negative, contain only. Tyr, place charges on the first floor near the entrance of the vehicle bay. Richards, stay here and watch the rear. I'll go back to the control room. We're about to have company."

Richards moved to Tyr, and Tyr tossed him a couple of auto-turrets. The metallic, brick-shaped objects were perfect for ambush or point defense.

Richards moved to each side of the hall and affixed them on the walls near the ceiling. They unfolded and swept back and forth, tracking for targets.

Tyr jogged out of sight into the second level of the vehicle bay.

Ban tapped Richards on the shoulder. "Call if you need help."

"Oh, you'll be the first to know," Richards said as he walked away.

Ban grunted in reply and moved back down the hall. "Becks, update."

"They're moving through the hatch now. One man stayed behind. You have five enemies headed your way."

"Tyr?"

A double burst of static signaled that Tyr had placed the charges and was in position.

Now we wait.

Ban watched on his HUD as Tyr broadcast footage of the soldiers. Two of them had entered the vehicle bay and were cautiously searching. The other three couldn't be seen, most likely in the hallway.

Ban had set up his position below the window of the overlooking room. He raised up with his light machine gun and opened fire; both men went down. One lay still, but the other crawled for the hallway.

Two more men came to the edge of the entrance and shot at Ban. He ducked down. At the same time, more shots were heard from Richards's direction.

Richards reported. "Boss, I'm engaged. At least three, no four enemy combatants."

Broken glass fell on Ban's helmet as bullets ripped into the room. "Tyr, blow the charges and push any survivors to Becks. Becks, fire at will. Richards, I'm coming."

The charges exploded as Ban sprinted from the small room. He looked below, seeing smoke and fire near the lower-level entrance.

Tyr had his back to the wall, firing around the corner into the hallway that led outside. Ban kept running toward the battle on the second level.

As he entered the second-level hallway, Richards fired blindly from cover behind a partition. The wall-mounted mini-turrets tracked as they fired further down the hall, into the darkness of the room beyond. Suddenly, a flash of light came from the end of the hallway, and Ban's HUD distorted, going dark.

Richards jumped back. "Ah! EMP grenade!"

With the loss of power, Ban's suit automatically opened his helmet's faceplate. He shuffled behind a partition on the opposite side of the hallway from Richards.

He pulled a flare from his belt, twisted it, and tossed it down the hallway. Bright green light ignited in the hall. He sneaked a peek around the corner, but he didn't see movement.

A panicked scream echoed from the room at the end of the hall, and several gunshots lit the room briefly. Ban watched as a man in light snow armor walked into view. Richards popped out and gave the man a three-round burst from his assault rifle. He dropped without a sound.

Ban and Richards looked to each other in question; the man hadn't even tried to raise his rifle.

A stammering voice called out from the room ahead. "D-don't shoot!"

After a nod from Ban, he and Richards came out, weapons drawn, and moved to the entrance. Ban kicked the flare into the room, revealing a man standing over the bodies of several soldiers.

The man walked forward with his hands raised, a blood-covered knife in his left hand. In his right hand he held a clear canister. Something jagged and black floated inside.

The terrified man tossed the knife to the floor. "They tried to kill me."

Unruly, mussed hair covered most of his face. He wore a white coat, slacks, and black shoes.

Ban saw another knife sticking up from the back of the soldier that Richards had shot. "Why would your own men try to kill you?"

"Because I was trying to save *this*." He held up the canister.

Ban lowered his gun. "What is it?"

The man clutched it close to his chest. "It's *everything*. The reason for this whole installation." He took a step back. "Who are you?"

Richards grabbed him by the coat and pushed him toward the vehicle hangar. "Your new best friends."

As Ban returned to the hangar, a chime from his suit let him know his systems had been repaired. He flicked his fingers and the faceplate closed.

The radio came back online. "—assist! We're getting killed out here!" It was Lieutenant Holland's voice. He sounded unnerved and more than a little angry. "Morgan, you moron! Are you reading me?"

Ban responded. "Yes. We have the target, and—"

"I don't give a damn what you have, *peasant*. Get your squad out here now! Do you—"

Ban cut him off and switched back to the squad channel. "Becks, report."

She sounded tense. "Ban, there's a lot happening on the other side of the base. Should we help?"

"I'm on my way to you. Are you clear?"

"Affirmative. Two targets emerged from the hatch and tried to run, but no one gets past me."

I believe it.

He pulled up his map and found Holland's location. He placed a new marker, gamma, at the spot where the road came closest. "Becks, I'll meet you near Holland." He looked to the map again. "All right, the rest of you load up."

He shouldered his gun and moved into the control room overlooking the first floor. With a few button pushes, the hangar's main doors began to open. Sunlight and snow fell through the opening along with a strong gust of wind. He headed to the stairs as Richards started down, motioning for the captive to go next.

Ban studied the engineer as the strange man made his way down the stairs. There was blood on both of his sleeves and on his hands. His black hair covered the right side of his face, and as he looked back over his shoulder, he smiled uneasily.

Something's off with this guy.

Tyr jogged back into the bay from the hallway that led outside. He moved to the armored personnel carrier and climbed into an open hatch on the front end.

After a few seconds, the engine started, and a hatch on the rear unfolded. Richards moved the captive inside and sat down.

As the hatch began to close, Richards opened a channel to the *Talon*. "ARN Talon, this is Wolf Squad. We have the target."

The same emotionless female voice from earlier responded. "Wolf Squad, move to epsilon. Extraction inbound."

A new waypoint appeared on the map, farther down the road from gamma.

Ban confirmed it. "Tyr, wait for us at waypoint gamma. After we rescue Holland, we'll meet you then head for extract at epsilon."

Tyr signaled affirmative. Once the vehicle-bay doors opened enough for the vehicle to fit through, Tyr drove out.

The vehicle shook in the wind. The once light snowstorm was becoming a blizzard.

Ban ran through the open doors, and when he was able, he moved deeper into the forest beyond the base. He took cover behind a large tree when he saw movement ahead. "Becks."

"I see them."

The Runians fired their guns, but nothing hit anywhere near Ban. They were shooting down into a depression.

Becks's sniper rifle fired twice. "They're down. But I think they were shooting at someone else."

"Stay here and cover me." Ban rounded the tree.

He ran to the edge of the depression and eased down a snowy hill. At the bottom, a fallen marine lay face down in the stream. The back of his helmet held the triple-dot insignia of a lieutenant.

Ban's display marked the body as KIA. He lowered his gun. "Shit."

"What is it?" Becks asked.

"It's Holland. He's dead."

"Dammit . . . you know we'll take the fall for this."

"I'm sure we will." Ban sighed. "All right, head to gamma. I'm right behind you."

"Already on my way."

As Ban neared the body, it moved.

Still alive?

Holland struggled to lift himself. "Morgan? Is that you?"

Ban looked up. Blurred forms approached through the trees further upstream. Because of the snowstorm, he couldn't see them clearly, but he could have sworn there were flashes of purple.

They'll overtake us if I carry him. And I'll be damned if I die for him.

Ban opened a private channel that only Holland could hear. "Something I've wondered for a long time, Lieutenant." He knelt, machine gun over his shoulder. "Do you feel remorse?"

Holland grabbed at his stomach. "Remorse? For . . . what?"

Ban laughed bitterly. "For ruining my life."

Ice and mud slipped through Holland's fingers as he tried to crawl. "You chose that."

Ban nodded slowly. "I faced the consequences. Now it's your turn."

Holland pulled himself forward. "Help me!"

Ban watched him struggle. "I don't think so."

Holland paused and looked up. "Revenge?"

Ban stood. "Maybe." The unknown soldiers were coming dangerously close.

Holland coughed and collapsed into the icy water, lifeblood flowing away in the stream. "Don't . . . leave me . . . here."

Ban twisted his lips in disgust. "Apologies, *my lord*." He brought his rifle down from his shoulder and turned away. "But as far as I'm concerned, you're already dead."

He closed the channel and started up the hill, never looking back.

FAITH TAKES MANY FORMS

TIEGER TOOK A FISTFUL OF THE PRISONER'S long blonde hair and jerked his head up, staring fiercely into his wide, hemorrhage-stained eyes. "Another *lie*."

Sweat dripped down the beaten man's face, forcing him to blink and squint. His breaths came hard and fast as he pleaded. "Please. Please! I told you I don't know anything! I was—"

Tieger silenced him. "The *truth*." He spread the clawed fingers of his armored gauntlet, tips threatening the soft skin of his throat. "I will not ask again."

The man cried as he tried to pull away. "I'm not lying!"

Tieger's heart quickened, muscles tensing. "*Death*, then."

Inquisitor Corva coughed as she walked out from behind Tieger. "Honored One, that might not be the most *efficient* method of inter-rogation." She moved into view, prolonging the doomed man's life. Her violet robes hung open, enfolding the Flame of Elcos that burned upon her white linen amice.

She had prominent cheeks, a long neck, and thin black lips that drew back over her teeth as she spoke sanguine. "Lieutenant . . . Holland, was it?" She held up her bony index finger and nodded. "Ah, yes. I remember now. A royal name, is it not?" She smiled. "The Hollands of Craigholde?" She glanced down at Tieger's hand and walked away, smile growing.

Tieger released the prisoner and backed away. "Very well, *Inquis-itor*." He sat down on a nearby bench, nearly collapsing it with the weight of his white heavy-grade powered armor.

The Alidian lieutenant pulled forward against his chains. "Is this about my brother? You have to understand! My father disowned him! When we found out he had those . . . those *viae*, we—"

She turned suddenly, walking back to him. "We will discuss the sins of your family later." She squatted on the soles of her boots, pointing to the bloodstained floor. "Tell us about your mission *here*, in *this* place."

Holland looked down, pink-tinged tears streaming down his cheeks. "Why won't you listen? I'm not a sympathizer! I—"

Tieger had watched all he could stomach. He stood from the metal bench and walked over. "You waste time, Corva. Only pain will loosen his tongue."

Holland shook his head back and forth and pulled violently against the chains. "No, not that! No more, please!"

The *Vox Dei* of Elcos surged like a tangible bonfire in Tieger's chest. His faith was strong, and the power of Elcos flowed through him. He held up his hand, and the power manifested.

Violet light coursed over Holland's skin. His screams intensified as the light grew, building with Tieger's rage.

Tieger watched him writhe; he knew the man felt as though he were on fire. In a way, he was.

The lieutenant gurgled and convulsed, eyes open, grunting.

Weakling.

Tieger walked to his side. "Pathetic frailty." He took the lieutenant's head between his palms and infused him again, deeper than before.

The man's shaking lessened, breathing less ragged, but it was not long before he wailed again.

Corva looked at Tieger in question.

"He will not die." Tieger twisted his lips in disgust. "But there is no reason the healing should be pleasant."

She nodded. "He brought this upon himself with his lies."

Tieger let the power fade and took Holland by the throat. "Now you will speak. What do you know about this base?" He squeezed the vulnerable neck.

The man blinked. "We came here . . . to find out . . . what they were doing."

"Who?" Tieger asked.

"The Runians."

Corva tapped the bridge of her beak-like nose. "Bold. An act of war, some might say."

Holland shook his head weakly. "No. No, they . . . weren't supposed to be here. The Accord—"

She paced behind Tieger. "And did you know this *illegal* Runian base had received an item from inside the Frontier?"

"Yes . . . we knew. They were collecting secrets. We came to . . . put a stop to it."

Tieger's grip tightened further.

Corva sighed. "Lieutenant, I do not know how much longer I can hold him back. He really does want to kill you."

The prisoner seemed to consider his position, searching the room frantically. He tried to make eye contact with the nearby trooper, but the helmet hid the soldier's face. Another, in the control room above, was motionless, devoid of emotion.

Holland must have realized he had no hope of escape. "There . . . there was something special."

Tieger's murderous expression was unchanged, but he relaxed his fingers a little.

The prisoner twisted his head, trying to swallow. "Some artifact. A piece of something they found . . . in the Frontier."

Corva knelt beside Holland, speaking softly. "This *artifact* . . . you found it?"

"I don't know. The plan went to the Void. I was left behind." He pulled against the chains. "They'll be looking for me!"

Corva feigned pity. "I do not believe they will, but we will make sure you are returned to them, Lieutenant. We are neutral and have no interest in your political squabbles."

His eyes lit up with sudden hope. "Oh, please, you won't regret it. I won't tell a soul!"

She touched his cheek with one of her nails. "There is just one more thing, Lieutenant."

The prisoner held his breath, eyes fixed on her.

Corva's expression hardened. "We require the security codes for the *Talon*."

He blinked multiple times. "What? Why would you . . . I don't understand."

She leaned in closer. "This is very simple. Your countrymen took something we want. Give us the codes, and you will go free."

"No! I can't do that. They're coming back for me!"

She looked up, smiling. "They did search for you, but unfortunately, there was no body to retrieve. Only the ruined remnants of your broken armor were found, and only then, just fragments. To them, you are most certainly dead."

The lieutenant looked around the room and mumbled to himself inaudibly, considering his options. His eyes widened again at some internal revelation. "You aren't going to let me go, are you? You say you will, but you won't! I know it. I know it . . ." He trailed off into tears.

Tieger released Holland, dropping him to his knees. "No more games, Corva. It is *my* way now."

The lieutenant had begun to give up. It showed in his muscle tone and posture.

Tieger's eyes closed for a moment, then he threw his right arm back, flinging his cape aside. The air near his arm distorted, warping the light around it. He reached through the wavering space, and with a twist of his torso, brought his arm back through.

In his right hand, he held his great-hammer. The twisted, Godan-wood haft was black, as if charred by fire. The head of the hammer was silver, shaped like a truncated pyramid, burning with a violet, inner fire. Opposite the hammer's head, a long, slender silver blade curved down the haft a forearm's length, inscribed with burning violet letters from a long-lost language.

Its name was *Janus*.

Tieger came forward, spinning the weapon as he walked. Without hesitation, he drove the blade down through the back of Holland's left knee, into the floor.

Both the stump and the floor sizzled. Holland screamed in agony as he tried to reach back for his leg. The burning continued, even after the blade was withdrawn.

Tieger walked back to where Holland could see him and tossed the smoking leg to the floor. He grabbed Holland's head and pulled it down. "Look at it!"

Holland couldn't breathe. He cried silently, eyes wide with anguish, unable to make a sound.

Tieger walked away. "You have very little time before I take another piece of you."

Holland wailed in torment. "I don't . . . I don't . . ."

Tieger moved to Holland's side and ripped the sleeve from his black sub-armor shirt. He placed the hammer's blade on the man's arm and pushed, sharp edge drawing boiling blood. He spoke through bared teeth. "*The codes.*"

Corva knelt close to Holland's face and stroked his hair. "Oh,

Lieutenant." She spoke softly. "Tell him the access codes, and it all stops. Don't you want to be free?"

He sniffled and cried in short bursts like a small child. Already down to the bone, Tieger yanked his arm violently and moved his weapon toward the underside.

Holland came to life again. "I'm just a lieutenant . . . they wouldn't give me something like that! Ah! Stop! No! Stop it!"

Corva almost whispered. "But you *do* know the codes. You are a member of the royal family. You have access to things a normal lieutenant would not."

The burning blade touched Holland's arm near the inside of his elbow. The skin popped and bubbled as it split.

Tieger's eyes were wild with fury, and spittle flew from his mouth. "Give them to me!" He pushed down at an angle, shearing the muscle away from the bone.

Through slobbering speech, Holland finally gave up his codes.

Satisfied, Tieger stood and began to walk away.

"Wait! Wait, damn you! I told you the codes!" Holland was shaking again, and apparently, he had soiled himself.

"Think carefully." Corva stood, frowning as she looked down on him. "I am a woman of my word. But do you really wish to be set free on this freezing moon, injured as you are, with no means of escape?"

Holland seemed to think about that for the first time. His next words seemed nearly impossible to say.

Corva moved closer with her hand to her ear. "I am sorry. I did not quite hear you."

He looked up, mucus dripping from his nose and mouth. "I said, I will take my chances."

"At the end he decides to show some spine." Tieger looked to the nearby trooper. "Take him to the *Forge*."

Holland's panic returned. "What!? No! I did what you . . . I did what you . . . I did . . . "

Corva placed her hand upon his head and patted him. "Please, Honored One, may I spend but a little more time with my new friend once we've returned?"

The distortion in reality appeared next to Tieger again, and he returned *Janus*. "Do as you wish, so long as he is ready when the time comes." He walked to the workbench, picked up his helmet, donned it, and walked toward the vehicle hangar's doors.

They opened, and Tieger walked out of the Runian listening post. The snow had stopped falling, and the wind had died. He stepped onto the waiting transport ship, turning to look back at Holland as he held onto the bar overhead.

The defeated prisoner cried out one last time. "Who are you, you evil bastard? I'll kill you, I swear!"

Tieger laughed at his ignorance. "I am Tieger of Westmarch! The *Malleus Maleficarum* of Elcos!"

Holland struggled against his chains. Corva held out her hand, and the trooper pulled a rod from his belt. She accepted it then jabbed it into Holland's neck. He stiffened and went still.

Tieger watched the woman's eyes as she surveyed her new project.

All must serve, one way or another.

The transport lifted away, carrying him high above the snow-covered trees of Nix.

Tieger jumped down as the transport landed. His heavy boots hit the solid deck, and he felt the ship's strength run through him. The Harbinger had given him a glorious vessel, a ship that would allow him to carry the will of Elcos into the Frontier and beyond.

The main hangar bay of the *Forge* was massive, running almost one-third the length of the colossal ship. Starfighters, bombers, troop trans-ports, orbital drop pods, and other various craft lined the periphery of the bay. Crewmen, pilots, and ancillary staff moved between the ships like busy ants, working at their various tasks.

Is it fear or faith that drives them? It matters little. Fear and faith are two faces of the same coin.

A second transport landed. It had open sides with a mounted gun and seats for the troopers. It was large enough to hold a full squad yet small enough to drop into tight spaces. Its armored hull was violet, like the Flame of Elcos.

Corva exited, continuing on without pause. Two troopers jumped down and turned to pull Holland to the deck behind her. They dragged his limp form away as he mumbled, already succumbing to fear.

Fear that will become faith.

Tieger walked forward, and an honor guard led by Captain Gault met him. Gault was flanked by a pair of officers and a small squad of troopers.

The captain was middle aged, with gaunt cheeks, gray hair, and deeply set wrinkles. He tried to hide his apprehension at Tieger's presence.

He wore the uniform of the Elcosian Navy, a deep-violet coat that overlapped itself and closed to the left of center. One white stripe ran around the collar, continuing across the lapel and down the lapel roll to the bottom of the coat; the other white stripe went down the front of the coat on the other side, almost a mirror image of the first.

White trousers with a violet stripe down each lateral surface were tucked into knee-high black boots. There was a service pistol on his hip.

The honor guard halted, and Gault continued on alone, kneeling before Tieger. "Honored One. We can be underway as soon as you order it."

Tieger looked forward, above Gault's head. "Excellent. Do you have the course of the *Talon*?"

"We do. They are leaving the Skine system, en route to the Ivo system T-Gate."

"So, they mean to go deeper into the Frontier?"

"Yes. I believe they will act upon the information they recovered on Nix."

Tieger looked down. "Await my instructions on the bridge."

"Yes, Honored One. May the Light of Elcos never go dark." The captain rose, hurrying away, and his honor guard followed closely.

Tieger walked again. He would not waste any more time; the Harbinger of Elcos would be expecting news of the shard.

He continued across the bay and exited through a set of doors that opened when he approached. Officers saluted and bowed their heads as he passed, and troopers, in their medium-grade powered armor, moved aside, making way for their leader.

Violet armor covered almost every surface of their bodies. Their helmets contoured closely to their skulls, two halves coming together in a seam to form a sharp, narrow crest.

The chest armor mirrored the helmets, bearing a central crest with five, three-dimensional chevron plates. The arms, abdomen, and legs were similar with added space between the segments for flexibility.

Heavy belts went across their waists, and from those belts hung white rectangles of cloth in the front and rear, triangular near the far end and trimmed in violet, each bearing the image of the Flame of Elcos.

They carried compact carbine rifles as well as small cylindrical grenades attached in pairs at each left hip.

The shock troopers of the Elcosian forces, known as embers, were raised to be fearless. Entire worlds were dedicated to their breeding and training. They were taught in the most rigorous environments to never give in or surrender, and they would follow orders that most men would not.

The perfect embodiment of faith.

Tieger continued on and entered a lift, taking it to the command deck. The bridge was near his quarters, and he looked in as he passed. At least a hundred sailors and soldiers manned the bridge, all of them stopping to bow their heads as he strode by.

A central platform, like the blade of a great sword, extended straight ahead, and Captain Gault stood there, calling out orders. Before him, a metal ring built into the floor projected a holographic view of nearby space with the *Forge* in its center.

The expansive bridge had multiple levels built into its walls that extended inward toward the central platform. Each held dozens of duty stations, and on the levels above and below the captain, crewmen toiled busily.

Tieger continued on to his chambers and entered. He lit several of the half-used candles scattered around the room then began to strip down, placing the pieces of his armor on a stand to the side.

His bone-white armor was similar to that of the embers, but where their armor closely contoured their bodies, his was far more monstrous. The armor at his shoulders, elbows, and knees stuck out further than the bones they protected, like curved spikes, and the fingers of his gauntlets formed claws. His helmet swept up and back like ashes blown by the wind, and his long, flowing, violet cape had the Flame of Elcos embroidered upon it.

Nearly naked, he stretched, flexing and extending his muscles. He then knelt before a metal ring embedded in the floor and waited. Even as he closed his eyes, the glowing violet mark on the back of his right hand burned into his vision. He could see the hammer and fist, brighter as he concentrated.

Before long, the circle hummed with energy, and the Harbinger's holographic image appeared.

The old man wore a circlet of silver over his short gray hair. He had violet-and-white robes with a bright, burning, violet flame on his breast, and that same intensity flared in his eyes. He held out his ringed fingers to his sides, palms facing forward. His face was stern, yet welcoming, like a father.

Or so he would have me believe.

"Tieger, my son. I see you have not forgotten humility."

Tieger lowered his head farther. "I am but an instrument of Elcos's will."

"And his most excellent one at that. Report."

Tieger looked up. "The shard is lost."

The Harbinger's smile faded. "Explain."

"I kept the *Forge* in shadow as you planned. Your agent, that contemptible spy, failed to retrieve the shard in time."

"The Alidians have it?"

"Yes," Tieger said in disgust.

"Where is my spy?"

"He was not recovered."

The Harbinger nodded in thought. "He has gone with them then. He continues the mission."

"That may be, Harbinger."

"Tieger, you will follow, but give him time to secure the shard."

Tieger shifted his position. "I believe there is another way."

"Oh?"

"I have captured a member of the royal family. One who has access to the *Talon*'s operating systems."

"Interesting. He has given you this access?"

"I have *taken* it."

"Hmmm. For now, you will follow as I have commanded. No doubt my agent will contact you when he is ready. Only then, use what you have learned to assault the *Talon* and retrieve the shard."

"And afterward?"

His eyes shot down to Tieger's. "Kill them all. They should never have intervened."

"Yes, Harbinger. I will do this."

"See that you do. Without the shard, we cannot find its parent."

Tieger bowed his head. "It will be done."

The image faded away, and the circle's humming ceased. Tieger stood and walked to his communications panel. "Captain Gault."

"Yes, Honored One?"

"Set course for the Ivo system, *ahead* of the Alidian ship. Remain inside the Never. Prepare to attack, but do not do so until I command it."

"As you wish, Honored One."

Tieger walked around the room, smile growing as he quenched the flames of each of the candles with his fingers.

As he knelt in the darkness, Tieger allowed his mind to wander out of the room, through the ship, and beyond into the vast sea of stars.

In all the Vagrant Sea galaxy, in all of its arms, star clusters, sectors, systems and worlds, there was only one region that held true civilization—the Fathom.

All the planets and territories of Humanity lay inside the Fathom. Everything beyond was Pelagos. As Humanity expanded deeper into the Pelagos, the unknown black of space receded and the Fathom grew.

The nearest edge of the Pelagos was a perpetual frontier state, wild and lawless. Such areas of unexplored space surrounded the entire Fathom, though not all of those areas were equal. Resources were distributed unequally, and not all areas of space were suitable for colonization.

One particularly world- and resource-dense area on the edge of the current Fathom-Pelagos intersect was known as the Aeturnian Frontier. A number of nations bordered it, and by extending into the Frontier, those countries had become quite prosperous. Two large countries in particular had arisen as dominant forces in the region.

First, there was the Republic of Rune, with its exalted senate and rule by the people. They held a sizable amount of territory in the Fathom, and their military might was considerable.

They boasted a vast network of habitable planets, most notably the capital, Doan. And as a country of artists, merchants, and scientists, they had made more technological advances than any other. Rune was surrounded by many smaller nations which made for buffer states and trade partners, but Alidia, their largest neighbor and largest trade partner, was also their biggest rival.

The Principality of Alidia was ruled by Hayden the Third, Patriarch of House Eld and the Star-Born Prince, from the throne world of Aridor. It was a nation of noble houses, each containing small feudal territories under the ultimate authority of the prince.

Their society was militaristic, and honor was held as a critical virtue. Service was required for citizenship, and their penal system relied heavily on absolution through conspicuous valor.

In contrast, the quagmire of politics between the noble houses could at times become less honorable. But in spite of such internal machinations, they were viewed favorably by most of their neighbors.

In the regions between those two dominant nations, a host of smaller countries lay. Most had no more than a token military force to protect merchants and travelers, but each thrived economically. Trade between the greater powers and the smaller countries was successful in many ways.

Rune, Alidia, and the surrounding nations had actually once comprised a larger kingdom known as the Kingdom of Doan. But as often happened in history, the Doanian Civil War had left the supernation splintered.

The Eld branch of the royal family had been set up as lords and protectors of the region that would become known as Alidia, and as the old kingdom fell apart, Eld consolidated its territories into a principality that ruled in the absence of a king.

The various remaining states of the kingdom continued to war for many decades until the ancestors of the current citizens of Rune ended those conflicts, forming a republic with the old capital, Doan, as its center.

Over the next few centuries, Rune and Alidia expanded into the Frontier, fortifying their territories. In order to stem the aggression on both sides, a third-party mediator from the nation of Valen sponsored peace talks. The small country was located between the two larger ones, recently suffering from the decrease in trade during the conflict.

With the help of Valenen diplomats, Alidia and Rune agreed to cease all military expansion into the Aeturnian Frontier. Private corporations and parties were allowed to continue their exploration and colonization of the Frontier, but neither nation could send military forces beyond their borders unless justified by agreed-upon emergency contingencies.

This treaty, known as the Accord of Valen, helped to limit military conflict between the two neighbors and to reopen trade.

While things had briefly calmed, Rune and Alidia were two estranged siblings who might never again walk together in peace. But there was still one tie that bound them on a fundamental level, stronger than any treaty—the Elcosian faith.

Humanity had worshipped Elcos since the dawn of history. Whatever mankind had been before that time, they had lived in darkness as wanderers and scavengers, roaming whatever worlds they happened to blindly stumble upon. Elcos provided knowledge and purpose. Trillions of men, women, and children prayed to Elcos each night as the darkness closed in.

Yet, however united man was in this belief, there remained one group that refused to be dragged into the light. They were the damnable, heretical arcanists—followers of something only known in rumor as *the Code*.

Tieger had hunted its members, pursuing them into the dark corners of the Fathom. He had silenced their teachings, and he had spread the Light of Elcos by burning them alive on dozens of worlds. And yet, the arcanists had managed to find a refuge in the Aeturnian Frontier. They had found a hole to crawl into, a filthy world shrouded in secrecy—Endi.

The few arcanists that remained had eluded Tieger for a frustrating number of years, hiding on their undiscovered planet. But recently, the Runians had stumbled onto something in the Frontier. It was ancient, a small piece of a greater whole, something which held a forbidden power.

The Harbinger claimed the shard would lead back to this *source*, a thing of true evil. If that were true, surely it would lead to Endi as well. The texts were clear—where there was an arcanist, darkness would not be far behind.

And yet Tieger had reason to doubt the Harbinger's sincerity when it came to the shard. Too often the old man had made moves to increase his power. Too often he had let heresy go unpunished.

Unforgivable.

Whatever the Harbinger's motivation, Tieger's purpose was most certainly pure, a literal execution of the primary mandate of Elcos.

I will spread the will of Elcos, burning the arcanist witches wherever I find them. They will be as bright as torches, lighting the hidden path to Endi. And when I am finished with them, many others will share their fate.

INTO THE FRONTIER

FALL STEPPED ONTO THE *MORNING RAIN'S* bridge, and the lift doors closed behind him with a soft whoosh.

He stood there for a few seconds, but no one acknowledged him. Between the competing melodies of computer alerts and the steady drone of overlapping conversations, the sound of his arrival had gone unnoticed.

He breathed deeply and took advantage of the moment to center himself.

Be where you are.

The bridge's layout was fairly unique, essentially a hollowed-out sphere with three levels, each lower than the one before. Manned duty stations lined the levels, all oriented toward the center. At four equidistant locations, lifts like the one behind him sat at the top of stepped paths. Those paths led down to the center.

Situated at the lowest point was the focus of the room, an incomplete ring of visual readouts surrounding a large black chair. A man sat in the chair, rotating this way and that, accepting reports and giving commands.

That must be Captain Hughes.

Fall made his way past busy crewmen as he went down the steps, studying the captain as he went.

Hughes stood out from the rest of the crew. He was dressed in the same blue jumpsuit as the others, but he wore a long emerald-green coat trimmed with gold embroidery, part of a Runian naval uniform.

A veteran?

The coat had a high collar, hiding some of the captain's face, but on the other side, there was a neatly trimmed, thick, dark mustache. He had a powerful nose, and his brown eyes were lined with wrinkles around the edges.

A green captain's hat covered his salt-and-pepper hair, cloth top tented up to a point near the front above the black bill. A narrow gold strap went across the bill and affixed to the front center of the hat was the winged, gold-and-green Runian Dragon.

Hughes sipped from a white teacup, decorated with intricate green designs. He barely turned his head as he spoke. "Plan on standing there all day, son?"

"No, sir." Fall stepped forward. "I'm Fall Arden. Your guide."

"Mmmm," Hughes mumbled as he looked through the gap between the teacup and the bill of his cap. "Fall. That's one I haven't heard before." He lowered the cup. "A Frontiersman's name?"

Fall shook his head. "My father's favorite season. I'm from Valen."

"Ah." He sipped the tea again. "In any case, welcome aboard, Mr. Arden."

Fall opened his mouth to accept the gesture but was interrupted as a woman behind him cleared her throat. "Captain, all preparations have been completed. The *Morning Rain* is ready for departure."

Fall turned to look at the source of the voice. The stiff-postured woman manned a special station jutting out from the second level. Her long black hair was cut straight across in the front, and her skin was nearly the color of sand. Her striking, exotic eyes shot toward him for a split second, unfriendly at best.

"Very good, Lieutenant Commander Endo," replied the captain.

Roshanan? No, the name sounds Furosatan.

The captain addressed the bridge. "All hands prepare for departure. Operations, full status report. Engineering, prepare the Inos drive. No mistakes now, people. I'll be watching."

He sent a sideways glance at Fall as he pushed his cap up with the index finger of his left hand. "She's a civilian ship, I know, but I run her tight." He went to sip his tea again but stopped. "You'd better have a seat." He motioned to a padded cloth chair against the edge of the lower level, not far outside his circle.

Fall reached behind his back to pull his sword and scabbard forward and around. He noticed a panel on the chair's right arm. A soft white light pulsed as he sat, signaling the possibility of device synchronization.

He retrieved the communicator from his belt and placed it into his right ear. After it adhered to his skin, the light on the chair pulsed brightly one final time, confirming the earpiece was linked.

His retinal implant activated, and its translucent display hung in the air, visible only to him. The interface responded to his hand and eye movements, allowing him to select an external view of the ship. The *Morning Rain*'s sensors created a three-dimensional, disembodied view of the ship and its surroundings.

Fall moved over its surface, following the curves. From up close, the rounded hull of the sea-creature-like vessel was even more alluring than what he'd seen before.

Someone on the bridge spoke. "We are away, Captain. All stations report green status. Engineering reports the Inos drive is at ninety-six percent efficiency."

Fall watched as the *Morning Rain* released from its moorings and moved away from Crossroads Station. Once clear, the ship accelerated.

"Approaching the Crossroads T-Gate, Captain."

He heard the captain's voice. "Good, good. Query the gate, Ensign Fulton. Our destination is the Hamar's End T-Gate."

"Aye-aye, Captain. Gate responding . . . distortion complete. The gate reports all clear on the other side."

There was a pause, and Fall focused past the display.

Captain Hughes looked around the room. "We have a rare chance to make a name for ourselves and for our people. Here, we prove to the nations of the Fathom that in the Frontier, Runians will always lead the way. That Frontier is waiting, but it won't wait forever." He paused with a growing smile. "Lieutenant Steppes, take us in."

"Aye-aye, Captain."

Fall shifted back to his display again. The T-Gate was a small metallic sphere about three meters in diameter. As they approached, the gate broke apart and expanded to a diameter large enough to envelop the ship. Space distorted among the exploded parts, and starlight from beyond bent around the edge of it.

As the ship entered, its image warped and wrapped around the surface. About halfway in, Fall's display suddenly showed the ship exiting rather than entering. The stretched image that had spread around the sphere coalesced to the intact form of the ship as it exited. The stars he saw were different than the ones from only a moment ago; transit between gates was instantaneous.

The captain rotated in his chair, looking up to the second level. "Lieutenant Commander?"

Endo reported. "Scan complete, Captain. No other ships detected. I've deployed a probe, which is now relaying data. If anyone enters or exits through the gate, we will have a record of it."

The captain nodded. "Very good, Lieutenant Commander." He turned toward Fall. "Perhaps our guide would care to orient us?"

"Yes, Captain." Fall cleared his throat. "Hamar's End is a common entry point into this region of the Frontier. It's fairly well-trafficked, so security is less of a concern here than some of the places we may visit soon."

The captain nodded. "Why the name?"

"Hamar's End?" Fall asked.

"Yes."

"It was named after a jumper, Edvard Hamar. He made blind jumps through the Rift for almost ten years before he went missing here."

"What happened to him?"

"No one knows. Maybe he went through the T-Gate. More than likely he blind-jumped again and never made it back. His final marker buoy was found here with a journal and a last will."

"An aptly named system, then."

"Yes, sir."

Endo looked to the officer beside her and spoke softly, voice carrying derision. " . . . wasting our time."

Fall looked up. "It's wise to know the history of a place. Keeps you from repeating past mistakes."

Her eyes went wide, and her mouth opened to respond, but the captain beat her to it. "Quite right, Mr. Arden." He sipped his tea. "Did you have a system in mind for our first destination?"

Fall nodded. "I thought we might try the Wetria system. It has four planets, one of them a gas giant. None of the planets there has been completely catalogued, and there's sure to be a wealth of resources to discover."

Endo disagreed. "Captain, that system is tagged with a class three warning due to the radiation output from its star." She worked the screens in front of her. "I suggest this more suitable system instead."

Fall focused on his display and looked at the system in question, SX4765. "No. That's Maw-space."

The captain raised an eyebrow.

Fall continued. "Ships go missing near the Maw, Captain, far more frequently than by random chance."

Endo smiled. "This is a *professional ship*, not some Frontier junker. I hardly think we'll get lost."

Fall sighed. "Didn't you read the reports I uploaded? Empty ships stripped for parts, missing crews . . . "

"Ghost stories," she said with a wave of her hand.

"Eye-witness reports from sources I trust."

Endo looked past him. "Captain, SX4765 has been tagged by Vaughan-Heighas as an A-type, high-priority system. There are five worlds, two within the star's habitable zone. There's an asteroid belt perfect for mining operations. Local parameters match other systems in which T-Gates have been discovered. All in all, the rewards outweigh the risks. Plus, it's not actually in this *Maw* of Mr. Arden's, just on the edge." She shot him a satisfied smile.

Fall turned to the captain. "A perfect place for a trap."

Hughes calmly sipped his tea and stared up through a viewport on the upper level. "Mr. Arden, our goal is to explore and catalogue worlds suitable for life or for exploitation." He sipped again. "However, wish though I might, we aren't on a warship, Lieutenant Commander Endo." He worked at a screen near his right hand, and a new system marker appeared on the star map. "As a compromise, we will travel to this system, Ro-Art, and send an advance probe into SX4765. Ro-Art should be safe enough."

Endo nodded. "Aye-aye, Captain. Lieutenant Steppes, plot a course for the Ro-Art system. Prepare to engage the Inos drive on the captain's command."

"Aye-aye, ma'am."

She cleared her throat, and Fall looked up. She smiled ever so slightly at her victory then turned to her screens, dismissing him as an afterthought. "Ranger Arden, you've been a great help so far. I'll be sure to let you know when we need you again."

Fall looked to the captain, who was occupied with another officer. He sighed again, stood then started up the steps. "Don't mention it . . . "

As the lift doors closed, he heard the captain's order. "Lieutenant, take us into the Rift."

Fall lay stretched out on his bed; arms crossed behind his head. He wore his earpiece, synchronized with the room's network access and his retinal implant.

The Runian ship held few distractions. No pseudarus, no liquor, and an understocked library must have been Captain Hughes's idea of a *tight ship*. In the absence of an alternative, Fall rode the ship's virtual surface, experiencing the journey in first-person.

Above the ship, through the semi-opaque, bluish-green haze of the Rift, he could just barely see the stars of the Vagrant Sea. Below, he saw the nebulous, violet abyss of the Never.

Terribly beautiful, the Never stirred primitive emotions. It was the storied realm of a god, somewhere beneath reality, out of reach but not out of sight.

Formless objects swam just underneath its surface. Some were small, nearly invisible, but others were massive, sending ripples as they moved. Thankfully, they were held by the outer boundary, never rising above.

But that wasn't so for the erini. Reminiscent of small fish, the darting blue shards shot up from the Never and followed alongside the ship as it traveled. Old stories held that the creatures were good luck, ensuring safe passage for lost crews. Whatever they were, the sight of them was comforting.

Fall had no idea what any of these creatures were or how they came to be. What he did know was entering the Rift allowed travel to distant destinations in much less time than could ever be achieved through conventional means.

Reaching the speed of light was impossible but not when traveling through shortcuts underneath space. The physics-defying feat was made possible with the Inos drive, though no one really knew how it worked; the technology had existed long before recorded history, a hand-me-down from a forgotten age.

It was essentially a potential space between two realities, only existing once entered. Once inside, ships could move faster than if they were outside, allowing travel between planets in minutes or hours and between star systems in days or weeks.

For longer distances, travelers were forced to rely upon an even more poorly understood technology—the T-Gates, devices which stabilized artificial connections between two distant points in space.

Each gate linked to a small network of relatively close gates, meaning multiple transits were needed to travel across the Fathom and the Frontier. And when it came to previously unexplored areas, no one knew where a new gate might be found, requiring jumpers to blindly journey through the Pelagos in order to find them—an incredibly dangerous practice.

Rewarded with a short, lonely life.

Fall felt a change in the vibrations produced by the ship's Inos drive. *Finally . . .*

The erini sensed the drop in power as well and fell away, mixing into the blue-green haze that rolled underneath the *Morning Rain* as it resurfaced and left the Never far behind.

Fall sat down in the padded chair and synchronized his earpiece.

"Good of you to join us, Mr. Arden." The captain held out his teacup as a man filled it with fresh, hot tea. "I have a feeling today's the day."

Fall sincerely hoped he was right. After four days of Rift travel to Ro-Art and three more waiting for the advance probe to reach SX4765, he was anxious for something to happen.

Captain Hughes sent a copy of the morning briefing. "Look that over, but don't waste too much time on it. In short, we have around eighty percent of SX4765 pre-catalogued. We should be able to move into the system in the next few—"

Ensign Fulton interjected, "Captain, we're being hailed."

He set his teacup down. "Lieutenant Commander?"

Endo worked quickly. "Captain, a small ship just cleared the third moon around Ro-Art III. The transponder registers the vessel as the *Rìluò*. Configuration is unknown, but it appears to be a large starfighter."

"*Rìluò*, eh?" The captain rubbed his chin. "That's a Roshanan word if I'm not mistaken. Isn't she a little far from her side of the Fathom?"

Fall studied the ship. It was elegant and slender with a single elongated fuselage. Near the rear, two swept-back wings flared away. Above those, on the dorsal surface, two airfoils projected upward.

It was mostly red, but along the sides, stylized waves of orange water led up to the feet of a black heron, silhouetted against a setting orange sun. The cockpit was located near the nose. It had two seats, side by side, but only one of them was occupied.

Fall spoke without thinking. "That's a Ranger's ship." The bridge crew turned to look at him. He sat up straighter. "What I mean is, the pilot of that ship is an Aeturnian Ranger, like me."

The captain nodded. "Ensign Fulton, open a channel."

The pilot's image was projected on Fall's retina. The middle-aged woman wore red-and-orange light armor with black sub-armor extending up her neck. The armor over her chest held small orange lights on each side that ebbed and flowed in rhythm with her breathing. Over her left shoulder, he could see the edge of her red cape, and the armor on her upper arms extended up a little past her shoulders.

A black device covered her right eye, and her black hair was pulled up into a high bun. She had a well-healed scar that ran along the right side of her face just below the device, right above her full ruby-red lips. On the left side of her neck, just below the jawline, there was a tattoo of a heron, the same as on her ship. Her one visible eye, slanted almost like Endo's, held a steady, intimidating gaze.

The moon shrank behind her as she approached. Fall selected a split-screen view of both her and Captain Hughes.

"*Xìng huì*, Captain. My name is Mei of the Flowing Lands of Roshan. I am at your disposal." Her accent was Roshanan, and it was clear that Doanian wasn't her first language.

The captain bowed his head slightly. "I am pleased to meet you as well, Ranger Mei."

She seemed pleasantly surprised. "You understand some Roshanan?"

The captain nodded with a smile.

"And you wear the uniform of a Runian sailor. How interesting."

"The *Morning Rain* is a private vessel, unaffiliated with the Runian military."

"I see. Does your private vessel have an escort?"

"No, Ranger Mei, we have no escort." The captain shifted uncomfortably. "Though we aren't defenseless."

She smiled and shook her head. "Of course, Captain. I only wish to mention that this area of the Frontier can be significantly more dangerous than the average."

"Yes, we've been warned." The captain motioned to Fall.

Fall stood. With his right fist on his left breast, he bowed slightly. "*Ab aeturno.*"

She responded with a nod of her head. "*Ad infinitum.*"

She sighed and looked back to Hughes. "Captain, I am relieved you brought a Ranger with you on your journey, but my warning still stands." She turned her head toward Fall again. "I mean no disrespect, but I do not know you." She looked more closely. "Though, you do seem familiar."

"I apprenticed under Thane," Fall told her with a hint of pride.

Mei's eyebrows rose, unable to contain her surprise. "I see."

The captain seemed more than ready to end the exchange. "Mr. Arden is our guide. He has sufficiently warned us of the Maw-space and its dangers."

"And yet you continue on . . . " She shook her head. "Do as you wish, Captain, but I will say it one final time. Enter Maw-space at great peril to your ship and crew." She paused to let the warning set in. "On an unrelated subject, I am currently searching for a lost freighter, the *Orchard Run*. I will be in this system for several more hours, and I have left communications probes in the surrounding systems. If you discover any signs of the freighter, a message would be appreciated." She paused again and turned her head slightly. "I do not advise anything heroic."

That was meant for me.

She nodded to the captain, then to Fall. "Farewell, Captain. Ranger."

The transmission ended, and the view of her ship returned. It maneuvered and moved further into the system with a flare of its engines. After a few seconds, the ship disappeared in a flash of blue-green light.

Hughes sat down, jaw tense. No doubt the conversation had left him feeling chastened.

Lieutenant Commander Endo stood up again. "Captain, we have received this morning's data packet from the probe in SX4765. I think there is something you should hear." She tapped her fingers on her console.

A prerecorded robotic voice played in Fall's ear. "Distress. The *Orchard Run* has experienced a catastrophic malfunction. The crew is unable to repair the ship and may require medical attention. Immediate assistance is required. Distress . . . " The message repeated on a loop.

The captain leaned forward in his chair. "Do we have any data on the source?"

Endo frowned. "The scan was cut short in order to transmit the packet right away, but from what I can see, the freighter is adrift near an asteroid belt. Her engines are cold, but the hull appears to be intact. I am unsure of life signs. There is no other evidence of activity in the system, but, as I said, the scan is incomplete."

The captain rubbed his chin and leaned back. "Lieutenant Steppes, set course for a distance of fifty thousand kilometers from the *Orchard Run*. Engage the Inos drive immediately."

"Aye-aye, Captain. Should I prepare a communication burst for Ranger Mei's nearest probe?"

He didn't hesitate. "No."

Fall stood. "Captain Hughes!"

"Sit down, Mr. Arden!"

"Sir, you can't just go in blind! You aren't ready for—"

"Sit down, or leave the bridge." The captain tugged on his coat. "The laws of naval custom are clear, and this ship is *quite* ready."

Fall sat back down, furious at the rebuke. He looked around at the cutting-edge bridge and all its comforts, staffed with bright-eyed men and women who didn't have a clue about the dangers they were about to face.

It's not the ship I'm worried about.

DERELICT

THE *ORCHARD RUN* WAS A LONELY MOTE OF dust, dwarfed by the drifting asteroids of SX4765. It was disabled, engines cold, and its crew was probably dead.

Fall looked out beyond the belt to the light-years-wide Maw-space nebula, blood-red, open and waiting like a hulking teranak's jaws. He suddenly felt as if the *Morning Rain* and all its crew might be drawn inside and lost.

What would you say then, Thane? I told you so?

He was pulled away from his thoughts by the straining whine of heavy machinery. He turned away from the nebula after one last look.

The *Morning Rain's* shuttle bay was tall and wide with five landing pads, a control room on the second level, and one continuous repulsion-field wall separating it all from the vacuum outside. It was busy that morning.

Technicians climbed underneath and inside shuttles on four of the five landing pads, making last minute adjustments and repairs. Automated drones with rounded bodies and multi-jointed arms hovered in the air, assisting or relaying messages. Up on the ceiling, a heavy orange crane moved along the tracks, carrying its cargo toward the last empty landing pad, right beside Fall.

He stepped closer as the crane deposited the shuttle. The elegant craft was blue and gray with twin engines and a rounded frame, just like its oceanic mothership.

After the shuttle was secure and the crane's claws lifted away, a technician in a greasy jumpsuit walked over. He took off his cap and rubbed the sweat from his brow. "Goin' over?"

Fall nodded. "Against my better judgment."

The technician looked to the shuttle. He tapped a command onto his wrist-mounted controls, and the rear door opened. "Okay, well, she's ready." He leaned over and pointed. "We fixed the anterolateral thruster array. Had a little jiggle."

Fall reached out and touched the shuttle's hull. "Something wrong?"

"Nah. Always a few adjustments to be made. Routine maintenance, that sort of thing."

"Makes sense." Fall looked up. "Weapons?"

The tech seemed genuinely confused. "On a shuttle?"

"Tell me it at least has shields."

"Well . . . no. It's a people-mover. There and back."

"So it's fast?"

The tech's shoulders relaxed. "Yeah. Real fast. No one's gonna catch her."

Fall frowned at the shuttle's smooth hull, watching his reflection warp as he walked alongside it. "As long as she sees them coming, right?"

The tech grimaced. "Uh, yeah, right." He put his cap on and backed away. "Excuse me."

The bay's main doors opened, and three crewmen entered. Fall recognized Olivia, and he'd seen the other woman two nights ago in the ship's lounge. But he'd never seen the man before.

Olivia smiled when she saw him. "Hey! I was hoping you'd come."

Fall shrugged. "Might as well earn my pay."

"I'll feel much better having you with us. We might need you over there."

He shook his head and smiled slightly. "I sincerely hope you *don't*."

The other woman cut between them, and Fall stepped back to avoid her. Olivia motioned toward her with a frown as she went by. "Fall, meet Corporal Wright."

The unfriendly woman had black hair, shaved short on the back and sides. She wore blue, polished medium-grade armor with the Vaughan-Heighas Expeditions Corporation comet painted on the chest plate. She had a carbine rifle slung over her shoulder.

She dropped the crate she was carrying and gave him a once-over. "Who are you supposed to be?"

Fall glanced sideways at Olivia. "Supposed to be?"

"Yeah." She looked him up and down. "You the mercenary?"

Fall's jaw tightened. "No, I'm the Ranger."

"Huh. Got a briefing about you." She leaned to the side. "Nice knife."

Fall reached back and pulled the sword's grip, exposing the silvery blade before he resheathed it with a *click*. "It's not exactly a knife."

She looked back up, eyebrows raised. "Any good with it?"

Fall crossed his arms and shrugged. "Good enough."

"Hmmm." She searched his hips. "No sidearm?"

"I don't carry one."

"Why not?"

"Don't need one."

She uttered a stunted laugh. "Some mercenary."

Fall's expression went flat. "*Again*, I'm not a mercenary."

She tilted her head and twisted her lips. "You gettin' paid? If so, you're a mercenary."

Fall opened his mouth to tell her exactly what he thought about corporate cutthroats like her but closed it as the other crewman passed behind her.

The wiry man had messy brown hair, glasses that magnified his eyes a little too much, and a tiny round bandage stuck onto his face. His jumpsuit's shoulder had a stitched set of interlocking gears, one large and one small. He carried a duffle bag in each hand, stooped over with the weight of them.

He looked at Fall then to Wright and sighed. "When you two are done, the adults are ready." His accent lacked the normal Runian flair, more akin to the tighter speech of an Alidian.

Olivia leaned over. "And this is Eddie, our tech."

He threw his bags onto the shuttle with a couple of grunts and turned, hands behind his back. "It's *Edward*. Edward Faunt. And actually, I'm an engineering specialist."

Wright walked over and patted his shoulder a little too hard. "You fix stuff, *Eddie*. Don't make it out to be more than it is."

His face turned red. He counted to five under his breath then turned and followed Wright inside the shuttle.

Olivia shrugged. "It won't be boring." She reached for her medical backpack.

Fall moved toward it, hand out. "Let me."

She picked it up and slung it over her shoulders. "I got it, tough guy."

Fall saw the pistol at her side as she adjusted the pack. It was sleek, marred with scuffs as if used many times before.

She followed his eyes and smiled wryly. "What? Gotta earn my pay too."

Fall returned the smile, shaking his head as he followed her inside.

Once everyone was on board and the gear stowed, Wright sat down at the flight controls. Fall sat across from Edward and Olivia, fastening his flight harness.

Wright received clearance confirmation, and the shuttle took off, effortlessly passing through the repulsion field.

Fall looked out through the forward viewport as they closed in. He'd only had a moment to look over the *Orchard Run's* schematics, but he had the general idea.

It was a medium-sized cargo vessel, meant to bring in ore from small moons or asteroids. Mostly gray in color, it had an elongated, cylindrical core that housed the bridge, crew quarters, engine rooms, and other facilities necessary for extended runs.

Rectangular cargo modules wrapped around the core in three evenly spaced groups. The modules appeared to be fine. In fact, there was no visible damage.

He couldn't see most of the engine array from his point of view, but the first sensor scans had shown it to be offline. Though he could see the bridge, it was dark.

He looked across to Olivia. "What's the plan?"

She retrieved her personal data manager, a white rod, from a pocket on her left forearm and pinched a small tag on the side. As she pulled, the flexible material inside slid out like a scroll. The ship's schematic overlay resolved on the thin screen.

She circled the engine room with her fingertip. "We need to find out what the problem is and fix it if we can. That's where Eddie comes in." She changed the display to show headshots of the *Orchard's* crew. "I'll lead the search for any injured crew members and triage them for treatment and transport." She looked up. "Wright makes sure it's safe for the other teams to come over."

Fall sat back. "No offense, but aren't we a little light, numbers-wise?"

Wright glanced over her shoulder. "Worried?"

"Concerned. From what I've seen, you think this is a salvage run. No one's asking any questions about what happened."

Edward snorted. "Well, that's our job, isn't it? To find out?"

Fall shrugged. "I'm just saying this doesn't feel right. I learned a long time ago to listen to my feelings."

Wright turned around with a huff. "A merc with feelings. Imagine that."

She brought the shuttle to a docking hookup one-third the ship's length from the bow. After a few quiet moments, Fall felt the vibrations of the two ships connecting. A red light on the pilot's console turned green.

"We're good to go." Wright removed her headset and stood. "Computer reads standard atmosphere on the *Orchard*."

She moved to the rear and opened the hatch. Olivia stood up and slung her medical supplies over her shoulder. Wright walked ahead with her gear, and Edward fell in behind her. Fall took up the rear.

They moved inside the ship's airlock, and Wright closed the outer doors. A slight breeze blew across Fall's face when she did. It smelled stale.

Edward moved forward and placed a device on the wall terminal. After a few beeps, the bypass was complete, and the inside airlock doors opened. "We're in."

Wright raised her rifle, switching the mounted flashlight on as she leveled it on the entrance. "About time. Let's go."

Wright's flashlight swept across the darkened cargo bay as she moved through its center, shadows tilting, rising and falling.

Fall reached down to a pouch and took a small vial. He removed its tiny black stopper and took a sip. The chemicals in the potion affected the rod cells in his eyes almost instantly, similar to a few minutes spent in a dark room, except to a greater degree.

Olivia activated her wrist lamp, and Fall turned his head. Normally, his night vision would have been ruined, but the potion maintained its effects.

"What's that?" Olivia shined her light on the vial.

"Night-Sight. Helps me see in the dark."

She looked up into his eyes. "Your file says you have a retinal implant. It can't do that for you?"

"No. Basic information interface only." He tucked the potion away. "Night-Sight can't be tracked or disabled. Less risk of cancer too."

"Hmmm." She nodded and turned away.

The rest of the search revealed nothing out of the ordinary. Supplies were scattered randomly around the bay, but there were fewer than Fall would have expected for a crew this far out.

They moved farther into the ship. Per usual on a deep-space

freighter, the corridors had an unfinished look, with visible support beams and loose wiring tacked down wherever it happened to run.

Olivia looked to her scroll. "I'm receiving faint life signs from toward the bridge." She turned to Wright. "You and Eddie get the engines running before we hit an asteroid. Fall and I will follow the signal."

Wright glanced at Fall, doubtful. "Your choice, Doc." She nudged Edward, and they walked down the corridor toward the engine room, around a corner and out of sight.

Fall turned to move toward the bridge, and Olivia followed. Since most of the ship was aft of the cargo bay, they only had to travel a short distance.

She motioned to a hatch. "Hold on. There might be someone in there."

Fall moved to the hatch and entered. The room inside appeared to be a mess hall. He motioned to her once he saw it was clear.

She shined her light around the room. Though there was no one inside, the mess hall's condition was suspicious. Tables were pushed to the walls, turned on their sides. Junk was scattered around the room.

Fall looked up and noticed the ceiling had collapsed in several places. He moved to a pile of debris and kicked at it. There appeared to be scorch marks.

Is that a bullet hole?

"Fall, get in here, now!"

He ran into the mess hall's galley, sword unsheathed.

"What is it?"

"The closet! Whoever's in there, they're in v-fib!"

Fall had no idea what that meant, but he ran to the closet, sheathed his sword, and tried to open it with his fingers.

"Hurry, he's . . . what?"

He looked back. Olivia stared at the data manager's screen, confused. "What's wrong?" he asked.

"I . . . don't know. One second I have v-fib, then I have v-fib broken up with normal heart rhythm."

"What?"

"It's like the scanner is malfunctioning." Her eyes widened. "Wait! There it is again!"

Fall pulled his sword from its scabbard and stuck it in between the door and the frame.

Olivia spoke behind him. "It's gone again. No, now I have two distinct rhythms, not including the v-fib."

"Yeah." He grunted as he pushed. "Us plus him, right?"

"No, I blocked our rhythms when I first started scanning. It's almost like—"

The door slid open, and Fall backed up slowly.

An ugly man with dented, patched-together armor pressed a pistol to Fall's forehead. "Like there's two other people in the room?" The nasty grin widened on the man's greasy, crooked face as he spoke.

Fall heard another person enter the galley.

"Ah, ah. I wouldn't, lady."

Fall couldn't see what was happening, but he guessed Olivia had been reaching for her gun.

The pistol tapped once against Fall's forehead. "Drop the sword, asshole."

If I do, we're dead.

Fall smiled. "Sure thing, *ugly.*"

He jerked his head to the right, and with a swift movement of his left arm, deflected the pistol off to the side.

The two flew into the closet. Fall had his left hand on the man's gun arm, trying to keep from being shot in the face. The ugly man's free hand had Fall's sword arm. They vied for leverage, deadlocked.

Fall turned his head and saw that Olivia was in trouble; the other man had her in a hold from behind, knife to her throat.

Enough.

Fall turned back and slammed his forehead into the man's nose. He let the pistol arm go and pushed the sword with both hands, razor-sharp blade piercing the man's neck as he gurgled and thrashed.

Fall turned and rose. "Killer."

He had his hand to his bow as the man behind him sputtered and choked but froze as two more men entered the galley.

The huge one had a shotgun pointed at Olivia. He carried someone over his left shoulder.

"Do it." He watched Fall's hand as it hovered over the open bow holster. "Do it, and she's dead."

The man struggling with Olivia let go and backed away. "Shit, Gor. How 'bout lettin' me get outta the way first?"

The small man next to Gor was Edward. His face was bloodied and bruised, glasses missing. He fell to his knees, and the man dropped the person on his shoulder to the floor with a heavy, sickening thud.

It was Wright—minus half her face.

Fall stood there, sword in hand, with his other hand still hanging over the holster. He looked at Wright then back up. "Killing her was a mistake."

Gor pointed the shotgun at him. "Don't make me blast you, pretty boy. Nice price for guys like you, long as you're mostly in one piece."

Fall flipped the sword over, blade back. "Not going to happen."

Gor smiled, unimpressed. His bloodshot eyes narrowed as he looked down the barrel. "Go for it. Let's see what you got."

Both of them stared, waiting for the other to go first. Fall had bluffed, knowing full well he'd be dead as soon as he made his move, but surrender wasn't an option.

Just when he'd decided it was now or never, an impossible noise came from the mess hall—the bowel-emptying roar of an angry Rab cat.

Wide-eyed, Gor spun around and fired the shotgun. The furious beast, unfazed, tore through the mess hall. Gor fired again and again, backing up as he did.

In the confusion, Olivia drew her pistol and shot the man beside her. Gor spun to shoot her, but Edward kicked his knee from behind, knocking him off balance.

Gor cried out, and Fall's arrow shot right through his open mouth, dropping him as the arrowhead drilled through his brain stem.

Down you go.

Olivia stepped away slowly as the bulky, dark-green tiger stalked into the room. She had her gun leveled on it, shaking, with a look of utter confusion on her face.

The giant cat moved closer, heavy paws thudding and sharp claws scraping like hooks as they dug into the floor.

When it seemed she couldn't hold her breath any longer, the tiger let out a rumbling laugh from deep inside its chest. It sat down on its behind, swishing its tail like a docile pet, and looked to Fall, mouth opening in a fanged grin. "Works every time."

Edward winced as Olivia treated his injuries. "So, which would you care to explain first? The tiger or the demon?"

"*Imp.*" Hermes lowered his red ears, legs dangling from the galley counter.

Fall rubbed his chin. "His name is Hermes. He's . . . a shapeshifting artificial lifeform."

Edward tilted his head and nodded. "Of course. How perfectly normal."

Hermes turned his nose up. "Hmph. Lucky for you. I pretty much saved the day."

"Hermes . . . " Fall pinched the bridge of his nose. "Not everyone made it."

Hermes dismissed him with a wave. "Big deal. She was a bully."

Edward nodded. "No argument here." He sucked in harshly as Olivia pressed some chemical to a cut on his cheek.

She frowned at them both. "She died trying to protect you, Eddie."

"No, she died running her mouth. Neither one of us saw that Gor coming."

Fall interjected, hoping to change the subject. "That reminds me. How'd they fool Olivia's scanner?"

Edward held up the small device he'd found. "I can't be sure, but I believe this was designed to simulate false life signs while masking the signals of others. It must have been malfunctioning."

Fall leaned in to take a closer look. "Too bad it's ruined."

Olivia stood with a sigh. "Eddie, if you can walk, we should get back to the ship."

Fall helped Edward to stand. "What about the engine array?"

Edward rubbed his newly healed face. "From what I could see before the ambush, it might be salvageable. My guess is these men must have sabotaged them."

Olivia picked up her bag with a grunt. "Without a way off the ship? Not very smart."

Fall pulled the arrow out of Gor's throat and returned it to his quiver where the arrowhead was recycled. "Their ship is nearby."

Olivia's eyes grew wide. "*Nearby?* We have to warn the *Morning Rain!*"

Fall shook his head. "It's no good, I already tried."

Edward took the earpiece out of Fall's hand and put it up to his ear. He pulled it away with a scowl. "Jammed."

Hermes hopped down from the counter and ran out of the room. Fall followed him. In the corridor outside the mess hall, the red imp hung from the lip of a viewport, looking through it.

He dropped down. "Well, that explains it."

Fall ran to the viewport and looked out.

The enemy ship lurked like a predatory insect, ready to feast on the *Morning Rain*. Its uneven red-and-black hull was built from salvaged materials, stolen from other ships. In contrast with its prey, the ugly ship bristled with weaponry.

Fires burned along the *Morning Rain's* surface where gas escaped, and massive chains held it like a harpooned whale.

Fall backed away. "I tried to tell them."

The others ran forward to see. Edward gasped. "How?"

As they watched, an attack craft left the ship, heading toward the *Orchard Run*. It was blood-red, jagged, and heavily armored.

Fall moved toward the mess hall.

Olivia followed him. "What are you doing?"

He came back out and tossed Wright's rifle to Edward. "Know how to use it?"

Edward checked the rifle and nodded. "Better if I had my glasses, but I think so."

"You won't need them. It'll be close-quarters fighting."

Edward sighed. "Wonderful."

They ran down the hallway, back through the cargo bay and up to the airlock. Edward went to the door, and after a second, he turned back. "The shuttle is missing."

"Damn." Fall ran his hand through his hair. "Gor and his men must have uncoupled it. Can you seal the airlock?"

Edward leaned against the wall. "If I had my tools, maybe."

"We don't have time to get them."

Olivia and Edward jogged back to the cargo bay entrance. Fall looked through the airlock. The attack craft was about to hook up. He looked down at Hermes. "When they're clear of the craft, get in behind them and secure it."

Hermes rubbed his red-furred hands together. "Got it."

"Stinger." Fall pulled the arrow from his quiver and set it on the floor next to the lip of the airlock. "When you shut the hatch, I'll hit the stinger."

"All right." He pointed up at Fall. "Don't blow it early."

Fall pointed back. "*You* don't blow it." He ran to the others.

Edward knelt just beyond the open hatch, and Fall put his back to the wall in the corridor. Olivia drew her pistol and stood behind Fall.

She edged closer. "Whatever happens, we can't let them take us."

"Believe me. I feel the same way."

"I'm serious. I'd rather die first."

"It won't come to that."

The attack craft locked into position, and the outer hatch cycled.

Fall looked away. "Everyone close your eyes!"

The inner hatch cycled open, followed by a loud *bang*. Edward raised his head and opened fire. The bullets ricocheted off of the heavy shields carried by the raiders. The invaders moved forward slowly, impervious to frontal attack.

Fall waited. Once the last man was inside, Hermes closed the airlock behind them.

Now!

He activated the arrow, and arcs of electricity shot out from it. Three men in the rear were electrocuted outright, and the men in the front stumbled forward. By the time they could move again, it was already too late. Fall was there between them, sword drawn.

The one on Fall's right raised his arm in defense and lost it at the elbow; he fell back to the deck screaming. The other man slammed his shield down toward Fall, and Fall dove away to avoid being crushed.

The heavily armored man reached for the weapon he'd dropped a moment ago, a nasty, mangled club. Fall rose and, rather than retreat, lunged forward with a burst of speed.

The club swung, but the man's piecemeal armor made his movements awkward, and Fall drove his sword into the gap in the armor near the knee. Injured, the man fell under the weight of his bulky gear, and Fall finished him off with a thrust to the neck.

He backed up and leaned against the wall, breathing heavily as the last raider died. "Okay . . . I think . . . that's it for now."

Olivia came to check on him. "Are you hurt?"

"No." He walked to the airlock. "Hermes, open up."

The airlock cycled, and Hermes walked to the opening. "Wow. You didn't blow it."

"Yeah, yeah. Let's get out of here."

Hermes put his hands behind his back and rocked on his heels. "About that . . . "

"What?" Fall asked.

"It doesn't have flight controls."

Fall walked on board to see for himself. "Great."

Edward came over. "What's the problem?"

Fall rubbed his face. "It's a drone. It has to be piloted remotely."

Edward slung the rifle over his shoulder. "I bet I could rig something up with a little time."

"Are you sure there's nothing you can do with the freighter's engines?"

He shook his head. "In a few days, maybe. Nothing right now."

Olivia holstered her gun. "We have to do *something*. Eddie, go ahead and start working on this pod. We need to get back to the *Morning Rain*."

"I'm on it." Edward jogged out of the bay, carefully avoiding the dead men.

Olivia turned. "Fall, I want you and Hermes to come with me to the bridge. Let's see if we can get in touch with the captain."

"Sure thing." He sheathed his sword, and they left the bay together.

"*Morning Rain*, come in. This is Ranger Fall Arden. If there's anyone alive over there, come in."

After a few seconds someone replied. "Ranger . . ."

It was Ensign Fulton from the bridge. The sounds of klaxons and small-arms fire could be heard over the communicator.

"We've been boarded. Please—"

There was an explosion. Static broke up the signal, but a check revealed the channel was still active.

Fall looked to Olivia uneasily. "Hello? Hello, is anyone there?"

"Mister . . . ah . . . ugh . . . Mister . . . Arden." It was Captain Hughes.

"Captain, we know you're under attack, but we can't get to you right now."

He coughed. "I want you to stay away. I'm going to scuttle her."

Olivia ran over next to Fall. "Captain, no! We can get to you, we just need more time!"

"Doctor, is that you?" The sound of pistol shots came through, loud enough to assume it was the captain firing. "She's full of the bastards. They . . ." He coughed a few more times. Fall could hear the bridge's fire alarm. "I won't let them take my ship."

A new type of klaxon came through the channel. As Fall watched, the raider ship released the chains and began to pull back from the *Morning Rain*.

He activated the self-destruct.

"Stay away." The captain's breathing was shallow and labored. "Mister . . . Arden. Help the survivors. Doctor . . . I—"

The captain fired his pistol, and there were sounds of a struggle. After a few moments, there was a new voice. "Shut off the destruct sequence. I don't care how, just do it!"

There was inaudible speech from the background, and then the original voice returned. "Shit. Looks that way. Now now, Captain. You won't be getting off that easy. In fact, I think you'd be worth a nice ransom. Just so happens there's a lady who—"

The channel cut out.

Olivia pounded the communications console. "Captain? We have to do something!"

Fall looked up. "We can't. Not yet."

As they watched, the last attack craft flew back to the retreating ship. Once on board, the ship disappeared into the Rift, leaving the crippled *Morning Rain* behind.

Edward called in. "Okay, I have a remote transmitter installed. The pod's software isn't security protected, so we should be able to control it."

Fall turned to Hermes. "Can you set it up on this end?"

Hermes spun around in his chair. "Leave it to me."

"Good. Olivia, let's go." He jogged toward the exit, and Olivia followed after him.

They went down to the attack pod. Edward was there waiting inside it, ready to go. They ran inside and retracted the bulky metal door.

Fall called the bridge. "Hermes, are you seeing it?"

"Ummm, yeah. Got it."

"Try not to kill us."

"No promises . . . "

The attack pod released its clamps and floated away with a thruster burst. It turned slowly then jumped forward suddenly when its engines engaged. Fall grabbed a handhold then caught Olivia by the arm as she stumbled.

The pod covered the distance quickly, and Hermes took them into the *Morning Rain*'s shuttle bay. The repulsion field held as they passed through and landed. The pod's door opened, slamming down to the deck with a *clang*.

Burning chunks of debris littered the bay. More than one shuttle was overturned, having fallen from their pads or the crane. Slumped over a waist-high control panel, a dead man stared back at Fall, skin burning on his back.

Fall looked away. "He fixed the shuttle."

Edward twisted his lips in disgust. "What?"

"Before we left. Seemed like a nice guy."

Olivia averted her eyes and ran forward. Fall and Edward ran after her, weapons drawn and ready. They went to the nearest lift and tried it. It worked.

Olivia turned when the doors closed behind them. "Where should we go?"

Edward looked up. "I can deactivate the countdown from the bridge."

"All right. Computer, bridge."

The computer's voice stuttered and cut out as the lift rose. "Ac . . . kn . . . dged, Com . . . der."

When they reached the bridge, the doors opened slightly then stuck. Fall sheathed his sword and moved forward to pry them open with his fingers. Beyond, smoke and the smell of burned-out electronics assaulted his senses.

The bridge was wrecked. Small fires crackled at the stations as thick black smoke rose to the ceiling. Bodies lay scattered over the levels, both raiders and Runians.

Olivia covered her mouth and went down, checking each corpse. Edward ran down to the second level to a station that appeared to be operating.

He sat down and started typing. Fall walked to him and looked over his shoulder as he worked. The harsh klaxons ceased, replaced with a shorter, standard alert.

"That does it for the self-destruct sequence." Edward cycled through the screens. "The systems are shot. Engineering is in shambles. The engines themselves . . . dammit. Disabled in the attack."

Fall sighed. "Dead in the water."

"It's worse. The shield generators are toast. Sensors are down. Life support is failing."

Fall looked up at the smoke swirling along the top of the spherical room. "We shouldn't spend much more time in here."

Olivia came back up the steps, eyes red and watery, her voice wavering. "All dead."

Edward looked back to the screen. He typed. "Actually, they aren't. The computer registers us as the only living crewmembers on the ship, but out of eighty, twelve others are unaccounted for."

Olivia looked at the screen. "Unaccounted for?"

"They're not here, dead *or* alive."

Olivia read the screen. "Captain Hughes, Endo Kumi, Stad Vern . . ."

Edward looked down. "Taken . . ."

Olivia slumped into a chair in disbelief. "Kidnapped."

Fall placed his hand on her shoulder. "The raiders might circle back around. We need to go." His words weren't the most sensitive, but they were necessary.

Olivia's misplaced anger boiled through in her question. "Where *exactly* should we go?"

Fall searched his boots for an answer. Surprisingly, he found one. "Mei!" Olivia seemed confused, so he explained. "We met a Ranger looking for the *Orchard Run*. If we find her, she'll help us for sure."

Olivia stood and walked a few steps then turned around. She stared off for several moments before sighing with a shudder. "Meaning we'll have to abandon the *Morning Rain*."

"I know. I'm sorry, but it's the only way." Fall's earpiece vibrated. He took it from his belt and put it into his ear. "Hermes?"

"How is it over there?"

Fall walked a few steps away. "Not good."

"Guess that means we're fired."

"That's a safe assumption." Fall rubbed his eyes. The Night-Sight potion's effects were starting to fade. "Doesn't mean the job's finished."

"Without pay?"

Fall looked down to the captain's station on the lowest level. On the floor next to it, underneath some fallen wires, he saw something white. "Yeah." He walked down the steps to pick it up and brushed the ashes away, revealing the cracked remains of Captain Hughes's ornate teacup. "Some mercenary . . ."

THE STORIES WE TELL

BAN TOOK A DRINK OF HIS PALE SYNTHETIC ale and stared into the flickering flames of the fireplace, slipping deeper inside a place he tried never to go. No hope, wisdom, or light could be found there.

Only fire and acid.

The sounds of soft music faded. Darkness crept in around the edges of his vision. The room shrank until there was only him and the fire, face to face.

Mud and death.

The burning logs split, screaming as they did. They disintegrated to ash in agony, falling apart. Their little hands reached out to him.

Save us!

He ran to them, but all he could do was fall to his knees and watch as boiling bones dripped between his fingers.

"Ban."

He jerked his head up, startled. "What?"

Becks frowned and crossed her arms. "I said, you lost."

He looked down at the holographic Vogi board, remembering the game. "What? How?"

"You're out of moves."

He sat up and leaned forward. "I can move my Resh Gal." He reached for the piece, hesitant.

"Covered with my dreadnaught."

"Then . . . I'll destroy your scout."

"My missile cruiser too? Surely you weren't counting on that hidden ephmere?"

He pulled his hand back and sighed. "Saw that, did you?"

"How could I not?" She leaned into his field of view. "What's wrong with you?"

He looked up, avoiding her relentless gaze. "Nothing. I just need another drink."

"You sure that's it? You seem distant."

"I'm fine."

She sighed. "All right, I'll get you another one, and while I'm gone, think about what you're going to say when I return." She pushed away from the table and stood up.

He reached out and took her hand. "Hey."

She looked away, impatient. "Yeah?"

"I love you."

"Mmmhmm."

"Really."

She turned back. "Then what's wrong?"

"Nothing."

"I don't believe you."

"Well, I'm sorry, but it's true."

She shook her head. "The only thing you're worse at than Vogi is lying." She let his hand fall away as she left.

He looked back to the Vogi board. He could almost see the writhing black tentacles of the ephmere as it lurked inside the game's nebula.

On the other side of the board, his Resh Gal hologram thrashed about in rage at its apparent defeat. Its head was lowered, but its bright, slit-like eyes glowed yellow, casting shadows over the bony black features of its face. The eyes always seemed to focus on him, no matter the angle.

Just my imagination.

He downed the remainder of his ale. The rest of the squad was a few tables over, not far from his own, so he stood up and walked over.

Richards sat across from Tyr, talking loudly with a mouthful of crispy pot pie. He pointed his fork as he chewed, dropping a steaming flake onto one of his playing cards. "...which is why...I think...you owe me twenty-eight glenns."

Tyr shook his head. He pointed at Richards, then back to himself.

Richards swallowed. "*Me?* No way. I won."

Ban sat between them at the small square table. "What about last week? And the week before that?"

Tyr crossed his arms and smiled smugly.

Richards shot Ban a wounded look, then tossed his fork into the bowl. "Fine. Will a glass of Theresian cover it?"

Tyr made a show of thinking about it then held up two fingers.

Richards rolled his eyes. "Fine, a double." He wiped his mouth and stood up, mumbling to himself as he walked toward the bar.

Ban looked down at his hands then back up to Tyr. "You did well."

Tyr raised his eyebrows in question.

"On Nix, I mean. Same as you always do."

Tyr shook his head and pulled the small rod-shaped necklace from underneath his shirt. He held it out.

"That may be so, Tyr, but even with divine protection, you did your job."

Tyr closed his eyes with a smile before tucking the rod back under his shirt.

Becks sat down with two mugs of ale, setting one of them in front of Ban. "There you are."

Ban grimaced when she caught his eyes. "Sorry. I decided to find the guys."

"All good." She smiled at Tyr.

Richards returned and sat, getting right back to his pot pie. "Drink's coming." He chewed another bite. "But there's trouble at the bar."

Ban looked over his shoulder, following Richards's line of sight.

Three marines stood near the bar, drinking. They turned when he looked. One of them motioned toward the table and laughed.

Ban turned back to the others. "Griffin Squad."

Becks leaned forward and spoke softly. "Rumor is, they blame us for Holland's death."

Richards washed his food down with a gulp of ale. "Hey, we did our job. That spoiled brat couldn't wait for the distraction."

Becks furrowed her brow. "*Keep your voice down.*"

Richards shrugged. "What? I'm just saying Holland blew it, not us."

The three men walked over. Their leader, Haskel, a short and stocky man, stepped up behind Ban. "Shouldn't you be resting after such a hard week, Morgan?"

Ban took a drink. "That's exactly what I'm doing."

"I meant back in your quarters, where it's quiet. *Safe.*"

Ban swished his ale around in the glass. "No, I feel fairly comfortable here."

"I think you'd be more comfortable someplace else," Haskel said.

Ban looked over his shoulder. "I'll be staying right here. Why don't you go back to the bar? Where it's . . . *safe.*"

Haskel scowled, frustration growing. "Maybe I'm not being clear, *bondsman.* We don't want you here."

Ban put his glass down, knuckles turning white. He turned slowly and deliberately in his chair. "Haskel, maybe *I'm* not being clear. Scurry back to the corner like the cockroach you are, before I embarrass you in front of what's left of your squad."

Haskel balled up his fist, face turning red. "You fu—"

Tyr gripped the table so hard it creaked, rising up to his full height. A shadow fell over the frightened man as Tyr eclipsed the hanging light above him. His neck bulged and his jaw tightened like a press.

Haskel stepped back, voice caught in his throat.

Ban held up his hand, and Tyr waited. "Bondsmen are free to use the enlisted lounge, Haskel. If you don't like it, file a complaint. Until then, keep your mouth shut, and keep your distance. I won't warn you again."

Haskel nodded with a devious smile as he backed away. "All right, but your squad won't always be there to protect you, Morgan. Watch yourself, traitor."

Traitor?

"That's right. I know what you did down there." Haskel pointed at Ban. "You'll answer for it."

The men turned away, and Tyr sat down with a heavy grunt.

Ban turned around, and Becks grasped his hand. "Ban, you know we can't have that kind of trouble."

"I can handle him."

"That's not what I mean. He's in Griffin for a reason. He can make life very hard for us."

Richards let his fork go and wiped his face before wadding up the napkin. "What'd he mean about the mission?"

Ban looked down at the table. "No idea."

Becks glanced sideways at Ban while she spoke. "He's talking about what happened to Holland."

Richards sat back. "We all heard the same report. The Runians swept in with reinforcements just as we left. What were we supposed to do, get our asses shot off for a corpse?"

Ban hit the table with the bottom of his fist, harder than he meant to. The squad looked up, surprised. "*We* got the artifact. *We* captured the engineer. *We* got it done."

Richards nodded. "Damn right. I'll drink to that." He did.

Ban looked over Richards's shoulder as two men in uniform walked in. They wore pistols on their hips, tense as they scanned the room.

The lead man found Ban and walked directly toward him. He put his hands behind his back. "Bond-Sergeant Morgan."

Ban stared ahead. "Yes?"

The other soldier stood back, at least an arm's length away from Tyr.

The head soldier looked down. "Finish your drink and turn in for the night."

"Why?"

"I'm asking, Bond-Sergeant. Don't make me tell you."

Becks looked up. "We were just leaving. Come on, Ban."

Ban stood up and looked back to Haskel. The man smiled and waved as he laughed with his squadmates.

Coward.

Ban took a deep breath and flexed his fingers. "We'll go."

The uniformed man relaxed. "Thank you, Bond-Sergeant."

Ban followed Becks to the exit, Tyr and Richards behind them. After they exited, the military policemen stood guard in front of the lounge.

Ban turned, watching Haskel and his men laugh even harder.

Becks squeezed his arm. "Not now, Ban."

He looked down to her and nodded. "Sure." He turned to walk away. "Not now."

The *Talon's* halls were empty. Each footstep echoed, clanking on the deck's metal plates.

"You aren't going to say anything?" Becks looked up at Ban as they walked.

"Like what?"

"I thought you'd want to talk about what Haskel said."

Ban opened his mouth to reply, but a couple of officers passed by in uniform. He stopped and turned to salute.

He noticed the crisply starched, royal-blue jackets with silver buttons and rank insignia. The men had shiny black belts with silver buckles and black leather straps. They wore matching slacks with polished black knee-high boots, each armed with a pistol at their side.

He felt shoddy in his gray T-shirt and blue cargo pants.

The officers walked by without so much as a nod, never pausing their conversation.

When they'd passed, Ban turned to Becks, leaning on the thick rim of a blast door housing. "You mean him calling me a traitor?"

"Yeah."

He shrugged. "You know as much as I do. We did our best."

She nodded slowly. "Still, why would he specifically single you out?"

"Holland and I had history. He had to have known that."

"You think he'll try to use that against you?"

"Probably. I'm not sure what else he could have meant." He stepped up to an open hatch. "I don't think I can sleep yet. Hang out for a little bit?"

"Sure." She followed him inside the room.

The ship's observation deck had two levels. The upper floor held couches, chairs, and short tables, separated by an opening in the center. The lower had a wet bar, more tables, and chairs. The area could host a fairly large party, but it was unoccupied so late at night.

They walked up the steps to the second level and looked out. The far wall was transparent, providing a good view of the Rift and the Never below.

Becks leaned on Ban's right arm, wrapping her own around it. It felt good to have her so close.

She sighed. "I feel like something's wrong. Are we okay?"

He looked down. "We're better than okay. I love you."

"I love you too," she said as she looked up.

"I know."

"So let me help you."

He watched one of the glowing erini streak by outside the viewport. "You can't."

She let go of his arm. "If there's anyone who can, it's me. We don't keep secrets, remember?"

He took a deep breath and told her a half-truth. "It's Holland."

"What about him?"

"Well, his death is bothering me."

"It's bothering all of us."

"It's more than that."

"Feeling guilty?"

"I am."

"Why? Because you didn't like him?"

"That's exactly why. I feel bad saying it, but I'm glad he's dead." He looked down into her eyes. "I know I shouldn't feel that way, and it bothers me."

"You had every right to hate him. He tried to ruin you."

"He *did* ruin me. He cost me my career. My dream."

She nodded slowly. "He didn't have to come down so hard on you, that's true. But mistakes were made. You had to own up to them."

He stepped back. "You think I don't know that? I've been paying for it for years."

She rubbed her forehead. "Don't get mad at me. I'm on your side."

"Then act like it."

Her eyes narrowed. "Watch your tone. You don't get to talk to me like that. Not after what we've been through."

He turned his head. "You're right, I'm sorry. It's just frustrating."

"Of course it is. We've all had to endure absolution. But this is the way it is."

"I know that. It just burns me deep inside. I had my own squad. I was on my way to captain."

"So? I was on my way to a noose. Richards would still be rotting in a prison. Tyr would . . . well I don't know what Tyr would be doing, but the point is, this is how we make atonement. Through absolution."

"It's not the same."

"How is it not the same? We all needed a second chance. We got one."

"But I didn't make the mistake they punished me for."

"What does that mean?"

"It means what I said."

"Ban."

"What?"

"You made the biggest mistake out of all of us."

He smiled as he looked down and shook his head. "I did, but not the one you think."

She blinked. "I'm waiting . . . "

He turned around and walked a few steps before turning back around. "I didn't give the order to kill those people."

She was taken aback. "You don't have to—"

"Holland did."

She walked closer, quieting him. "By the Void. What are you trying to say?"

"I helped cover it up."

"How?"

"By taking the fall for it."

"Wait. You're telling me you stood there and got convicted of manslaughter, and you didn't do it?"

"Yes."

"Why would you do that?"

"It wasn't my choice initially. After it happened, I filed my report. The report was changed without my consent. When I asked why, I got pulled into a backroom meeting. I was told that if I took the fall for it, I'd get a slap on the wrist and a few months later, after everything calmed down, a promotion. I'd have a grateful royal in my pocket."

Becks leaned in and looked up into his eyes. "That mission went all over the networks. Dead children. Dead parents. Why didn't you leak the real story?"

"Because I fired my gun, the same as the rest of them. Besides, Holland was never *there*. All the records of him being on the mission were purged. Communications logs, the video footage, all of it . . . erased."

"What about your squad?"

"They turned on me. Tav, Carde, Falke. They all testified I gave the order to torch the facility."

"But Holland was the one?"

"Yes. I expressed my doubts. The intelligence was incomplete, and we hadn't verified the target. He overruled me and forced the assault."

"Ban . . ."

He stared over her shoulder. "When we realized, it was already too late. We couldn't help them. Holland said they were terrorist sympathizers and that they'd made their choice."

She touched him. "I didn't know."

"How could you?"

She looked up. "Why didn't you tell me?"

"Because I was complicit. The shame of it was too much."

"So why tell me now?"

"Because he's *dead*." Tears welled up in his eyes. "I'm finally free of him."

She came in close, softly touching her body to his. "You shouldn't keep things from me. You can always tell me." She put her arms around his neck, pulling him down for a kiss.

If only I could.

After a few seconds, a bright flash of light caused him to open his eyes.

Through the viewport, he saw millions of stars spinning out of view as the ship turned. The *Talon* had dropped out of the Rift and was maneuvering.

They finished the kiss, and Becks rested her head on his chest. "It's going to be okay."

He closed his eyes, resting his chin on the top of her head.

I wish I could believe that.

Becks lay curled up next to Ban, her cheek on his chest and her arm across him. Her breathing was slow and rhythmic, and he knew she'd fallen asleep.

For the longest time, he thought about the events of the last week and a half.

He watched a battered dropship fall through the sky as wind blew fiercely through snow-covered trees. He saw a bloody knife and a shard of crystal, black as space. He watched Lieutenant Holland reach out to him as he died in a freezing stream.

Ban pushed himself up on his elbows, realizing he wouldn't be able to rest. After he was sure that Becks was sleeping deeply, he gently moved out from under her. She lay there naked with a smile on her face, peacefully dreaming.

The sleep of the guiltless.

He walked a few steps and folded his small desktop down from its alcove and sat to read. He picked up the holoreader, powered it on, and flipped through a few of the news headlines that vied for his attention.

NEGOTIATIONS WITH RUNE CONTINUE DESPITE RUNIAN AMBASSADOR'S GAFFE. *No . . . How about,* END OF AN AGE: THE DECLINE OF THE DOANIAN KNIGHT. *Depressing. Maybe I'll go for a walk.*

He went to the main screen of the reader and typed a note for Becks, letting her know he was going out, then placed the reader on the bed next to her. After getting dressed, he kissed her on the cheek and left his quarters.

Walking the corridors of the *Talon* was a familiar thing. Like many other sleepless nights, he walked aimlessly, going from deck to deck. Up through the ship he went, passing by the main security hub, the gymnasium, and the medical bay.

He didn't stop at any of them, and without knowing it, he'd returned to the lounge. It was closed, its patrons long since gone to bed. The artificial pavilion outside was quiet, so he took a moment to look it over.

It had grass and trees, but no birds. It was another piece of home, meant to relax or inspire, but it did neither for him. It always bothered him that there weren't any birds.

Before he realized, he was looking through the lounge's window, toward the bar. He could still see Haskel's smile.

That little bastard.

He turned away and walked again, restlessly going over the details in his mind.

How could he know? I wiped the data from my suit. No one could have found it.

He entered the lift and rode it down.

I'll be exiled. Everything I've regained will be taken away. They'll finally kill my dream.

When the lift doors opened, he walked out, no real destination in mind.

As he passed the mess hall's open doors, a few men came rushing out. "Hey, traitor!"

Ban stopped and turned to face them. There were three of them.

"I told you I'd find you." Haskel took the lead, speech slurred and eyes red. Synthetic alcohol would have worn off by then; he must have gotten into the real stuff.

"You're drunk, Haskel. Go home," Ban said.

The two men behind Haskel were taller, but not much larger. The one to the left, Keen, clenched his fists. He was tense, trying to appear more muscular than he was.

Keen laughed. "Scared, Morgan?"

"Of a bunch of drunks? Piss off."

Haskel looked like his head was about to explode, veins bulging on his ruddy forehead. "You're a dead man, Morgan. I saw what you did."

The man to the right focused on Haskel. He was hesitant, seeming to hang back. His eyes darted back and forth, beads of sweat building on his forehead. His name was Corelle.

Corelle reached for Haskel's shoulder. "Hey, maybe we should just go back inside."

Haskel slapped the hand away. "No. We do this now."

Ban watched every move, preparing. "Don't get yourself hurt, Haskel. It won't end well."

Keen spit. "You're pretty cocky for a bondsman criminal."

"Criminal?" Ban looked at Keen. "Then you know who I am. You know what I've done before."

Haskel took a step forward. "No one here's scared of a kid-killing—"

"You're first, Haskel," Ban said, interrupting. "Whatever happens here, win or lose, I'm making sure your next meal comes from a tube."

Haskel's eyes grew large, and he looked back for support. He grabbed at his pant leg. When he turned around again, his arm shot toward Ban's belly, finger-length knife in hand.

Ban's training kicked in. He turned and took Haskel by the wrist then shoved his other palm into the waiting elbow. The knife fell end over end to the floor, and Haskel screamed, crazed eyes focused on the deformity in his arm. Ban took advantage and threw a punch as hard as he could. Haskel collapsed to the floor, unconscious, with a broken jaw to match his arm.

Keen backed away, hands up in defense. But before he could escape, Ban grabbed him by the shirt then by the hair on the back of his head. "Still want this?"

Keen pulled at Ban's wrist, searching for Corelle. "Help me!"

Ban leaned in. "He can't." He punched Keen in the gut, hard enough to drop him to his knees. "Now, pick up your boy and get lost."

Ban stepped back. Once Keen had stumbled to his feet, he and Corelle picked the drooling Haskel up from the floor.

Corelle looked back as they struggled to carry him away. "You only made things worse for yourself, Morgan."

They all turned to the sound of a new voice.

"I don't think so, Corelle. In fact, I think Haskel just gave him a way out." It was Lieutenant Garret. "Attempted murder is a serious crime, even against a bondsman."

Corelle fought for something to say but only stuttered. "B-b-but—"

Garret walked closer. "Get Haskel to the medical bay. If you know what's good for him, and for you, you'll make up a convincing story."

"Y-y-yes, sir!" Corelle almost fell down trying to back away.

The two men moved as quickly as they could while carrying Haskel's dead weight. They disappeared around the corner at the end of the corridor.

"Bond-Sergeant."

Ban turned and came to attention. "Sir."

"Trouble sleeping?"

Ban nodded, fingers still in a fist. "Yes, sir."

"Understandable." Garret looked down then back up. He appeared to be slightly uncomfortable. "Relax, Ban."

Ban did.

Garret went on. "I'd planned on waiting until tomorrow, but the computer showed you walking the halls."

"What is it?" Ban asked.

"I heard about your confrontation earlier tonight."

Ban winced. "It was nothing."

Garret blinked at the understatement. "Haskel tried to kill you. It wasn't nothing."

"It's settled now."

Garret furrowed his brow. "Ban, Haskel was handpicked by Lord Holland to accompany his son. His son who *died*. I don't think you understand just how much trouble this has caused." He stepped closer. "If Haskel pushes this, you'll be stripped of your rank and discharged from the military—for the last time."

Ban turned his head. "For what reason?"

"Griffin Squad's report states that you left Lieutenant Holland to die." He held up his hand to stop Ban's reply. "I know you didn't. On top of that, they also submitted a report that you harassed them at the lounge. That you gloated about Holland's death."

"That's *not* what happened."

"There were credible witnesses. You made a threat."

Ban crossed his arms. "This is ridiculous."

"I'm sorry, Ban. I'll try to speak to the captain about it, but I can assure you he won't defy Lord Holland. In fact, he'll likely go well out of his way to please him."

"Lord Holland . . . " Ban nodded in disbelief. "He'll never let me be."

"No, he won't. You made a powerful enemy."

Ban exhaled. "Sir, you can't let this happen. I'll be disgraced forever."

Garret placed his hand on Ban's shoulder. "It's not over. Later this week, once things have calmed down, we'll go in together, try to sort it out."

Ban sighed. "Yes, sir."

"Try to get some sleep." Garret nodded and walked away.

Not much chance of that happening.

Ban waited a few moments then took the nearest lift back to his deck. When he entered his quarters, Becks was sitting at the desk.

She held the holoreader in her hand. "Couldn't sleep?"

"Not really." He sat on the foot of the bed across from her, subconsciously rubbing his sore hand.

She reached out and took it, frowning. "What happened?"

"Haskel and friends decided to get a little payback."

"And you convinced them otherwise?"

He smiled weakly. "No, but I feel much better."

Becks nodded. "There's something else?"

"I'm in trouble."

"Yeah, I'd say you are. But it'll blow over."

"No, not for the fight. I ran into Garret. Lord Holland wants to pin the loss of his son on me."

"That's crazy. He got *himself* killed."

"It won't matter. My career's over."

"We'll fight it."

"No. I don't want you or the guys getting caught up in this. I have to do this alone."

She pulled his hand closer. "You know, that's the single dumbest thing you've ever said, Ban Morgan. Wherever you go, or whatever happens, you know I'm always with you."

"Even if it means exile?"

"Yes. Anything. Anywhere."

He pulled his hand free. "I hope you really mean that, Saira," he said as he looked up into her eyes, "because I need to tell you what really happened on Nix."

OUT THERE

IT WAS LATE IN THE EVENING, TWO DAYS AFTER the attack, when Edward called the bridge from the *Orchard Run's* engine core.

"Hello? Mr. Arden, are you there? Ranger Arden, will you *please* answer?"

Fall sat up in the pilot's chair and rubbed his tired eyes. "I'm here." He shook himself awake. "What's going on?"

"Oh, good," Edward replied. "Well, it's taken a series of small miracles on my part, but the engines are finally Rift-ready."

"The thrusters?" Fall asked.

"Good to go. And there should be plenty of fuel to get us clear for a jump."

Fall stretched out. "Nice."

Edward laughed. "Better than *nice*. Amazing by anyone's standards."

Olivia's voice came through the same speaker. She sounded fatigued and slightly annoyed. "Fall, go ahead and get us moving. I'll come up after we finish, but Hermes should be on his way up now."

"Sounds good. I'll jump us once we clear the belt."

Fall turned to the controls and plotted a course out of the asteroid field. With the plan laid in, he engaged the thrusters. The ship's inertia compensators were slow to kick in, allowing a few moments of discomfort each time the thrusters corrected.

"Smooth flying, *ace*."

Fall turned to the bridge's hatch. Hermes was there, holding on with his tiny hands.

Fall smiled. "Just shaking the cobwebs off."

Hermes climbed up into the copilot's seat and braced himself. "Do you have to shake 'em so hard?"

"Quit whining." Fall input a course back to the Ro-Art system. "There. We're clear."

Hermes sniffed. "I'm holding you personally responsible for any explosions."

Fall smiled. "Go for it. You'd be the only survivor." He held his breath and activated the Inos drive. A few seconds later, the Rift opened, and space faded away.

Hermes hopped down. "Huh. Still alive. How 'bout that?"

Fall stood up and yawned. "Sorry to disappoint you."

"Eh, I've gotten used to it." He walked over and climbed up into the pilot's seat with a few exaggerated grunts.

"Your life is so hard." Fall walked to the exit and yawned again. "Call me if there's trouble. Otherwise, I'll be in the bunks trying to get some rest."

Hermes waved him away in dismissal. "Sleep tight, sweetheart."

Fall turned around and walked out with yet another yawn. "On this bucket? Unlikely."

"Get up, already!" Two tiny, persistent feet hopped up and down on Fall's back.

Fall opened his eyes halfway and mumbled through his smushed lips. "Hermes. Get off."

"No! Wake it up!"

Fall rolled over slowly as Hermes jumped down. "Come on, I just fell asleep." He rubbed his eyes and sat up, stretching the stiffness out. The bunk's mattresses were less than fresh, so he'd settled for cold metal floor and a ratty blanket.

"You've been asleep for *nine* hours." Hermes looked back as he walked out of the room. "And Olivia's been asking where you are."

Nine hours?

Fall nodded groggily. "Tell her I'll be there . . . " He yawned. " . . . in a minute."

He stood up and stumbled into the small bathroom to get a shower. Freezing cold water did the trick, waking him up as he rushed to dry off and be warm again.

After he was clean, dressed, and geared, he went back to his corner of the room. He knelt and inspected the items he'd gathered the night before.

There was a small black velvet bag with a white string, a golden necklace with an emerald gemstone, and a distressed, wrinkled piece of paper.

The paper showed a hastily scrawled message in smudged black ink. He read it again.

You were wrong about the mansion. That damn dog almost got me! It got Rame's leg and damn near the rest of him too. I sincerely hope this trinket was worth it.

It was unsigned.

The bag held the necklace. Its small emerald stone and gold chain reminded him of something his mother would have liked. He decided to keep it in case they ever found the crew or someone who might claim their remains. He tucked it into a pouch on his belt and headed for the bridge.

Olivia waited there with some freshly brewed coffee she'd found in Wright's ration kit. From the look on her face, it was bitter. "Sleep well?"

Fall rubbed his hands together. "Rock-hard deck without a pillow? Never better."

She sipped. "That good, huh?"

"Like a dream."

She smiled. "Hungry?"

He touched his belly and grimaced. "Now that you mention it, I'm starving."

She stood up. "Me too. Let's go see what we have."

"Right behind you."

They left the bridge for the mess hall. It was neater inside than before; the debris had been pushed to the side and one of the tables sat upright with a few surrounding chairs.

Fall continued on to the galley. "I saw some supplies in here before. There might be something we could eat."

They searched the cabinets and the food closet. Dried blood still covered most of the closet's floor, but up top it was relatively clean. Fall walked out with a few containers and put them on the counter.

He'd found some freeze-dried eggs, a can of mixed fruit, some nuts, and a package of bread sticks. All Olivia found were some basic seasonings.

Fall frowned. "They didn't leave us much."

"No problem. With the rations Wright had, I can whip up something decent," Olivia said.

"You can cook?"

She nodded. "Kind of. I picked up a few skills from my dad over the years."

Olivia opened the containers and moved a pan and utensils around the countertop. "So, I have a confession to make."

"Oh yeah?"

"Mmmhmm. I didn't just ask you here for breakfast."

"Okay." Fall reached up and rubbed the back of his neck.

"Relax." She glanced over with a wry smile. "Now that I have you all alone, I think it's time you make good on your promise."

"My promise?"

"Yeah. Back on Crossroads Station you said you'd tell me more about your past."

"I don't remember promising anything."

She shrugged with only a hint of a smile. "Pretty sure you did."

Fall leaned back against the counter, palms on the edge of it. "Trying to fill those gaps in my file?"

"Maybe. Maybe I'm just curious."

"About?"

"Your life. Who you are."

"Is that all?" He looked up at the stained ceiling. "From birth okay, or is that too late into the story?"

Olivia raised an eyebrow. "Sounds like someone wants to make their own breakfast."

Fall held his hands up in surrender. "Whoa. Say no more. You've broken me."

She laughed. "I *am* known for my interrogation techniques." She adjusted the heat of the stovetop burner. "I just want to know what brings someone all the way out here."

He thought for a second then shrugged. "A chance."

Olivia poured oil into the pan. "A chance for what?"

Fall looked down, crossed his arms, and then looked back up to her. "Life? I don't know. For something real."

"Something real? I'm not sure what you mean."

"Well, let me ask you this. Back home, how often did you feel like you'd made a difference?"

She tilted her head. "That's hard to define. Most of the time?"

"See, I could have answered that instantly. Never."

She tasted the tip of her finger. "That can't have been true. Didn't you have a family? Didn't anyone rely on you?"

He grunted. "No. My mother died several years ago. I don't have any siblings."

"What about your dad?"

"He was a jumper."

She stopped stirring for a moment. "Was?"

"He died when I was young. A short life, but a good one, as he used to say."

She went back to cooking. "He must have seen some crazy things out here."

Fall nodded. "He mostly jumped out into the coreward Frontier, pretty far from here. I used to read his logs."

She stopped stirring the eggs. "It's a sensitive subject. Let's talk about something else."

He waved his hand. "No, it's fine. It was a long time ago. Such is life, right?"

"I suppose it is." She nodded. "I've lost family too."

"Sorry to hear that. One of your parents?"

"My sister. Though, to be honest, I'm not actually sure she's dead."

"What do you mean?"

"She went missing. Out here, actually. She might be okay, but I guess there's no way to know."

"Hmmm. What's her name?"

"Elizabeth."

Fall looked up. "I like it."

Olivia smiled. "It's kinda silly, but I hoped the *Morning Rain* might somehow come across her or some hint of her."

"That's not silly at all. There's always a chance."

Olivia sighed. "Especially now that *I'm* missing too." She shook her head. "Enough about that. We talked about your dad, but what about your mom? You said she passed away?"

"More like faded away. She was never the same after my father didn't come home. I remember she used to sing when I was small. She was . . . *quiet* after he died."

Olivia tasted a spice then added it to the eggs. "Sounds lonely."

He nodded. "Yes. But Hermes was there."

She looked up from the stove. "Oh yeah. What's his story? I don't think I've ever heard of anyone owning an AI before."

"Own him? Don't let him hear you say that." Fall looked down at the floor and laughed to himself. "It sounds ridiculous, but I found him in the forest near my house."

"He was lost?"

"Not him. Me." Fall's smile grew slowly as he spoke. "We had a small house. More of a cabin, really. I had this itch to wander, and it was nice to get out of such a dark, quiet place. My mother certainly didn't mind." He looked out into the mess hall. "I liked the feeling of solitude, and I liked animals. Birds, deer, tyks—"

She pointed to the paint on his shoulder armor and raised an eyebrow.

He nodded. "Yes, foxes too. Actually, that's a pretty good segue." He leaned against the wall near the door, moving his hands as he told the story. "There was this fox. I saw it every few days, hiding deep inside a log or sitting on top of a rock. It was different than the other animals. It only ran from me if I got really close, and it always seemed to want something I didn't have." His eyes moved as if he were seeing the story as he told it. "I followed that thing for kilometers and kilometers, going farther each day until one time, I'd gone too far to make it home before dark."

Olivia frowned. "You got stuck out there all alone?"

He looked up and nodded slowly. "I thought so at the time."

"Hermes?"

"Right. He was the fox. No surprise there. But back then, I had no idea."

"So what happened?"

"I got lost. Completely and utterly lost. For several days."

"That's awful! Poor kid."

"Eh, I was fine. Every time the sun went down, I'd see a campfire in the distance. When I'd wake up next to it in the morning, there'd be berries and fresh water sitting next to me."

"He protected you."

"He did. When I finally made it home, Hermes was there in my room. He's been around ever since."

"Amazing. Though, I have to admit, I never would have pictured him as a *caregiver*. He seems . . . "

"Stupid? Arrogant?"

She snorted. "Well . . . yeah."

"That's his way. His form changes along with his mood." Fall tapped his cheek with his index finger. "Or maybe it's the other way around."

She laughed then tasted the tip of the spoon. "So you grew up in a forest? No school?"

"Just home modules I taught myself. I never had a teacher until Hermes. He taught me everything else I needed to know."

"Seriously?" Olivia asked.

"No joke."

"You never went into town? You didn't have any friends?"

"Nope. The nearest city was on the horizon, and I had to climb pretty high up into the trees to see that. But I didn't miss out. You'd be surprised what a shapeshifting teacher can teach you."

She opened the oven and placed the dish inside. "I didn't think about that. Now I'm kinda jealous."

"Of me? You're a doctor. I could never do that."

"I bet you could. You seem smart enough."

"Maybe. It's the studying though. I'm too impatient."

She nodded. "It *is* a skill."

Fall tapped the heel of his boot against the wall as the conversation took a natural lull. "So. What makes someone like you come all the way out here?"

She shook her head with a playful scowl. "Like me?"

"I meant that to sound nicer than it did. You know, someone with a life. A career."

"Mmmm, if I really had to put my finger on it, I'd say boredom. I fell out of love with the routine. Frontier medicine, going places no one has been before . . . I thought it might be just what I needed."

Fall smirked. "Maybe you should be a Ranger."

"Oh no. Not me."

"Why not?"

"Too dangerous."

He spread his hands and looked around. "You're doing a wonderful job of playing it safe."

"True. But I'm not looking for any more trouble than I already have."

"Hey, trouble finds us all, one way or another. Might as well embrace it."

"I may have to at this rate." She bent down to open the oven door. She wafted some of the hot air and smiled. "In the meantime, I'll settle for breakfast. Would you mind getting Eddie?"

"Sure thing."

"Good." She tapped the spoon on the side of the pan. "Let's eat!"

"You made *this* from rations and leftovers?" Edward pinched off the tip of a breadstick.

Fall agreed but couldn't speak with his mouth full; he was already on his second plate before Edward had made it halfway through his first.

Olivia watched Fall eat as she leaned forward, chin resting in her hand. "I hope it's okay. I didn't have much to work with."

Fall spoke between bites. "It's great, Olivia. I'd like to see what you could do with a fully stocked kitchen."

She leaned back with a smile. "This might be the best we eat for a while. We have enough scraps left to get us to Ro-Art, but I'm afraid it's plain military rations from then on."

Fall chewed and washed his food down with lukewarm water. "I guess we should have saved some."

Olivia smiled. "No, enjoy it while it's fresh."

Fall nodded in agreement and took another bite.

Edward filled the silence as Fall continued to eat. "Oh. I've been meaning to ask. What were you and Endo Kumi fighting about on the *Morning Rain*'s bridge."

"The lieutenant commander?" Fall asked.

"Yeah."

"I wouldn't say we were fighting. We disagreed on the ignorance of wandering around the Frontier without a plan."

Olivia drank some water and wiped her mouth. "Sounds like you were right."

Fall shrugged. "Small comfort now."

"That may be, but you stood your ground. Bravo," Edward said.

Fall frowned. "I was only doing what I was hired to do. Power struggles don't matter to me."

"They do to *her*. She's gunning for captain before thirty. She'll step on anyone in her way."

Olivia laughed at that. "Yeah, she's ruthless." Almost as soon as she'd said it, her smile faded.

Edward shook his head. "Don't feel bad. She was mean."

Olivia poked at the scraps on her plate. "Still, I wish there was something we could have done."

Edward dropped his fork. "Call me negative if you wish, but I'd settle for getting *myself* back home." He stood up, wiping his mouth with his sleeve. "In fact, I'd better get back to those engines."

"Sounds good." Olivia pushed back from the table and stood. "I know I could use some sleep. Fall, you better get to work too."

Fall wiped his mouth and stretched. "Hermes has it covered on the bridge."

She smiled down at the table, looking up to his eyes as she backed out of the mess hall. "I meant the dishes."

Fall took a seat at the helm. "All right, looks like we're coming into the system. We should reach the outermost planet's orbit any minute now."

Olivia sat down behind him. "I've had Hermes working on the communications software. He thinks we can get a broadcast out to your friend, Mei."

Fall thought about that for a second and spun around. "It might be better if we knew exactly where her probe was. Broadcasting our location might get us into more trouble."

She took a sip of coffee and frowned. "I didn't think of that."

Fall keyed the communications panel. "Edward, any luck with the sensor array?"

After a few seconds, he heard some grunting, then a crash of metal parts, and then a curse. "This *absolute* piece of junk!" Footsteps approached the microphone. "It's not going well. We might be able to find something, but this thing's in bad shape."

"What kind of range are we looking at?"

"Range isn't the problem. Without good resolution, we might end up calling a lump of rock. Even if it replied, we wouldn't know."

"Just let us know when we can try," Fall said.

"You can try right now, but I can't make a promise on what you'll get."

"All right. I'm bringing us out of the Rift." Fall input the command, and the ship broke away from the Never and out of the Rift, back into normal space.

Hermes tapped a few keys on his console.

Fall smiled; it was hard to take him seriously while he sat on a crate to reach the controls. "Hermes, why don't you just take a taller form?"

The crate disappeared, and Hermes floated above the seat as if nothing had changed. He turned with a grin as the crate reappeared. "It's like you don't even know me."

Fall shook his head.

Hermes looked at the screen for a few moments then rubbed his chin. "I think I found something."

Fall and Olivia walked over. The screen displayed a two-dimensional representation of the system. Near the second planet, a small blip blinked.

Olivia leaned in. "Is it the probe?"

Hermes scratched again. "I can't tell from this. Could be."

Olivia looked up. "What are you thinking, Fall?"

"I'm thinking we don't have much of a choice. This freighter won't run forever."

She searched the display. "Couldn't we head for the nearest T-Gate?"

"There isn't one here. It would be a huge gamble to make the trip to the closest one."

She sighed. "Okay then. I guess we don't have a choice. Head for the probe."

They took their seats again, and Fall reengaged the Inos drive. It took longer than normal to enter the Rift, and something was strange about its appearance once they did. Several warning indicators flashed on the panel ahead.

"Are you seeing this?" Fall asked.

Olivia leaned over Fall's shoulder. "Yeah. The Rift looks . . . unstable."

The ship shuddered, and a siren sounded.

Fall found the communications panel and called engineering. "Edward?"

Edward responded. "The drive's giving me trouble. I'd shut it down for now if I were you."

Fall sat back. "Can we get a few more minutes out of them?"

"That depends on how you feel about explosions and decompression."

Fall looked forward through the viewport. The Rift seemed to be fading in and out of focus, faint stars becoming visible here and there. He turned. "Hermes, how close are we?"

"Um . . . the sensors seem . . . confused. No way to tell."

Edward spoke. "I'm shutting it down."

There was an audible power drain, and the lights flickered. The ship lurched to the side and Fall barely caught himself. Through the viewport, he saw the Rift disappear in an abrupt flash.

The planet Ro-Art III was suddenly there, closer than he'd have liked. Edward sounded panicked. "Not good."

Fall righted himself. "What happened?"

"The drive's fried. Worse yet, we lost the conventional engines."

The ship listed and moaned. The planet's gravity was pulling them in, and they had no way to escape.

Olivia squeezed Fall's chair as she held on. "There's no way off the ship. What do we do?"

Hermes laughed. "Sprout wings?"

They both turned to look at him.

He shrugged. "What? It's not like we have any other options."

Fall scowled. "This thing isn't exactly aerodynamic, Hermes. We're going down *hard*."

"Then I guess it's time you showed us what Thane taught you."

"Sure. I'll just go back to the lesson on riding a giant missile into a planet."

"A crash landing?" Olivia sounded unsure. "Can you do it?"

"We're about to find out." Fall turned back to the console. "I'm dumping the cargo modules. Edward, I need all the power to the thrusters you can give me."

"I'll do what I can."

Fall began the module jettison process. "All right, everyone strap in. Hermes, set up a distress call to Mei's probe."

Olivia snapped her harness buckles. "What should I do?"

Fall looked back. "Survive. We'll need a doctor." He looked out through the forward viewport.

Ro-Art III might have been beautiful in other circumstances. Along the northern edge of the continent below, a string of lakes was surrounded by dense forest landscape. If they were lucky, they could hit water.

Hermes gave Fall a furry thumbs-up. "You're good to go."

Fall hit the broadcast key. "This is Fall Arden of the *Orchard Run*. We have suffered catastrophic engine failure and are crash landing on Ro-Art III. If we can, we'll activate a distress beacon after the crash. Please assist if able." He hit the key again. "All right, it's sent."

Hermes turned. "You know, if it makes you feel better, I'll survive the crash, even if you guys don't."

Fall grunted. "Who'd be left to laugh at your stupid jokes?"

"You make a good point." Hermes looked up. "Still . . . might be worth it."

Olivia clicked the last buckle on her safety harness. "Hermes . . . "

"I'm kidding. You guys'll be fine. Probably."

Fall turned back to the viewport, making whatever adjustments he could as they fell toward the planet's surface.

Wish I could be so sure.

The ground rushed up to meet the *Orchard Run*, far more solid than it had looked from a few kilometers above.

The freighter hit and skipped with a terrible jolt, thrusters dying as the ship fell again and again. Fall braced, though he knew it wouldn't do any good, fearing each time the freighter came back down would mean his death.

He closed his eyes as it fell the last time, gritting his teeth against the horrible forces that threatened to rip him out of his seat. Suddenly, there was the briefest flash of fire as the bridge broke free, momentum like a catapult launch, then surprisingly, a gentle rest.

"Open your eyes," he heard from all around him.

Fall did, but he couldn't see. He reached out into the doughy substance that covered him. He started to panic and tried to get out, unable to take a breath.

"Hold on a second," the oozing voice said.

Just when he was about to lose it, the smothering material began to quiver. It receded away from him, and the fading light of a setting sun met his eyes.

The semi-liquid goo continued to shrink away, and Olivia tumbled out of it too. She was coughing, but she seemed to be in one piece. "Ah! What is this stuff?"

Hermes's voice came from the undulating dough as he returned to his red imp shape. "Excuse me, but this *stuff* just saved your life."

Olivia's mouth hung open. "You . . . saved us?"

"Yeah, Fall can't fly for crap. See that giant lake over there? *Way* over there? Missed it." He hopped down from a fallen tree trunk. "I guess it wasn't a complete loss. You might be drowning right now."

Fall looked back at the ship. They'd been ejected through the front viewport, chairs and harnesses included. The remainder of the ship lay closer to the edge of the forest, having carved a giant gash through the dense foliage.

He stood slowly and checked himself. He was intact and felt no pain at all. He went to Olivia, but she was already beginning to stand.

Then he remembered Edward.

The drive section!

Fall took off running, and Olivia followed. It took some time to cover the distance, and when they all made it to the aft of the ship, they paused for a moment to catch their breath. They carefully trudged up the wall of dirt and rock which sloped up to the edge of the ship.

There was a gaping hole in the hull near where engineering would be, and that's where they climbed inside. Luckily, vines had been ripped from the forest and were hanging from the hull, providing handholds on the way up.

Once he made it to the top, Fall reached down to help Olivia up and inside. Hermes was hanging on to her shoulders.

Fall turned to look at the forest. The sky was overcast, and shadows covered the dense floor. He squinted, and for a moment he thought he saw those shadows move.

That's the last thing we need.

They ran down the ruined corridor leading farther into the ship. Though Fall had never gone to engineering, he was certain he wouldn't have recognized it then. The hull was buckled, protruding into the room, distorting its shape.

Near one of the mangled walls, he spotted one of Edward's hands sticking up from the rubble. "There!"

They ran over, and Olivia bent down to take a look. "Oh no." She turned her head. "Poor Eddie . . . "

Hermes moved to the metal and changed, assuming the shape of a Rigian ogre-bear. Fall had never seen one of the brown four-armed bears in person, but apparently, Hermes had. He lifted the metal and threw it away with ease then reached down and cut Edward's harness with his claws.

Fall knelt down. "It crushed him."

Olivia dusted her hands off and backed away. "He probably died quickly. At least there's that."

"Quiet." Hermes turned around, large feet making heavy thuds, voice deep and resonant. "I hear something."

Olivia followed him. "What? Where?"

A grating noise echoed from down the corridor. Something heavy fell over.

They waited.

A more insidious sound followed. A growing chatter and a multitude of rapid taps flowed toward them.

Fall stood and pulled his mech bow from its holster.

Olivia looked to him, stiffened with fear. "What's that sound?"

"I have no idea." He walked to the mangled hatch that used to separate engineering from the rest of the ship. "Illuminator."

He reached up for the arrow, aimed blindly into the darkness ahead, and fired. With a tap of his fingers, the corridor exploded in light.

Along the walls, floor, and ceiling, clinging insectoid creatures recoiled from the blinding display. They dug their sharp claws into the metal of the hull, screeching in anger.

Fall ran back to the group. Olivia must have seen the urgency on his face, because her expression soon matched. "What is it?"

"Not it. *They*." He reached back to his quiver. "Boomer."

He fired the arrow at the opening of the hatch, detonating the explosive. Smoke and fire encompassed the area near the blast, and Fall drew another arrow. He nocked and waited for the smoke to clear.

He heard the noise above him just in time. He dove to the side, barely avoiding the mass of falling cables. A blur landed where he'd been standing, and sharp claws threw sparks in the darkness.

Olivia screamed and drew her pistol. Pieces of the beast's exoskeleton flew away as she fired, but it continued to advance toward her rapidly on its pointed appendages.

It raised a claw to strike, but never got the chance.

Fall's sword sang as it severed the arm. He leapt onto the beast with a downward thrust and drove it down to the floor. He twisted hard then pulled his sword from its thorax, and the animal's legs folded up near its body.

Olivia held her smoking gun in front of her, eyes wide.

Fall flipped his sword over and sheathed it as he spoke. "There's at least twenty more out there."

She lowered the gun. "What do we do?"

"We find a way out. Hermes, I need you." He retrieved his bow and nocked another arrow.

Hermes lumbered over, towering over Fall. His voice rumbled.

"What's the big deal? We can handle twenty."

Fall held the drawn bowstring next to his cheek, looking down the arrow's shaft. He whispered so only Hermes could hear. "The forest is full of them. Hundreds, maybe thousands."

Hermes opened his fanged mouth to speak but stopped and nodded.

Near the collapsed hatch, the insects tapped and probed as the weakened hull peeled away like paper. They squeezed and pushed through, legs scrambling to find a hold. As the first one rose up and started forward, Fall exhaled.

He waited until the last moment, when the swarm came in behind the lead insect, then released the arrow, praying Mei had heard the call.

FIRE AND LIGHTNING

SIDNA CURLED UP INTO A BALL, GRASPING THE frayed end of her blanket with her toes.

So cold . . .

After a few careful adjustments, she had nearly every part of her body covered. Satisfied and finally feeling a little bit warmer, she exhaled and began to relax. But just as she drifted off to sleep, her leg jerked, and the blanket shot free. The stored heat underneath rushed out, cold air taking its place.

"Ahhh!" She sat up and threw the worthless blanket against the wall. "Ugh!" She swung her legs out of bed, shivering, and hurriedly slipped on her pants, patched-up leather jacket, and insulated leather boots.

Once she was dressed and a little more comfortable, she opened her travel bag. Using her compact mirror and brush, she untangled her hair and wound it into a loose braid. Then she washed her face and brushed her teeth at the basin.

Anxious to be free of the frigid quarters, she left for the cockpit. When she entered, she found Mei busy at the *Rìluò*'s controls.

The Ranger continued to look ahead as she worked. "How was your rest?"

Sidna walked to the copilot's seat and placed her hand on the headrest. "Same as always. Terrible."

"Did you try the meditation routine I suggested?"

Sidna rubbed her temples. "*What?*"

"I left a summary in your quarters." The mechanical patch over her right eye hummed briefly. "I had hoped you might take advantage."

"You're kidding. Meditate inside this flying glacier?"

"If you would only try, you might learn to endure such minor difficulties."

Sidna plopped down in the seat. *"Or* you could keep the ship at a temperature the living prefer."

Mei smiled only in the slightest. "I am quite comfortable."

Sidna turned to the console. "Like I said . . ."

After a few moments of silence, Sidna warmed up, and her thoughts returned to the lost freighter, the *Orchard Run.*

Come on, please be out there.

Using the interface in front of her, she reviewed the sensor logs. Almost a week had gone by without a lead. If they didn't find it soon, she'd lose her last chance at going back to Veridian.

She sat back and sighed. "At this rate, we'll never find it."

Mei continued to study her display. "That was always a possibility."

Sidna turned to face her. "Then what are we doing? Let's widen the search. We're not paying you to—"

Mei paused and spoke matter-of-factly. "I am obligated only to the terms of the contract. Not to your whims. We will leave the system when I am convinced."

Sidna crossed her arms. "Ronin knew when to listen."

"I am sure he did. But he is gone. The job is mine now, and I plan to do it correctly."

Sidna grunted derisively. "Do it forever too."

Mei turned her head slowly. The imposing device covering her right eye made a whirring noise. "I have no desire to prolong this search any longer than I must. This mission has become . . . *troublesome.*"

Sidna rolled her eyes.

Yeah, sure. I'm the annoying one.

A short-lived chime sounded from the panel in front of Mei, and she looked to the pilot's display. "Ah, you see? Patience has been rewarded."

Sidna turned back to her own readout. "What? What is it?"

"A transmission from the probe. A distress call." She placed a command into her controls, and the recording played.

"This is Fall Arden of the *Orchard Run.* We have suffered catastrophic engine failure and are crash landing on Ro-Art III. If we can, we'll activate a distress beacon after the crash. Please assist if able."

Sidna listened, then turned to Mei. "Who's Fall Arden? He isn't on the crew roster."

"He is an Aeturnian Ranger."

"That doesn't explain why he's on the freighter."

Mei narrowed her eye. "I assume he is there because his captain refused to follow my advice."

Sidna thought for a second then leaned forward. "Yeah, or he's getting paid to find the glyph."

"I highly doubt that," Mei said.

Sidna furrowed her brow. "Mei. He's on the freighter. The odds of him being there for anything else are almost impossible."

"I agree. It is strange."

Sidna stared ahead for a few minutes then turned back. "If he has the glyph, you know I'll have to take it."

Mei faced her. "You may find that exceedingly difficult. Inexperience does not mean incompetence."

Sidna wasn't impressed. "A thief's a thief."

Mei turned back to her interface, silent.

Sidna studied her. "Okay. Don't just sit there stewing. Say whatever it is you want to say."

Mei looked down. "I was wondering what could be so important about this glyph that you would attack a stranger for it."

"You don't need to know that. All you need to know is that I will."

"Again, I think that would be unwise."

Sidna glared. "I don't care what you think, Mei. How about you concentrate on helping me find it, which is your actual job?"

"Very well." Mei nodded tightly, inputting commands into the touchscreen ahead of her. "I am setting a course for Ro-Art III."

Sidna laid her head back against the seat with a thud. No matter what Mei thought, she couldn't afford to let anyone get in her way.

I can't let anyone stop me.

The Rìluò maneuvered in space, and Sidna lost sight of the planet ahead. With an intensifying hum, the Inos drive activated, opening a Rift into the endless sea of stars.

No matter who they are.

The clouds parted, and the Rìluò descended over Ro-Art III. Night was falling, and the ship's running lights scattered on the clouds in fiery orange. Wind buffeted the ship, and a fine mist left streams of water that streaked away across the forward viewport.

Mei activated a visual overlay that started at the bottom of the viewport and swept upward. It enhanced the low light, letting them see the planet's surface as if it were late in the day.

Sidna watched as the landscape rolled by. The terrain undulated with high hills, most of them covered in a sea of trees and dense forestation. The thick leaves had just begun to change colors, showing signs of the shorter days and longer nights of autumn.

Her eyes followed the hills toward the horizon. Small lakes, strung out like beads on a necklace, came into view. Each lake was an isolated body, any links with the others lost in the forests nearby.

Near the edge of a large lake, the terrain was marred with a fresh, ugly wound, and at the end of that wound, she saw the smoldering wreckage of the *Orchard Run*.

Mei brought the *Rìluò* closer to the downed freighter. Its bridge was missing, and the ship had ruptured in multiple areas along the hull. Ejected materials and equipment were scattered along the ground.

Sidna stood slightly and leaned forward. "It looks like the surface of the ship is moving. What's wrong with the imager?"

Mei leaned forward, and the device covering her right eye emitted soft mechanical sounds. After a few moments, she sat up straight, and her hands worked the controls more quickly. "That is no malfunction."

Mei flew the *Rìluò* nearby, swinging the tail around as she passed over the hull. Sidna could see the beasts clearly then; green, man-sized insects with armored exoskeletons swarmed along the ship's surface. Some disappeared into holes in the buckled hull, while others tore into the softened metal nearby. The monsters were frenzied, rapaciously seeking something within.

"Open the ventral hatch. I'll get inside the freighter while you cover me." Sidna left the cockpit and returned to her quarters.

Moving to her bunk, she retrieved her brown leather belt, leg-strap holster, and engraved semi-auto pistol. Quickly inspecting the gun, she ejected and reinserted the magazine, racked the slide, and watched a shell enter the chamber. After fastening her gear loosely, she holstered the weapon, producing the satisfying sound of metal on worn leather.

There was one last item—Ronin's data module. She'd removed it from his armlet after he died and used it to replace her own.

Prepared, she moved through the small aft bay to the ventral hatch. She opened it, and once inside, manually closed it behind her. When she was ready, she gripped a nearby strap.

The ventral bay door opened downward with whining servos, and a gust of humid wind rushed up into her hair, flinging it back. Floodlights from the *Rìluò* activated and repositioned, illuminating the surface of the *Orchard Run* through swirling, misty rain.

The ship continued to descend, and Sidna picked a clear spot below. She wiped the moisture from the small screen of the data module and toggled the locator program. The glyph was far ahead, deep inside the freighter's innards.

She gritted her teeth and dropped down to the *Orchard Run*. The ruined metal was slick, with a surface much more uneven than it had appeared from above. As she steadied herself, beams from the *Rìluò* swept along the hull, revealing the alien creatures ahead.

One of the monsters slowed, turning to investigate the unexpected source of light. Its mouth parts moved eagerly, sampling the air. Tensing suddenly, it let out a high-pitched, unmelodious screech, and the swarm flowed toward Sidna.

She closed her eyes, fighting her instinct to run. Instead, she allowed her emotions to empower her. Focusing through the fear, she drew her pistol slowly and deliberately.

Beginning at her right shoulder, she hovered her left hand over her *viae*. Red-orange light emanated from between her fingers and spread along the curves of her *viae*, igniting under her jacket as her hand passed. Intense light spilled out from her sleeve, and when she reached the gun, the energy erupted along the metal grooves on its surface.

She fired into the nearest creature, and molten fragments exploded from the other side. The beast burned from inside the gaping wound then collapsed, engulfed in flames. She shot one insect after another, leaving a blazing line of carcasses.

The creatures beyond the line stopped, screeching at the fire. They bunched up, seeming to consider the risk of crossing.

Taking advantage of their pause, the *Rìluò* drifted alongside the hull. Its guns spun with a low-pitched hum, and scores of rounds ripped through the bunched-up creatures, shredding them instantly.

Sidna lowered her pistol, and the light along her arm dimmed. She ran ahead toward the ship's aft, avoiding holes and warped areas of hull plating. She was forced to stop suddenly as an explosion rocked the hull. Again and again more explosions came, blasting from deep inside the ship. Once the explosions subsided, she continued.

There were fewer of the beasts then, but several still tried to burrow through openings in the hull. Just ahead, one of the creatures lifted a broken section upward, moving inside.

She raised her pistol to shoot it, but before she could pull the trigger, the creature jerked back and collapsed. A high-pitched drilling sound came from its corpse, and a tight spray of liquid spurted up into the air.

The drilling halted as she walked closer. She looked down and saw a gray rod, with two encircling white stripes near something like feathers, sticking out from the wound. It was deeply lodged into the creature's vital organs, point still spinning.

Sidna looked to the right as the hum of Mei's machine guns resumed. The bullets threw showers of sparks as they tore into the hull behind her. The Rìluò hovered in place for an instant, and Sidna turned to see the ravaged forms of dead insects not far behind her.

Mei's voice boomed. "Move! This is no time for hesitation!"

The Rìluò turned and sped forward. An arc of fire from the machine guns raked the ground, moving away from the ship to the edge of the forest. Sidna's attention was suddenly snapped back to the freighter as a furious roar bellowed from below. She ran to the hole, and through the opening, saw a large, four-armed bear-thing wrestling with one of the creatures.

She cocked her head. "What the . . . ?"

The room appeared to be a large cargo area comprised of mostly open space. Small fires and emergency lighting weren't bright enough to see the whole area clearly, but there appeared to be other monsters in the room.

An insect's pointed appendages thrust into the bear, distorting its shape slightly. Somehow the bear didn't slow at all, destroying the creature with its own set of claws. The bear roared again and ran to fight another creature. It was a frightening thing to see, yet as it moved away, her eyes were drawn to something far more interesting.

Farther into the room below, a figure moved deftly in the darkness. He held a silver blade in his hands, flowing from monster to monster, dispatching each creature he met. The sword reflected the light from the nearby fires as it moved in the air, and for a split second, she saw the swordsman's face.

That's him.

Four of the beasts lay dead when he finished. He spun rapidly and unfolded a long object of some kind in his left hand. As she watched, it became a bow.

He reached up behind his head then brought his hand forward. He shot an arrow, and another explosion rocked the hull.

The explosions . . . he's the cause.

Turning to run, he looked up and saw her crouched there. He raised his weapon, ready to fire, but froze instead. His arms relaxed slowly. He was about to say something when the bear passed by him. A woman ran by as well, yelling something as she did.

He looked back to where he'd been firing, then bolted away, stealing a glance at Sidna before disappearing out of sight.

Why didn't he shoot?

She bit her lip, almost to the point of drawing blood.

Why didn't I shoot? Focus.

She pulled up the data module once again. The holographic indicator showed the glyph moving away in the same direction as the group.

He does have it!

She crouched under the opening and grabbed a bundle of hanging cables. After she tested their strength, she lowered herself down to a toppled-over shelf. Sliding down its surface, she came to the floor, never slowing.

She chased after the group, moving in the direction she'd seen them go, through a central work area with workbenches, crates, and repulsion lifts. Ahead, she heard more roaring, the sound getting closer and closer as she ran.

With a startling crash, a pile of metal and wires fell in front of her. Right after it, one of the monsters jumped down and raised its appendages. She stifled a stunted scream then cursed, angry at herself for being surprised.

The monster charged forward as she raised her arms. She didn't have time to infuse her pistol, so she used a little more energy for a quick response. A short-lived, blue-white flash lit the air between them followed by a wave of heat and rapidly expanding air. Her ears rang slightly from the bang, but the creature was instantly obliterated. Charred pieces of it scattered all over, and a haze of ash fell to the deck.

Her way clear, she ran forward, coming to a short, wide bridge. Below it, pipes and conduits ran perpendicular to her path, leading off to the side for several meters in both directions. She crossed over and entered the final area of engineering.

The upper sections of three huge engine cores stretched across the expansive room with two sets of metal scaffolding running between them. Those paths branched into upper and lower portions, half leading up and over the cores, and the others below.

Rainwater poured in through breaches in the ceiling, and light flashed intermittently as the Rìluò flew by. Dim yellow bulbs along the handrails provided meager visibility. She ran up the metal steps of the right scaffold, between the middle and right engines, chasing after the roaring bear.

She topped the steps and sprinted ahead, metal resonating with each footfall. When she came to the end, she reached a merger of the upper scaffolds, a final link to the ship's rearmost platform.

About twenty meters ahead, the Ranger and his friends faced a swarm of insects. A wave of the creatures had found them, getting there before she could, and they filled the bottleneck path, nearly pushing each other over the edges as they competed to advance. She took a quick look behind, seeing the other insects hadn't reached her yet, then watched.

The bear stood ready in the front, teeth barred and snarling. The swordsman was behind, bow at the ready. The woman knelt nearby him, hastily tending to a wound above his left knee. She yanked a strip of cloth into a tight knot, wiped the sweat from her brow as she stood, and unholstered her pistol.

As the monsters closed in, the bear turned to look at the swordsman then ran forward, throwing itself into the fight. Its arms swung wildly, slashing and crushing. The insects focused on the bear, and as they attacked, the swordsman shot his arrows. The woman held back, shooting only when a creature seemed to be gaining ground. Despite their injuries, the wounded animals continued to thrash, going still only when dead.

The Ranger fired several more times in rapid succession until his hand came forward empty. The bow folded into a holster at his side, and he drew his silvery blade. He moved back a few steps, spinning his sword around once, body winding up like a spring.

She returned her attention to the bear. Among the flailing claws, it continued to fight, assaulted over and over by relentless stabbing. But something must have happened then, because the bear's image began to shift and distort. With a short flash of light, it disappeared, and an incredibly small object fell to the deck, rolling away.

Not good.

Though she couldn't have explained why, Sidna instinctively ran forward, shouting at the insects. When she did, a few in the rear ceased their pushing and turned, strange heads lowering as they located her.

She walked backwards, imbuing her *viae* with fire and charged her pistol. The three creatures she'd alerted crept toward her, closing in for the kill. She took aim on the lead beast and gripped the trigger with her finger, holding her breath.

Before she could shoot, the scaffolding behind her started to shake, and the *clanks* and scrapes of the primary swarm flowed toward her. She turned to look back only for a second then ran forward, firing into the insects ahead. Each one jerked and shuddered when hit, catching fire, collapsing as they disintegrated.

She leapt over the burning chitin. When she reached the other end of the scaffold, she stopped and turned. The creatures crawled over the final bridge where she'd just been, nearly across.

She holstered her pistol and closed her eyes, palms forward and pointed down to the path. Bracing herself for a huge release of energy, she closed her eyes and opened her *viae*, channeling as much fire as she could.

A stream of flames ignited in front of her, roaring through the grated metal. Superheated, it began to glow red then white, dripping as it warped. As the first of the monsters swept the remains of the dead away, it rushed forward and fell, its weight collapsing the weakened structure.

Sidna swept her hands up and blasted the opposite side of the interspace for good measure then stumbled backward, head swimming. She stepped on something, which rolled underneath her boot, and lost her footing, falling onto her back. Her vision darkened, closing in from the sides.

No. Not now.

She looked up to see one of the monsters approaching, front legs raised as it opened its mouthparts. She held her hands up in defense, bracing for what came next. Instead, the Ranger crashed into it, silver blade flashing. He hacked at the head until the beast fell away, then turned to her. He looked her over quickly then ran away with a spin of his sword.

Sidna rolled onto her side to watch him go. He sprinted toward the woman, reaching her just as her pistol went dry. A group of the bugs surrounded her, and he jumped into them, cutting and stabbing. She was able to escape, mostly because they all turned on him. He flew out of the pile, stumbling backward into the bulkhead, clutching his side, hurt.

Three of the monsters remained, moving toward him slowly. They were injured too, barely able to walk on their battered limbs. When they got to him, he raised his sword, limited by his pain.

One of the creatures leapt forward. The Ranger deflected the claws with his blade and kicked a leg from under it. The leg splintered as the insect went down with a screeching wail.

The other two monsters rushed forward, and the swordsman stepped to the side as claws dug into the wall where he'd just been. He brought his sword down on the head of the one that had just attacked, killing it instantly.

The last creature shoved the twitching carcass away, never slowing. The Ranger readied his sword to defend, but as he did, the forgotten enemy near his feet stuck its claws deep into his left leg. He cried out, and as he did, the monster in front attacked. The Ranger twisted just in time to avoid a lethal blow, but the claws lodged into his chest, through the armor, somehow missing his heart. With his final effort, he managed to thrust his sword into the monster's gullet, killing it before it could kill him.

He tried to take a step but let the sword go and fell.

The woman ran forward then dropped beside him, desperately pressing her hands to his wound, trying to stanch the flow of blood.

Sidna pushed herself up and shook her head. She rose and rested her hands on her knees, looking back to see what had caused her to slip. It was the cylindrical object that had fallen from the bear. She twisted and reached out to take it, noting the gash in its side. She put it in her jacket pocket then stood.

Careful not to stumble, she walked to the Ranger and the woman, hand on her pistol's grip. The woman pulled something from her belt.

Sidna held out her left hand. "Drop it!"

The woman looked up, furious. "He needs it! Shoot me if you want!" She put it to his neck, waited, then looked up at Sidna. "My bag! Now!"

Sidna jumped. *"Listen, I—"*

The woman pointed. "There! Hurry!"

Sidna walked to the bag, picked it up by a strap, and tossed it to the deck near the woman. "Here."

The woman reached into it, searching and probing.

Sidna looked around. There wasn't a way out; she'd have to blast a way through. She picked a spot along the inner hull that looked weak, already damaged from one of the burrowing insects.

A crash near the scaffolding surprised her. Along the paths, burning corpses were pushed away, falling into the engine room's depths. Already, a new wave of monsters had arrived.

She raised her arms toward the broken hull and turned her head.

The woman held a canister over the Ranger's chest, injecting a foamy liquid into his wounds.

Sidna activated the communicator on her wrist. "Mei, I'm about to blow a hole in the rear of the ship." She raised her arms and fed her *viae* with searing power, already feeling the drain. "You should hurry. I think your Ranger friend might be dead."

WOUNDS

THE SENSATION OF FALLING STARTLED SIDNA out of her sleep. She sat up and rubbed her eyes, head pounding, absolutely miserable.

Mei cleared her throat from the pilot's chair. "Go back to the hold. Get some rest."

Sidna leaned her forehead on the console with a groan. "I already told you. There's no room back there."

"There must be somewhere to lie down," Mei said.

"No, there isn't. Not since you let that doctor set up a field hospital back there." Sidna sat back in the chair and sighed. "It doesn't matter anyway. Unless you happen to have some liadra root on hand."

"I am afraid not. Perhaps you should ask the doctor."

"I don't think she'd help me even if she could."

"Could it be she does not trust you?" Mei asked.

"Maybe."

"She did catch you going through a dying man's belongings."

Sidna turned her head. "I was looking for the glyph."

"Which you found. And took."

"Well . . . yes."

Mei laughed softly. "Not so long ago, it was *you* accusing *him* of thievery."

Sidna blushed. "I am *not* a thief. The glyph belongs to *my* people."

"Is that why you had to pay someone to steal it?"

Sidna crossed her arms. "Retrieve."

"Hmmm. I wonder who will retrieve it from *you*."

"They can try," Sidna said under her breath.

Mei smiled. "They will."

Sidna looked back toward the ship's hold. "Someone like Fall Arden?"

"No."

Sidna turned around and laid her head back. "You sound awfully sure."

"Because I am."

Sidna laughed. "You don't even know him."

"True, but I knew his mentor."

"What's that got to do with him?"

"I assume Thane must have seen potential in him, not only for skill in battle, but for something deeper."

"Like what?"

"I do not know. But if Thane trusts him, so do I."

Sidna sighed. "It doesn't really matter now." She stretched and yawned, eager to change the subject. "So what's the plan?"

"It is the same as the last time you asked. We are going to Crossroads Station. There, we will deliver Fall and his wards to the hospital. Then I will take you home to Endi."

"What about Veridian?"

"You must take the glyph to your elders. They will decide when to send an expedition back to Veridian."

Frustration welled up inside Sidna. "I found the temple. I'll be the one to bring back the tear."

"The tear?" Mei asked.

"The reason I went there in the first place."

"Then I would suggest you find another ship to take you. The contract explicitly states you are to return home after the path to Veridian is verified."

Sidna sat up and leaned over. "Come on, Mei. Now that I have the glyph, I can find a passage. All we have to do is fly right in."

"The difficulty of reaching Veridian is not the issue."

"What then? The temple? Ronin and I mapped half of it, and I *killed* the Guardian."

Mei turned back to Sidna. "How can you be so sure? From what you have told me, you barely escaped."

Sidna looked down. "I guess I don't really know for sure. But I know how to fight it now."

Mei seemed unconvinced. "I think you would say anything to go back."

Sidna sat back. "Fine. I'll just have to get there on my own."

She took the strange necklace from her pocket and turned it back and forth in her hands. It appeared to be a simple gold amulet with an expensive emerald, but it was so much more.

Sidna looked up from the glyph into Mei's probing eye. "What?"

Mei shrugged. "Nothing."

Sidna tucked the glyph away and stared ahead, looking out into the Rift. Her hand brushed the other object in her pocket, the one she'd picked up on the freighter after the bear disappeared.

She pulled it out. Strangely, it looked different than it did before. There'd been a slice where the casing was pierced, but the gash was almost closed.

Is it . . . healing?

She turned to Mei. "Hey, back on the frei—" She was cut off by an alert from the alarm system.

Mei looked down and tapped commands into the interface.

Sidna queried her own display as well. "What is it now?"

"A collision warning. A massive gravitational disturbance has appeared. I must deactivate the Inos drive."

Mei took the ship out of the Rift. As reality reappeared, Sidna saw the source of the disturbance.

A warship sat directly in their path.

It was elongated, like a giant blue cannon with flattened sides. There was a fortified bridge on the top, hangars that ran down the side of it, and menacing guns all along the surface.

Alidians.

"What are *they* doing here?" Sidna asked.

Mei looked up at the ship. "Impeding us with a gravity phantom. It has tricked the navigational sensors into showing a large body in our path."

"Why would they do that?"

"I could not say, but they are here illegally."

"Huh?" Sidna asked.

"No military forces from Alidia or Rune are allowed to enter the Frontier. There is a treaty against it."

Sidna squirmed uncomfortably. "Which means they might not be happy about being seen. We need to get out of here."

Mei pointed to the console screen. "Too late."

Sidna looked at the sensor readout. The display showed a starfighter squadron approaching from behind.

On the communications panel ahead of Mei, a light flashed, and she tapped a button near it.

An authoritative voice spoke. "Starship Rìluò, this is Lieutenant Reade of the ARN Talon. Please state your intentions."

Mei responded. "We are on a course to Crossroads Station."

"For what purpose?" the pilot asked.

Mei's jaw muscles tightened. "Our purpose is our own business. By what right do you detain a private starship in the Frontier?"

The pilot's voice conveyed his annoyance at Mei's challenge. "We have reason to believe Runian agents are active in this region. All ships are to be stopped and scanned."

Mei shook her head. "Lieutenant Reade, the Rìluò is a registered Ranger vessel. The Alidian government declared long ago that Ranger ships are to be respected and to be aided if necessary. Has that changed?"

There was no answer. The lead fighter closed in on the Rìluò, almost nose to nose. The blue snub-nosed ship was heavily armed.

Sidna looked to Mei. "He's scanning us."

She could see the pilot from her seat. He looked up from his console, closed helmet obscuring his face. "You have a wounded man aboard."

Mei closed her eye. "We do."

A few moments went by.

"You will be brought aboard for medical evaluation and treatment."

Mei slammed her fist down. "We will do no such thing!"

"That wasn't a request, Rìluò." The starship maneuvered and pulled away. "Form up and do not deviate. For your own safety."

Sidna reached up and muted the transmission. "We can't let them take us in!"

Mei scowled. "We have no choice. They have no intention of letting us go, and we would be unlikely to survive the escape attempt." She reopened communications. "Very well, Lieutenant. We will comply."

Mei cut the channel. She pressed another button and activated the ship's intercom. "Doctor, we have been intercepted by an Alidian warship."

There was a delay, then the doctor responded. "What? They shouldn't be out here."

"Yet they are," Mei said. "You should prepare Fall for the medical transfer."

"Okay." She sighed. "I'll get him ready."

Mei deactivated the intercom and brought the *Rìluò* in behind the Alidian starfighter formation. She turned to Sidna slightly. "We will be fine as long as we do nothing suspicious."

Sidna subconsciously touched the *viae* on her arm. "Such as?"

"We must not give any indication we are aware of the illegality of their presence."

"Well, I didn't know until a few minutes ago, so that shouldn't be too hard."

Sidna watched through the forward viewport, realizing just how large the Alidian vessel really was. By the time they reached the hangar's repulsion fields, the ship occupied her view in all directions.

The Alidian starfighters banked and flew away. "*Rìluò*, continue your current course into the flight deck. You will be directed to the correct landing space upon entry."

Mei did so, taking the *Rìluò* through the shimmering blue repulsion fields. She landed with the guidance of a wand-waving technician in a cap and padded naval fatigues. Once the landing sequence finished, she activated the ventral bay door, extending the ramp.

She stood and moved to the rear. "Come. And do not say a word."

Sidna followed her. "I know what to do."

They moved into the rear hold. The doctor was working on a medicine pump and its tubing, bundling them next to the Ranger on his bed.

Mei started down the ramp, and Sidna followed. When they reached the bottom, an Alidian officer approached, flanked by two soldiers with powered armor and bulky rifles.

The officer wore a crisp blue uniform with black leather belts and a holstered pistol. He was young but carried himself with confidence. Behind them, two medical technicians in white jackets and slacks pushed a repulsion sled.

The officer signaled the two soldiers to stop then advanced with his hands behind his back. "I am Ensign Walter. I understand you have a wounded man aboard?"

Mei walked forward to meet him. "Yes. Our doctor is preparing him."

"Very good. Our medical team will go on board and retrieve him. That is, if we have your permission?"

Mei narrowed her eye. "You do not." She turned aside. "Though I doubt it will change anything."

The ensign waved the medical team ahead. "No, Captain, I'm afraid it does not."

Mei twisted her lips. "So much for Alidian honor."

One of the marines tightened up. The ensign turned his chin slightly while looking down, and the marine stepped back. The officer looked back up. "You will come with me."

"Where?" Mei asked.

"To answer some questions."

"And my crew?"

"The rest of your crew will report to sick bay for evaluation."

Mei stepped forward. "Are we under arrest?"

"Not yet. For the moment, you are restricted guests. If your ship and crew check out, you will be released."

"I have your word on that?"

"Yes."

Mei's eyepiece made a whirring sound as she stared ahead. "Very well then, Ensign."

"Thank you, Captain. Please follow me. As for your crew, the medical team will escort them." He turned to take a step but hesitated. "Oh, and welcome aboard the *Talon*."

He motioned to one of the soldiers, who stepped forward. The armored man remained silent.

Mei looked back at Sidna without expression then followed the ensign.

Sidna crossed her arms and sighed. After a few seconds, she turned and looked up and behind her. She had the feeling she was being watched.

On the level above, leaning forward on the railing, a man in a white coat stared down at her. He was thin, with long dark hair, but other than that, she couldn't make out any other features. Alidian soldiers and technicians walked past him, but he stood still, like a predator perched in a sea of waving grass.

Sidna squinted, trying to make out his hidden face. He didn't move, seemingly staring back, but she couldn't see his eyes.

"Coming through!"

She turned and moved in time to not be run over by the medical team. The two technicians jogged with the sled between them, and the doctor ran beside the Ranger as she held up a bag of clear fluid.

Sidna's escort stood beside her. His voice was firm. "This way."

She nodded and followed him. After a few steps, she turned to look up to the second level.

She searched all along the railing, but the strange man was gone.

"I'm fine, really."

"Doctor, you have wounds that need treatment, so please sit down." The bossy, heavy-set nurse tried her best to make a patient out of Doctor Hansen, but she was having a tough time of it.

The doctor sat down reluctantly. "You expect me to sit here while you have my friend back there doing Elcos knows what to him?"

"He's in surgery. You need to—"

Doctor Hansen stood up. "What are they going to do to him?"

"Sit down. *Now.*" The nurse motioned to a nearby soldier, and he stepped forward.

The doctor looked at the soldier and sat down again. "This isn't right."

The nurse straightened her uniform. "You two will remain here. Everyone that comes on board the *Talon* must have a full medical screening. If you cause further trouble, you *will* be sedated."

She paused a moment, waiting for a reply, then stood up and left the waiting room. Once she'd gone, the soldier moved to the other side of the room and looked outside.

Sidna rubbed her head.

If they find my viae . . .

The doctor looked over and whispered. "What are you gonna do?"

Sidna looked up at the guard. "About what?"

"About your *viae*. Isn't that what you're worried about?"

Sidna looked at her with complete surprise then scowled. "Worry about yourself."

The doctor leaned back in her chair, sighed, then looked at Sidna again. "I am." She waited for the soldier to look away. "You'll get us all turned in."

"Your compassion is overwhelming."

The doctor looked at Sidna's jacket pocket. "Why'd you take it?"

"Take what?"

"That necklace. I saw you take it from Fall."

Sidna's lips drew tight. "It wasn't his."

The doctor smiled incredulously. "I happen to know he found it on the freighter."

"So you condone looting the remains of the dead?" Sidna asked.

"As if stealing from the dying is any better."

Sidna looked up to the white ceiling. "If you must know, there was a friend of mine on that freighter. He was supposed to bring that necklace to me. It's mine."

"Interesting. Fall said there was a note indicating it was stolen."

"Maybe it was. I don't care."

"Who was it stolen from?"

"No idea. Not that it's any of your—"

The guard walked a few steps closer. "Hey. Would you two shut up? It's bad enough I'm stuck here without hearing you argue."

They both sat back. After the guard walked away again, Sidna leaned over slightly. "Look, Olivia, right?"

"Yeah," Olivia said quietly.

"Bottom line is, I'm sorry I took it like that, but I had to."

"Fine. It's just some stupid jewelry anyway."

The door opened across the room, and the nurse came back in. She motioned for them to follow her. "We're ready for you both."

Sidna stood up slowly. She looked at the guard.

I could take him, easy, but then what?

She followed Olivia through the door and through a winding hallway. The floors, walls, and ceiling were white and shiny with a single blue stripe running down the middle of the floor. It split off toward rooms to the side.

The nurse stopped at a door, and it opened. "You're in here." She looked at Sidna and pointed inside.

Sidna stepped inside, and the door slid shut, leaving her alone.

There was a single table, hard and metallic, without any padding. A small computer and chair were attached to the wall facing away from the bed. Otherwise, the room was empty.

She tried to open the door. It was locked. The panel nearby was protected by a numeric code.

I have to get out of here!

The door slid open rapidly, and she nearly fell backward as a man walked in. The door shut behind him.

He placed something in the pocket of his white coat, a thin metal bar with a loop on one end and two flat extensions pointing down on the opposite end. She looked up. He had long black hair that hid most of his face, and he wore glasses.

He smiled, showing the most perfect teeth she'd ever seen. "Hello."

Sidna backed up to the table, startling herself when she bumped into it.

The man walked over to the computer and sat down. "There's no need to be alarmed. I just want to talk."

Sidna looked at the door then back to him. "Talk?"

"Yes. Let's talk about *you*."

"Listen, Doctor, I—"

He laughed then coughed into his hand. "Oh, I'm not a doctor."

"Then who are you?"

He stood up. "Who are you? Or should I ask, *what* are you?"

Sidna panicked, edging toward the door like a caged animal.

The man laughed. "Where are you going?"

She held up her hand. "Don't make me hurt you. I will."

"Yes. I bet you would." He looked at her hand. "What might you be hiding under that jacket?"

She narrowed her eyes. "Let me out of here."

"Are you sure you want that? What if these Alidians find out what you are? Would they accept you?"

"I'll take my chances."

"I have a better idea."

"No thanks."

He clicked his tongue twice. "So angry." He turned and sat down at the computer and accessed a program. He input several commands then turned back to her. "There. I'm happy to report you're in excellent health."

"Why would you—"

"I want you to be free."

She let fire fill her *viae*, holding it in her hand. "Tell me why."

He stood again and spread his hands. "I find you very interesting. In fact, I think you're exactly what I've been looking for."

"Let me out of here."

"You're free to go anytime you want."

Sidna looked at the door's control panel. The screen indicated it was unlocked. She touched the panel, and the door slid open.

"Stay away from me."

He nodded. "Of course. I only ask one thing. Call it a favor for helping you just now."

"What?"

"Don't let him catch you."

"Who?"

He smiled. "You'll see."

She backed out into the hallway. "Don't follow me. I'll kill you if you do."

The door closed. She backed up, waiting for it to open, but it didn't. She realized she was still holding fire in her hand and quickly put it out.

"Excuse me?" Another nurse walked toward her. "What are you doing?"

Sidna swallowed and did her best to look normal. "I just finished my exam, and I'm looking for my friend."

The nurse studied her suspiciously. "Come this way."

Sidna followed her, turning back every so often to make sure she wasn't followed. They passed a large window overlooking a room below.

The room was hexagonal with blue-green walls and floors. It had a sterile appearance, and everything was ordered and in its place. In the center, a patient lay on a table, connected to tubes and wiring.

The nurse stopped. "Lucky guy."

Sidna looked through the window. "What's going on down there?"

"That's the operating room. Your injured companion is having his wound closed."

Sidna watched as four tiny machines, like five-legged mechanical scorpions, moved over the surface of his body. A tail extended from each, curving over the central core. The machines moved gracefully in pairs, like the hands of an artist, carefully sculpting the flesh and tissue below.

One of the machines bent its tail underneath itself as a prop while it used the five appendages to manipulate tissue. The other member of the pair then used its tail to fire a laser over the area. The other set of robots swept behind them, their legs a rapidly moving blur as they laid down healthy material.

Fall seemed to be at peace. He looked vulnerable there, very different from when she'd first seen him.

"He nearly died."

Sidna looked up. "Huh?"

"The patient. I've seen worse, but it was bad enough."

"Yeah. I guess it was."

Serves him right for poking his nose in where he shouldn't.

The nurse looked up. "Looks like they're almost finished. I'll take you back. I'll bring your other friend there too."

They walked back toward the waiting room. Thankfully, there wasn't any sign of the strange man along the way. The nurse showed her inside, and Sidna took the same seat as before. She waited for a few minutes, then the door opened again.

Olivia's eyes went wide when she saw her. She came over and sat. "How'd you get out of there? I thought you were screwed."

"They didn't notice. Must've gotten a lazy doctor."

"Really? Mine was pretty thorough." She shivered.

"Just lucky, I guess."

Olivia looked back toward the door. "I didn't see Fall."

Sidna leaned over. "I did. He's fine."

"Was he out of surgery?"

"Almost."

Olivia's shoulders relaxed. "Oh, good."

"Yeah." Sidna squirmed and looked at the guard then back to Olivia. "I wanted to ask you something."

"What is it?"

"It's about Fall, actually. Do you trust him?"

She nodded. "Definitely."

"Why'd you hire him?"

"I didn't. He doesn't work for me."

"So you don't know why he was hired?"

"He was our guide. But that mission's over."

"Then why's he still around?"

"We were trapped on that freighter after the raiders attacked."

Sidna turned her head with a tight smile. "Ah, that explains it."

"What?"

"Don't you see it? He wanted the necklace. He probably tipped off the raiders, hoping to make some extra profit off you at the same time."

Olivia drew back. "You're way off. Like ridiculously way off."

Sidna shrugged. "If you say so."

The door opened, and the overweight nurse came inside. "All right. You two check out. You've been assigned separate quarters for the time being."

Olivia stood up quickly and shot Sidna a dirty look. "Fine by me."

Sidna stood up. "Me too."

Olivia walked toward the door where the soldier waited. She turned back. "You know, I was going to give you the benefit of the doubt, but I can see I was right the first time."

"You should learn to listen to your instincts. Too bad they failed you on Fall."

Olivia laughed bitterly. "You're a miserable person."

Sidna watched her go. "Maybe I am." She walked out as her own escort arrived at the door.

But at least I know who my friends are.

Sidna ran through the door, desperately chasing the fading light ahead. If she could just catch up, she'd be safe, but the light was always just out of sight, always around the next turn.

"Wait, damn you!"

She heard herself yell, but the sound was distant. She was falling behind, and before long the nightmare would find her.

A musical hum suddenly permeated the chamber, coming from every-where at once. It resonated through the stone walls and the bones of her skull. Her stomach dropped, and she knew she'd been found. She stopped and looked around.

Nothing was there, but she knew it was watching her. Unwilling to run endlessly, she summoned her energy, fed by fear, and blasted a burning hole in the wall ahead. She kept running with the wave of fire ahead of her, breaking through room after room.

At last, she reached a large, open chamber with a small central pedestal. The room was pitch black except for a thin beam of light that shone down from some distant point above.

On the center of the pedestal's surface, there was a clear crystal. It gleamed in the sunlight from above, scattering prismatic light onto the stone surfaces nearby.

She watched as a silhouetted form moved toward it. He held a shining white light in his hand, and he moved with a fluid grace that made him seem to float.

He continued to move toward the tear, and she became angry. Refracted light moved along the floor, throwing multiple colors in his path.

"Stop." Her voice sounded distant.

The faceless man said nothing and continued to move toward it. She reached for the tear, but it was so far away. No, she was far away, suddenly across the room.

The man stopped his advance.

From the other side of the darkened chamber, she saw another moving form. Its shape was nebulous, engulfed in violet flames. It plodded ahead, burning, toward the central pedestal.

She tried to yell again, but she heard nothing. She watched the flaming form advance, stopping opposite the center, just like the man with the shining light.

She was suddenly back at the pedestal, and both forms advanced.

She was furious. The tear was hers, not to be taken by anyone else, certainly not the newcomers. She reached out for the tear, but it was gone.

She looked around and realized that she had taken its place. But where prismatic light once shone, a dark, creeping substance roiled on the stone floor. It fed on her anger, pulsing in time with her heartbeat.

She looked up, and she saw that the man with the shining light had passed her, standing between her and the flaming form.

The violet flames advanced but slowed when they reached the edge of the light. The light dimmed slightly, straining against the surging fire. Slowly the man was pushed back toward her, and with each step, the flames grew in intensity.

Her anger grew as well. The undulating black tendrils of hate spread out ahead, reaching around the light, moving to quench the flames.

The light continued to dim, sputtering as it did. The man was forced down to a knee, struggling to hold both the flames and the darkness at bay. When the darkness reached the flames, both forces grew, and an explosion sent burning globs of the dark material all around.

She watched the light dim to a small point, surrounded on all sides as it was crushed.

But just before it could be snuffed out, it changed. It swirled and spun like a small spherical hurricane, faster and faster. The darkness recoiled toward her as if terrified.

The light was like a storm, but instead of affecting the air, it seemed to change the very essence of the world around it. The flames could not burn, and the darkness could not hide.

She held her hand up to shield her eyes, stumbling backward. A hand gripped her shoulder, and everything disappeared. The light and the flames and the darkness were gone.

It was all gone.

OBJECTS OF DESIRE

THE SPY'S IMAGE FADED IN AND OUT of focus, wavering in the darkness as he made his report. "So far they've found nothing."

Tieger stood before the circle in his chambers. The holographic emitter's white-blue light cast jagged shadows behind him. "These Alidians are ignorant, incompetent fools."

The spy interlocked his fingers. "Oh, they aren't ignorant. Not anymore."

Tieger narrowed his eyes. "Explain."

"At first, they didn't understand what they'd taken from Nix. They knew it came from somewhere deep in the Frontier. It seems they were worried the Runians might gain some new advantage from its study, so they decided to strike preemptively and steal it." He took a deep breath. "What they've learned since my capture is that such a shard can be used to find its parent crystal, if only one knows how to listen."

"You have given them that knowledge?"

"It seemed reasonable, considering my incarceration and lack of alternative transportation."

"Foolish. In doing so, you have made things difficult for your true allies."

The spy looked down. "Yet, think of the insights you have gained. Better to have me here, where I can report on their movements."

"They continue to believe you are a Runian engineer?" Tieger asked.

"They do." The spy smiled as he looked up. "I assure you, I only revealed the shard's unique properties when the interrogations became . . . aggressive."

Tieger allowed himself enjoyment at the thought of the spy's torture, but he did not show it outwardly. "The shard is irrelevant. What do they know about the parent crystal itself?"

"Half-tested theories. I told them only as much as an engineer with limited access would know. They will not be able to pinpoint the parent crystal's location precisely."

Tieger stared at the spy, frustration returning. "Curious how a spy knows what an engineer should not."

"I know only what the Harbinger tells me." His voice was laced with false sympathy. "You mean, he hasn't told you the parent crystal's true purpose?"

Tieger tightened his fists. "He tells me I have the *Forge*, and with its overwhelming power, I can erase you and your ill-gained knowledge from existence any time I choose."

The spy's lips split only enough to show he had received the threat. He nodded. "The *Forge* is indeed a great power. But only one of many."

Tieger advanced on the hologram. "One I will use to take the shard by force if you continue to test me."

The spy nodded, head slightly turned. "You *could* do that. But why, when you could let the Alidians do your work for you? Let them spend their strength taking the parent crystal from the Runians. The *Talon* will make an isolated, easy target, battle-worn and so far from home."

Tieger waved his gauntlet. "The difficulty is irrelevant."

"Nonetheless, it would be prudent to watch and wait."

Tieger grunted. "I *have* been watching." He held up his index finger. "In fact, you might be interested to know what I have learned."

The spy's hands fell apart from each other. "Yes, of course. Terribly."

Tieger watched carefully for the spy's reaction. "I have seen a little ship, all alone, plucked from the Rift like a fly caught suddenly in a web."

The spy smiled. "Fascinating. It seems there must be a spider about."

Tieger's jaw muscles tightened. "Tell me what has happened to the crew of this captured vessel."

"They eat well and sleep soundly."

Tieger laughed harshly. "I can only assume you have made plans to ensure they do not survive."

"You assume correctly." The spy tapped the side of his nose. "I make such plans for everyone I meet."

Tieger nodded. "I have seen the fruits of your research in the past. I want to see what you have learned."

The spy did not move. "The details would bore you."

"I will be the judge of that. Send them *now*."

The spy reached into his sleeve. After a few movements of his fingers underneath the white material, he looked up. "Very well . . . "

Tieger accessed the data. Facial images and medical information scrolled through the air. "Two Aeturnian Rangers. The male is gravely wounded, expected to recover."

"Yes, the Alidian surgeons are quite skilled."

Tieger searched. "The other Ranger has no biological information."

"She has avoided the Alidian screening process so far."

"No matter. In spite of the surgeon's expectations, neither patient will survive." Tieger read on. "A Runian civilian?"

"Yes," the spy said.

"An agent?" Tieger asked.

"A possibility. I am watching her closely."

"Kill her and be done with it." Tieger pointed. "This last one. A woman. Who is she?"

"No one of consequence. She is a migrant who bought passage to Crossroads Station."

"How can you be sure?"

The spy paused before answering, his voice tight but only just so. "I know my trade."

"Still, there is something . . . familiar about her," Tieger said.

"I don't see how. She is from a remote world, a place even I had never heard of."

Tieger leaned in closer, until his lips nearly touched hers, studying. "The *eyes*. Somewhere, I've seen these eyes. Defiant . . . fearful . . . " His words caught in his throat as his pulse quickened. "An arcanist's eyes!" He turned on the spy's image. "Know your *trade*, do you? That *girl* is a witch. The only one to ever escape me."

"That seems highly—"

The hologram disappeared abruptly as Tieger ended the transmission. He stormed to his communications panel and called the bridge.

Captain Gault answered almost immediately. "Yes, Honored One?"

"Intercept the *Talon*."

Gault was surprised. "Has the Harbinger given the order to attack?"

Tieger's wrath seethed through his teeth. "Do not question me, Gault. I swear to you, you will only do so once."

"No . . . no of course not, Honored One! It will be as you wish."

Tieger walked to his armor stand and took his helmet. He brought it down over his head, and the pressure seals activated. As the armor linked with the helmet, his desire surged—the witch would finally burn.

He left his quarters and strode through the hall toward the

Forge's bridge. His embers lined the corridor, falling in behind him as he walked.

As he entered, the crew stood quickly. None of them returned his gaze. The sight of his bone-white heavy armor with violet embers trailing behind was truly fearsome.

Captain Gault made his way to Tieger, bowing his head as he spoke. "We are ready to exit the Never on your orders."

"Do it now." The sound of Tieger's voice, rendered artificial by his helmet, echoed throughout the silent bridge, carrying the terror of his malice to every heart. "Bring them death."

Sidna sat up in her bed with a start as she awoke from her nightmare. She blinked and rubbed her eyes, trying to escape the nagging sense of impending danger.

It wasn't real. Just get up.

She pulled her blanket away and swung her legs over the side. By the time she stood up and stretched, the dream and its unpleasant images had begun to fade from memory. She rubbed her sleepy eyes and reminded herself how bad her real-life situation was.

Her temporary quarters were much like the rest of the *Talon*—boring. The only decoration on the wall was a framed Alidian flag, blue with a white crown-within-a-crown and white stars above. Everything else in the room had sharp angles in some variation of blue or gray.

Man, I can't get out of here fast enough.

She used the modest lavatory to get a shower and freshen up, washing away the grime of the previous day. Her clothes had been laundered for her, and they were fresh too.

She looked in the mirror and touched her cheek. "Huh. I actually look pretty good for once."

Though she'd had trouble sleeping that morning, it was still the best night's sleep she'd had in a long time. It showed in her eyes more than anywhere else.

The faint smell of cooked meat wafted into the room, and her stomach growled audibly. "Ugh, I'd kill for breakfast." She threw on her jacket and headed for the exit.

On the other side of the door, the shared dining room and its long wooden table waited. To the left there was another door, closed. To the right, there was an outer wall of transparent viewport.

Fall sat at the other end of the table beside Olivia. They both looked up from their plates, nearly done. Fall produced the hint of a smile. Olivia looked away from Sidna flatly.

The Ranger wore his armor, and he followed her eyes down to the narrow hole in the front.

Before Sidna could say anything, the steward, a young man in a tight-fitting blue uniform, approached. He stood with his hands behind his back, never quite looking in her direction. "You may help yourself."

Sidna went to the tabletop. There were three meager trays of food—fluffy, pale eggs, white potato hash with a crisp on top, and some sort of greenish-brown sausages, likely cold. There were two carafes, both half-filled with water, ice melted down to tiny floating remnants.

She took one of the metal plates from a stack at the end of the table. "I'd rather help myself to my things."

The annoyingly proper man glanced toward her without any change in his expression. "As I've told you before, that will be impossible until the captain releases you. Your items will be delivered to your ship at that time, no sooner."

Sidna poked at a sausage with a frown. "You could at least let us out of these . . . rooms."

The steward coughed. "These *rooms* should be quite enough for the likes of you. The diplomatic suites are usually reserved for dignitaries."

Sidna laughed. "They're little cubes with a cot and a shower."

The steward scowled. "Might I remind you this is a warship? To have your own shower is *absurd*."

Fall took a drink of water. "So why all the special treatment? Afraid we'll tell someone we were taken prisoner?"

The steward turned on him. "I merely do as I am told. If you wish to speak with an officer, I'm sure one will be along shortly. Until that time—" The steward squinted and leaned forward as he walked around the table toward the viewport wall. "—enjoy your . . . "

Sidna looked back down at her food. The white potatoes turned red as the lighting shifted. A low-pitched alert sounded from the audio system for several seconds, paused, and then resumed in a loop.

A wave of dread rose up as it had only minutes ago in her dream. Fall and Olivia looked to each other in question then turned around to the viewport.

The room's hatch opened, and an armed soldier entered. He followed the steward around the table.

A look of disbelief crossed the soldier's face, and Sidna had to see what he'd seen. She ran to the viewport, shouldering her way to the front. Her mouth started to open, wordlessly giving voice to the sinking feeling in her gut.

Out in space, a rolling nebula of smoke and lightning bloomed. From the cloud, a violet light shone from deep within. The edge of the cloud broke, and a pointed projection advanced, stabbing into the black before it. The shape widened as it came through, and the burning Never trailed away from its surface.

Kilometers long, it was a gargantuan spaceship, the colors of ash and bone. Violet flames shot into space from the engines along the hull, and armored plates formed chevrons along the dorsal and ventral surfaces. It was full of fire—a white-hot engine—roaring its way into reality.

Sidna's knees weakened, and her breath caught in her chest at the sight of the *Forge*.

Tieger had found her again.

Richards secured the last of his armor as he jogged after Ban. "Boss, what's the plan?"

Ban looked back as he ran. "We've been ordered to the starboard flight deck."

"Expecting trouble?" Richards asked.

"At this point, you know as much as I do," Ban said. "Just be ready."

They entered the middle section of the flight deck. A few other squads had already assembled, and Sergeant Din of Puma Squad, stood nearby.

Din was older, an experienced veteran of many campaigns. His quick eyes instantly evaluated Wolf Squad then shot to Ban. "Morgan. Good to see you."

Ban shook Din's hand with a subdued smile. "You too. What's going on?"

Din shrugged. He nodded toward a crowd of medical personnel and officers.

Ban looked. "Incoming wounded?"

"Possibly. Someone important's coming over."

"What makes you think that?"

"Overheard one of the officers. Seems the higher-ups made contact with the Elcosians. Purple bastards have a prisoner."

"An Alidian?"

Din nodded. "Apparently, they want to turn him over."

"We're going to let them on board?"

"Looks that way."

Ban frowned. "That's not a good idea." He pointed out into space. "That's hardly a missionary transport."

"Agreed, but I'm not paid to think," Din said. "Bet they've caught some fugitive. No doubt they want to gain a little influence with the prince by handing him over."

"That wouldn't surprise me. The problem is, we aren't supposed to be here."

"Bah. The Elcosians usually stay neutral in things like this." Din leaned in. "Unless you're hiding an arcanist under your bed?" He raised his eyebrows.

"That sounds more like something you'd pull." Ban sighed. "Anyway, I guess we'll find out soon enough."

"Sure." Din put his helmet on. "Stay sharp, Morgan." He walked away.

The flight deck's doors opened. Lieutenant Garret walked in.

Ban met him. "Sir."

Garret avoided eye contact. "Is my squad ready, Bond-Sergeant?"

"Yes, sir."

"Good." Garret looked out over the bay.

Ban watched his face. "Is something wrong, sir?"

Garret rubbed his chin. "Not now."

Ban swallowed. "Haskel."

"That's right. He can't say much with that broken jaw, and he's not able to write very well with the arm, but he managed to get his story across."

"Is it bad?"

Garret moved past him. "It isn't good."

Becks touched Ban's shoulder. "Ban?"

Ban turned to watch Garret as he walked to the center of the bay. He lowered his helmet's faceplate. "We knew this would happen. Stay focused."

She lowered her faceplate as well, staring for a second longer in silence before she nodded.

The low-pitched alert brought Ban's attention to the bay's repulsion fields. An armored Elcosian troop transport entered, hovering for a moment before it touched down.

A man stood inside, weight supported by two Elcosian embers. His head was shaved, and he wore a ragged white jumpsuit over a blood-stained shirt. His left pant leg was shorter than the other, rolled up to reveal a crude, metal prosthesis. He seemed weak, requiring assistance to step down.

Ban watched as the crowd of Alidians dispersed. Captain Howe, along with his senior officers, walked forward with an escort of marines.

Becks gasped. "Ban ... he's ... "

"What is it?"

She paused. "That's Lieutenant Holland."

Ban used his HUD to zoom in on the prisoner's face. Through the swollen skin and bloody stitches, it was him. "It can't be."

He's been alive this whole time?

An angry murmur rose as the other squads recognized Holland. The captain turned with his palms facing downward, signaling for calm. It seemed he'd known ahead of time.

Holland stumbled forward. The ember who'd helped him let him go and stayed behind with the dropship.

When the captain reached Holland, he put his arm around him. They walked back to the group of officers as more and more Alidians gathered around.

Ban searched for Garret. He found him, standing in the small crowd, transfixed on the resurrected Holland.

Everyone in the room suddenly turned to the transport as a loud thud echoed throughout the bay. A hulk of a man in heavy white armor had jumped down, his presence previously unnoticed. His armor gave the appearance of some kind of beast or a demon, whose thick white bones had caught fire then instantly froze.

Howe released Holland and turned toward the transport. He spoke as he walked, but the armored man ignored him and raised his arm toward the group of Alidians behind him.

Ban watched as Holland cringed and bent over, clawing at his gut. No longer weakened, he rose up, eyes wide and mouth trembling. He lunged and grabbed the captain from behind then pulled him back toward the other Alidians.

Just before he got there, he threw his head back. "Only in Fire will we find absolution!" He suddenly erupted, bursting into intensely burning, violet flames.

The group of Alidians around him screamed and writhed as they too caught fire. Agony gripped them; flesh fell from their bodies as they tore it away. Within a few seconds, their terrible wailing died out, and there was nothing left of them, except for melted mounds of slag, bodies, and sizzling armor. The survivors stared at the horrible scene in disbelief.

Unopposed, the armored man walked forward, terrible laugh penetrating the stunned silence. His embers spread out behind him as he advanced. The Alidians came to their senses, rushing for cover—everyone but Ban.

He stood there, unmoving in the face of death, paralyzed by the weight of his guilt.

Olivia leaned forward, forehead almost against the viewport. "What am I seeing right now?"

Fall turned to look at the steward, whose eyes grew wide with fear. He turned back to Olivia. "Nothing good."

The steward must have agreed. He backed into the table and felt his way around it, never taking his eyes away from the ship. He pushed past the soldier and Sidna then ran out of the room. The soldier followed after him.

Olivia backed away from the viewport. "Think we still have a ride?"

Fall tightened the straps of his pauldrons as he spoke. "Mei wouldn't leave us behind."

Olivia turned away from the viewport, looking back once before she spoke. "She's still in the brig. I'm starting to worry."

Fall looked toward the exit and trailed off. "Me too . . ."

Olivia followed his eyes.

Sidna walked to the hatch. Surprisingly, it opened, and she ran through without hesitation.

Olivia sighed. "Someone's in an awfully big hurry."

"I'm guessing she came to the same conclusion we did."

"Then we don't have much time."

Fall frowned. "She wouldn't take the *Rìluò*, would she?"

Olivia put her hands on her hips. "Oh, she totally would."

He shook his head. "She won't be able to get past the *Rìluò's* security, but we shouldn't give her too much time to try."

"What should we do?" Olivia asked.

Fall moved around the table toward the exit. "We have to find Mei. We can't leave without her."

He stepped into the next room. It was like an office, with a desk and chair, a boxy weapons detector, and lockers. One of the lockers was open, keycard sticking out from a slot above it. "Unlocked?"

Olivia moved past him and pulled the card. She put it into another slot above the next locker. There was a beep and a click. She opened the door. "Maybe they left it without thinking."

Fall looked inside and saw his bow holster, quiver, belt, and sword. As Olivia opened the last locker, he reached in for his gear and rearmed himself.

Olivia checked her pistol. "Find Mei. I'll follow Sidna."

"Splitting up is risky."

"True, but if she takes the ship, we're screwed."

Fall nodded. "Fine. Just stay out of sight."

"No arguments here."

Fall moved to the hatch. "Ready?"

Olivia took a deep breath and nodded. "Yeah."

The hatch opened, and Fall peeked out into the hall. "It's clear."

"Meet you there." Olivia stepped out and jogged down the hall. She looked back. "Be careful!"

Fall nodded and ran the other way. There were posted directions to the nearest lift, and he followed them. When he got close, he noticed a group of soldiers crowded around it.

A man in powered armor stepped out in front of him. "No civilians allowed on the lifts during alerts."

Fall looked up into the helmet, seeing his own reflection stare back. "I'm looking for another Ranger. She should have been released by now."

The man didn't move at all. "Like I said, the lifts are reserved for Alidian military personnel. You'll have to wait."

"Is there another way to the brig?"

"There is, but you wouldn't be allowed inside. Matter of fact, I'm surprised they released you."

"Your captain decided holding me illegally wasn't in the best interests of Frontier diplomacy."

The soldier turned his head. "Go to the lounge around the corner and sit tight until your friend is released." The soldier looked down at Fall's sword and gripped his own rifle a little tighter. "You don't want to make anyone nervous right now."

Fall sighed. "Looks like I don't have a choice." He decided to continue on before the soldier or his colleagues became more suspicious.

He jogged around the corner and through a series of corridors. After a few long minutes of searching for another route below, he saw the lounge. He walked over, looking up to the high ceiling and the multiple decks exposed to the tall, open space in the middle.

How am I supposed to find anything on a ship like this? This deck alone is massive.

The area outside of the lounge looked like a miniature park with a small grove of trees. The ground underneath the trees had fragrant soil and was covered with a species of silvery-blue grass.

Is this what Aridor looks like?

He was nearly knocked from his feet when an assault pod tore through the hull and ruined the rear of the lounge.

He instinctively dropped into a crouch and spun around, scanning the room. The bar top, tables, and chairs had been destroyed.

Panels on the sides of the pod popped opened, and Elcosian embers leapt out, guns firing. There'd only been a few patrons in the bar, but the embers showed no mercy, shooting them dead where they lay.

Fall pulled his mech bow from its holster. He couldn't be sure that the bystanders were all dead, so he decided against a boomer arrow.

"Killer."

With the arrow nocked, he stepped out and released it into the nearest ember's helmet. The ember went down, and Fall jumped back just in time to avoid retaliation from the remaining invaders. He sprinted for the trees and hid behind the most central one.

The embers slowly moved through the ruined bar and set up along the inside of the entrance. One of them went prone and shot a few rounds into the tree, right beside Fall's face. Tiny fragments of bark hit his cheek, stinging sharply.

"Son of a bitch!" He blinked a few times and rubbed his eye.

Enough!

"Stinger."

He pulled the arrow, nocked it, and shot it into the ground at his feet.

"Fogger."

He pulled the arrow and nocked it, and while resting the bow on the tree, blindly fired it near the embers. When it detonated, a thick fog dispersed through the area, causing the embers to take cover.

He holstered the bow and ran to the edge of the grass then dove to the deck, just below the rim of the tiny park.

He looked back and saw an object fly out from the fog and land near the trees. The small sphere unfolded into a mechanical crablike robot, and it walked under the trees before scanning the area with a visible beam. After the scan, it chirped to the embers.

The embers moved rapidly through the dissipating fog, guns leveled on the tree. When they were close, one looked up into the tree and the others circled around it.

When the time was right, Fall activated the stinger arrow he'd left behind. Arcs of electricity traveled outward to five of the embers, and they fell to the grass, convulsing. But one ember wasn't hit. He turned just in time to take Fall's sword in his neck, thrust with the full force of a running charge.

Fall inspected the others then wiped the blood-covered blade on one of their waist cloths. He took a few seconds to catch his breath then jogged back to the lounge. A quick search there confirmed that all the patrons and staff were dead.

Elcosians. No wonder Sidna panicked so hard.

He shook his head and ran back outside, resuming his search for the brig.

Sidna scrambled to her feet and barely managed to turn the corner as a barrage of bullets bit into the floor and walls around her.

She felt the vibrations from the other side of the wall, centimeters from where she stood. She ducked to the side and sprinted down the corridor, farther away from her pursuers.

She was approaching another intersection when she heard shouting behind her. She dove to the floor as more bullets shot over her head. She rolled and arced her lightning back through the cloud of dust. One of the embers was able to dive away, but the other was hit. He fell to the deck, dying as smoke rose from his charred armor.

Sidna pushed herself up and ran. When she reached the next intersection, she coughed and looked left.

Alidian marines were retreating toward her under heavy fire, falling back in groups. The attacking embers advanced aggressively, pressing the advantage of overwhelming numbers. She ran in the opposite direction.

She was dashing down the corridor, looking over her shoulder, when she suddenly found herself on the floor. Her vision blackened, and her skull pounded.

Something pressed down on her, making it hard to breathe. She looked up to see a blurry violet boot on top of her chest.

The ember must have been hiding in a room to the side of the corridor, and he'd hit her in the head with something—most likely the rifle pointed at her face.

"Take that jacket off," he demanded. "Now!"

"Go fu—"

He kicked her in the ribs.

"Ah! Damn!"

"I won't tell you again."

Sidna started to take it off, but the pain slowed her down. When one of her arms was free, the ember grabbed her by it and examined her *viae*.

"I knew it. The Honored One was right."

Sidna heard a metallic *tink* on the floor just beside her.

The ember pulled her arm. "Get up."

"Not a chance."

"We'll see about that." He shouldered his rifle and grabbed her by the hair. But as soon as he'd started to pull, he let go.

Sidna rolled over and looked up.

A tiny red hand reached across the ember's helmet. Another hand grabbed at his neck, and the ember stumbled backward, struggling to get the thing off.

Sidna took the opportunity to pull her pistol, kindle a fire, and shoot a round into the ember's neck. The soldier's body burned from the inside, popping the seams of his chest armor. Dead, he fell forward to the deck without so much as a grunt.

A fluffy, red creature fell along with him. It steadied itself on the ember's back, hopping from foot to foot.

It jumped off and sat down then patted its feet. "Ooo! Hot, hot!"

Sidna stared at it, unsure if she should laugh or scream.

The thing looked up with an embarrassed grin. "Um, hey. Looked like you could use some help."

Sidna stood up and looked around cautiously. She put her jacket back on and stuck her hand into her pocket. The tiny metal object from the freighter was gone. "What are you?"

He shrugged. "Whatever I want to be."

Sidna touched her throbbing head. "Not sure why I expected a straight answer out of a stuffed animal ..." She opened her mouth wider and winced as her jaw clicked.

The creature smiled. "I'm Hermes."

"Whatever." She walked a few paces and turned. "But thanks for the help."

She jogged down the hall, careful not to pass any open hatches without a little space to spare.

Behind her, she heard padded feet running with the occasional click of a claw on the floor. "Hey! Wait for me!"

Sidna never looked back; the weird little thing could find its own ride. And if Mei wasn't at the *Rìluò* soon, she could too.

Tieger walked forward slowly, positioning nevergates between himself and incoming gunfire. Hundreds of bullets entered the disk-shaped distortions in reality, disappearing somewhere into the Never.

As he advanced, the Alidian marines fell back deeper into the *Talon*. But retreat was futile. The shields had fallen, the engines had been disabled, and his embers had begun to spread.

Yet they resist.

Holland's surprise explosion had ensured light resistance in the hangar, though a single squad continued to slow his progress.

Tieger motioned to the embers taking cover nearby. They stood up without hesitation and concentrated their fire on the squad's machine gunner.

The ember to Tieger's left fell to a sniper's bullet, and a rocket flew through the air, heading directly for Tieger. He raised his nevergates, but just before the rocket reached him, it took a dive toward the deck.

Small jets of fire and debris blasted between Tieger's distortions, blinding him momentarily. When the air cleared, he caught sight of the last Alidian survivors as they escaped from the bay.

How very clever ...

His embers lay dead around him, but he would not be alone for long. Two additional troop transports entered the bay, and fresh embers jumped to the deck, opening fire immediately on the retreating soldiers.

The last Alidian marine who remained, the machine gunner, fell back through the exit, dragging a wounded soldier along as he fired. Tieger signaled for his embers to hold their fire as the doors closed.

Three more transports entered the bay, and the embers set up defensive positions away from the door. They knew the marines would most likely seal the hatch and trap it with explosives.

Tieger allowed his nevergates to collapse and stepped up into the middle transport. Two embers had remained inside, waiting to accompany him. The side doors closed, and the ship lifted away.

Tieger watched from a viewport as the transport exited the bay. All along the *Talon*, explosions bloomed and escaping gas erupted. Assault pods rocketed toward the ship, more and more making it through the Alidian flak screen. Starfighters from both forces were dogfighting, rolling and turning, trying to gain the advantage.

An Alidian fighter, triangular and blue, flew by, flames spewing into space. It exploded just beyond the transport, and its killers, two Elcosian slivers, passed by. The slender white starfighters, like splinters of bone, banked and penetrated deeper into the conflict.

The *Forge* loomed beyond the skirmishes, far from the fray. Tieger smiled. No doubt Gault was anxious to enter the battle, but Tieger would not risk any real harm to his true target.

She belongs to me.

The transport continued along the surface of the *Talon* and turned around the other side of the ship, facing away from the *Forge*.

A sliver flew into the launch bay ahead of Tieger's transport. He watched as it hung in the air, sweeping from left to right as its guns fired. Small-arms fire returned in answer, and the starfighter's shields shimmered in violet.

Tieger's transport came in behind, taking advantage of the distraction. The side doors opened, and one of the embers manned the mounted gun, spitting gunfire around the bay. Between the mounted gun and the sliver, Tieger met no resistance as he dropped to the deck.

Dead Alidian marines and debris were scattered around, and fires consumed the ruined hulls of starfighters and transports. He turned. On a landing pad not far away, a small orange-and-red starship sat alone, unharmed.

Tieger smiled.

Let her come to me.

A MURDEROUS PURPOSE

FALL MOVED SWIFTLY THROUGH THE *TALON'S* embattled corridors, avoiding skirmishes as they erupted all around him.

Arrow drawn, he backed his left shoulder against the wall and angled around its edge. The hall was clear. He relaxed his draw and jogged ahead.

Halfway down, he heard incoming movement and shouts. Unable to make it back to the corner in time, he ducked into an unoccupied room. After the Alidian marines charged by, he slowly moved back into the light.

Across the hall in a recess, a closed hatch bore the words *Emergency Access.*

There. That's what I need.

He pulled on the bar attached to the hatch, and both sides of the double door opened with a quiet hiss.

The short, narrow hall inside led to a small hexagon-shaped room with a central ladder connecting the decks above and below. A diagram, like a map, was affixed to the wall behind the ladder. Fall took a moment to study it, noting the brig was down below.

He descended the metal rungs then stepped up to the exit hatch three decks down. He listened. He heard nothing. After a few seconds, he opened the hatch and stepped out carefully into the middle of another hallway that branched left and right.

There were hatches at each end. Both doors were closed, and he had no way of knowing which way led to the brig.

Pick one.

When he wasn't sure which way to go, he usually went right, and so he did. He opened the hatch at the end.

Unlike the decks above, this floor was eerily quiet. He could hear the distant sounds of what must have been explosions, but they were muffled and far away.

There was a smell there too—almost metallic, offensive and familiar. *Blood.*

Fall drew his sword. He walked through the deck, catching sight of two bodies.

The men were unarmored, yet they had been armed. One leaned against the wall, sitting down, one arm across his belly. The other lay face down, a pool of his blood having spread out to meet the other man's.

Fall got closer and noted the sitting man's wounds. He'd been stabbed neatly in the chest and belly, thin wounds placed precisely to lacerate the aorta in two places. The gray skin had been completely drained by the hemorrhage.

Across from the sitting man, a reinforced, double-doored hatch was wide open. Inside, the antechamber held a desk, a weapons scanner, and a protected guard station behind thick glass. Another soldier lay dead inside that shielded area, blood congealing underneath her.

Beyond an open hatch, there were two rows of cells, separated by a hall between them. Each cell was small, large enough to hold a hard cot. They were enclosed by shimmering blue repulsion fields, all except for the second on the right, which was open and empty.

"Fall Arden? Is that you?" Mei's calm query came from the third cell on the left, the farthest one.

He sheathed the sword and walked to her.

Beyond the blue field, she stood from kneeling. "I knew you would come. Even so, it is appreciated."

"Hold on while I get you out." Fall jogged back into the main area and searched the sitting body for a card. He found it then went back to Mei. Inserting the card in the slot next to her cell did the trick, and the repulsion field vanished.

Mei stepped out and audibly sighed. "I do not think I will ever get used to confinement." She looked up to him. "She is not with you?"

"Sidna? No."

Mei looked to her wrist. "Ah. Three decks above. She seems to be moving about randomly."

Fall raised his eyebrows. "You put a tracker on her?"

Mei looked up without moving her head. "Almost immediately after I met her. You would have done the same."

"Nice."

She nodded. "Where is your doctor?"

"Following Sidna, I hope."

Mei lowered her wrist. "We will go after them together then retreat to the Rìluò."

"Sounds good. Something's bothering me, though. What exactly happened down here?"

Mei looked back into her cell. "I was interrogated, held here against my will to delay the complications of our arrival."

"What about these Alidians? Why'd the embers kill them but leave you?"

"Not embers. It was another prisoner, though I do not think that description entirely applies." She turned to the middle cell on the other side. "He wore nondescript clothing, a wool shirt and gray pants. His skin was pale. His hair was long. The whole time I was here, he said nothing. There were times I would notice him gone, but no one had come to release him." She walked toward the exit while Fall followed behind. "Not long ago, he suddenly stood up and looked to the ceiling, as if he had seen something beyond it. Then he walked through the failing field of his cell, as though it had never existed." She stopped briefly to study each of the dead Alidians. "I heard them die. When he returned, I asked him what he planned to do. 'Murder,' he said." Mei turned to look back into the brig. "I asked him who he wished to kill. He did not answer. I asked him to release me. I remember exactly what he said next. 'No, I am afraid that would complicate matters ahead of my intent.'"

Fall rubbed his jaw. "His intent?"

"That is what he said."

"A mystery for later," Fall said as he turned away. "We can worry about it once we get out of here."

"I agree. Did you use the lift?"

"They're locked down."

Mei looked down the hall. "I noticed an emergency access hatch on the way into the brig."

"That's the one I used. Let's go."

Fall backtracked to the ladder, and together they climbed. They stopped three decks up where Fall had first come down.

"This is it," Fall said with a grunt as he stepped off.

Mei followed. "We must hurry."

They exited, and Fall peeked outside. "Any idea which way?"

"This way," she said as she studied her wrist display.

Mei went left, and Fall followed. They reached the first intersection. Fall held back. Something wasn't right.

"You feel it too," Mei said as she drew her red knife. The serrated edges slid from the sheath like thirsty teeth. Her right hand held her compact red pistol.

"I do." He drew his sword and took a step.

At just that moment, the walls and ceiling were harried in a storm of gunfire. Fall dove left, landing on his shoulder, surprised more than anything to still be alive.

He looked up to see a pair of embers rushing toward Mei. She'd gone the other way, now across from him at the four-way junction. She kicked one of the soldiers in the hip and caught the arm of another with her knife.

She pulled the attacker close using her knife's edge to grip his armor, jabbed him in the neck with her pistol, and then shot him through the faceplate as he stumbled backward.

She spun to shoot the other one, but his gun was faster. She deflected the barrel with her forearm as he shot then fired two shots of her own in return.

Fall was back to his feet then. An armored Alidian appeared, firing as he advanced from the hall to the left. He turned to shoot when he saw Fall, and Fall slammed into the wall to avoid his aim. The Alidian turned to get another shot at Fall but froze when an Elcosian grenade bounced off his leg.

Fall saw it too and ran away as fast as possible. It exploded, and the shockwave hit him in the back. When he rose from the floor, he turned to see the burning mess at the intersection.

He held his hand up, choking on the smoke. "Mei!"

Nothing moved beyond the fire and smoke.

His communicator vibrated. He reached for his belt and fit it to his ear. "Mei?"

"Fall? Are you all right?"

"Mei! I thought . . . "

"I am fine. Where are you?"

"Directly across from you."

She coughed. "I do not see a way through." There was static. "Listen to me. Sidna is behind you, moving away from us. You must get to her."

"What about you?"

"I will find another route."

Fall turned around and started walking. "I'll get her and find a way to the hangar. Go ahead and get the ship ready. Olivia might already be there."

"It is a good plan." She sighed. "Fall, I am trusting you. Please do not let anything happen to Sidna."

He picked up the pace. "I won't."

Ban advanced the barrel of his gun around the corner, watching the view from its tiny mounted camera. Nothing moved.

Bodies of both marines and embers were scattered throughout the corridor, but smoke and the failing emergency lighting made it difficult to tell who'd won the battle.

How did they get through our defenses? Where are the shields? Why aren't we withdrawing?

He looked up. "The bridge."

Becks inched forward, staying low. "What about it?"

"If we can get there, we can retreat or at least put up a decent fight."

Richards shook his head. "We're just soldiers, boss. We can't run a ship."

"Still, we have to try. Unless you have a better idea?"

Richards shook his head. "Don't get me wrong. I'm with you. Same as always."

Ban looked to Becks and Tyr. They nodded in agreement.

He activated his communicator. "This is Bond-Sergeant Ban Morgan calling the bridge."

There was no answer.

"Calling any command staff."

No one answered. The communications suite of his armor was tethered to the ship's main hardware. It should have automatically broadcasted to each officer registered with the ship. Either it wasn't working properly, or they were all dead.

Richards turned his head. "Sounds like no one's home."

Ban stood and edged around the corner, gun raised at the ready. His helmet's low-light mode revealed the darkened corridor, and the squad walked through it, stepping over bodies and debris.

The bridge was on the first deck, but the lifts were inactive. Each deck had access points to maintenance tubes that ran throughout the ship, so they made their way to the nearest one, and once inside, began climbing.

The tubes were hollow cylinders that honeycombed throughout the ship. At each deck access point, Ban could hear fighting beyond the hatches as his fellow marines fought to save the ship. He wanted to help, but unless he could take back the bridge, it would matter very little.

After several minutes of climbing and walking, they finally made it to the first deck. Tyr moved to the hatch and opened it slightly.

He reached to his left arm and pulled out an optic cable. He worked it through the opening, and as he moved it back and forth, it transmitted visual data. Ban could see from the transmission that the corridor outside was clear.

Wolf Squad moved through and made their way toward the bridge. Like many areas they had passed, bodies lay strewn around the deck. But something was different there as they approached.

Becks walked over. "What is it, Ban?"

Ban knelt to take a closer look. The dead marine's neck had been slashed through the flexible sub-armor mesh. He moved to another nearby marine, seeing stab wounds under one of the arms and near the groin.

"It looks like they've been killed with knives or some other kind of bladed weapon."

Tyr rolled one of the corpses over. He looked up to Ban in question.

"Yeah, I see it."

Richards leaned over. "I don't get it. I don't see anything."

Ban turned to him. "That's the point. No bullet wounds. On *any* of them."

Richards looked around. "There're bullet holes all over the place."

"But not on the fallen."

Becks walked over. "Where are the embers?"

Richards stepped over a body and turned. "What are we saying? These guys got killed by someone who dodges bullets and doesn't use a gun?"

"I'm not sure." Ban stood up. "I do know I'm sick of looking at this."

Becks nodded. "Agreed."

Ban walked to the main bridge hatch. He motioned for Tyr, but as he neared it, it simply opened.

Ban backed away, surprised. "Why isn't this locked?"

He looked forward and saw the answer.

Crewmen lay scattered around the room or at their stations, all dead. Most were officers, explaining the lack of a reply to Ban's calls.

Wolf Squad moved around the bridge, searching for survivors.

The combat command area was a huge rectangular-shaped area with two smaller areas forward and down some steps. Down even further, between them, steps led to another central platform. The forward wall was made of segmented viewscreens, showing the space ahead of the ship.

Along the periphery of each work area, crew stations were set up with displays, and in the center of the main area, a set of workstations surrounded a huge table, complete with holographic representations of the ship and its systems.

Ban moved around the table and checked the bodies there. None of the people he found were alive. "Richards. Get me access to operations. I want a status report on the ship's systems."

Richards stared at a mutilated dead woman. "Uh . . . yeah. Sure."

He moved to a terminal near the center of the bridge. He plugged a cable from his wrist into a port and opened a panel on that same wrist, typing in commands. Before long, he stood up and unplugged the cable. "It's a no-go. I'm locked out."

"What?" Ban asked.

"Malicious program. It'd take hours to break, even if I knew how. Software registers the code as . . . Runian."

"That doesn't make any sense. How would . . . "

Ban thought back over the last few days.

The ship we captured?

Becks faced him. "What are you thinking?"

"I'm thinking we had the enemy on board long before the Elcosians arrived."

Becks thought for a second. "The civilians?"

"Yes."

Tyr tapped Ban on the shoulder and walked toward one of the lateral exits from the bridge. He stopped just before the hatch.

Ban followed him, curious. Tyr pointed to a bloodstained handprint near the hatch. Someone had left the bridge, headed toward a lift.

A survivor? Or the Runian saboteur?

Ban looked at Tyr then turned back to the others. "Let's follow this. Either we'll find someone who needs help, or we'll find the one who did this."

Becks went in ahead of him. "If it's the latter, I have a few things I'd like to say."

"No more than I do." Ban followed her, and Wolf Squad left the bridge, following the trail left in blood.

Sidna sprinted down the hall, strange shapeshifter flying closely behind her. Unable to keep up with her longer legs, he'd changed into a scaled lizard with flapping, leathery wings. Behind them, pursuing embers shouted as they narrowed the distance.

The corridor made a fork to the left, and the way ahead was clear. Bullets shot from the left path, ripping holes in the opposite wall. Sidna stopped, almost falling as she did.

Two Alidians in powered armor staggered backward from the left. Rounds ricocheted from their thick armor, but some of them found their mark. One of the marines was killed, and the other went to a knee, breathing heavily. She struggled to raise her rifle but succumbed to the incoming gunfire before she could pull the trigger.

Sidna charged her *viae* with lightning, and when the two embers who'd killed the woman jogged into the corridor ahead, she unleashed the stored energy, electrocuting them. A third ember jumped out from around the corner, rifle raised.

Sidna didn't have time to react.

The lizard folded his wings and surged over her shoulder, hitting the ember directly in the chest, lifting him off his feet and into the air. With a roll and a flap of his wings he released his grip, throwing the ember into the wall with a *crack*. The beast corrected his flight path with a few flaps, never losing momentum.

She followed him around the turn ahead, but at the last second, she looked back over her shoulder. A squad of embers was right behind them, barely slowing as they jumped over their convulsing comrades. She pulled herself around the corner and sprinted ahead.

About twenty meters in front, she saw the lizard come back into the corridor, flying at full speed toward her from the opposite direction. "Go back!" it screeched.

She stopped halfway down the corridor next to an open hatch. Four Alidians came around the corner in pursuit. They stopped and raised their weapons toward her, and she leapt through the hatch. A storm of bullets filled the corridor behind her.

The shifter came flying into the room with a quick twist and a flap of his wings, somehow unharmed. As he did, Sidna heard returning gunfire from the pursuing embers.

Good. Kill each other.

She stood up and ran to the hatch controls. With a few commands, she was able to close and seal it. The door wouldn't hold against any real attempts to open it, but the lock might buy her time. She looked around for another way out.

The room had two levels. It looked like a lounge, with furniture, a bar, and a transparent outer wall. She ran up the stairs leading to the second level. Her attention was drawn across the room to the viewport.

Outside, a battle raged. She could see the distant lights from explosions, and beyond, the massive *Forge*. It was a place of torture and death. The thought that she might be taken to it again made her shiver.

I'll die first.

Knocking sounds came from the hatch below, so she hastened her search. A check of the hatch on the upper level revealed it was sealed; she couldn't get it open.

The sounds from the lower hatch ceased, but after a few moments she heard a grinding noise.

She moved to a couch on the nearest wall and yelled, "Help me flip this!"

The lizard landed beside the couch and took the form of the massive bear she'd seen before. He easily flipped the couch, and Sidna took cover behind it.

The hatch below opened forcefully, and voices from the soldiers echoed upward. She looked to the sealed exit on her level.

Blowing a hole through it would take a lot of force. She might destroy the viewport, exposing the lounge to vacuum. She'd have to make her stand there instead.

One of the soldiers slowly climbed the stairs. She drew her pistol, filling it with hot orange fire from her *viae*.

Cornering me was a big mistake.

Ban tried to calm his nerves as he watched Tyr break through the hatch. Not only had his home come under siege, but there were flying reptiles on board. He sincerely hoped he was having a nightmare.

Hope. Wisdom. Light.

The usually comforting words rang hollow. He knew he'd betrayed the meaning behind them with his actions on Nix. The people he'd seen burn in the bay screamed in his mind, reaching a crescendo as the mole broke through the door.

Tyr forced the hatch, and Ban rushed inside, weapon raised. He went left, and Richards went right.

Ban swept the left side of the officers' lounge. "Clear!"

Richards echoed him. "Clear."

Becks pointed her rifle up through the second floor's opening. "Top's clear from this viewpoint."

Tyr covered the rear, making sure the corridor outside remained empty. Ban moved toward the stairs, signaling for the rest of the squad to stay below and hold the lower level.

He took each step slowly, trying to be quiet, but his powered armor wasn't made for sneaking. He had no doubt he'd be heard if any Runians were waiting above. When he was close to the top, he crouched down and raised his light machine gun, allowing its camera to take the risk.

And risky it was. A flash of light made him pull it back down. The camera was fried, and the top of the gun sizzled.

"Ban!" Becks shouted from below. "Tyr, give him some cover!"

Within a split second, Ban heard the hiss of a rocket flying up through the opening in the floor. The ceiling above exploded, and debris came crashing down.

Ban wasn't sure the viewport wall would hold, but his powered armor was vacuum-rated. He was certain the lizard and the girl were not.

He rushed up the last few steps and took cover behind a large chunk of fallen ceiling. The girl fired, and the debris melted and popped where it was hit.

A quick check confirmed his gun was in working order. He raised it over the debris and fired toward the girl's hiding spot. He came around the edge and continued firing.

To his surprise, a monstrous bear ran toward him, roaring loudly. Without thinking, he reached to his belt and took a grenade, activated it, then tossed it forward before diving back behind cover.

The grenade exploded, and the floor trembled, weakened even further. He crawled forward and looked around his cover. There was no sign of the bear, but he saw the lizard creature skitter behind a chunk of ceiling. The girl was nowhere to be seen.

Magic bullets. Flying lizards. Monster Bears. To the Void with this!

Ban took the metal sphere hanging at his waist and dropped it to the floor. It activated, and the holographic image of an armored marine took cover.

Ban got to his feet and moved to another chunk to the side. He watched as something slithered out on the other side of the room, heading toward the hologram.

The hologram poked its head up, trying to draw attention. A few of the bullets hit near the hologram's head, and one or two went through the hologram.

It worked; the girl stood out in the open, confused.

With both enemies distracted, Ban advanced and leveled his gun on her. "Hold it!"

She jumped in surprise but didn't turn her pistol.

"Drop it! Now!"

She reluctantly dropped the pistol and slowly turned toward him.

"On your knees!"

She hesitated. His trigger finger tensed. He didn't have time to play with her, and whatever else was in the room. He decided to give her a count of three.

"One."

Her eyes closed, and she breathed deeply. The hologram deactivated, not by his command.

"Two."

The girl opened her eyes. Red-orange light spilled out from under her jacket sleeves. The flying reptile perched on the debris near the hologram, wings unfolded. Ban squeezed the trigger.

"Thr—"

The three of them froze as a bolt of electricity shot up and coursed through the rubble near the opening in the floor.

Ban kept his gun on the girl, and she stared him down.

"Ban?" Becks sounded uncertain.

He shuffled sideways, careful not to lose sight of the girl. He looked back and forth between her and the lizard. They both seemed ready to attack.

"I'm a little busy, Becks."

"It's . . . ugh . . . it's important, Ban."

She sounded like she was in pain. He edged backward behind some fallen ceiling and looked through the open floor.

Tyr and Richards stood very still, faceplates open. They'd both put their guns down, hands up. Becks also had her faceplate open, and he could see her unease. Something in front of her neck twisted, reflecting silvery light.

Behind her, someone stood in the shadows, just in front of the hatch. Ban could make out light armor and a bandana, but the face was shrouded.

He activated his low-light mode. The man was one of the civilians, holding a razor-sharp sword in front of Becks's throat.

Ban fought down panic, which quickly turned to anger.

The man spoke. "All of you. Stop."

He must have been the one who attacked the bridge. That blade was the evidence, now held threateningly to his lover's neck.

"We aren't enemies," the murderer said.

The girl waved her hand. "Fall. Look around. We aren't exactly friends."

The lizard hopped down to the floor. Its shape changed fluidly into a small, red, furry creature. It raised its hands in surrender and walked slowly to the edge of the hole. "They're about to kill each other up here. You might want to speed it up."

Ban looked back to the man. "Drop that sword, or your friends up here will die."

The man slowly lowered the blade and took a step back. "All right, I didn't come in here to kill anyone."

Ban gritted his teeth. "Put your weapon away, and we'll talk."

The Runian sheathed his sword and raised his hands. The lights in Becks's helmet came back on with a flicker, and the faceplate closed.

"Now, Becks!"

She broke away, and Ban swung his gun around, opening fire. The man dove backward and out of the room. Ban jumped down to the lower level and ran to the hall, but the man was nowhere to be seen. He was deciding which way to go when an explosion rocked the room behind him.

He ran back inside and followed Tyr up the stairs. The hatch had been blown open. The girl and the creature were gone.

He turned toward the viewport. Cracks were beginning to spread along its surface.

Becks topped the stairs. "The wall won't hold much longer." She ran to the blown hatch, and the squad exited, everyone except for Ban and her. He stared out to the battle outside.

"Ban?"

He walked forward a few steps. "The Elcosians."

"Yeah?"

"They've killed us," he said.

She walked over and hefted her rifle. "We aren't dead yet."

"They aren't even using their main ship. They're just picking us apart from the inside." Ban looked down at his hand. "I helped them. I gave them—"

She smacked him in the helmet, hard. "I said, we aren't dead yet."

He stared at her for a long moment while the viewport continued to fragment. Without a word she patted her rifle and backed up toward the hatch.

He nodded and followed her through, giving one last look to the space battle.

Not yet.

CRUCIBLE

SIDNA LOOKED UP AS SHE DESCENDED THE ladder's lowest rung. "I never asked you to follow me, you little weirdo."

Hermes jumped down and shrugged. "You need my help."

She turned back as she exited the emergency access hatch. "I really don't. Seriously, go bother someone else."

His ears dropped, and he frowned, adopting an exaggerated expression of hurt feelings. "You know, that's pretty ungrateful. If it hadn't been for me—"

His mouth kept moving, but she didn't hear the rest.

An intrusive sensation bore suddenly into her mind—the cursed connection shared between her and the one she feared so much.

Though she couldn't see him, she could have pointed right at Tieger through the wall. She backed away, slowly at first, then ran as Tieger's presence continued to grow—he was coming closer.

Hermes cried out as she went the wrong way. "Where are you going? We were almost there!"

Sidna ran even faster, but the feeling kept up. She rounded a few corners, randomly sprinting through the halls of the hangar deck.

Hermes yelled for her, but she wouldn't slow down. The little shapeshifter was too far behind, and Tieger's presence was at its strongest yet.

You're on your own.

She turned her head just in time to slam full force into the man ahead. "Ah!" She bounced off and fell to the floor.

His gloved hand extended toward her. "Sidna?"

It was the Ranger, Fall.

He took her arm and pulled her to her feet. "Come on. Those Alidians are close by."

"I don't care about them!" she yelled. "Tieger's coming, and he—"

Hermes dashed around the corner, never slowing as he passed.

"Must run!" he said breathlessly. "Must run, must run, must run!"

Fall went to the corner and looked around it. He jumped back and hugged the wall, eyes closed tightly as bullets shot past him.

"Embers!" He pulled Sidna by the arm. "And something else!"

She jerked free. Her anger swelled at the thought of being weak. She didn't need anyone's protection.

Not this time.

Filling her *viae* with fire, she turned to walk back toward her pursuer.

"Sidna! What are you doing? You can't—" Fall's voice fell away, suppressed by the overwhelming force of the presence.

She pushed it away as best she could, back into the recesses of her consciousness, and focused solely on her hatred for Tieger.

"Sidna! What are you doing? You can't go back!"

She walked around the corner, out of Fall's sight.

"Dammit!" He ran after her, drawing his mech bow on the way. "Boomer." He rounded the corner, arrow nocked and drawn.

The end of the corridor was engulfed in flames, and embers staggered forward, burning alive. Sidna stood a few meters ahead of Fall, breathing heavily as fire surged in her hands.

The flames before her parted as a heavily armored man walked through them. Sidna's fire leapt up from the deck and flared around him, but he never slowed, undeterred by the heat.

Sidna backed away, red-orange light fading from her hands. Electric, blue light took its place, and the air crackled around her. "Damn you! Die!"

The man stopped and did something that should have been impossible.

He reached into nothing. When he pulled his arm back out from the absence, he held a dark wooden haft, revealed to be the grip of a large hammer. The head was silver, like Fall's sword, with a long blade on the opposite face and violet energy that flowed from inside. Letters, ancient and unreadable, were inscribed in its surface.

He held the weapon with both hands as he walked. Sidna unleashed a fury of electricity, but the bolts seemed to fizzle out, absorbed by the hammer.

He laughed and spoke with a terribly deep voice. "Do you feel it, witch? Do you feel it in your *bones*? You will *die* here."

Fall raised his bow. "Sidna, move!"

She didn't. "I'm not going anywhere!"

"Fogger!" Fall took the boomer arrow from the bowstring and replaced it with the fogger arrow.

He fired it into the wall beside her and activated it with a double tap on his palm. As the burst of fog rapidly expanded, he holstered the bow and ran ahead.

He threw the boomer arrow past her, end over end, and grabbed her around the waist with both arms, lifting her off her feet as he twisted. Once he was between her and the arrow, he detonated it.

The explosion never came. He had just enough time to spin around and draw his sword as a sharp blade came thrusting for his throat. The two weapons connected, and Fall pushed the other away. He ducked under the next swing and ran the opposite direction, pulling Sidna along with him.

"Let me go!" she screamed.

The corridor's structure trembled as the hammer's head slammed down behind him.

Fall and Sidna ran back around the corner where they'd been before. The fog wafted after them, glowing with a violet hue.

The man's deep, bone-chilling voice echoed down the corridor. "Here, witch, let me show you *true* fire."

Fall drew his bow. "Boomer." He nocked the arrow and drew back. "Stop!"

Violet flames danced over the man's armor as he cleared the corner. "More tricks."

Fall shot the arrow directly at his chest, but before it reached the target, it disappeared. The wavering air normalized, and the man still advanced, completely unharmed.

He laughed mockingly. "Your flying sticks cannot touch me, boy." He walked forward. "I will mount your ruined head on a pedestal in my chambers. It will make a fitting decoration after this day's victory." He flipped the hammer over, showing its silvered edge. "Come, let us match blades once more before your light goes out."

Fall holstered the bow, and his right hand went to his sword.

Ab aeturno . . .

He resigned himself and drew the sword with a flourish. "Sidna, you—"

She stepped beside him. "If you tell me to run, I'll shoot you in the leg, then actually do it." She raised her pistol, and fire coursed through her arms. "Shut up and fight."

The boy sprang forward, sword swept back, grim look of determination on his face. Capitalizing on the foolhardy attack, Tieger feigned a blow to the boy's sword side then delivered a powerful swing of the hammer's shaft to the other.

Impressively, the boy saw through the feint and dodged it deftly as he continued forward in a spin. His silver sword darted back and forth with expert skill, probing for weakness in Tieger's defense.

Good. Very good.

Avoiding a counterattack, the boy maneuvered away. Tieger felt invigorated, but the boy's frustration was beginning to show in his tightening movements.

The witch noticed an opening between the two and fired her pistol. One round flew past Tieger, sizzling as it burned into the wall over his shoulder. Others were swallowed by his nevergates, subconsciously summoned in his defense.

Tieger pushed forward, and the boy, perfectly balanced in his stance, matched pace. His retreat continued for several steps beyond Tieger's final attack, and Tieger seized the opportunity to attack the witch.

He raised his fist, and the Fire of Elcos burned brightly on her skin, causing her to drop her pistol as she screamed in pain. The boy saw her burning, but instead of running to her aid, he stepped in front of her, sword raised in defense. His face took on a hardness Tieger hadn't expected. It wasn't anger or fear, but as if all emotion ceased, a cold void taking its place.

Tieger released the flames, and the witch dropped to her knees, breathing heavily. "Yes . . . you will die first. It will make her dying all the more painful."

A series of distant explosions caused the ship to shudder around them. Main power failed, and the emergency lighting flickered.

Neither of them moved.

Another explosion was accompanied by a rush of atmosphere. The vacuum warning in Tieger's suit activated, and he stepped forward over a threshold. In response to the change in pressure, a blast door closed behind him, sealing the area.

The boy flowed forward to meet Tieger, graceful in his fury. The rapid exchange of blows sent sparks flying around them. Flashes from the flickering lights made their movements appear broken and stuttered, but neither faltered.

After halting the advance, Tieger edged forward, slowly pushing the boy back. He attacked high and low, and with each strike, the boy's blade appeared just in time. A few more steps and Tieger had closed the distance back to the witch.

Darkness fell.

Three more flashes of light broke the black as their blades connected, and a cry of pain echoed throughout the deck.

The lighting came back online, revealing the boy once more. He was down on one knee, grasping his left side with his right arm. He looked up.

Absurdly, he managed a pained smile, and his eyes shifted to Tieger's shoulder.

Tieger looked up, and he saw the boy's sword lodged between two plates of his armor. It glowed faintly, and for a moment, the air visibly stirred around it. Tieger reached up and grasped it, but the blade was stuck.

Wet warmth ran down the side of his chest, and his left arm went numb. Tieger looked back to the boy, enraged.

The witch was at his side. Blood ran from her nose down her face and neck, steam rising from her reddened skin. "You've got a little scratch there, Tieger."

He tried to pull the blade out again, but he had to stop as pain shot through his chest down to his knees. "This? It is only a little . . ." He grunted in pain. " . . . splinter."

The witch stepped forward, right arm extended, her perverse *viae* crackling with blue energy. "That's all I need."

Lightning found its way down the blade. His muscles locked, and his teeth ground near to the point of breaking. The force of the contractions was enough to cause his arm to pull the sword out, suddenly halting the flow of the electricity. Behind him, an explosion matched the combined intensity of his pain and rage.

Free of the forced spasms, Tieger threw the glowing sword down so hard it pierced the deck.

Just then, something gave way as the compartment decompressed, and a gust of air assaulted the front surface of Tieger's armor. He tried to take a step but lost his balance and stumbled; he was losing too much blood from his wound. He watched as *Janus* skidded past his feet, carried away by the escaping atmosphere.

He looked up in time to see a blur of motion. The boy's armored shoulder struck Tieger's chest, and Tieger, wounded and off balance, was pushed back.

The blast doors closed between them in response to the change in pressure. The last thing Tieger saw was the boy collapse to the floor, safe from any retribution.

Tieger held on to the deck as his armored claws dug in, suit sealing him against the vacuum. Darkness threatened the edges of his sight, unconsciousness grasping at his legs, defeat ringing in his ears.

But he refused to pass out, and the metal floor beneath him moaned as it tore, giving way to his unsated desire to rend flesh and bone—not only for the witch, but for the one who had dared protect her.

"She is *mine!*"

Fall blinked and closed his eyes, afterimage of Sidna's lightning still burning. He rolled to his stomach. Through the haze, he saw the faint glow from his sword where it stood in the deck.

He rose up without too much difficulty, but the first step didn't go as well. He fell sideways into the wall and clenched his jaw, forcing himself to take shallow breaths to ease the pain.

Sidna walked over and braced him underneath his right arm. "Is it bad?"

"I'm more or less in one piece. Here, walk me to my sword."

They hobbled over to it. Sidna's lightning had flowed along the blade and into Tieger's armor, but how the sword ended up stuck into the deck was a mystery. He let go of Sidna and walked to it.

The silver blade was completely unharmed, glowing faintly.

He braced himself and grasped the hilt. The sword came free easily. He held it up, and a twist of his wrist sent a point of light up the length of the blade. It looked as normal as it ever did.

Sidna was standing there, looking into his eyes as he lowered the sword. "How'd you manage to get through his armor?"

"No clue. Must've gotten lucky." He sheathed the sword with a grimace and turned to the blast door. "That was personal."

"It was. He wants me because I survived," she said.

"Survived what?"

"*Him.*" She closed her eyes. "His name is *Tieger.*" She rubbed her nose with the back of her hand and looked at the blood. "He captured me once, and I barely got away. He's been obsessed with me ever since."

Fall thought about the speed of his attacks, deep, unnatural laugh echoing in his mind. "I don't love the idea of him being out there, showing up at any time."

Sidna shrugged. "Welcome to my life."

Fall looked at her, dried blood under her nose, braided hair frazzled, full lips bleeding from where she'd bitten them.

She looked at him and did a double take. "What?"

He waved his hand and swallowed. "Nothing. I felt sorry for you."

She narrowed her eyes with a twist of her lips. "Don't." She turned and looked around. "We can't go back to the hangar. Dammit, Mei, where are you?"

"She's on her way to her ship. Olivia should be there too. We can ... " He turned around.

"What is it?" she asked.

"Hermes," Fall said as he looked around.

"Oh. Damn. Why didn't he come back?"

Fall looked down the hall, expecting the little red idiot to come running around the corner.

"No idea."

Ban's armored hand struck the wall, bracing him as the ship rocked with another explosion. He had the Runian fox's scent. He wasn't about to let him get away.

The problem at the moment was the large power signature just ahead. It matched the profile of heavy powered armor, but it wasn't Alidian and it didn't match an ember's trace either.

It has to be the man in the white armor.

Tyr had rigged a few EMP grenades to explode when the target came near. But the signal had stopped its advance. Ban had to decide what to do next.

Richards fidgeted. "Boss, it's possible he saw our signatures or maybe even the trap. What if we—"

The trap sprung suddenly, and Ban sprinted forward out of the cargo storage room.

He searched the area, confused. The grenades had exploded as intended, but there wasn't anyone nearby.

Richards walked over, spun around a few times, and shrugged. He started to walk back over when he accidentally kicked a small metal object with his boot. It rolled to a rest near Ban.

Richards cringed. "Explosive?"

Ban knelt and picked it up. "No. We'd already be dead."

He turned it over a few times in his fingers, but it gave no outward clue as to its purpose.

He stuck it in a pouch on his belt. "It's hardly powered armor."

His HUD showed that the large signature was moving away from its last location.

Becks turned. "Whatever it is, it's leaving. We need to focus on saving the ship."

Ban faced her. "Dammit, there's no way we're letting the Runians get away. We owe it to the crew to get revenge."

"No, we owe it to the crew to *save* them. Remember the crew, Ban? They aren't all dead."

Ban opened his mouth to speak but closed it. She was right. She was always right.

He rested his gun on his shoulder. "Richards. Set up a ship-wide broadcast. Tell the crew to—"

An explosion went off nearby, much larger than the previous ones. It came from the direction of the starboard flight deck.

Richards jogged over. "That one was ours, boss."

Ban nodded. "The explosives we set on the hangar bay hatch when the attack started."

Tyr pinched his fingers together in front of his face.

Becks agreed. "Tyr's right. If they board from both flight decks, we'll never clear the ship."

Ban lowered his gun. "Richards, coordinate with the survivors. Have all available squads report to the port flight deck to repel boarders. We'll secure the starboard bay."

"Sure thing, boss."

Ban made for the starboard bay at a jog. None of the blast doors were closing, and his suit read normal atmospheric pressure. The repulsion fields in the bay must have held against the explosion. The downside was the bay probably absorbed the full force of the blast.

"Hey, boss, wait a second."

Ban slowed and turned to Richards.

"The remaining squads are calling affirmative, but there aren't many survivors."

"Then we'll do what we can. It may not be enough, but we have to make a stand." Ban looked to Becks. "For the crew."

"Mei! Mei, come in!"

The sound of bullets ricocheting blasted through Fall's communicator. Shots returned, some from Mei's pistol and some that sounded like Olivia's.

"We are a little busy here," Mei said tightly.

A few more shots were fired.

Fall touched his ear. "Mei, listen. We can't make it back to the *Riluò*. We need a pickup at the other hangar."

"If I had my ship, I would be . . . pick you . . . "

Fall tapped his ear communicator.

"Mei? Mei, I can't hear you."

" . . . patient . . . embers here . . . up soon."

The signal degraded further, and Fall gave up.

He and Sidna were outside the port hangar bay, where he'd found some hastily placed explosives near the hatch. The devices weren't hidden, most likely meant to keep boarders from coming through the bay and into the ship.

Sidna stood a few meters away with her hands on her hips.

Fall walked over. "Any good with explosives?"

She shrugged. "Never needed them."

He nodded. "I guess you wouldn't."

"You?"

"Not unless it fits on an arrow."

She turned and walked away. He caught up. "What do you think?"

She rubbed her jaw and winced. "I'm spent. It's all you."

"All I can do is blow them up."

"Go for it."

He jogged ahead and turned around to face her. "Are you serious?"

"Yeah. You want out?" She pointed back. "That's the way out."

They reached what seemed to be a safe distance, down the hall and around the corner. "Boomer." Fall drew his bow. "All right . . . "

The arrow flew into the area around the hatch and exploded. The energy of the shockwave blew through the hall.

Sidna pulled at her ears. "Damn."

Fall holstered the bow and shook his head. "Looking back, that was stupid."

"Yeah, but it worked. Come on."

They had no difficulty getting inside the bay as most of the inner wall had been disintegrated. Miraculously, they hadn't caused a hull breach.

They walked to the center, surveying the results. Anything within a few meters of the hatch had been obliterated, and almost everything else was on fire. The few shuttles and fighters left in the bay were toppled over, and none looked flight ready.

Sidna turned to him, visibly frustrated. "Great. Just great."

He raised his eyebrows. "How is this my fault?"

"Are you serious right now?"

"It was your idea!"

She put her hands on her hips. "You do everything you're told?"

He pointed to the entrance. "We could still be out there, waiting—"

They turned back to the blown-open wall. The four Alidian marines from earlier were standing there, weapons trained in their direction.

Fall slowly raised his hands. They weren't in any shape for another fight.

The marine with the big gun appeared to be the leader. He turned his head slightly. "If either of them moves, shoot."

Sidna hadn't put her arms up. "Shouldn't you meatheads be worried about the Elcosians taking over your ship?"

The marine lowered his gun and walked across the bay toward

Sidna. She stood up tall, smugly daring him to hit her.

A few steps away, he transferred the gun to his left hand and held out his right. A flat shock-rod extended well past his hand from his forearm. He thrust it toward her abdomen.

But just before it could make contact, the rod halted. Fall's blade held it, sizzling and popping where it touched the electrified surface.

The marine with the sniper rifle sidestepped into view. "Drop it, Runian. Unless you want your brains all over the far wall."

Fall looked to the leader's helmet. He tried to see through to the eyes, but he couldn't. Reluctantly, he dropped his sword to the floor and braced for the inevitable shock.

Instead, the rod retracted, and the man stepped back. "You're fast. Very fast." The marine pointed at him. "Unlike you, I don't attack unarmed men."

Sidna grunted.

The marine turned his head toward her. "*Your* type is never unarmed, witch. Now, both of you, turn around and get on your knees."

Sidna stepped forward. "Or what?"

The metal rod came back out, and Fall grabbed Sidna's left shoulder. "Cool it. Save your strength."

The marine paused. "Listen to your friend."

She shrugged Fall's hand away. "He's not my friend."

Fall shook his head and turned around to face the repulsion field. *Come on, Mei.*

He saw it then—a glint of light, rapidly closing in.

He spun and tackled Sidna to the deck, flat as possible.

She fought him. "Get off!"

He grabbed her wrists. "Look!"

The *Rìluò* flew through the field and into the bay, guns blazing.

Fall rolled and scrambled to his feet, grabbing his sword on the way. He looked back to see the marines scattering for cover.

Sidna passed him, up and running. He ran after her toward the *Rìluò*.

After the sweeping barrage forced the soldiers down, the ship spun around, ventral bay open. Olivia was there, reaching out. Fall and Sidna leapt aboard with help as the ramp began to close.

The marines began to shoot back, and Mei banked hard, accelerating rapidly into space.

Sidna never stopped moving, headed straight for the cockpit.

Fall stayed in the rear area, and Olivia came over, leading him to a bench. The ship finally settled, and he was able to catch his breath.

Olivia looked him over, hands moving all around his chest. "Are you okay? Where are you bleeding from?"

She reached under his arms and started undoing the straps of his armor. He winced as each piece came away, though it felt good to have the weight removed.

"I don't know why you even wear this! Honestly!"

He rested his head on the wall behind him as she worked, looking back toward the rear hatch.

Somewhere beyond it was a man in jagged white armor, so powerful he could shrug off lightning bolts, immune to flames hot enough to melt steel.

Tieger.

◈

Sidna braced herself in the copilot's seat as Mei darted between the remains of destroyed starfighters.

Fortunately, the ships engaged in battle ignored them, and the *Rìluò* went unchallenged. As they cleared the perimeter, Mei activated the Inos drive, and they entered the Rift.

Mei relaxed. She turned to Sidna. "Are you all right?"

Sidna stared ahead. She took a deep breath and let it out slowly. "They found out what I am."

Mei nodded slowly. "All the better we made our escape."

Sidna closed her eyes. "Ran away, you mean."

"You would prefer I turn around?"

Sidna squeezed the arms of her chair. "No. What I'd *prefer* is Veridian."

Mei turned further, anger on her face. "With the Elcosians in pursuit? Madness."

Sidna bit her lip, realizing Mei was right. She opened her eyes and rolled them. "Fine. Whatever. We hide for a while. Where?"

"I have contacts on Parsera."

Sidna laughed. "So some Elcosian spy can turn us in? No thanks. We'd be better off on Dar Van-el."

"In the Maw? I will assume you are joking."

"Barely." Sidna crossed her arms. "What about Gyre?"

Mei looked ahead and shifted in her seat. "No."

"Oh, come on. It's not so bad. Let's get lost there for a little while." She pointed behind her with her left thumb. "Those two can catch another ride."

Mei seemed skeptical.

Sidna shrugged. "What? They can handle themselves."

Mei sighed. "I am sure they can."

"So what's the deal?"

Mei blinked, suspicious. "Who are you meeting there?"

"What?"

Mei shook her head with a slight smile. "Before I found you, you were planning to find your glyph and return to Veridian."

"And?"

"And I know you did not plan to go alone."

Sidna laughed. "You don't know anything."

"Perhaps . . . " Mei looked down to input coordinates into the pilot console. "Very well. We will go to Gyre."

"Huh." Sidna stared. "I didn't expect you to give in so easily."

Mei turned. "As always, I will do what I think is best. You should consider doing the same before you associate with the wrong sort of person."

Sidna raised her eyebrows. "Wrong? Maybe." She stood up to go back into the hold. "But he's much better company."

Klaxons wailed between iterations of the automated broadcast message.

As far as Ban knew, there wasn't anyone left on the ship to hear it. Repeated tries over the radio had been met with silence.

"Alert. This is not a drill. The ship has sustained critical engine damage. All personnel report to the nearest escape craft."

Ban hid behind a shelf in the half-destroyed quarters. Embers stalked through the corridor outside the room, sweeping the ship for survivors. The last one passed, taking a moment to shine a light into the room before moving on.

Ban relaxed a little. "Becks."

She looked up, and though he couldn't see her face, he knew her eyes were filled with tears. "We can't leave him. It's not right."

"We have to. You know we do. He's dead."

Tyr held Richards's body in his arms, kneeling on the floor. Richards's faceplate was open, and Ban saw nothing reflected in his normally smiling eyes.

Richards had taken a few hits from the escaping Runian ship, and while the squad had hidden from the Elcosians, he'd quietly bled to death. The field narcotics had made it a peaceful event, but nothing could take the fear away. Richards had joked his way through many dangers in the past, but this time he simply squeezed Becks's hand as he faded away.

She looked up. "All right. I'm okay."

Ban held out his hand. "We have to go."

She nodded and stood. Tyr laid Richards on the remains of the bullet-ridden bed nearby. After one last look, he closed Richards's faceplate and drew his pistol, nodding to Ban.

Ban walked to the door and looked both ways. The hall was clear, so he stepped out, building to a jog. The nearest lifeboat wasn't far. He broke the glass in front of the emergency lever, and the lever came out with a pull. The hatch opened, and Ban moved inside.

Tyr and Becks followed, and once they were in, Ban closed the hatch. They hastily fastened themselves into their seats, and Ban hit the launch button on his armrest, slammed into the seat as the lifeboat exploded away from the *Talon*.

He linked into the lifeboat's external cameras, watching the spiraling form of the *Talon* as it shrank from view. Its battered surface hemorrhaged, expelling crystalizing gas and debris from multiple sources.

There was a bright flash, and a narrow beam of light cut through the hull, barely missing the lifeboat. The *Talon* nearly split in half at the site of the wound. Ban watched in shock as another beam hit the rear of the ship, slicing through the drive section. The engines exploded, devastating the remaining wreckage.

When Ban's suit adjusted to the intensely bright light, he opened his eyes to see that the *Talon* had been completely obliterated.

Behind him, he heard the worst sound he'd ever heard in his entire life—Becks let out a moaning wail, deep from within her chest.

Tyr leaned forward against his harness and pounded his armored fist into his chest. His body shook with spasms as he grieved silently, unable to make a sound.

Ban could only watch helplessly as they suffered, unable to grieve with them. His own pain was too great, and if he took on more, he might fall apart.

He shut off the external camera's feed and sat there in the enshrouding darkness.

Ashes and death.

Violet flames licked and sputtered around Tieger's shoulder, burning away necrotic flesh. Underneath, new tissue was born, and the taint of the witch was purged.

The pain would have been terrible if not for the persistent thoughts that clawed their way to the fore of his mind.

Tieger of Westmarch, the *Malleus Maleficarum* of Elcos, had been defeated.

No.

Tieger stood, shirtless, and walked from his chambers.

No more of this.

The time for self-doubt and self-pity had come and gone.

He entered the bridge. Captain Gault was there on the central platform, receiving a report from a junior officer. The officer saw Tieger and left hurriedly with a quick bow.

The captain lowered his head and spoke. "Honored One, we—"

Tieger held up his hand. "Survivors?"

"There were a few pods, yes. Should we hunt them down?"

"No, leave them to starve. We hunt the witch. Have you found the trace?"

"We have, Hono—"

"Where?"

"The Ko gate seems most likely."

"And then?"

"There are many systems beyond that—"

Tieger held up his hand again, fury building. "I do not need your fumbling guesses, Gault, I want an answer."

"They'll go to Gyre."

Tieger turned to see who had spoken out of turn.

It was the Harbinger's spy. His black leather coat opened slightly to reveal light armor, dressed with leather straps and an array of throwing knives. His arms and legs were lightly armored with knee-high boots and open-fingered gloves. A hood obscured his face.

Stepping forward, he pulled the hood back, smoothed his hair away, and flashed a toothy white smile. His yellow reptilian irises reflected the ambient light.

Tieger sneered. "I see you have survived. Not surprising for a snake."

"That I did." The spy studied Tieger's shoulder conspicuously, as if he could still see the wound. "And without a scratch."

Tieger squeezed his fingers into fists—it was that or strangle the man. "Gyre?"

"It's where I would go."

"I know it not."

The spy nodded. "A world without law and order, completely untamed. You wouldn't have been there before."

"And yet, you knew it straightaway."

The spy bowed slightly, flashing his perfect smile. "Gyre is a deep, dark hole. And as you said, I am a snake."

DREAMS AND WHAT LIES BENEATH

FALL STALKED THROUGH THE TREES, USING his ash-wood longbow to sweep away the damp, low-hanging branches. He wound through and underneath the limbs as he followed the natural forest trail, careful not to slip on the leaf-covered roots below. He held his hip-quiver close, feathers forward, thumb encircling the shafts so they didn't rattle together. His worn leather boots flattened the wet grass near the base of the last tree.

The clearing beyond was isolated, its own little world, shaded by the dripping leaves above and penetrated by a beam of light that punched through an overcast sky. A bird pecked at a trunk, and an animal's call echoed through the dense air.

The fox, who sat on top of a broken log, turned toward him.

Fall smiled. "Ready?"

The fox stared with a slight swish of its bushy tail.

"Go."

The fox leapt from the log.

Fall sprang forward and climbed the rotting wood, slipping once on the bark before he reached the top. He balanced on the fallen tree as it bent under his weight, searching, but the fox was nowhere to be seen.

He lowered to a crouch and swung his legs over the edge to sit. As he did, the log collapsed, and he fell through the top, landing in the mushy filth inside.

He struggled but couldn't right himself. When he'd given up on flailing, he looked up to see a familiar smile. "I'm always rescuing you."

Fall reached up, and a strong hand yanked him free of the mound then set him on his feet. He picked up his bow and brought it down over his head, string forward on his chest, then looked up as he brushed the muck from his pants.

Thane was middle-aged, with salt-and-pepper hair, yet his face was youthful in appearance. His light armor was black, with a black-and-white-checkered cape that hung over the left shoulder. The hilt of his longsword stuck up over his back, and his revolver hung lazily at his right side. White owls decorated the armor at each of his shoulders.

He stood there, arms crossed, with a smirk. "What? Don't look at me like that."

"Thane?" Fall looked around the glade. "Why are you here?"

"I should ask you the same. Your mother will be worried sick."

Fall rubbed his red nose with a sniffle. "She doesn't even know I'm gone. She never does."

"Hey now. What did I tell you? Don't talk bad about your family. They're all you've got in the world."

Fall lifted his chin. "Not me. I have the fox."

"Nothing lasts forever."

Fall sighed and looked down again. "I know that." He looked up again, eyes brighter. "Oh! You could help me! With you here, that fox won't get very far."

Thane shook his head. "Sorry, kid. I have my own problems."

Fall frowned. "Like what?"

"Well, there's that, for one thing." He pointed back to the log.

A creeping darkness reached out from the hole on top and through cracks at the base. It was more an absence of light than anything else, but it did have a form. Soft wood fell away as thin vines of oil reached out, widening as they lengthened.

Thane backed away, stepping over a stone half buried in the forest detritus. "You know me. I have to keep on moving." He saluted Fall with two fingers to his brow then walked off into the trees at a brisk pace.

Fall turned back to the growing horror, now free from its stumpy confinement.

He looked inside it, knowing somehow that the pulsing darkness meant to grab him and drag him down somewhere. Deep feelings of dread suddenly took root in his gut, primordial and absolute.

Fall looked around frantically. The sun had gone dim, and the air had chilled. All the animals had fled, leaving the once-peaceful woods eerily silent.

He turned in a slow circle. "Something's not right. This isn't how it was."

Past the pulsating black jelly, he saw the fox, watching him from a distance. It seemed to be waiting for him to do something.

"What should I do?"

The fox looked down from Fall's eyes to his body.

Fall looked down too, seeing that his coat was covered in blood. Inside, his chest was bleeding profusely. Panicked by the sight, he turned and ran into the woods and tripped over a broken branch. He scrambled back to his feet then nearly fell again.

As he fought to escape through the tangling forest, he heard something like laughter closing in behind him, a hideous sound only a creature of nightmare could make.

Fall opened his eyes and sat up with a groan.

Again?

For the last few mornings, he'd had some variation of the forest dream. And no matter what happened, Thane and Hermes were always there.

But the darkness was new.

He rubbed his face and exhaled deeply as he transitioned back into the waking world then fumbled for the light switch on the wall. It was lower than he remembered, but he found it eventually. He kicked the wadded-up blanket at his feet and swung his legs over the edge of the bunk. After another minute of staring at the floor blankly, he stood up and reached down for his suit.

There was a knock at the hatch as he zipped up. "Yeah?"

Olivia answered. "Hey. It's me. I saw your light and thought you might like something to eat."

He pressed the key, and the hatch slid open.

She was waiting there with a steaming bowl of plain, warmed-up oats. "Mornin'. Hungry?"

He blinked a few times. "Always."

She looked up into his eyes. "You still aren't sleeping well. Are you hurting?"

He touched where Tieger had cut him, now a tingling raised line in his skin. "Not really." He stepped past her into the *Rìluò*'s rear hold.

She followed him to her makeshift gurney and handed him the food as he sat. "Bad dreams?"

He stirred the oats. "Yes."

She frowned. "Something on your mind?"

Fall took a bite and grimaced at the lack of flavor. "An understatement."

Olivia drank coffee from an old, dingy mug. "Might help to talk about it."

"Hmmm. It might." He poked at the mush in his bowl as he started in the middle of his thoughts. "You know, I've done a ton of missions on my own. Without Thane, I mean."

Olivia nodded.

"Some went better than others, but I've always managed to pull off the job. This one . . . " He put the bowl down. "I failed."

"How?"

Fall's eyes widened. *"How?"*

"Yeah." She sat down next to him. "What was your job?"

"To guide the crew."

"Which you did."

He laughed bitterly. "It was implied they'd survive the trip."

"Was it? You weren't hired as a fighter. You were hired as a guide. The captain ignored his guide's advice. Ultimately, he's responsible."

"I doubt Vaughan-Heighas will see it that way."

"To the Void with Vaughn-Heighas. We know what really happened."

Fall nodded. "I can't help but think that Thane might have managed to do more."

Olivia swung her legs back and forth. "I don't see how anyone could have."

Fall sighed. "Me neither. It's just a nagging feeling."

"I bet it'll pass."

"I hope so." He picked the bowl up. "If for nothing else, so I can get some sleep."

Olivia watched him eat. "What about Hermes?"

He shrugged as he chewed. "What about him?"

She raised an eyebrow. "Don't you wonder where he is? What happened to him?"

"Not really." He swallowed, throat dry. "Got any coffee?"

"Yeah, I'll get you a cup as soon as you answer my question."

"She applies her torture tactics yet again." Fall sat back. "I'd be worried, except this is fairly normal. A few years ago, I lost him for a whole month. He just showed up again one day, two T-Gates away like nothing ever happened." He turned to her. "He always comes back."

Olivia walked over and took a cup from the sink. "I hope you're right. I kinda like him." She poured the steaming caffeine and handed it over.

"What else?"

"Huh?"

"That can't be all that's buggin' you."

"That isn't enough?"

"Nope. Spill it."

He smiled wryly. "Why should I? Got my coffee and my food. You'll have to up the stakes."

Olivia narrowed her eyes. "Tell me, or I'll tell Sidna you actually *like* her."

Fall paused. "I'm sorry, what?"

"Yeah, I've seen you. You get quiet when she's around. You stare when she can't see you."

"Because she's unpredictable."

"Uh-huh . . . "

Fall sat up. "Fine. If you're going to go making stuff up, I'll tell you. I dreamt about a monster."

Olivia made an exaggerated move toward the forward hatch. "Oh Sidna, I've got something to tell you."

Fall put his cup down and jumped up. "Hey! I'm serious. It was black, and . . . well, *ominous*."

"Ominous?" she asked, doubtful.

"Yeah. It's stupid, but things get to you in dreams that normally wouldn't."

"Hmmm. Okay, I guess that's good enough."

"All right. Now be reasonable."

"Oh, I'm reasonable, there's just something you should know about me."

"What?"

She smiled as she walked away. "*I'm* unpredictable too."

"Ronin went. Why won't you?" Sidna asked, voice muffled slightly.

"Veridian was never part of the job," Mei replied, also distant.

Fall held his finger just in front of the cockpit hatch entrance key, listening carefully.

Veridian? A city? A planet?

"When I am sure we are free of pursuit, I will take you and that glyph of yours back to Endi."

"Ugh. They'll just debate like they always do, right up until Tieger kills them all."

"That is possible. But since your elders will be the ones to pay, I will do as they wish." She paused. "Hold a moment."

The hatch opened suddenly, and Fall stared inside at the two women. "Oh . . ."

Mei turned her head slightly. "Exactly how long were you going to stand there?"

Fall looked up to see a small camera pointed at his face. "Sorry. It didn't seem like a good time to come in."

Sidna turned in her chair. "I guess you heard all of that?"

He shrugged. "Just the parts about your elders, a glyph, and some place called Veridian."

She threw her hands up. "Great, Mei. Just great."

Mei ignored her. "What was it you needed?"

He entered, and the hatch closed behind him. It was tight inside the cockpit, so he took a knee behind the two women. He looked out into the Rift. "Just wondering where we are."

Mei looked ahead. "We are approaching Gyre."

"Nice. Good timing on my part."

Sidna grunted.

Or maybe it wasn't.

He moved to turn around. "I'll wait in the back."

Sidna turned around and stood. "No, stay. I need to get ready, and there isn't enough room back there with all the extra . . . *passengers.*"

Fall moved aside to let her pass. After she left, he sat in her seat and turned to Mei. "Veridian?"

She waved her hand. "A dream."

"I don't understand."

"Veridian . . . is a planet. A place she has been to once before. Or so she claims."

"You don't believe her?"

"I do not default to trust with her."

He raised his eyebrows. "Why not go with her? See what's there."

Mei looked at him incredulously. "A dangerous experiment."

"Probably. Why don't her elders want her to go?"

"I am not sure she has even asked them. She hardly submits to their authority."

"Are some of them arcanists too?"

Mei turned to look him directly in the eyes. "They *are* the arcanists—the last living enclave."

Fall whistled. "So, she can't go home, and you won't let her go to Veridian?"

"Correct."

Fall sat back in his chair. "She'll probably ditch you the first chance she gets."

Mei's lip rose at the corner, the hint of a smile forming. "She will try. But I will never be that far behind her."

Fall furrowed his brow. "That's a time-heavy investment. I hope her elders are paying enough."

She nodded. "They will. Though I admit I *have* thought of asking for more." She released the ship's controls. "What about you? What will you do on Gyre?"

He reached up and rubbed his neck. "To be honest, I was hoping I could rely on your charity for a night or two. I'm all out of virtua. I keep hard currency for places like this, but it won't last long."

"You plan to hire a ship?"

"Eventually, if I can raise the fare."

"What about your ward, Olivia?"

Fall tapped his finger on the armrest. "I'll get her home, but she's stuck with me for the time being. I'd be grateful if she could stay on your ship while I look for a new contract."

"As long as Sidna remains in the city, I have no problem with it."

"Thanks, Mei. Add it to the list of things I owe you."

"You owe me nothing."

"No, I do. And I always pay my debts." He smiled. "Even if it takes a little while."

She stared for a few moments. "Interesting."

"What's that?"

She smiled. "From time to time, I see a little bit of him in you."

"Who?"

"Thane."

"Really. How so?"

She closed her eye in thought. "I am not quite sure myself. But I do see it." She opened her eye. "As he was when we were young."

"You knew him back then?"

"Oh yes. Our paths have crossed many times."

"Huh." Fall interlocked his fingers behind his head. "Small galaxy."

She turned to the Rift, smile widening. "Yes. I suppose it is."

The conversation paused naturally then, and Fall soon lost focus on the Rift. He looked to the internal camera feed and saw Olivia rummaging through her medical backpack.

There was something about the Runian doctor. She was beautiful, that was for sure, but there was more. She was intelligent. And she was talented too. Her drive and optimism were infectious.

Fall watched as Sidna came out of her quarters and passed through the rear bay.

Sidna. He remembered his hand around her wrist and her arm around his waist, helping him walk after the fight. He thought about her scowls, and her biting comments, and the way her fiery nature was undeniably sexy.

"Perhaps you could use Sidna," Mei said.

Fall sat up quickly. "Um, what?"

"She has spent a considerable amount of time on Gyre. She might have a contact in need of a Ranger."

Oh. Right.

He did his best to relax. "I might do that. Believe it or not, I've never been there."

"I am unsurprised. Thane avoided it when possible." Mei looked up. "As do I."

"Well, you probably won't be there long."

"That all depends upon Sidna." She sighed and flicked two switches. "But for the moment, we are here."

The Rift destabilized at her command, and the *Rìluò* returned to normal space.

In the distance, superimposed on the stars of the Vagrant Sea, Fall saw a gray world marked with swirls of bright white. As they approached, he saw that the swirls were massive storms, many the size of an entire continent on his forested homeworld. The rest of the strange planet was covered in dense, irregular clouds with only the slightest hints of deep, dark blue on the other side.

He cycled through the sensor displays. "I'm not seeing a station in orbit."

"There are none. We are going to the surface."

"Through all of that?"

She smiled. "It will be fine."

"All right . . ."

They flew closer, and just before they reached the atmosphere, they were hailed. What they received was only a numeric code as far as Fall could tell, and Mei responded in kind. After a few seconds, she received a stream of complex data displayed on an overlay which appeared on the cockpit viewscreen.

Mei activated the internal intercom. "We have arrived at Gyre. Prepare yourselves. It will be rough going in."

The space around them started to dull. Soon, the ship was enveloped in the thick atmosphere, and he lost sight of the stars. Mei had to make constant corrections for the buffeting winds, but as the storm seemed to reach its greatest fury, the view ahead cleared and the *Riluò* broke through.

Not far below the clouds, Fall spotted a large, gray, cylinder-shaped projection sticking up at an angle from a violently tossed ocean. Rain fell heavily, blown in all directions, and everywhere he looked, he saw lightning and dark clouds from horizon to horizon.

Mei flew the ship into the hollow metal cylinder, and the sounds of spinning turbines drove away all other noise. The walls were at first broken up by gaps in the metal with foaming water spilling over their edges, thrown inside by the churning ocean. Further inside, the walls became solid with streams of water running down the sides. Those metal walls gave way to layers of gleaming, wet stone.

Fall's breath caught as they passed into a gargantuan underground cavern. Suddenly his viewing distance changed from a few meters on each side to several kilometers all around.

Massive lanterns lit the spaces between incredibly large columns of stone that stretched from darkness above to darkness below. At first, the columns were irregular in shape, yet natural in appearance, as if they had been formed by dripping stone. But as the ship moved deeper into the cavern, the columns became more uniform, and the faint lines of man-made designs could barely be seen on their smooth surfaces.

Mei navigated the spaces between the columns. "Sidna, you may want to come to the cockpit."

After a few moments, Sidna entered through the hatch behind Fall. She looked up at him as she knelt. "Most people never get to see Cisterne."

Fall turned his head slightly, unable to look away from the view ahead. "Cisterne?"

"The city." Sidna laughed and rolled her eyes. "You've seriously never heard of it?"

He leaned forward. "Yes, but I didn't realize it was underneath an ocean."

"All are welcome as long as they aren't welcome anywhere else—that's the saying, anyway. No police, no judges, and certainly no religion," she said.

"Sounds like the perfect place for Ranger's work."

Mei nodded. "As long as you keep your eyes open."

Far in the distance, past the forest of columns, a hazy luminescence grew in intensity. The *Rìluò* flew closer and closer until Fall could see that the radiance came from a large island in the middle of an expansive underground lake.

The lake stretched out of sight into the darkness, but there were lighted ships on the water, scattered around like stars in an upside-down nighttime sky. A few small stone islands poked up from the lake, each with structures and lights of their own.

But in the midst of it all, the sight of the main island had him transfixed, its surface covered in thousands and thousands of lights, all different sizes and colors.

It was the glow of a secret city, Cisterne, hidden beneath the ocean of a storm-shrouded world.

A PERFECT VESSEL

SHROUDED AND SECRET, THE NEVER LAY JUST below the surface of reality, its strange depths holding a path to every world. It touched the Vagrant Sea in all places, and with enough energy, could be breached and traversed. The *Forge* had that power, and Tieger used it.

He stood before the *Forge's* cathedral viewport, looking out into the mysterious realm, troubled as he often was.

The Never seemed to go on in all directions, fading into a sky of deep violet. It was full of transparent ether, breathable and warm, dense and nebulous far into the distance as it neared the edge of the normal world. There, it formed clouds of flammable gas, inhospitable to most forms of life.

Deep in the center, in the clear ether, there were suspended islands, each beautiful in their impossibility. There were thousands of them, many littered with the ruins of an ancient people who must have died long ago. The remains spoke of forgotten technology, elegant yet awesome in scope.

The island nearest the *Forge*, Teras Ni, had a winding river that fell over its side, ending in a waterfall that disappeared into the nothing below. Scattered forests lined the river, and lush green grasslands led up to the base of a mighty volcano, Cor Vod. It was there, at the peak, that the Harbinger communed with the mighty Elcos.

It was from there that the old man plotted and schemed.

The cathedral's doors cycled and opened. Tieger listened without turning, and the spy made no sound as he ascended the nearest of the two curved marble staircases leading up to the main platform. He continued to watch in the glass before him as the reflection of the shadowed figure walked to the center, next to the throne.

The seat sat isolated on the semicircular dais, worked into the shape of a burning pillar of flame. Around the chair, the floor was hewn from violet marble, its form a rolling, stony fire that caught along the rear wall and spread out to the periphery.

The spy placed his hand upon the chair's upper rim, then eased his fingers down the side. "Enjoying the view, *Honored One?*" The statement was soaked in derision.

Tieger ignored it. "It allows me to see a great many things."

"Oh? Contemplating the future?"

"Yes."

"Wise. It has become uncertain."

Tieger tightened his fist. "Indeed. It grows more perilous by the second."

"So true." The spy walked behind Tieger, maintaining his distance. "Why, even a girl can be dangerous if we let down our guard."

Tieger's shoulder burned with phantom pain. "I will repay that transgression. Many times over."

For the boy, even more so.

"You mean to attack the city?"

"Yes."

The spy shook his hooded head. "She'll escape in the chaos. I'd think you might have learned that lesson recently."

Tieger pointed his clawed, armored finger at the spy's shadowed face. "Concern yourself *only* with finding her."

"I am." He smiled. "I assure you she's become my only focus."

"The attack will proceed after I have spoken with the Harbinger." Tieger turned and watched the spy walk away in the reflection.

When the spy was just before the hatch, he turned. "Oh. I wanted to tell you something. You shouldn't trust Captain Gault. I've seen him speaking with the Harbinger in secret. I don't think you would care for what was said between them." He walked out without waiting for a response.

Tieger wanted to go after him, but the cathedral's recessed communications ring abruptly hummed with energy. He quickly turned and knelt.

The Harbinger's form appeared before him, oversized and looming. His expression was tense, and there was harsh disappointment in his voice. "*Tieger.*"

"Harbinger."

The Harbinger sighed. "Tieger, I have heard troubling news."

Tieger remained silent. It would be best to discover what the Harbinger knew before he spoke.

"Patience was never your greatest virtue, but I believed that through discipline, you might learn to restrain yourself. Now, I find you have spoiled my plans over a single arcanist."

"The witch—"

"She is nothing! You have yet to find the Runians or the parent crystal, and with the destruction of the Alidian ship, we have lost the shard."

Tieger looked up. "Your plan remains viable. The Alidians will search for their lost ship, and the shard—"

"The Alidians will never send another ship. Use your mind, Tieger. Or have you lost it?"

Lost my mind? You would shrink away in terror if you knew my mind.

"I only follow the mandates of our faith. Is that not our main directive from Lord Elcos—to find and destroy the witches?"

The Harbinger swelled. "How dare you remind me of the will of Elcos? I am his Harbinger!" He pointed down to Tieger, disgusted. "Your obsession has blinded you."

Obsession? It is my only purpose in life.

Tieger stood. "I have her now. With a little more time, I—"

The Harbinger waved his hand. "I will hear no more of it, Tieger. You will return your efforts to the Runians. Once they are found, you will take the crystal and kill them all."

No! I will not let her go! Yet he must believe that I will play by his rules as long as it takes.

Tieger bowed his head. "Yes, Harbinger. Your will is the will of Elcos."

The Harbinger sighed. "Tieger, you have never failed me before, yet now I find myself in doubt of your motives." He pulled an object out from his sleeve, black with a glowing violet strip encircling it near one end. "I truly wish this was not needed." He raised the rod.

Tieger suddenly had the wind knocked out of him. He fell to his knees. "No . . . do not . . . "

"It is already done. If your efforts prove fruitful, I will return the Vox Dei."

Tieger rose, gasping for air. He stumbled to the side and fell again, catching himself before he went to the floor.

"You . . . cannot. Give . . . " He stared down at his gauntlets, vision distorted and swimming. His ears pounded.

He rose to his knees and held his hand out. *Janus* did not answer the call. The air beside him remained intact, mocking him with its faithless integrity.

I am empty! He has taken the Flame!

"I have instructed Gault to take you back into the Frontier, where you will await new orders." The Harbinger put his hands together. "And Tieger. Do not fail me again." The circle was drained of power, and the Harbinger's image faded.

Tieger stood with effort and stumbled to the throne. He beat the top with his armored fist until the marble cracked and chipped.

He thinks I am cowed. That I am some broken thing. For certain, he has reduced me, but whatever I have become now, I am a warrior first. I have only ever needed my hands to kill.

Tieger moved around the throne and sat. There was one place he could always go when he needed to center himself—a place more genuine than the *Forge's* cathedral, a place where his true self could always be found.

The past.

The blasted wastes of Westmarch, unforgiving and unkind, rolled away behind Tieger as his transport sped through the plains.

Past dying trees with rings layered in radioisotopes and beyond depressions where water once flowed, stood a tower higher than any mountain on the flattened world.

The transport skidded to a stop, and Tieger rushed out with the other boys. Death was in the tower, but life waited if he could survive the climb.

An end to endless warfare, a T-Gate for the taking, a sector within reach—the defense grid held the key.

What was one more bullet-riddled corpse? What was one more festering wound? What was one more fight to the death, steel on bone, struggling in the dirt?

They said he could have it all if he won. He might even see his sister again. So he killed in order to see her face.

He would not be his father, dead on some no-name battlefield. He would not leave Ketta alone, hungry, frightened.

He would not let her die.

Tieger pounded his fist on the throne's arm, losing his focus on the exercise. He stood and shook his head then activated his communications software. "Commander Prime."

There was little delay before her sharp response. "Honored One."

"Report to the cathedral. Alone."

"Yes, Honored One."

He cut the channel and looked out into the Never, resuming his mental efforts.

The human brain—the essence of a man, his memories, his destiny—it lost something when scattered beyond the skull. A man's blood—it took all of his being as it soaked into the soil.

And what of victory? A victory for whom? At the end of the day, the defense grid belonged to another man. He had won, but nothing true could ever belong to a soldier.

A soldier owned spoils. Anti-rad chems, untainted food, and ... women.

The women were afraid that night, and rightly so. His fellow soldiers were not kind. But there was one who was unafraid.

She met his eyes. Slave. Sister.

More blood was shed. Brother and comrade fell. When it was over, only he and his sister survived, but not for long.

Ketta lay in the loss of her own being, whispering one final word in answer to his question.

Mother.

He went home. It was empty, except for the one who had emptied it. She pleaded, tears forced from her eyes by an iron grip. But she did not deserve the release of oblivion.

He left her there, alive yet dead, just as he was from that day forward.

For long years without end he wandered, searching, until the day they came to Westmarch—men of violet flame. They lifted up the burdened and the abandoned, the defeated and the weary.

Through personal trial, rage became passion, and a heart was made pure. And through the eyes of the Harbinger, Elcos took notice. A mighty gift was given, a gift to make a hammer out of a man.

To make a warrior out of a soldier.

"Honored One."

Tieger turned to see Commander Prime standing at attention. She held herself with pride, eager to learn his will.

Her violet medium-grade powered armor was similar to that of the rank and file ember, except she had a shield over her left arm and a sheathed broadsword at her left hip. The white-trimmed violet shield was wide enough to cover her torso, nearly flat at the top, tapering elegantly to a point near the opposite end. The white cape over her shoulders held the Flame of Elcos, and a short white crest of animal hair topped her helmet.

"Commander, it has come to my attention that complete loyalty on the *Forge* is a thing of the past."

She knelt. "Point me where you would strike, Honored One. I am your weapon."

"Today you will be my *shield*, Commander. A time is approaching when I need to know whom I can trust. You will gather those loyal to me, discreetly, and prepare to retake the *Forge*."

"As . . . as you wish, Honored One."

"Now rise, and go."

She stood and departed, cape trailing behind her as she moved with a practiced grace not common among embers.

Tieger turned back to the Never and the volcano, Cor Vod.

Beware, Harbinger. A warrior is coming.

Tieger left the cathedral, barely allowing the hatch to open before he stormed through. He walked to the nearest lift and entered, heading for the bridge. When he arrived, Gault was nowhere to be found.

An officer turned to Tieger and bowed his head. "Honored One, how may we serve?"

Tieger paused, reining in his anger before he spoke. "Where is Gault?"

"He is off duty, Honored One. I do not know his location."

Tieger turned without a word and left the bridge. He walked to the lift, setting the destination for the other side of the deck. Gault would most likely be in his quarters.

After the lift stopped, Tieger walked out. His fury was becoming difficult to control. If Gault had betrayed him to the Harbinger, he wouldn't be able to keep himself from killing the man.

No doubt he will snivel and beg.

Tieger moved around the last turn, only to find two embers waiting before the captain's quarters. They spread out and stood ready.

He stopped and looked them over. "Why are you here? I did not command such a thing."

An officer stepped forward from behind them. "You do not give the commands on this ship any longer."

Tieger stared at the fool. "Tell me then, dead man, who does?"

"Captain Gau—"

Tieger lifted him by his neck.

The embers nervously aimed their weapons at Tieger but held their fire. The officer kicked and jerked, trying to free himself, but to no avail.

Tieger looked from the officer's reddening face to the embers. "I see two more dead men."

Before the embers could fire, a voice rose from behind them—the voice of Captain Gault as he exited his quarters. "Honored One. The Harbinger has—"

"The Harbinger has done what, Gault? Told you to replace me?"

"No. He said that . . . he said that I was to contain you if you lost control."

"He wants you dead if he gave you such a command."

Gault drew his pistol, hands shaking. "I must follow his commands, even the impossible ones. Like you, I am his tool to be used as he wishes."

"He does not take care of his tools to throw them away so carelessly." Tieger's grip tightened.

The captain's eyes filled with panic. "Tieger, the officer, please release him."

Tieger looked back to the swelling face of the officer. "This one was dead the moment he questioned my authority." With the satisfying crunch of trachea, the officer's neck was ruined. Tieger dropped him to the deck with a dull thud.

A squad of embers mobilized behind Tieger, surrounding him. He turned his head slightly to see them. "It would seem that you foresaw my coming."

The captain looked back and forth between the groups. "I did not order this! All of you, stand down!"

Tieger laughed deeply. "There has been enough talk."

Behind him, there were shouts and the shuffling of feet. Cries of pain called out as Commander Prime's sharp blade found flesh.

"I have made plans as well." Tieger walked forward. The two embers backed up to the wall and dropped their rifles, bowing their heads, but they had chosen their fates. They fell to the deck, shot dead with two quick bursts of fire from behind Tieger.

When Tieger reached the captain, he knocked the pistol from his hands and took him by the neck, pinning him to the wall.

Tieger roared at Gault through his helmet. "Contain *me*? I cannot be contained, little man!"

"Tieger . . . I don't—"

Tieger thrust his clawed gauntlet into the soft tissue of Gault's chest wall, pushing deeper through the cartilage and bone and into his thorax. Gault's lungs collapsed before he could make a sound, his screams stolen by the air he so desperately tried to breathe.

"You have doomed your men, Gault." Tieger positioned his helmet as close to Gault's face as possible, staring into his eyes as the man suffocated. "You will not be the last to die by my hands this day."

MASTERS OF LIGHT AND DARK

Mei canted the *Rìluò* on its side, circling as she approached the hidden city of Cisterne.

Sidna watched as the island drew nearer. Many nights she'd dreamt of the square-roofed, multicolored buildings and the tall, far-reaching manors that rose above them. The city and its people had gotten into her blood long ago, the only place she could really be herself.

"Shipyards?" Fall leaned forward. "Those are the boats we saw moving across the lake."

Sidna leaned over a little more too. "Yeah. They run goods into the caverns."

An enormous cargo ship sat up out of the lake, with a gaping, jagged wound in its side. Workers lined the edges, welding the injured hull with bright, short-lived sparks.

Fall saw it too. "That one took a big hit."

Sidna nodded. "These caverns stretch on for hundreds of kilometers. It's a dangerous route to the outlying posts."

"Can't they map out the hazards?"

"Sure, but there's more than rocks in the water. I wouldn't go for a swim if I were you."

Fall's eyebrows rose. "I'll take your word on it."

Sidna looked out over the city.

The Entertainment District, the real heart of Cisterne, spread out beyond the shore. It was mostly full of taverns and restaurants, but whorehouses, gambling dens, narcotic lounges, and other vices were ever-present. She stuck to the taverns when she visited; the drinks were good, and her contacts in the city could usually be found there.

Rising above the lower parts of the city was the Residential District, where row after row of mostly identical buildings were loaded with cramped apartments. The city had a few thousand residents, most of whom were impoverished workers or indentured servants of some kind.

Higher on the island, the upper class lived in modern buildings, complete with all the comforts money could buy. Terraces with glowing gardens and pools of water lined the mansions above, reflecting the carefree lives of those fortunate enough to own them.

The plants of the gardens were nocturnal, genetically engineered to grow in the night, and for purely aesthetic reasons, they had bioluminescent bulbs that thrived in the darkness. Like everything else in Cisterne, they were there because they could survive.

As the Rìluò came around the backside of the island, Sidna saw the Wharf District projecting out into the lake. Dozens of marinas were comprised of moorings, some designed to hold sea vessels and some for space vessels, a necessity on the crowded island.

She watched as the Rìluò approached an available pad. Mei maneuvered the ship into position, bringing her down easily. The Rìluò settled, and the engines began to shut down. There was a persistent swaying due to the water.

Fall turned in his seat. "Smooth landing. What now?"

Sidna stood up and stretched. "Think I'll have a drink."

"Great. After the past few days, I could use one too."

"Oh, actually, I'm meeting up with someone. An old friend."

Fall smiled, cheeks reddening. "Sorry, yeah, of course. I probably shouldn't waste any time finding a contract anyway."

"Good idea." She started to edge toward the exit.

"Any advice on where I should start?" Fall asked as he stood to follow her.

She shrugged, impatient to move on. "No clue. Ask around, I guess."

"Damn." He seemed disappointed. "Mei said you might know someone."

Sidna looked to Mei. "Someone who could do what exactly?"

Mei glanced back as she completed the shutdown sequence. "I merely told him that you might help him find a client."

Sidna frowned. "Well, you told him wrong. If I'm seen walking around Cisterne with a Ranger, I'll end up with a knife in my back."

"What?" Fall asked. "Why?"

Sidna looked down and shook her head. "Because a lot of the people here are criminals. Or at least they would be. There's no law here, and that's way they like it."

"I'm not a policeman," Fall said.

"It doesn't matter. You represent order. That's how they see it."

Fall shot a sideways look at Mei. "Come on, it can't be *that* bad."

Sidna closed her eyes. "Look, I can't afford to lose anyone's trust here. I can't help you."

Fall sighed. "Fine. Could you at least point me in the right direction?"

Sidna pointed outside. "Yeah. It's that way."

He rolled his eyes. "Thanks for the insight. Hope that didn't cost you any credibility."

She scoffed. "Look. You got us into this mess. Help yourself out of it."

He pointed up to his face, eyes widening. "*I* got us into this?"

She put her hands on her hips. "If we hadn't been taking you to Crossroads, we wouldn't have been anywhere near those Alidians."

Fall threw his hands up. "Alidians? Are you kidding me? What about the Elcosians? And that maniac, Tieger?"

She crossed her arms. "Who says they were after me?"

Fall exaggerated a search of the cockpit. "I'm sorry, is there another arcanist around?"

Mei sat back. "Fall, that is not fair. Sidna—"

"He's after *her*, Mei. Not us."

"That may be so, but—"

Sidna silenced her with a raised hand. "You have a problem with arcanists?"

Fall shrugged. "Not particularly."

"So it's just me then."

His expression hardened. "Right now? Yeah."

Sidna smiled tightly. "Nice. Thanks for clearing that up."

Mei reached out for her arm. "Sidna, wait."

"Save it. I'm done here." She left the cockpit and entered the main hold.

She passed Olivia, who had gathered her things into a few organized piles. "Hey. Are we—"

"*We* aren't anything." Sidna walked past her without slowing.

She keyed the controls to open the ventral hatch and to extend the exit ramp. She started walking before the ramp was even halfway to the dock.

Cool, salty air rushed up onto her skin, and she took a deep breath. The smells of wood, oil, and seawater did their best to bring a smile to her face. Cisterne wasn't home, but it was just as good for someone who never stopped looking over her shoulder.

Three shadowed figures approached along the dock, silhouetted by the dim lights of the hanging lanterns running alongside. The dock creaked, and the wood transmitted the sounds of their thudding boots as they moved toward her. Two she didn't recognize but the other she knew instantly.

Lean and tall, he walked ahead with his arms wide. "Sidna! Is that your beautiful face I see?"

"Unfortunately for you, Gabin, it is."

He paused momentarily, frowning for an instant before his smile returned. "Feisty as always, pretty girl, but to you, it's *Gab*." He embraced her gently. His long red coat whipped about in the breeze, and his white cloth undershirt was open near the neck. He smelled faintly of perfume, most likely not his own.

Just the man I needed to see.

She pushed away slightly, pressing her hands against his bared chest. "All right, *Gab*. This pretty girl needs a drink."

He stroked the well-trimmed facial hair of his beard and mustache. "My dear Sidna, I'm sure you'll drink for free wherever you choose." He motioned to the other two men, clothed in more modest work attire. "See to this wonderful ship." He turned to the city, left hand resting on the pommel of the rapier at his waist and placed his right arm across her lower back. "And I'll see to this lovely girl."

"Which will it be?" Gabin gestured widely to the line of dens along the street known as The Starless Way.

"First one with a drink." She began to cross the cobblestone street to the nearest tavern.

He held his arm in front of her. "Why don't we skip the Winking Wench."

She looked at his arm and raised an eyebrow.

He dropped the arm and smiled. "It's not my kind of place."

"You pissed someone off."

He looked away. "I might have."

"Exactly how far do we have to walk to find one where you're welcome?"

"Not too far. The Mule should be fine. I think."

She crossed her arms. "It's been a really long day, Gab."

"Right this way." He turned to walk up the gently inclining street.

They wound through the rows of two-story buildings. Each was different in color, but most were brightly painted to take advantage of the low-light conditions. Gas lampposts lined the street, and swaying lanterns lit the sides of each building.

The doors of each den were wide open, and noisy, as drunken revelers moved from one to another. Small electric bulbs were strung along the buildings, crisscrossing above their heads. The air smelled of pipe smoke, alcohol, and something else Sidna couldn't quite place. The whole district had that scent, not unpleasant, just different from anywhere else.

They weaved through crowds of people, who laughed and drank on the street, and more than once, passed by a small group of entertainers that danced as they played their instruments for coin. They crossed the cobblestones when needed, all the while slowly climbing higher and higher.

Sidna stopped Gabin when they passed a place called Stormbreaker. At a small window to the side of the main entrance, a man sold drinks. For just a few silver coins from Gabin, she received a tall drink called the Iron Anchor. She sucked down half of it before he tried to stop her.

"Easy, girl. You won't last the night."

She pulled back the oversized cylinder of alcohol and held her palm out. "This isn't my first time down The Starless Way, Gab, but it'll be your last if you come between me and my drink."

He stepped back and, smartly so, bought her another. She finished off the first and started on the second as they walked.

Gabin smiled at nearly every woman who walked by and bowed to a few men, who nodded in return. There weren't many in Cisterne who didn't know him.

A few intersections later, he stopped outside a particularly rowdy establishment. Above its door hung a wooden sign, painted with the image of what she assumed was a mule, laughing as its owner pushed it from behind. "I'd wager it's your first time here, worldly though you may be."

"That's a bet you'd finally win, Gab." She walked past him and through the entrance.

The air was smoky, but it didn't sting her eyes and was pleasant to smell. Groups of men and women gathered at round tables built around poles that went from floor to ceiling, laughing and drinking.

A short, greasy man shuffled over and into her path, wiping his hands on a dirty rag. "What's your pleasure?"

Gabin came behind her and placed his hands on her shoulders. "This one's with me, Rath."

The man sneered but stepped aside, walking back to the bar with a disgruntled look.

Sidna walked to the wooden stairs in the corner and went up the creaking steps with Gabin following closely. When they reached the top, there was a room to the right with another full bar.

The bartender, a woman with long, bound, brown hair in a low-cut white blouse, nodded in her direction as she poured a drink.

Sidna walked over and leaned on the bar. "Give me something stout. And tall."

The woman nodded again and pulled a mug down. She filled it with amber beer and set it in front of Sidna. Gabin tossed a few coins onto the bar, and the woman snatched them up, already moving to serve the next customer.

He led Sidna to a table in the corner then sat down, facing the stairs, and Sidna pulled up a chair to sit opposite him. She took a sip of her drink and sighed contently; she was finally beginning to feel the warmth.

Gabin took out his electric pipe and prepared to ignite it when he caught Sidna's eyes and put it away. He smiled knowingly. "Feeling better?"

"Much."

He nodded. "Glad to be of service. Though, it's fortunate for you I was still here to receive you."

"Is that so?"

"Indeed. Not much longer, and I might have lost interest."

She grunted. "You would've waited another month if I'd asked you."

He looked up and smiled, leaning his head from side to side. "Two weeks. Maximum."

She smirked, eyes narrowing over the edge of her glass. "Mmmhmm."

He leaned back, grin widening. "So, tell me all about your adventures. And don't try to tell me you've been lying low. I saw the wounds on that ship." He leaned forward and pointed with a flirtatious smile. "You've been up to no good."

She returned the smile and shrugged. "Same as always."

He sat back and stroked his face in thought. "It's about your magic again, isn't it?"

She rolled her eyes. "It's not *magic*, Gab. The Code is . . . well I've told you before. There are rules. It's not a trick or a prayer or something stupid like that."

"No, of course not. Your fireballs are quite complicated."

She stared flatly. "You're annoying."

"Guilty."

"Ugh, stop smiling like that. Anyway, yes. I'm after something called a tear."

"As in teardrop?"

"Yes. I've never actually seen one, but it's like a small crystal."

He leaned forward, his eyes growing wider. "Ah, so it's valuable then."

Sidna looked around then leaned forward. "Shhh. Only to people like me."

He looked disappointed. "A shame, to be sure. Why do you want it then?"

"They contain information that allows us to use the Code differently."

"But you've never seen one?"

"Right. I can only use the Code in ways that have already been discovered."

"You're losing me, girl."

"Listen, it's easy. Before I had my *viae* tattooed into my skin, my affinities were determined. Fire and Air. My *viae* match my affinities."

"Your tattoos? You said before that they allow you to do your magic."

She nodded. "I provide the energy and the knowledge, but the *viae* make it possible."

"And these tears contain symbols for new *viae*?"

"Sort of. That's a little more complicated."

"But how do you know this tear will have *viae* symbols that fit your affinity?"

"I don't, but it could. If not, it would still be a huge discovery. No one has found a tear in several hundred years."

"I see. So where is it?"

"On a planet."

He smiled wryly. "Not very specific."

"I keep some things to myself."

"Of that, I have no doubt. But I'm curious. What keeps someone else from snatching it up?"

"I'm the only one who can get there."

"The route is hidden? Dangerous?"

"No, you just have to have the key."

"Which you have?"

She raised her glass proudly then took a triumphant sip.

Gabin smiled. "Who did you steal it from?"

She feigned offense. "Why would you assume I *stole* it?"

"I am a pirate, girl. I know these things."

She raised her eyebrows. "Good point." She leaned in again. "It doesn't matter."

"It matters to the owner."

"Too bad. They should have protected it better."

Gabin sat back and smiled. "My philosophy exactly." He tapped the backs of his fingers on the wall behind him. "If you have the key, why haven't you gone after this tear of yours?"

"Well, that's the problem." She took a long drink. "I went there once, not long ago, but . . ."

"What?"

"Nothing. I'm going back though."

"When?"

"When it's safe."

"Hmmm. It seems you've stirred up more than your fair share of trouble this time. Perhaps your old friend Gabin could be of service."

"Well, right now—"

The bartender walked over and sat two frothy mugs in front of Gabin. He nodded and tossed her another coin then smiled suggestively as she walked away. She bit her lower lip and somehow managed to blush.

Sidna crossed her arms.

Gabin shrugged. "What?"

"You're hopeless."

"Again, guilty. You were saying?"

"Ugh." She swirled her mug and took a sip. "Right now, it's the freeloaders holed up in my ship."

"*Your* ship?"

She glared over her mug. "That's right."

He leaned back and took a drink of his beer. "Ah, so you want them to leave?"

"Yes. Especially this stuck-up Ranger. He's such a—"

"Ranger!" Gabin caught himself and leaned in close, speaking much more softly. "You brought a Ranger here?"

She tilted her head, eyebrows raised. "Is there a bounty on you, Gab?"

"Probably. A big one, no doubt."

"Don't worry. They don't even know you exist."

"A hurtful thing to say. Surely . . . wait. Did you say *they*?"

She wiped her mouth as she looked up. "Mmm? Did I?"

"You did." He sat back and smiled. "Sidna, Sidna. Always the troublemaker."

She set her empty mug on the wooden table and crossed her arms again. "It's never bothered you before."

"Of course not. It's the main reason I enjoy your company. That and—" Gabin froze and looked past Sidna. His hand slid under the table, and his eyes narrowed.

Something hard pressed against Sidna's head.

A woman's voice came from behind. "That'll be enough, pirate. Put it on the table."

Sidna stayed very still, unsure of who was behind her but certain there was a gun. "Gab, whatever trouble you're in, I'd like to avoid it."

The woman behind her spoke again. "It's *your* trouble this time—Sidna."

Sidna tried to turn, but the gun barrel pressed even harder.

"The Maiden would like a word. You and your friend are invited to her manor."

Gabin slowly raised his hand back above the table. "Why not simply say so? Of course we'd be happy to drop by. Perhaps later this evening."

"*Now.* Get up."

Sidna edged out of her seat and stood slowly. The gun moved to her lower back with a forceful jab. "Ow, dammit!"

"Just a reminder. Now turn and walk." The woman took Sidna's pistol from her holster. "And be calm. No one in this shit town would dare cross the Maiden for you."

Sidna turned, and the woman moved with her, staying out of sight.

She walked to the stairs and started down. When she reached the bottom, the man from before, Rath, was standing to the side, cleaning a mug. He smiled, satisfied.

Sidna shot him her meanest look and continued out of the bar. Once outside, she followed the woman's directions. Two streets over, they finally reached a parked transport.

A door on the side opened, rotating upward above the small vehicle. The woman behind her pushed with the gun. "Get in."

Sidna thought about escaping, but she had nowhere to go, and she'd be dead before she could fill her *viae*. She got in and moved to the far side. The woman with the gun got in as well and sat across from her, adjusting her knee-length black coat.

The pistol she carried was compact but lethal nonetheless, and the woman could have been described the same way. She was short and thin with long black hair pulled over her shoulder, frigid blue eyes, and firm, thin lips.

Gabin was shoved in beside her, and another man sat down across from him. He was large, with a bald head, and even though it was nighttime, he wore dark glasses that obscured his eyes. He seemed to be seeing just fine, though; his large, long-barreled pistol was pointed directly at Gabin's crotch.

The door rotated down and closed, and the transport lifted away.

Sidna opened her mouth to speak, but the woman shook her head.

"Save it for the Maiden."

The transport touched down, and the side door swung upward. After the engines went quiet, the woman stepped out and pulled Sidna's arm, less than gentle with her grip, causing her to stumble out of the car.

All right. I'll remember that.

A breeze blew her hair away from her scowling face, and she looked out into the night. They were near the highest point on the island, looming over the streets and buildings below. She could see the docks and the Rìluò, a small orange spot underneath a pale distant light.

Too far away.

An artificial waterfall to her side produced soft white noise, and the plants in the garden behind it rustled in the cool sea air, bioluminescent flowers lighting the water bright blue and green through the foaming cascade. The wind stirred again, and the ever-present city smell was gone, replaced by that of wet rock, just like in a cave.

You are in a cave. Now focus.

She turned to follow the woman, who motioned with her gun. Gabin and the large man followed, scuffing the stone with their boots. Tall wooden doors were set into the old rocky walls, and as they approached, those doors opened with deep, resonating groans.

Inside, an expansive, darkened hall led deeper into the manor. Low-burning torches lined the walls, casting light up onto the landscape paintings above them. Red carpet ran down the center of the hall with bare, worked stone on each side.

They continued until they came to a set of lifts, anachronistic in their modernity. The woman moved to a lift and waved a card in front of a reader. She placed her palm on the panel, and the lift doors opened.

They all stepped inside, and Sidna and Gabin moved to the rear. The man and woman said nothing, but kept the guns pointed at their prisoners. The lift sped upward, and after a few silent, tense moments, the doors opened.

Sidna and Gabin walked forward past their captors, stepping into a large, open foyer. Its appearance differed from what she had seen so far, with reflective marble floors and polished white stone columns. Tapestries depicting shadowy figures lined each square column, lit by the smoldering fires of coal braziers. Beyond the columns, to the sides, the room continued for a meter or so before disappearing into darkness. Ahead, down the long red carpet, another set of large wooden doors stood open.

Sidna and Gabin walked on, prodded from behind. They went through the open doorway and into the next room.

The room was like the last, except for a raised black stone platform with bright white flecks that sparkled as Sidna came closer. A white shining chair sat on top of the platform, in the shape of a half moon, with a black seat built into the cradle.

Beyond the extravagant seat, a dimly lit balcony wrapped around the rear wall. There was a brief flash from it, almost like reflected light or the sharp glint of metal. Sidna tried to focus on it, but it never returned.

A shadowed form rose from the floor in front of the platform, standing on four legs. It was muscular and thick, with a wide neck and bulky head. Its fur bristled and stood like spiked razors, and a rumbling growl vibrated in its chest. Slit-like red eyes moved from her to Gabin, and yellow fangs appeared from beneath curling black lips.

"Ghidro, sit," a woman's voice projected from the chair.

Sidna looked up from the monster to the voice, yet she still saw no one sitting there.

As if from nowhere, the woman stood from the dark, gliding forward. The beast sat with a heavy thud and laid its head down with a whimper.

The woman wore a long black coat with a tight black corset trimmed in silver that flared out around her form-fitting black pants and knee-high boots. Her silver blouse had a high collar, open in the front, revealing her ivory skin. Her hair was long and red, flowing in waves over her shoulders. Intricate silver patterns, like flowering vines, ran the length of the coat from top to bottom.

She stood there for a moment, studying Sidna, then spoke. "Do you know who I am?"

Sidna looked to Gabin, who had his eyes locked on the woman, legitimately in awe. She looked back ahead. "The Maiden," she said impetuously.

"Yes. And you are Sidna Orin." She smiled and narrowed her eyes. "You have something of mine."

"What are you talking about?"

"In the coat. Inner pocket. Right side."

The woman behind Sidna stepped to her right and held out her hand, pistol in the other. "Let's have it."

Sidna stood there, staring past the Maiden. Everything she'd worked for was about to be taken away; she couldn't let that happen.

She stepped forward and looked up into the Maiden's eyes. "No."

The beast at the Maiden's feet stood and began to growl, folding its ears, but Sidna didn't back down. "I'm not about to hand it over to you. Not to anyone. It's *mine*."

The Maiden stroked the creature's head and stepped to the edge of the platform, directly above Sidna. "Are you sure you want Veridian that badly? Do you even know what awaits? You might not rush there so quickly if you did."

Sidna raised her chin defiantly. "I've seen the dead halls of Fel Kno'a. I've faced the evil master inside."

The Maiden leaned forward, arms behind her back. "No, you

haven't." She walked back to the creature and picked up a thick, sturdy chain. "I assume you refer to the Guardian of Fel Kno'a? It's no more the *master* of that place than Ghidro is here."

"How would you know?" Sidna asked.

"I know because I've studied it my entire life. I too seek the tear."

Sidna hid her surprise. "Okay, if you know so much, who *is* the real master of Fel Kno'a?"

The Maiden tugged at Ghidro's chain, pulling against its fixed end. "Someone who very much *wants* to be chained. Or rather, wishes to be anchored." She gestured to the woman behind Sidna. "Seph, I'll take my glyph now."

The woman reached for Sidna's pocket, and when Sidna tried to push her hand away, she caught Sidna's wrist and twisted. The pain took her breath away and dropped her to her knees. The woman holstered her compact pistol and reached inside Sidna's jacket, taking the glyph. She let go and walked to the platform.

Sidna rubbed her wrist, tears welling in her eyes. "No! It's—"

"It never was *yours*, Sidna." The Maiden walked back to the moon throne and sat down into the darkness surrounding the seat, disappearing once again. "You should have known you wouldn't be the only one to seek it. More than that, you were incredibly stupid to bring it to a city of thieves."

Sidna's *viae* began to glow fiery red-orange under her coat sleeves.

Gabin stepped toward her. "Sidna, no! That's the worst thing you could do right now."

She stood up and raised her arms. "I'll burn this place down to the water before I let her have it!"

The Maiden laughed.

Sidna cocked her head. "What's so funny?"

The Maiden raised her arm as well. The area around her seemed to dim, and Sidna's vision failed. She couldn't see anything, not even a hint of light.

She reached out for Gabin's arm. "I can't see! Gabin!"

"Relax, girl! You're fine." His voice did nothing to calm her.

She heard the Maiden laughing again in the darkness. "There is one more thing you should have known, Sidna. You should have known there's only one reason I would want the tear."

She's an arcanist!

"Seph, please escort her to a cell."

Sidna heard two footsteps approach then felt a sharp pain in her head as she was knocked to the floor. The last thing she heard before losing consciousness was Gabin, yelling something about a girl.

OF RUST AND RUIN

THICK MUD, RED WITH CLAY, SUCKED AT Ban's armored legs as he walked. He trudged through miserably, vaguely aware of the ugly chorus behind him.

Crude air rushed in, filling holes as boots came free from the mud, men complaining and groaning, sick of the swamp that tried its best to swallow them whole.

The squad continued until a mound began to rise out of the filth. Hanging branches with drooping leaves parted as they climbed the sloping hill.

"This way," a voice commanded.

Ban's men looked to him for confirmation. He waved them on as he followed the lieutenant's command.

Near the top of the mound, they looked out, seeing a haze of white rising above the mire. In the distance, a settlement sat defiantly, alive in spite of the hostile world.

Ban watched a drop of cloudy green slide down his faceplate as the acrid fumes of the bog world Fugelaese condensed on the cold material. One touch meant horrible pain. One inhalation would mean an agonizing death.

Back down into the muck they went, closing in on the settlement. It was a refinery in some ways, the products of which were weapons of war, illegal in the Fathom, designed to kill in terrible ways. Ban and the others were tasked to put an end to it.

But where were the condensers? Where were the munitions labs? Where was the defensive perimeter? Where was the orbital launch platform?

The facility looked quite different than it had in the briefing.

The lieutenant raised his arm. "Target the filter stacks."

Ban knew it was wrong. He asked the lieutenant if they shouldn't withdraw. Shouldn't they ask for clarification? Something wasn't right.

"Do as you're told, peasant."

Ban lowered his rifle. So did the men behind him.

"You stupid grunts. I didn't track through two kilometers of shit so you could suddenly develop brains. If any man doesn't fire in the next ten seconds, I'll be sure to ruin him for life. Believe it."

The men exchanged silent glances, faces obscured. They all looked to Ban.

"Morgan. What about your dream? You'd sacrifice it for a few terrorists in a Void-kissed slime hole?"

He was right.

So Ban did his duty. He and the men fired, and oxygen flared red then green in the thick fumes of Fugelaese.

Ban opened his eyes, awoken by sudden pain in his chest and shoulders. He winced at the blaring sounds of the lifeboat's collision alarm.

What?

He looked around. Weapons and armor, previously stacked, lay scattered against the forward wall. Orange lights flared and faded. Outside the viewport, the stars were fixed in place.

He turned to look at the others.

Tyr blinked hard and shook his head.

Becks was out of sight. "What did we hit?" she asked.

Ban flipped the panel open on his seat's armrest. He deactivated the collision alarm then scrolled through status readouts for each of the lifeboat's systems. "I can't tell. There's minor damage, but it's structural."

Becks unbuckled her straps. "It looks like we're sitting still."

"We are."

Ban unfastened his harness and stood carefully. The lifeboat shifted, and he sensed acceleration.

He searched for his helmet, put it on, then synchronized it with the craft's control software. When he looked through the external camera, he saw a thick cable. As he followed it, it led into a rapidly approaching ship's bay. The ship was black, almost invisible in space.

Becks walked to his side. "What do you see?"

"A ship."

"A rescue?"

"I don't know yet."

As they passed by the bay's outer edge, they entered an expansive hold. A bulky mechanical boom captured the lifeboat with its claws and brought it up to a platform then locked it into place.

The camera feed's quality degraded, but right before it went out completely, Ban saw armored men running toward the platform.

He ripped the helmet off. "Boarders!"

Tyr unbuckled his harness then ran to get his pistol. Becks did the same, and they moved to the front row to take cover behind an empty seat. Ban knelt behind his own seat, bracing his light machine gun on top of the armrest.

Several muffled sounds echoed through the lifeboat, metal parts interlocking and clamping down. A high-pitched whine cut through the craft's speakers then settled into static.

An authoritative male voice spoke through the noise. "Disarm and move to the rear of the pod. Comply, and you will not be harmed."

Ban recognized the accent. "Runians."

"This will be your final warning. You will be treated fairly under the articles of the Accord, but only if you surrender peacefully."

Ban looked down the barrel of his light machine gun. He imagined what the fight would be like, close-quartered and ugly—a massacre.

Tyr and Becks looked to him for reassurance.

Not this time.

"Do as he says."

Becks seemed to want to protest but quickly realized the impossibility of the situation. She backed up and raised her hands in disgust. Ban and Tyr joined her.

After a few seconds, sounds of grating metal came from the other side of the hatch. The doors opened swiftly, and two Runian marines rushed inside.

Drakes.

They stood firm like desert-weathered statues in medium-grade powered armor, green with gold accents, and dark-brown sub-armor suits. Their helmets were rounded, having segmented faceplates of something hard and shining like golden metal or thick glass. Angled armor covered their jaws and chins, curving up to form rounded crests over the ears.

Loose sub-armor cloth bunched up around the necks and between armored plates, reminding Ban of something a lone wanderer would wear. Shoulder guards crested just above the arms, rounded slightly at the tops. The chest and abdomen armor contoured with the upper body, leaving space underneath the arms. The thigh and lower leg protections matched those of the upper body, leading down to dark, scaled, heavy boots fastened with straps that flared out to the sides.

Dark-green capes flowed over their shoulders down to the middle of their calves. Rough leather pouches lined their belts. Painted green-and-gold Runian Dragons perched imperiously on each shoulder. Each soldier had a combat knife mounted over the left chest, angled downward, and carried a bullpup-style assault rifle.

The two drakes focused those rifles on Ban and Tyr, electric-green targeting lasers piercing the lifeboat's dim interior.

The soldiers moved apart slowly as another man entered between them. He was an officer from the look of his tented cap, also adorned with the dragon insignia.

His uniform was lightly armored across the chest, shoulders, elbows, knees and boots. The rest was crafted of green cloth with gold trim. He had thick brown gloves and boots, coming halfway up his forearm and just below his knees, respectively. There was a long pistol on his left hip and two bullet clips on the right side of his dark-brown belt. His shoulders and collar held rank insignia.

A major.

Glowing green light shone from under the cap, and when he lifted his head, Ban saw the source—the semitransparent screen of a head-mounted device. He was a young man, perhaps in his early thirties, with a faint scar running down his right cheek. His eyes were hard to see, but his jaw was firmly set.

He walked forward, left hand on his pistol's grip. "Alidians. I would chastise you for your illegal presence, but well . . . I'd have to take some of that reprimand myself." He turned slightly to look behind him. "Enter."

Two medics in white suits entered the lifeboat and stopped just behind him.

The officer stepped forward again and held his open hand out to the side. "Would you mind if they have a look? There's a large debris field not that far from here, and the signs of a battle are evident."

Ban coughed and cleared his dry throat. "Our ship was destroyed."

"Your ship?"

"Yes. Destroyed by Elcosian forces. But you already know that."

"How would *I* know that?"

"Your spies should have checked in by now."

The officer's hard expression went unchanged. "I assure you, sir, I know nothing about any spies."

"So, you just happened to find our lifeboat?"

"I'm afraid that's something I'm not allowed to discuss with you."

Ban straightened up. "Discuss your secret base, you mean."

The officer was stunned momentarily, but only barely so. "I see. This is unfortunate." He tapped his foot and rubbed his chin. "Listen, soldier to soldier, I wish I'd never found you. I don't want to detain you, yet I clearly can't let you go."

Ban nodded. "Honestly, I only care for the safety of these two. If you give me your word that no harm will come to them, I swear there'll be no trouble from me or from them."

The officer lifted his hand from his pistol and smiled slightly. "You have my word."

Ban moved aside and let the medics through. They went to Becks, placed a blanket over her shoulders, and tried to have her sit. Tyr waved a medic away when she came near. Ban did the same.

The officer walked to Ban. "I want you all to come with me for a little while. I apologize, but I must turn you over to one of my superiors. No doubt you'll be transported back to the Fathom and released upon contact with the proper Alidian authorities." He did his best to smile reassuringly. "I'm sure you understand our activities here will need to remain secret for now."

"As I said, take care of these two, and we'll do whatever you ask."

"Thank you . . . um . . . ?"

"Ban Morgan. Bond-Sergeant Ban Morgan, formerly of the *ARN Talon*, Alidian Royal Navy Marines."

"I see, Sergeant. My name is Major Stephen Garland. I'd heard about the honor of the Alidian soldier, but now I see it firsthand. I promise you you'll be treated with the utmost respect." He removed his cap, revealing short, shaved hair. The scar on his face continued up into the hairline. "And might I ask why you and your ship were out in the Frontier? I'd understand if you couldn't say."

Ban laughed bitterly. "We were searching for you. You and your base."

Garland was visibly taken aback. "Well, Sergeant, I can honestly say I'm glad your *Talon* didn't find me first." He turned and motioned to the exit. "If you'd allow my drakes here to escort you, we'll welcome you aboard. You'll be confined to quarters, and I'll also need to confiscate your equipment for the time being."

Ban nodded once. "If you have to."

Garland nodded. "I'm afraid I do."

The Alidian marines followed Garland out of the lifeboat and onto the ship, escorted closely by the Runian drakes.

The bay outside the lifeboat was impressive, with multiple shuttles and heavy mechanical arms for lifting equipment. A few meters away, a group of men in hazardous materials gear was carefully working on a pile of what appeared to be debris.

The corridors leading away from the bay were narrow, hexagonal in cross section. Soft green lamps were interspersed along the path at shoulder level, which left the path darkened, yet adequately illuminated.

They were taken to crew quarters as promised. The drakes ushered them inside, and the hatch doors closed behind them unceremoniously.

Becks sat on the bed, sinking into it slightly.

Ban sat on the foot of the same bed. "Another failure."

Becks stretched out. "There was nothing else we could have done."

"Not you. But I could have," he said as he rubbed his temples.

"At least we're alive."

Ban lay down and closed his eyes without responding.

Becks moved over. "Are you taking a nap? Don't tell me you plan on keeping your word."

He opened his eyes. "Why not? Say we take the ship. What then? Fly it back to Alidia and hope they forgive me for losing the *Talon*?"

"That wasn't your fault."

He turned his head. "Wasn't it?"

Her eyes shot to Tyr then back, and she said no more.

Tyr lay down on the opposite bed, rolled away, and exhaled forcefully.

Ban watched the ceiling for a few moments then closed his eyes again.

No. For me, the dream is over.

"Ban. Ban, wake up."

He opened his eyes.

Becks's hand gripped his arm tightly. "It's Tyr."

Ban sat up and rubbed his face. The quarters were lit by a small lamp built into the wall next to the bed. The bed across from his was empty, sheets folded, fit for Alidian regulations.

He got out of bed and stretched. "Where did he go?"

"I don't know. I woke up just now, and he was gone."

Ban got dressed and walked to the sink. He used the small amount of water available to wash his eyes and splash his cheeks. He felt like he hadn't slept at all.

Once he was a little more awake, he went to the hatch. He pressed a button on the nearby panel, and one of the drakes outside answered.

"What?"

Ban cleared his throat. "I want to know where my man went. He's not inside the room."

"He was summoned by Major Garland. He should be back soon."

Ban leaned on the wall and rubbed his eyes. "I would prefer to see where he's been taken."

There were a few minutes of silence. Ban was beginning to become agitated when the drake finally returned.

"Sergeant Morgan, Major Garland will see you now."

The hatch opened, and one of the drakes stepped inside. "Please come with me." He motioned to Becks. "The corporal must stay behind."

Ban stopped. "No, she comes with me. We don't split up."

"Those are Major Garland's orders." The drake gripped his rifle tightly.

Becks smiled weakly. "Ban, it's okay."

"No, Becks, it isn't."

"Right now, it has to be."

Ban sighed and looked up into the surface of the drake's helmet. "Okay. I don't like it, but fine. I said I'd cooperate."

The drake stepped aside. "After you."

Ban walked into the corridor. The drake came out of the quarters and pushed a button on the door panel, closing the hatch.

He walked past Ban. "This way."

Ban looked back at the hatch then followed the drake through the corridors leading to Garland. They passed a viewport on the way, and the Rift was visible outside.

A mobile base. No wonder we couldn't find it.

They walked a little further, approaching a set of large doors marked *Lab Alpha.*

The drake used a nearby panel to call for access. After a few moments, locking mechanisms disengaged, and the doors began to retract. Air rushed out onto Ban's shirt and skin; the room was positively pressurized.

The drake stepped inside, and Ban followed. After they were through, the doors closed and sealed behind them. He could feel the pressure normalize shortly thereafter.

The lab had three levels, each comprised of assembled scaffolding. In the center of the lab, extending up to the ceiling, was a large bluish-black crystal with unidentifiable objects buried underneath its surface. Equipment was arranged around it, and men in lab gear moved about, busy at work.

The drake led Ban up the steps to the second level. Garland was seated at a nearby table, reading a report.

"Ah, Sergeant Morgan, I was just about to call for you." He motioned for Ban to sit.

Ban sat slowly, noticing the drake remained close by. "Major Garland, I came about my man, Lance Corporal Tyr."

"Yes, that was explained to me. First, I'd like to show you Artifact 110." He motioned to the black crystal.

Ban leaned forward. "If I could just—"

Garland continued. "It's something we found in an asteroid field just over half a year ago. At first, it had us quite baffled. Why would a crystal, so regular in shape, be in a place like that? Why would it also contain technology so advanced that its purpose was unknown? And lastly, why were we able to interface with it so easily?"

Ban's impatience must have been obvious. Garland continued, smiling. "What we found, and this is really interesting, is that the devices inside have software very much like our own. The base programming language is different of course, but the logic is similar and relatively simple to extrapolate, though the crystal's devices are likely thousands of years old. Do you know what this means?"

Ban leaned forward. "That our technology is based upon this technology or that we have a common technological ancestor."

Garland's expression shifted to one of surprise then of disappointment. "Well, yes. That's probably what it means."

Ban placed his hands on the edge of the table. "Now, are you going to tell me about Tyr?"

Garland stood. "Come this way."

Ban did and looked back at the drake who continued to follow in silence. Garland circled the crystal, stopping just before a row of four black, roughly egg-shaped objects.

Garland motioned to the objects. "Pseudari. We've found that the best way to communicate with the device was not through traditional human interface devices, but through artificial reality."

He walked to the nearest pseudarus and placed his hand on it. "There's a whole world inside the crystal. We sent men and women inside, through their minds, but all of them died."

Ban tensed, and Garland reacted. His hand went to the pistol at his left side. The drake behind Ban raised his rifle, taking a step back.

Ban turned back to Garland. "What is this?"

Garland pressed a few keys on the pseudarus's surface. The pod split down its seams and opened. Fog rolled out across the scaffolding, and Ban saw a man inside. It was Tyr, wearing a headset with multiple wires running into the walls of the pseudarus. He wore a black full-body suit, and a tube ran from his nose to a syringe lying on his belly. His breathing was slow and regular.

"Get him out of there now!"

"No, Sergeant. He will die if I do. In fact, no one has ever left the simulation intact. Something is . . . alive in there, as ridiculous as that sounds." He pointed to a nearby screen. "We can observe what the participant sees, but the feed goes out when the thing approaches. Your man encountered the presence, and surprisingly, has somehow survived."

"You said no harm would come to us."

"There will be no harm from us, as promised, if you continue to comply as he did."

"Are you saying you didn't force him?"

"That's correct."

"Why would he go in there?"

"For the same reason you will."

"And that is . . . ?"

"Inside the crystal, I believe there is information of some kind, probably guarded by the intelligence within. I will send your group in, one by one, until it is retrieved. Tyr volunteered to enter so that you and your woman would not."

"And now I have the same choice."

"Yes."

Ban paced a few steps then turned on Garland. "You'd never let us out, even if we did whatever it is you want."

"That may be true, but you have no other choice. Go inside, rescue your man, and find my information, or I can shoot you now and put your woman in there."

Ban looked at the crystal, then back to Tyr. "I'll do it."

"Good. If you manage to survive, I will free you both."

Ban walked to the second pseudarus. "You'll only get what you want if you do." He stepped inside and sat down.

And then I'm going to kill you.

After the disorientation passed, Ban opened his eyes.

He was on his knees, dirt filling his clenched fists. Wind gusted over his back, warm and dry, and his ragged, dingy shirt flapped over his arms and chest.

He lifted his head. The planks of the wooden roof were collapsed, open to the sky above, dark and overcast. The clouds lit up with lightning, and thunder shook the stone walls.

There was an open window ahead, so he stood to walk to it. His feet were uncovered, and his pants were torn in several places down the legs. The floor was covered in dirt and molded wood fragments, rough and gritty on his soles.

When he looked out through the narrow window, he saw a bleak landscape below. There were patches of dead grass; gnarled, leafless trees; and dried, cracked basins that water had abandoned long ago. Just below him, a worn flag, gray and tattered, whipped in the stormy air, and mortar fell from the crumbling walls.

Multiple tall towers rose from the shadowed, rocky ground, separated by a few kilometers each. They were black and cylindrical, with square, toothlike projections along the tops. By his surroundings, he figured he must be in one such tower.

In the distance, past rolling hills, he saw a great, black fortress. Its walls appeared to be intact, somehow immune to the decay. The wooden gates of its courtyard were open, yet the entrance was anything but inviting. A ring of forest, barren and foreboding, surrounded it on all sides. A paving-stone road led to the castle, formed from the smaller paths that ran from the bases of each of the towers.

He turned back to the room and saw a hole in the floor that led to a descending staircase. Its steps were narrow, jutting from the inside wall of the tower. He went down slowly, huddled away from the edge, and continued until he reached the bottom.

The bottom of the tower was covered in the same debris as the top floor, along with broken stone, splintered wooden crates, and filthy sacks of foodstuffs. The smell of decay was stifling, so Ban jogged through the stone doorway as quickly as possible.

The pockmarked paving-stone road led away from the tower and wound through the low-lying hills surrounding it. He decided to walk the road to the castle, sure that the information he sought would be there. As he walked, he was shoved around by powerful gusts of wind. The smell of rain was in the air, promising a change in the already restless atmosphere.

Considering the dust that blew across the road and up into his face, there couldn't have been rain for quite some time. He thought about that as he walked.

Why should it rain now?

He passed a ruined, broken-down cart with a missing wheel. The wooden frame was fractured in several places, and the metal axles were rusted to the point of disintegration.

Does time pass here?

He was a few kilometers from the black fortress when he saw movement in a nearby roadside tower, much like the one he'd set out from. As he came closer, he realized it was the shifting of shadows cast by a small fire inside.

He looked up to the sky.

It's darker than it was when I started out. There must be a day and night cycle in here.

The tower had an entrance identical to the one before, but more intact. He went inside and started up the wooden steps to the higher level, moving as quietly as possible in case there was someone inside.

Turning just a bit when he walked up through the opening in the floor, he saw a pile of objects near a well-built campfire. The smoke from the fire rose into the air of the tower and left through gaps in the roof above.

He inspected the area near the fire. The pile beside it was well organized, a collection of clothing and metal armor. The armor looked similar in form to the powered armor he normally wore, though it was made of dented metal, primitive and in poor condition.

He knelt to touch the helmet but froze when he heard movement behind him. He twisted around on his kneecap.

A large man stood at the entrance to the steps, one foot still on them, a bundle of wood fragments in his arms. A large club with a diamond-shaped metal head hung at his waist, and a small axe was balanced atop the wood.

The fire made it hard for Ban to make out the man's features. He squinted and held his arm up to block the firelight. "Who's there?"

The large man laughed with a deep, resonating voice that reminded Ban of the flexing of a sturdy old tree. The shadowed figure walked forward confidently. To Ban's surprise, he recognized the man's scarred face.

"Tyr?"

Tyr tossed the wood and axe beside the fire and dusted off his gloved hands with a subdued smile.

"Hello, Ban."

TRUTH TAKEN ROOT

BAN STOOD SLOWLY, BARELY BELIEVING what he'd just heard. "Tyr? How?"

Tyr smiled and removed the gloves from his hands, one finger at a time. "I can hardly believe it myself."

Ban searched the man's still-scarred face. "Is that really you?"

Tyr tucked the gloves into the top of his pants and shrugged. "Everything feels normal."

Ban sighed then sat next to the fire and warmed his hands. "Same. Except I'm freezing."

"It's warmer during the day." Tyr sat down too. "A little."

"Hmph." Ban nodded once.

The night air had a chill on it, worsened by the cool stone bricks they sat upon.

Tyr took a stick and poked at the fire, prodding the wood to burn. "Sorry."

Ban blew into his hands, trying to warm them. "For what?"

"Getting you drawn into this place."

Ban grunted. "Neither one of us had a choice."

"True." Tyr tapped on a smoldering log. The coals underneath it flared, and the heat intensified. "Becks?"

Ban scooted forward. "Safe when I entered. For Garland's sake, she'd better stay that way."

"Garland . . . " Tyr tossed the flaming stick into the fire and grabbed another. "Did he tell you why we're here?"

"He wants some secret information."

"Mmmm. No mention of the monster?"

"Barely. He said something here killed his men. I assumed he was motivating me to rush in after you."

Tyr looked to the window. "I'm afraid not."

Ban's attention went to the steps, barely visible. Suddenly the tower seemed less safe in the dark of night. "Are you saying there's something dangerous out there?"

Tyr nodded. "In the fortress. The black one down the road."

"You saw it?"

"Only a part of it. I tried to enter the fortress, but the shadows inside attacked me. Not sure how I made it out."

"Shadows that move . . ." Ban edged even closer to the fire despite the rising heat. "We shouldn't go out at night."

"Agreed."

"What about this tower? Is it secure?"

Tyr inhaled deeply then tossed another log onto the fire. "The shadows followed me up to the edge of the forest then turned back. Nothing else came out this far. Not until you, anyway."

Ban stared, watching the flames lick at the newly added fuel. "If we don't get what he wants, he'll send Becks in too."

Tyr nodded.

Ban pulled his feet back from the heat. They were sensitive from the walk to the tower. "Find any extra boots?"

"I did. That armor over there's for you. Too small for me."

Ban stood up and walked to the pile. There was a breastplate, leather pants, long brown gloves, and a pair of rough, old boots. He picked one of the boots up and set it next to his foot. "They might fit."

Tyr came over and raised the breastplate. Ban turned, and Tyr helped him into it. He tightened the straps and stepped back.

Ban moved his arms and bent over slightly. "Not very comfortable, but it'll do." He looked up at Tyr. "*What?*"

Tyr shook his head with a smile. "For a moment, you looked like one of your old Doanian knights."

Ban looked down. "Hardly." The armor suddenly seemed heavier. "Help me out of it."

Tyr worked at the buckles. "There's a village off the road, maybe a few kilometers away. I didn't want to go alone."

"Understandable." Ban knelt and carefully laid the breastplate back down. "I think we should stay here tonight then get up early and go to the village. See what we can find. After that, we can make our way up to the fortress."

Tyr held out his hand to help Ban up. "Sounds good . . . boss."

Ban looked up quickly. "Don't . . . "

Tyr shrugged. "It's what Richards would've said."

Ban stood on his own. "I'm sure he would have." He picked up the blanket lying next to the armor and moved over to sit close to the fire. "But it doesn't seem right anymore."

Tyr sat down and brushed some dirt from his pants. He waited, seemingly lost in thought. After a moment, he took in a deep breath. "Becks told me."

Ban looked up, eyes narrowing. "Told you what?"

"About Holland. How you took the fall for Fugelaese."

Ban looked away, jaw tight. He closed his eyes and exhaled. "Did she tell you I left him on Nix?"

"She did."

Ban reached up and ran his fingers through his hair. "I guess it's better you know."

Tyr looked down between his legs to the floor. "Why didn't you tell us?"

Ban thought for a moment. "Shame? Self-loathing? Take your pick."

"But we're your family. You should have told us."

Ban wadded up the blanket and wrung it in his hands. "Well, now you know. Your squad leader's a traitor."

Tyr twisted his lips. "For Nix? You never swore allegiance to House Holland."

"No, but I did to Alidia. To the *Talon*."

Tyr waved his hand. "The Elcosians bear that responsibility. Not you."

Ban shook his head. "We could've saved her if we'd had the command staff. That *was* my fault."

Tyr opened his mouth to reply, but Ban threw the blanket down. "No! Enough with the excuses. Enough with the denial. The lies." His eyes burned. "I'm a *murderer*, Tyr. And a traitor. Even worse than that, a coward."

"Ban . . . "

"I'd be better off dead."

His words echoed from the walls then hung in the silence. Neither man spoke for several seconds.

Ban eventually rubbed his face with both hands then exhaled. "I'm just *tired*, Tyr. The guilt. The nightmares. I wish it would all go away."

"You think dying would fix that?"

Ban looked up, despondent. "Even if it would, I have to pay for what I've done."

Tyr leaned back and looked up into the sky. "You're already serving absolution for Fugelaese. It's true you took on too much of the blame, but that's its own punishment."

Ban looked up too. A few stars peeked through the clouds. He watched until they disappeared again. "I marooned an officer. How should I pay for that?"

"Death," Tyr said. "Or exile."

Ban's eyes lowered down to Tyr's. "Not sure which one's worse."

Tyr nodded. "I know which one Becks would prefer. Me too for that matter."

Ban shook his head, laughing bitterly. "Fools."

Tyr's eyebrows rose. "Excuse me?"

Ban coughed. "I said, you're *fools*." He shifted his weight. "I always got blind loyalty from the three of you, though not once did I earn or justify it."

Tyr squeezed the stick, causing coarse clumps of dust to fall from his fists. "Don't say that."

"Why not? I deserve it. In fact—"

The stick snapped. "I said stop!" Shadows rose and fell on the walls, and the wind whistled as it passed the windows in the stone. Several seconds went by before he spoke again. "A man gets to decide for himself who he follows."

Ban watched him, moisture building in his eyes. "Even if he's wrong?"

"*Especially* then. It means that man sees something the leader doesn't."

Ban interlocked his fingers and rested his forehead on top of them, elbows on his knees. He couldn't speak, knowing full well he'd probably break down if he did.

After a moment, he felt a strong hand on his shoulder. "You need rest, Ban. You'll see things differently in the morning."

Ban suddenly felt the weight of his fatigue, almost pulling him down to the floor. "I doubt it." He raised his head, vision blurred. "But I think I'll try."

"Good." Tyr patted Ban's shoulder once and walked away. "That's all we can do."

Ban balled the blanket up and set it next to him, preparing to use it as a pillow. It wasn't very soft, but it was better than cold, dusty stone. He looked up to see Tyr standing by a window, arms crossed as he peered outside.

After a few moments, Tyr sighed. "It may seem strange to say, but there's true evil here. I've seen it."

Ban rolled over, fire warming his back. He was nearly asleep when Tyr spoke again.

"Remind me. What's that your old knight's creed says?"

Ban closed his eyes again, words trailing off. "In the darkest night of faith long forsaken, the light will forever shine."

Tyr shifted his weight, scraping his boots on the floor. "I always took comfort in those words."

"Me too." Ban rolled over again, falling asleep. "Back when I believed them."

The dawn brought little more than muted sunlight and a chill in the air. No rain had fallen during the night, and the simulated world remained a rocky, barren place.

Tyr bent down to pick up the rusted remains of a broken tool. "It's no paradise."

Ban smiled. "No. I guess not."

"Still, impressive."

Ban nodded as Tyr threw the old tool away from the road. "I've seen some really good sims before, but nothing on this level."

Tyr raised an eyebrow. "Wait for the monster."

Ban kicked at a small half-buried rock. "I've been thinking. It can't really be a monster."

"What then? Some hostile program?"

"It must be. In the context of the sim, it just looks like a monster."

"Still, we should be careful." Tyr looked up to the sky, squinting. "From what Garland said, we can die here."

Ban gripped the axe tightly. "Right. Death is death. Doesn't matter what kills you."

Tyr grabbed at his stomach. "Might be hunger that does me in."

Ban smacked his dry lips with a smile. "Thirst for me."

The village came into view as they walked, rising up in the valley between the hills. As they approached, Ban saw houses arranged in rows with paved roads that ran between them. Each of the buildings was made of dark wood with tiled roofs of clay. Most of the homes looked the same, but there was a larger two-story structure right in the center of town.

Where the road met the town, there was a broken old signpost. Ban picked it up and brushed the dust away.

Tyr looked over his shoulder. "Oak Manor?"

"Maybe it refers to the largest house. Or to the village as a whole."

"What does *oak* mean?"

"No idea." Ban tossed the painted plank away. "It must have meant something to the programmer."

They walked into the village and passed between the houses. Each of the wooden cottages had paned windows made of milky glass. A quick look into the first small house revealed scattered furniture and broken items. Its door lay on the ground, having fallen from its ruined hinges.

"Try another?" Tyr asked.

"I'm sure they're all the same. I'm curious about the larger house though. There might be something of use inside."

They walked over and entered. The main space was a dining room, much like a tavern back home.

Ban wiped the large, dusty wooden table with his finger. "It doesn't look like anyone's been here for decades."

A stranger's voice confirmed Ban's observation. "Longer than that, if you care to know."

Ban and Tyr spun around to search for the source.

An old man with long unkempt hair and a bushy white beard stood in the doorway. He leaned on a gnarled, wooden walking stick, dressed in a moth-eaten cloak and tattered, worn rags.

Ban held up his axe defensively. "Who are you?"

The old man stood a little taller. "I may have forgotten my manners in the long while since I last saw another face, but surely *that* was a poor greeting."

Ban looked to Tyr. "It makes sense there might be setting-appropriate characters programmed into the sim."

The old man laughed, dry and wheezy. "I'm no *sim*. In fact, I was wondering whether or not I'd hallucinated the two of you."

Tyr stepped forward cautiously. "Tell us who you are."

The man thrust the walking stick down to the wooden floor, looking up with a fury that made him seem almost as tall as Tyr. "And just who are you? You've come to my home. Have some respect."

Ban stepped forward as well. "This crystal's been floating in an asteroid field for thousands of years. There's no way you've been here that whole time."

The man's eyebrows rose. "That long, eh? Time gets away from you in a place like this." He laughed to himself.

Ban scowled. "Old man, we don't have time for this. We came seeking a certain . . . intelligence. Are you the one we're looking for?"

"Well, that would depend on what sort of intelligence you're after. I suppose I have some of my own, but I hardly think you've come searching for mine." He seemed proud of that little joke. When no one laughed, he coughed into his hand and moved on. "Could be you came for one of the other villagers. I wasn't the only one to live here, though I'll likely be the last." He gestured out to the town. "Long ago, there were many people here."

Ban nodded. "Simulated programs, you mean."

"No. And don't tell me what I mean." He pointed his walking stick at Ban. "I mean *real* people. Flesh and blood. They lived their lives in this world."

Ban looked at Tyr with a smirk. "Stubborn thing thinks it's real."

The dense stick rapped against Ban's knuckles. He pulled the hand away in pain. "Ow!"

"How's that for *real*?"

Ban shook his hand. "Don't do that again."

"I assure you, the people who lived here were very much alive." With effort, the old man slowly walked over to a nearby window. He turned and held is arm up, gesturing to the village as he leaned on the walking stick. "The wood is wood. The stone is stone. Every particle, wave, and force is faithfully recreated. Your bodies, though they aren't original, are genuine copies."

Ban looked at Tyr then back. "Copies? We gained access through pseudari."

"Your consciousness is here in this body. But your old body was left behind."

"What are you trying to say? That this place actually exists? Inside the crystal?"

"Yes."

Ban shook his head and touched his breastplate. "If these are copies, they aren't that great. In the real world, Tyr was injured. He can't speak."

The old man walked to Tyr and smiled. "The creator of this world was known far and wide as a healer. When people entered, most major injuries or ailments were cured. Your copies underwent the same treatment."

Ban rubbed his forearm. "I broke my wrist when I was a child. It's as stiff as always. And Tyr still has his scars."

The man frowned. "The crystal isn't perfect. Not anymore, anyways."

Tyr took the conversation over before Ban could argue further. "Where are the others? The people who lived here."

The old man looked down solemnly. "Unlike you two, the people of this world left their bodies behind forever—an easy matter for the master of this place. The consciousness—the essence—of each person was stored inside. It was a one-way trip intended to grant immortality. They weren't ever supposed to die, but they did, and when they did, they died *here*."

Tyr wrung his large hands together. "The monster?"

The old man's face took on an expression of sorrow. "Yes." He walked to the table and sat on the wooden bench. "Under Thenander's care, this world flourished, and all remained ideal. Things continuously changed, of course, but the people went unmarked by time. When Thenander left, all of that began to change."

"Thenander?" Tyr asked.

"Yes. Thenander the Healer. A god, though he refused to be called one."

Tyr looked at Ban, hand rising slowly to his neck. "A . . . god?"

The man looked up. "Yes. One of many, now lost."

Ban leaned back and laughed. "Maybe you've been here too long, old man, but there aren't any gods." He looked at Tyr apologetically. "At least not in the way *he* means it, Tyr."

The old man nodded with a knowing smile. "Of course, you're right. They weren't some mythical creatures from the afterlife. I'm talking about beings risen from the bonds of living flesh, able to bend space and time. The masters of realities."

Ban shook his head. "A programmer of a world like this might seem like a god to the people inside."

"Then your reality must be a program too. The gods had power over the outside world as well."

Tyr stepped forward. "But where did they go? Did they lose their power?"

Ban furrowed his brow. "Tyr ..."

"Please, Ban."

Ban sighed, shaking his head as he looked down with an uneasy smile.

The old man's eyes lingered on Ban as he spoke to Tyr. "They no longer hold sway over the universe as they once did."

"Why?"

"They were forgotten."

Tyr shook his head. "Not all of them." He walked to the wooden table and used his weapon to carve the image of his necklace, the twisted metal rod he carried in the real world. "Do you know this?"

The old man didn't hesitate. "Hesfarde the Unyielding—god of strife and perseverance, among many other things. It is good to see she still has followers, though I'm sure you didn't know her name."

"There are many things I don't know about her."

"As I said, forgotten."

Ban rubbed his temples. "You're saying Tyr's god was real?"

"Is real. Was real. Will be real. She is lost along with the rest."

"Lost? Where?" Ban asked.

"I'm not even sure that's the right question. They simply aren't *here*." The old man motioned to the other side of the table. "Sit. Please." He walked to the cupboard. "Are you thirsty?"

They walked over and sat. Ban placed his axe on the tabletop. "Very."

The man went inside the closet and returned with two glasses. He unscrewed metal lids from their tops. "Wine. I think."

Tyr took a careful sip, pleased with the result. "What else?"

The old man sat. "I'm not sure I know much more. I know the gods need us in order to exist in any meaningful sense."

Ban tapped the axe with his finger. "You said they rose from their bonds. What does that mean?"

The man rested his chin on his folded hands. "We thought they must have been human once, but no one knew for sure. Their power was, at most times, incomprehensible."

"You'll have to forgive me, but it still is."

The old man nodded. "I'll admit, it would be hard to believe if I hadn't seen it for myself."

"Then show us."

His eyes lit up. "*That* I can do. What would you like to see?"

"How about the information we came for?"

"What you seek is in the castle."

"Where the monster is?"

"Yes."

Ban looked into the old man's rheumy eyes. "What is it? The monster, I mean."

The old man leaned forward. "A nightmare. Pure evil in its most concentrated form."

Tyr nodded. "Yes. I saw it."

The old man looked at Tyr without moving his head. "No, you didn't, or you'd be dead."

Ban pinched his nose impatiently. "But what is it really? Some security program?"

The man's eyes went back to Ban. "Something from beyond this galaxy. There are many more like it, and there was a time when the gods fought them for the hearts of mankind."

Ban smiled wryly. "The hearts of mankind?" Tyr shot him a frustrated glance. Ban stifled his amusement as best he could. "Okay, why not? We've listened to everything else so far. Tell us more about your monster."

"It's an ephmere. A terrible—"

Ban stopped him. "Wait. An ephmere, like in the game of Vogi?"

"Yes . . ."

"That's . . . impossible."

It was the old man's turn to smile. "Impossible? You're sitting on a bench made of particles inside a crystal. Are you sure you know what that word really means?"

Ban laughed in acquiescence. "Apparently I don't."

The old man continued with a wave of his hand. "An ephmere—a terrible thing of darkness, black and writhing, full of hate and at the same time, supreme intellect. This once perfect world was appropriated in order to be its prison. To contain its mind."

Tyr swallowed. "Why would that seem like a good idea?"

"Because it's incredibly hard to kill, if it even can be." The old man shifted uncomfortably. "But that isn't the worst of it. The prison is degrading."

Tyr looked to Ban. "So, this world really is falling apart."

Ban looked back to the old man. "Your monster has something we need."

"Yes, it does, but not even the one who sent you knows what that is."

Ban narrowed his eyes. "But you do?"

"Indeed. There was a woman here, the Champion of Thenander. She held his blessing and watched over this place in his stead. She must have been killed. I believe the ephmere took that blessing from her."

"A blessing?" Ban looked to Tyr then back to the old man again. "I bet that's what we're after." He moved his hand from the axe. "Will you help us find it?"

The old man smiled. "I'm glad you finally asked for help, young man. I've come to like your friend, and it would be a shame if he died."

Ban watched the old man with contempt. He walked too slowly down the road, and night would fall soon. "Shouldn't we have stayed in the village? Tyr said it isn't safe at night."

"Tyr is right. There is no safe place at night. Except for one."

"Where?"

"A shrine of Thenander. In the forest near the castle. The ephmere hasn't grown strong enough to breach its wards. *Yet.*"

They continued. Tyr turned to the bent man. "What is your name?"

He walked on. "Hermes."

"I'm Tyr. This is Ban."

Hermes looked back. "Yes, I know. Oh, don't look surprised. You both said each other's names before."

Ban cocked his head slightly. "Hmmm. I guess we did. Tell me, how'd you survive when all the others were killed?"

"I slept."

"You . . . slept?"

"Oh yes. I slept for many, many years. I was found by a traveler—a man far from home."

They finally reached the edge of the forest. Though the trees were barren, they were mighty and thick. Dead underbrush made the trek ahead daunting, but there appeared to be a walkable path. The old man followed it, and they walked behind him in silence, stepping over the fallen branches.

"A great time had passed while I slept, and the traveler told me of the world in which I'd awoken. It was a different reality, godless, full of doubt and ignorance. I was dismayed, but grateful to be awake again."

Tyr brushed a low-hanging branch aside. "That man came here?"

"No. He never could've found this place. He traveled the galaxy as you know it, outside the crystal. A jumper, you would call him. He'd left his family, not sure if he would ever make it home again."

Ban looked at Tyr, and Tyr returned the questioning glance.

Hermes continued. "In gratitude for my awakening, I asked him what I could give him in return. He wanted me to travel with him, since he was supremely lonely. I agreed, of course, and for a time, we searched the stars beyond his maps."

Ban held his axe more tightly.

The old man just admitted he isn't from this world. His story is changing. He's not what he seems.

"But the jumper eventually grew sick, as all men do. He wished to return to his family, so he could see them before he died. He had a disease, you see, one that I couldn't cure. Unfortunately, he grew very ill before we returned, and he did not want his family to see him in such a state."

He's leading us into a trap, distracting us along the way with this tale.

Ban signaled to Tyr that he should be ready to attack. "So, what did he do then, *old man Hermes?*"

The man paused for a moment as he walked, then continued with the story. "He asked me to leave him and go home to his son. He begged me to watch over him, to make sure he grew up with his father's sense of adventure. There's a great power within him, he said."

Ban spread out from Tyr. "You raised his son?"

He chuckled. "No. I wouldn't dare replace him as a father. I was simply there for the boy as a companion. I watched him grow into a fine young man, full of spirit and with his father's drive."

They came to a clearing. It was covered in the same debris, but instead of a path, it widened out into a large circle. Before Ban knew it, he was inside its edge.

It was odd, but Ban thought he saw a hint of green underneath the dead leaves.

Hermes turned his head. "Though you probably wouldn't agree with my assessment of him now, Bond-Sergeant."

Ban tensed and raised his axe. "I knew there was something off about you. What was your plan? Lure us to the monster? Or are *you* the monster?"

The old man turned around. "Everything I've said is true. I just played a little loose with the details of where and when. The ephmere awaits you in the castle."

"How did you know my rank?"

"Because I've met you before, and so has the jumper's son."

Before? On the Talon!

Ban felt anger rise inside. "You mean the swordsman."

"Yes, Fall Arden."

Ban rushed forward, full of blind rage. The old man caught the axe with his walking stick and sent Ban flying over his outstretched foot. As Ban recovered, Tyr fell to the ground too, holding his right knee.

The old man stood taller, no longer bent. "Here, under the withered branches of this circle, the truth will be heard."

Ban rose to his knees. "Whose truth?"

The old man pointed the walking stick at Ban. "Oh, give up your skepticism. You live in a world much greater than you."

Tyr raised his hand, breathing heavily. "Ban. We should listen. He's not lying."

The old man softened. "Thank you, Tyr. Sorry about your knee. Don't worry. You'll find that your aches and pains leave quickly here."

It was true. Ban's shoulder had throbbed only moments before, but it was already beginning to feel better. There was something about the circle, there in the otherwise dead forest, that made things seem brighter, if only just barely.

Hermes nodded proudly. "I'll let you decide if what I say is the truth, but you *will* hear it first."

Ban rose to one knee with a grunt. "If we must."

"I think you should. I don't know how the Elcosians knew about your ship or how they disabled it so quickly. The girl we were with, the arcanist, they were hunting her. It's possible they were tracking her, but I assure you, she would've loved to have been anywhere else."

Ban stood slowly. "And your friend's son, Fall? The Runian?"

"Valenen, not Runian. It's a long story, but he was badly wounded trying to protect a friend. His condition was the reason we agreed to come aboard."

Ban wouldn't relent. "What about the dead on the *Talon*'s bridge, murdered with a blade? What about the Runian code that disabled our ship? What about my friend, my *brother*, Rowan Richards?"

The old man leaned forward on the walking stick, sympathy in his eyes. "I don't know the answers to those questions, Ban. Maybe Fall does, but I can tell you without a doubt he had nothing to do with the attack. Your anger is misplaced."

Ban looked to Tyr. "Tyr?"

Tyr looked into the forest then back to Hermes. "I want to believe it."

Ban looked down and kicked away the decaying leaves. Green grass pushed up through the stones below. He couldn't deny there was something right about it all. "All right, Hermes. I'll agree to one thing. I'll meet your friend's son and ask him about his part in the attack. If I believe him, I'll leave it alone."

The old man tapped the stone below his feet with his walking stick. "It's a start." He turned around and walked to the edge of the circle. "You should gather wood quickly and have a fire before nightfall. The circle will protect you, but not if you stray outside."

Ban walked toward him. "Wait! You're leaving?"

"Yes. I must take steps to ensure you two can get out once this is over. Plus, I need to watch over Becks."

"Watch over her?"

"Yes. I would bet the video feed cut out when we stepped inside the circle. If they think you're dead, they might try to put her inside the crystal. I'll try to keep that from happening."

Ban looked down at the grass again, suddenly embarrassed by his outburst. "You . . . have my thanks."

He nodded. "I should. You wouldn't survive this night otherwise. Don't forget that when the time comes. Now, do as I say and try to sleep if you can. I'll come back in the morning at first light. The castle is a way yet, and we have to get there before night falls again."

The old man suddenly disappeared without a trace, and the two men stood there alone.

Ban walked to Tyr. "You really believe it all? About gods and monsters?"

Tyr stepped up to the circle's edge and grunted. "Enough to hurry."

"Well, I'm still not sure." Ban looked out into the dead forest. It was already harder to make out the branches than it was a few minutes ago. He shivered at his sense of foreboding. "But I'm sure not going to waste any time."

DEEPER STILL

FALL ROSE UP FROM HIS ARMORED ELBOW and leaned back in the creaky wooden chair. The flame above the table flickered as its candle shifted, casting shadows on the walls of the isolated backroom.

He sighed. "That's all you can tell me?"

The woman who sat across from him was pale, appearing slightly ill, as if she were malnourished. Her hungry, sunken eyes narrowed. "Times are tough, Ranger. There's a freeze on contracts. You know that, or you wouldn't be here."

"Right, but who froze them?"

"If you don't know, I'm not telling."

Fall leaned forward and motioned to the small bag of coins in front of him. "For what it cost to get in here, I'm owed an introduction."

She smacked her lips, looking at the bag. "I might be convinced, *for a friend.*"

Fall shifted in his seat. "And we aren't friends yet, is that it?"

She leaned over the table. "It's *gold* that makes friends here, Ranger."

Olivia crossed her arms. "We've been a little too friendly if you ask me."

Fall held up his left hand and grabbed the coins with his right. "Olivia, it's okay."

"We won't have enough left."

"Hold on a sec." Fall held up the gold. "Look. Do you need a Ranger or not?"

The old lady smiled. "*I* don't."

"But you know someone who does?"

She nodded. "As a matter of fact, I do. I can set it up."

Olivia walked closer. "When?"

"Tonight."

"Where?"

"Out past the wharf. Row of Ga'rue. Look for a man called Foran. He'll take you down."

Fall glanced at Olivia then back to the woman. "Down?"

"That's what I said."

"Why? What happens below the city?" Fall asked.

"See for yourself." She reached forward and snatched the gold from his hand. "Now go."

Olivia watched the woman empty the bag onto the table. "Wait a minute. You expect us to give you a sack of coins and just take your word on it? Who's to say you aren't sending us out to get robbed?"

The little old woman smiled and tapped her index finger on the table. A shadowed man walked forward, holding a makeshift scattergun.

The woman shrugged. "I could rob you now . . . "

Fall stood up slowly. "Fair enough."

She nodded curtly. "Don't keep Foran waiting, Ranger."

"Olivia." Fall held out his hand, motioning for her to follow.

"Yeah . . . " She walked backward toward the door, eyes on the scattergun.

Fall opened the door, and Olivia went through. He backed out, taking one last look at the small woman, eyes gleaming as she counted her candlelit coins.

Fall flipped a silver coin to the bartender. "Thanks, I guess."

The taciturn man caught it then waved it over a scanner behind the bar. Satisfied, he pocketed it, nodding as he went back to cleaning the glassware.

Olivia hurried through the exit, dodging a few patrons as they entered.

Once Fall caught up, she tapped her wrist display and pointed down the street. "That way."

Fall stayed close, keeping his eyes on her as they walked. More than one man turned to look her up and down, and he found, surprisingly, that it angered him. He felt embarrassed considering he'd done the same thing more than once himself.

As they came up on a nearby intersection, Fall spotted the orange-and-red lights on Mei's armor. Olivia led the way, and once they got a little closer, Mei saw them too.

The Roshanan Ranger leaned on the wall outside a fragrant smoke shop, arms crossed as she looked up. "What did you find?"

Fall and Olivia looked at each other uneasily, and Olivia grimaced. "Well..."

"What?" Mei asked.

"There's a guy we need to meet," Olivia said.

"This worries you?"

"He's in a different part of the city."

"How far away?"

Olivia turned to Fall in question.

Fall frowned. "Other side of the island, back near the wharf."

Olivia sighed. "We're getting short on money too."

Fall nodded. "Yeah, we almost spent my whole stash greasing all those palms."

Mei tapped her fingers on her elbow. "You have no other leads?"

Fall crossed his arms too. "None. It should be easier in a city like this, but no one's posting contracts."

Mei kicked the toe of her boot into the sidewalk a few times. "Odd."

He nodded. "How's it going with Sidna?"

Mei stared down the street. "I should have heard from her by now."

"Aren't you tracking her?"

"I am, but I will not interfere just yet. I will go back to the ship and wait a little longer."

Olivia smiled. "I'm sure you'll find her."

Mei's eyepiece hummed. "You may count on that, Doctor."

"Thanks again for the help, Mei," Fall said.

"Do not mention it. Olivia, will you be staying on the Rìluò?"

"No, though Fall already tried to ditch me."

Fall placed his hands on his hips. "It would be safer if you did. It's rough out here."

She turned on him. "Don't think I can handle it?"

"It's not that." He shook his head. "I'm grateful for the help."

She narrowed her eyes and nodded. "You'd better be."

Fall sighed and looked to Mei. "I'll let you know what we find."

"Please do. And I will do the same." She nodded and walked away.

Fall popped his knuckles as he turned back to Olivia. "We need a ride. Preferably a cheap one."

Olivia pointed over Fall's shoulder. "What about that?"

Fall turned to see. She'd pointed to a roofless metal carriage with four tall wooden wheels.

On the frame, there were two rows of benches and a forward seat for a driver. Its flowing sides had small mounted gas lamps that shone softly on the step bars. From the front, a length of curved rod reached out to a harness.

The harness attached to an animal, a female artus. She was a little skinny for her size, but her thick coat looked healthy with a silvery sheen. Her ribbon ears stood up tall and rotated in different directions, and blinders covered her six eyes, three on each side of her slender face.

She stamped her padded, clawed feet and flexed her powerful muscles. The three tufts of her flowing tails swished. She snorted and held her head high.

Fall and Olivia went over, and the carriage driver walked around the rear. He wore a short, dirty gray coat with holes in the ratty fabric. His hair was greasy, and his fingertips were black.

He adjusted his flat gray hat. "No virtua and *absolutely* no credit." His eyes widened when he saw them, probably due to the quality of their clothing and weapons. "But we take gold, of course. Anything of value, really." His searching eyes spent a little too much time on Olivia.

Fall stepped between them at the side of the carriage. "Gold will do."

"Very good. Yes, that's good." He averted his eyes and went wide around Fall toward the front.

Fall pulled himself up then reached back to extend a hand for Olivia. She smiled as she took it, pulling herself up as well. They sat on the forward bench.

The carriage driver tossed a little morsel to the artus then jumped up into his seat. He turned around and propped his elbow over the edge of it. "Where to?"

Olivia crossed her arms. "By the wharf. Row of Ga'rue."

The tiny man's mouth dropped open, and he turned around quickly. "Yes, masters. Yes, of course."

He flicked the reins, and the creature walked forward slowly, working up to a slow trot. Her rough feet rubbed on the ground, and her claws clicked. The carriage rolled along behind her, bouncing roughly over the ancient paving stones below.

Olivia spoke softly from the corner of her mouth. "Masters?"

Fall shrugged. "No clue."

The artus slowed, and the carriage came to a stop. Fall and Olivia steadied themselves then scooted down the bench.

Olivia grasped the hand bar and turned, lowering herself to the ground.

Fall moved forward, just behind the driver, reaching into his belt pocket for his last gold coin. "A smooth ride. Thank you, sir."

The driver took the coin, looked at it, and seemed to think better of insulting Fall with a test of its quality. "Thank you, master. Eh, will you be wanting a return trip?"

Fall looked out into the district. It was the lowest point on that side of Cisterne, except for the wharf just beyond at the water's edge. He remembered seeing the nondescript buildings and unlit streets from the Rìluò, but being in the middle of that darkness was worse.

"I don't think so. At least, not any time soon," Fall said to the driver.

"Fair enough," the little man replied.

Fall hopped down nimbly and stepped back. The driver turned the carriage, and it rocked up the uneven street, back toward the glow of the city above.

Fall turned to Olivia. "Let's get going. I don't like this place at all."

All around, the darkened buildings of the Row of Ga'rue crouched in wait. The narrow alleys seemed to hide any number of dangers, each a path to an uncertain end.

Olivia moved closer to him, hand unconsciously going to her pistol. "Yeah. This might have been a mistake." She looked ahead. "Is that it?"

Down the street, next to a solitary lamppost, a man leaned against a doorway. He was mostly shadowed, though the lamp's light shone down to reveal his boots.

Fall walked around Olivia. "Foran?" His voice carried in the silence.

The man backed through the doorway, disappearing. After a moment, his arm reached out, motioning them inside.

Olivia sighed. "Well, that seems completely safe."

Fall walked ahead, hand on his sword's grip. "No choice."

When they stepped inside the strange doorway, an empty room greeted them.

They walked through that first small room to another door. Beyond it lay a much larger space, like a repair garage or a warehouse. Far across in the corner, the man leaned on the wall next to a tall lump of machinery.

He wore a brown jacket, frayed near the bottom, over a loose shirt with buttons going down the center. His hat had a short brim that circled the rounded top. He held a lantern in his hands. "This way."

His voice was unfriendly and untrustworthy, which somehow made Fall feel better. He'd had enough of smiling swindlers for one day.

They walked to the man's corner, aware of every echoing footfall in the spacious, barren room. As they came closer, Fall could see that the machinery was meant to operate a cargo lift.

The man raised the lift's gate and stepped inside.

Olivia hesitated. "Are you Foran?"

"I am."

"Where are we going?"

"Down to the Town."

"A town?"

"*The* Town."

"And the guy we're meeting is down there?"

He spat. "How should I know?"

Olivia looked back at Fall. Fall nodded.

Olivia turned back to Foran. "Okay, we'll go. But we're watching you."

He tipped his hat and smiled. "Be my guest."

They entered the lift, and Foran shut the gate. He pressed a button on the lift's control panel, and the machinery sputtered. The lift started to descend.

Fall looked up and watched the ceiling disappear from sight as they went down.

Does this planet ever end?

The rickety lift lurched one final time then came to rest. The doors opened with a few shrieks and a prolonged, scraping moan. Foran lifted the gate.

Fall looked at the others uneasily and stepped out.

The rough stone tunnel was narrow and short, forcing them to walk single file. The air was humid, and water dripped from above. After a few meters, the tunnel gave way to a small chamber, hewn from the rock. Flickering torches lit the area, and the smells of burning hydrocarbons and smoke filled Fall's nose. A creaky ventilation fan spun just above the center of the room, barely doing its job.

A man in a black coat, with long hair and an uncut, stubbled face leaned against the wall on a rusted metal chair. He looked up as they approached. "Who's this?"

Foran waved his hand from Olivia to the man and looked at Fall expectantly.

Fall coughed and swallowed before he spoke. "Fall Arden, Olivia Hans—"

The dark man raised his dirty hand. "Which one's the Ranger?"

"I am." Fall stepped forward. "What is this place?"

The grumpy man only stared back as he pressed a button on the wall. The doors behind him opened, moving apart with the grace of the lift; Fall had to grit his teeth to stand it.

Beyond the doors, a dark tunnel sloped downward and to the left. Golden lamps activated in series, mounted along the tunnel walls. The sounds of heavy machinery and hissing steam echoed up into the small room.

A mine?

Foran walked through the doorway and down the passage. Fall and Olivia followed under the harsh gaze of the doorman. When they'd passed the threshold, the doors began to close, thundering shut and locking behind them.

Fall tensed as the sound vibrated through his bones. The tightness in his shoulders remained, even after it was quiet.

Locked in.

They followed Foran further and further, down narrow rock-hewn steps that spiraled around a central core. Every so often, there was a notch in the outer wall, most times empty, but sometimes holding a lamp or a set of tools.

They reached the bottom and walked out into a square-shaped room with blue stone bricks. No lamps hung along the walls; the bricks shined their own faint light.

Fall looked down at his boots. The metal caught the strange, otherworldly glow and reflected it. The rest of his clothing was darker than normal.

Foran smiled at Fall's curiosity. His teeth shone in the light, and his eyes were a tint of blue.

Ahead, a broad stone staircase led down to the floor. Several wooden doors, made sturdy by flattened bars of thick metal, lined the edges of the room, none giving any hint as to what lay beyond.

Foran walked to the right, to an exit like any other. "This way."

He opened it, and Fall heard the distant sounds of a multitude of voices. On the other side was another room that stretched out farther than he could see.

Olivia was growing impatient. "Is there an end to this any time soon?"

Foran nodded. "Just a little further."

They went into the room and saw that there were small buildings inside.

They were constructed of the same strange rock, but of larger bricks. The tops of them were made of clay tiles, and the four-paned windows were made of something clear yet cloudy. Many of the small places had openings in the side, and people crowded near them.

The people were dressed in a mix of dirt-stained uniforms that glowed faintly. There were men, women, and children of many ages.

One of the children, a young girl with a shaved head, ran over when she saw them. She looked up at Fall with something like awe. She didn't speak.

Foran kicked dust at her, and she ran away, looking back to Fall one more time before she disappeared into the throng of adults. "Don't worry. They're mostly harmless."

The group walked on for hundreds of footsteps, through wooden doors and stone spaces, by people who slept on piles of straw or waited in lines near the small buildings.

Fall looked around at the different groups. "Who are these people? They don't look healthy."

Foran kept walking. "Workers."

"Who do they work for?"

Foran looked genuinely confused by the question. "The same person we all work for. Did you hit your head on the way down?"

The largest part of the mine they'd seen, one that went on for what seemed like a kilometer, widened out and slanted at a sharp downward slope. Along the sides, conveyer belts carried piles of rocks and ore. Workers at the top pulled the loose fragments free and loaded them into carts on tracks that ran out of sight.

None of their clothes looked like the type anyone would wear for a job like that. And each time he made eye contact with one of them, they looked away hurriedly.

Foran shrugged with a slight movement of his head and turned to another door. "This is it."

He opened it and motioned for them to enter. Inside, it was dark, the only place they'd seen so far that didn't glow.

Foran held up the lantern to show that nothing waited inside.

Fall walked through first, hand on his sword.

But something was wrong. It was the stillness of the air. The silence spoke of hidden dangers.

He paused, drawing his blade slowly.

"Is it true?" A rumbling voice vibrated underneath the darkness ahead. It was ominous, artificial. It made Fall's stomach drop.

To his left, sharp metal, narrow and triangular, cut through the air, barely betrayed by a short-lived glint along its edge.

Fall turned, swiftly unsheathing his sword as he leaned and pushed off the floor. He deflected the spear then instantly moved to attack the one who held it.

"Wait!" the strange voice cried out.

Fall held, suspending the silver blade's edge less than a hand's length away from the spear wielder's vulnerable elbow.

Again the voice spoke. "So, it *is* true."

The spearman moved away. It was then that Fall noticed it wasn't a man at all.

A . . . *machine?*

Artificial joints whined quietly as the fleshless body straightened up and moved back into the corner. Its emotionless, transparent blue eyes matched the color of the walls outside, following Fall with swift, unnatural movements.

Fall slowly relaxed, turning to face the end of the room. His eyes began to adjust, and he could see a little farther.

The voice sat forward in its chair behind a wide desk. "Only a test, my friend. A *Ranger's* test."

Fall looked back to the entrance. Olivia walked through with her hands raised. Behind her, Foran entered with a white pistol drawn. He closed the wooden door, standing there quietly.

Fall sheathed his sword, and lines of light activated in a grid pattern along the floor, intensely blue in color. The square-shaped areas between the paths were black, almost invisible. As the lines spread, they continued up the wall and along the room, revealing the same smooth black material between them.

The light tracked up to the desk, rising into it, pulsing like a breathing thing.

The voice leaned forward into the luminescence, eyes shining orange, metal plates clicking as its hand beckoned Fall forward. "Come, Ranger. I have a job for you."

"You should know we never take jobs without pay," Fall said.

The voice was synthetic, a low, humming imitation of human speech. "I know everything I need to know about you, Aeturnian Ranger."

Fall narrowed his eyes. "I doubt that."

The machine cocked its head. "You dislike me."

"Is that a question?"

"No."

Fall crossed his arms. "I'm leaning toward mistrust."

"A common reaction from a human." The machine held its open hand up and watched with electric eyes as the fingers reached higher. "Creation of artificial intelligence in the god-image is man's greatest possible heresy."

Fall recognized the quote from the Elcosian *Truth and Fire.* He shook his head. "It's more about your minion trying to stab me when I walked in."

The philosophic machine leaned forward, synthetic voice dropping deeper. "*Your* motives are also unclear."

"I'm looking for work."

"Hmmm. For work or *workers?*"

"What in the Void does that mean?"

"I checked the records, Ranger. You have an open contract."

Fall sighed. "That job's over."

"Is it? Your employer does not seem to know."

"They will soon."

The machine stared for an uncomfortably long time. "You have come for them. They must be valuable . . . "

"You aren't making any sense."

The machine stood from its chair and walked beyond the table.

Various parts spun and clicked as it did, yet it moved smoothly in spite of its complexity. "You are here for the Runians. I will release them, but only if you complete a task for me."

Olivia started forward and struggled against Foran's grip. "What does he mean? What Runians?"

Fall turned back to the machine. "Runians? Here?"

It walked closer, inspecting him. "You must have known. Why else would you have come?" It turned around. "It does not matter. I have your compatriots. Do you want them or not?"

Does he mean . . . ? It can't be.

Fall hid his surprise. "First, tell me how you . . . *obtained* them."

"I bought them. The same as all my captives. They were *not* cheap." The machine looked at Olivia. "Fathomers fetch a high price."

Olivia pulled forward. "You son of a—"

Foran kicked the back of her knee, and she went to the floor. "Easy, little lady. The grown-ups are talking."

Fall forced himself to relax. "Will you get to the point?"

Thin metal plates on the machine's face moved in crude approximations of emotional display. "Below us, there is a structure. Inside it, there is a lost device that my employer desires."

Fall shifted impatiently. "Can you be more specific?"

It placed its hands behind its back. Fall could see through the gaps in the frame of its body; the fingers danced rapidly. "The device appears to be a transparent stone, such as a small crystal, containing a burning fire."

"Who wants it? Why?"

"Your acquisition of that information is not necessary to complete the job."

"I'll decide what's necessary. Otherwise, find someone else."

The plates above its eyes lowered. "Very well. My employer is the master of this city, the Maiden. What she wants with the device, she has not said."

Fall looked down. "So, I get you this crystal, then I get my . . . compatriots?"

"Yes."

He looked back up. "Sounds easy enough. Why hire a Ranger?"

The machine nodded. "There is a significant obstacle against which my workers have proved . . . inadequate."

"You sent your captives to get it?"

"Yes."

Fall stared at the machine, waiting for more information. It only stared back. "Well, what happened to them?"

"They died. Although, I will admit, I have extrapolated that conclusion based upon the available data."

"Meaning?"

"I have not recovered their remains. But I should mention that survivors from other expeditions have returned in the past."

"What did they say when they came back?"

The machine emitted a sound like laughter, and the faceplates tried to show amusement. "They said there was a *demon*."

Fall smiled. "You don't believe them?"

"Oh, certainly not. Though, something *is* killing them. The survivors were quite traumatized. It was some time before suitable replacements arrived."

"Suitable?"

"It's not every day I manage to buy a Fathomer crew. Laceras really outdid themselves this time."

The raiders . . .

Fall managed to hide his anger. "Why not send one of your fighters if it's so dangerous?"

The machine imitated a shrug. "Supposedly, the device is complex. Acquisition may require a complex mind."

"I'm no scientist."

"Of course. I have sent enough scientists. Now, I will send a *hunter*."

Fall stared then nodded, contemplating his options. "How do I find the crystal?"

The machine reached down to the desk and flipped a switch. A portion of the wall behind him slid open, grinding stone, to reveal a round floor panel.

"Step inside. You will be taken to the structure instantaneously."

Fall searched the alcove's interior from top to bottom. "Some sort of lift?"

"Not quite. You will see." The machine went back to its chair and sat down. "You may return the same way once you have the device."

"Hold on. I'm not leaving my friend here."

"She will be fine. No harm will come to her. As a matter of fact, I could use her help too."

Fall reached for his blade. "Leave her alone."

"Be calm, Ranger." Its hands remained beneath the desk's edge. "Some of the Runians were injured in their . . . procurement. I have a few medics, but your doctor will prove far more useful I think."

Doctor? How'd he know?

Fall looked at Olivia, who was equally surprised.

The machine waved its hand. "If you need to know anything, it's this: the Maiden knows everything that happens in Cisterne."

Olivia stood up. "I'm going with him."

"I think not." The machine continued to look at Fall. "You would be better served to meet up with any potential survivors already in the structure."

"There's someone still alive down there?" Fall asked.

"It is possible, though unlikely."

Fall looked to Olivia. He did his best to reassure her as he stepped onto the platform. "She'd better be safe when I get back."

"That all depends upon the manner of your return." The machine pressed something under the desk.

A new light built around the panel, bright red-orange. The black metal beneath Fall's boots liquefied and rippled under his weight. There was a tingling sensation, and his skin felt wet. He looked up. The room and everything inside broke apart, swirling and mixing in colors of blue, black, red-orange, and white.

As if through a pool of water, he heard the machine's garbled voice. "Kill the demon, Ranger, and your friend will go free. If not, I'm sure I'll find some other use for her."

Fall tried to reach out, but the colors of his suit—gray, green, silver, and orange—mixed in with the whirlpool and were swept away, down into the deep.

BROKEN WORLD

FALL WAS SOMEWHERE ELSE.

The swirling palette changed, electric-blue fading into burning red-orange. His own colors flowed into the mix, yet his consciousness remained apart from it all.

As he watched, the colors migrated past each other and gathered together in likeness, rearranging into a warped, wavering image. Gray, silver, orange, and green came toward him, separating from the newly added black and red-orange. It all slowed and settled into place, slightly out of focus.

He stumbled from the pad and fell to his knees. When he opened his eyes, he saw his gloved hands, bracing him above the smooth black material below him.

He looked up as lines of bright red-orange spread out before him in a grid. On the wall ahead, the lines rapidly turned and crossed each other, tracing an image from top to bottom. They formed a tall twisted tower with a tiny pulsating square about one-quarter from the bottom.

A map?

Fall stood up and looked to each side. Two black halls stretched out in opposite directions. The red-orange grids continued to spread, following the shapes of the walls and floors.

He listened.

Nothing.

He went right. At the end, the hall made a ninety-degree turn. As he walked, the grid of light suddenly moved away in all directions, giving the illusion he was standing upon nothing—as if he'd shrunk to the size of a bug and was floating in the center of the hallway.

A trap?

He closed his eyes and reached down to his belt, searching for the right vial. After he found it, he took it out and opened it, brought it to his lips, and drank the Night-Sight. A few moments passed before he felt the slight tingle behind his eyes.

When he looked again, the scene was very different. Where there had been black, there was a faint gray hallway. The red-orange lines burned intensely, squares spreading and shifting from their previous positions. He walked again, and the lines continuously changed location and size. Without the potion, it would have been debilitating.

He jogged to the end and followed the hall to the left. The next thing he saw was overwhelming in a new way that no potion's chemicals could counter. After a short stretch of floor there was a huge open space. He walked out to the floor's edge.

He stood on one flattened section of a path that sloped down to the left and up to the right. Above and below, the structure corkscrewed for hundreds of stories around the central chasm, lined by openings like the one behind him.

He heard a scream, panicked and confused.

He looked up, across the empty space, and saw a woman, two levels above. She ran through an opening, indistinct from any other.

I need to place some sort of marker.

He reached down and activated the mech bow. "Killer."

He nocked the arrow then raised the bow, compensating as best he could for the distance and elevation. The missile flew, arcing before it dug into the wall near the opening.

Up the floors he jogged, closing in on his target. He paused only for a moment to holster the bow, retrieve the arrow, and catch his breath. Then he ran through and turned the corner. Halfway down the next hall, he saw her, shuffling along with her hands pressed to the wall.

The red-orange lines ran vertically, revolving around her. She looked back and screamed again.

Fall called out to her. "Wait!"

She stopped, shaking. "Stay away!"

"My name is Fall Arden. I can help you if you just wait."

Her voice broke. "The Ranger?" She almost fell to her knees. "Get me out of here!"

He ran to her and took her by the hands. She looked up.

He recognized her long black hair and her eyes. She was Lieutenant Commander Endo Kumi, the unpleasant officer from the *Morning Rain*'s bridge. She smelled strongly of sweat and fear.

Fall reached down for the potion vial. "Here, drink this."

She pulled away. "What is it?"

"It's okay. It'll help."

She relaxed slightly and took a careful sip. She screwed up her face and nearly gagged. "It's disgusting."

Fall tipped up the bottom with his fingers. "All right, that's enough. Now, close your eyes." He put the vial away.

He helped her stand. "Do you feel it yet?"

"I think so."

"Open them."

She slowly opened her eyes and let go of his arm.

"Better?"

"Yes. Much."

"It's temporary, but I have more if we need it." He searched her for injuries, finding none. "What are you running from?"

"I'm . . . not sure. It killed Peters and Byn." She pulled on his arm. "We have to go."

He grabbed her hand. "No, I can't."

"What? Why?"

"The machine that sent me has the rest of your crew. He won't let them go unless I kill whatever's down here."

A cool gust of air blew across Fall's neck, wet with mist. He started to turn but was lifted from his feet and pinned to the wall.

He looked down into the face of the thing that had him. It spoke. "A human? Kill *me*?"

It was covered in jet-black fur, gray in the Night-Sight, with pointed white incisors and a nose somewhat shaped like a man's. Its eyes were alien, deep gray, with two concentric rings of bright white where each iris should be.

Fall grabbed its forearm. The muscles underneath the fur were hard as iron. The hand was tightening.

He reached down to the bow holster on his left hip, and it opened. The creature turned, looking down at the shifting mechanism, unable to grab it without loosening its grip.

Fall used the distraction and reached up with his right hand to jab the thing in the throat. It dropped him and stumbled away.

Fall drew his sword; the blade's edge sang in the silence. He held it back, ready in a striking stance.

The beast recovered, shaking its head with a cough. "You're a tricky little thing." It was taller than Fall, with open robes and dark clothing underneath.

Fall stared into the white rings in its eyes, ignoring the pain in his neck.

The creature seemed amused by his confusion. "You don't know what I am, do you?"

Fall swallowed, throat dry. "I know you're not a demon."

"Really? How can you be so sure?"

"Because I don't believe in demons."

It laughed. "Then you're a fool."

Fall held perfectly still, fighting the almost irresistible urge to flee. Kumi didn't share his composure.

The creature pointed at her. "Not another step."

She froze.

Fall narrowed his eyes. "Leave her alone."

It smiled menacingly. "As you wish."

It evaporated, and a stream of something fluid, transparent, shot to the right of Fall. He felt the same cool mist from before as it took the shape of the beast and its raised blade.

Fall turned and swiftly deflected the incoming slash then braced as it came on again.

The creature's gray blade pushed against Fall's. Its eyes widened with surprise. "You saw me . . . " It jumped back, lowering the curved knife. "Impossible. Only *she* could see the *Fyd Wyr.*"

Fall took the initiative and rushed ahead, flipping his blade forward for a thrust. He stabbed through the air as the black beast dissolved and flowed behind him.

Fall dove forward and rolled across his shoulder, twisting on his knee to face his opponent as its knife slashed over his head. His momentum brought his sword around for a backhand cut, passing through another burst of cool vapor.

A few meters ahead, the mysterious thing reappeared. "You have some skill."

Fall stood up, letting his blade hang down by his side. "We can't all teleport."

"Never say never, human."

Fall grunted with a smile. "If you're going to keep calling me that, you could at least tell me what you are."

He bowed slightly, never lowering his eyes. "I am Sostek. The voidstrider."

"Well, I'm Fall. The *human*."

Sostek sheathed his knife and nodded toward Fall's side. "Where did you get it?"

"What? My sword?"

"Yes. None of the humans I've seen here have carried one, much less a solsynth blade."

"Solsynth?"

"Yes, solsynth. The metal. I didn't know any of you champions still lived."

Fall furrowed his brow. "It was a gift from my father."

Sostek cocked his head. "Strange. A champion's weapon is supposed to be sacred."

"My father wasn't religious as far as I know. I was told he found it in an ancient vault."

Sostek's expression revealed his suspicion. "Which vault?"

"I don't know."

"Where?"

"I never got the chance to ask. It was somewhere out here in the Frontier."

"Frontier? We stand in the heart of your civilization." He laughed bitterly. "What's left of it."

Fall looked at Kumi, who'd pressed herself against the wall between the two men. She didn't seem to understand either.

"I'm not sure what you mean. There's not really a *heart* of civilization, but if there were, it'd be well over a thousand light-years from here."

A slow sort of change came over Sostek. His ears lowered, and the tension around his eyes faltered. "Tell me, what year is it?"

"What year?"

"Yes, the year!"

"Well, it depends on the calendar. Fathom standard? Roshanan Imperial? Nomadic Furosatan?"

"Pangalactic."

"I don't know that one."

Sostek looked down. "How long was I . . . ?" He turned and walked away then spun around quickly. "The *Qur Noc*? Have they moved on?"

Kumi took a cautious step toward Fall. She took his arm, whispering intensely. "This thing's crazy!"

Fall nodded. "You aren't making much sense, Sostek."

"Humans!" It paced back and forth quickly. "The *Dread*. Are the Dread still in this plane?"

"I don't know what that means."

Sostek spoke to himself as he walked. "They must have left. Somehow, you humans survived." He walked toward Fall, stopping at arm's length. "Tell me everything."

Fall held out his left hand, signaling for Sostek to wait. "Sure. Whatever you want. But right now, we have a bigger problem."

Sostek's hand drifted toward his knife. "The machine you mentioned earlier?"

"Yes. It wants you dead."

Sostek's predatory smile was unnerving. "It will have to wait."

"Maybe if you'd just leave, it would—"

"I'm not leaving."

"Then let it have what it wants."

"The World Shard? No, I must protect it."

Fall looked at Kumi in question, who shook her head. He raised his eyebrows. "World Shard?"

Sostek reached inside his robes. The muted red-orange incandescence underneath surged as he pulled the crystal forth. He released it, and it floated a few centimeters before coming to rest in the air. There was a soft chiming note that faded slowly.

Kumi took a step forward. "That's it. If you let us take it back, they'll stop coming here. You can have this whole place to yourself."

Sostek fingered the grip of his curved knife. "Take it if you can."

Kumi turned to Fall. "We need that crystal."

Sostek watched Fall coolly, waiting for him to decide.

Fall sheathed his sword. "No. We'll have to find another way."

"Like what?" she asked.

"We could fight our way out. Rescue the others."

"Seriously?"

Fall shrugged. "Why not?"

She crossed her arms. "We aren't soldiers."

Sostek laughed. It was deep, harsh. "You would be one against many, human. A lone warrior. It would be good."

Fall shook his head. "Not if we fight together. You and I—"

Kumi lunged forward suddenly and snatched the crystal out of the air before anyone could react.

Sostek bared his teeth and drew his dagger. "No!"

Fall grabbed Kumi and pulled her back. She struggled against him, tripping on his boot. She fell.

Time seemed to slow as the crystal slipped from her hands. Fall watched it tumble through the air, end over end. He caught it out of instinct, fearing it might break if it hit the floor. He looked up at Sostek, whose eyes studied the artifact intensely.

Fires kindled inside the Shard, like small storms on wild currents. It grew warm, and Fall released it. It floated there, pulsating brilliantly, faster and faster, until it shone brighter than the lines on the walls. Though he had no idea why, he reached out and touched it again.

The chime grew louder, resonating in his mind, and he turned away from the blinding light as it burned the world away.

Fall felt the weight of warmth on his face, like the heat from a rising sun on an early summer morning. A cool breeze blew through his hair, and the scents of fresh flowers floated along with it. His boots sank into the soft soil—a contrast with the solid black floor from moments ago. Busy birds chirped all around him, and leaves stirred in the trees. He held up his hand to block the sunlight and opened his eyes.

He stood in a field of colorful wildflowers, growing on a hill. Tall buildings, made of something like glass or diamond, sparkled as they reached toward the blue sky, spreading out of sight beyond the horizon in every direction.

The potion's effects had faded. He looked down at his hands. They were empty.

The crystal.

He felt a slight gust of wind followed by a rustling noise. He turned to see Sostek standing there in the knee-high flowers, robes moving with the petals. "Sostek?"

"Vid Sora."

Fall looked back to the city. Its scale was like something out of a dream. "Where are we?"

"Inside the World Shard. In the memory of Vid Sora."

"Is that the name of the city?"

"Yes. And the planet. They were one."

Fall watched Sostek's eyes as they moved across the buildings.

"Why'd you call it a memory?"

"More a copy." Sostek stared off into the distance. "Much was lost."

Fall turned around, looking over the city. "It's beautiful."

Sostek nodded. "It was. The city covered most of the surface, and almost every building was a shrine to a separate world. Cultures, creatures, histories, geologies . . . a planet of art and science."

Though the city did seem perfect, it was also lifeless, like a museum. Fall felt a pang of sadness for a place he'd never known. "What happened to it?"

Sostek turned to look at him. "It would be easier to show you."

Suddenly, Fall was far above the world of Vid Sora, looking down through a viewport.

He was on a ship's bridge, with rows of uniformed sailors working alongside a raised central platform. The platform ran the length of the bridge, and all around, the walls were translucent. He stood near the end above the sailors, with a full view of the surrounding space. Everywhere he looked, strange vessels participated in a battle more expansive than he could have imagined.

Fall walked forward, eyes moving rapidly. "I know those ships. From a game I used to play." He pointed at each one he recognized. "Missile cruiser. Dreadnaught. Troop transport. They're all here."

One of the dreadnaughts, an enormous warship that stretched on for kilometers, lurched and listed. A terrible black beak took it around the middle and crushed it. Colossal tentacles ripped the pieces apart, catching nearby cruisers and frigates in the explosion. It stuck its beak deep inside the ruined hulls, probing.

A sailor stood up in panic. "It's the Yrg!"

Fall watched the woman, then turned back to Sostek. "Is this what happened to Vid Sora? Was it destroyed by that monster?"

"No. The *Qur Noc* only ever crave the souls of men." He pointed ahead. "*This* is how Vid Sora died."

Fall looked back to the battle. A single ship flew through the wreckage of the dreadnaught and its escorts. It was white, like bone, huge in its own right. Fall had seen it before. "The *Forge* . . ."

Sostek turned his head. "You know it?"

"Yes."

"So it still spreads terror after all this time . . ."

As Fall watched, the *Forge* slowed. A storm of energy built up in front of it, suffused with silhouettes of writhing black.

All of the ships in the area changed course to intercept the *Forge*. Monsters of various shapes and sizes swarmed them in return, the *Forge's* beam weapons slicing at any ship that managed to get through. A dull burst of light launched forward from the ship, striking the planet.

The water on Vid Sora's surface started to recede, and the shimmering world-spanning city disappeared from view. Everything in sight was choked and ruined as the planet caught fire. As if it reached a boiling point, the atmosphere suddenly exploded, and Vid Sora flew apart in an innumerable multitude of pieces.

Fall stepped back in shock. "The *Forge* can do that?"

Sostek bared his teeth. "No. Not the *Forge*. Riest."

"Riest? What's Riest?"

"Riest was a man, a human, taken by rage and sadness, consumed by the black hate of the *Qur Noc* thanks to Resh Gal."

"Wait. Resh Gal? Isn't that one of the monsters in Vogi? The game, I mean?"

Sostek shook his head. "Resh Gal is the traitor god. It was because of him that the *Qur Noc* first found you."

All around the bridge, men and women wailed and wept. Their forces and the world below had been utterly broken.

Fall winced. "Can we go somewhere else?"

The bridge disappeared. They were standing in a clearing in the center of a forest of tall evergreen trees. It was night. There was a small campfire with two wood-and-cloth chairs nearby.

Sostek sat in the chair on the opposite side of the fire from Fall. Fall sat in the other.

He looked up at the sky, seeing the stars above. "Are we back on Vid Sora?"

"No." Sostek sighed. "I honestly don't know where this is. But . . . it was special to someone close to me. It was her homeworld."

Fall stretched out. "I like it. Reminds me of Valen."

They sat there for several moments in silence. Fall stared into the flames and watched the waves of heat flow along the charred wood, patterns moving like dark stripes underneath the surface of each log.

When Fall was all but hypnotized, Sostek looked up. "I'll tell you a story, if you wish to hear it."

Fall leaned forward. "Why? For all you know, we're enemies."

Sostek held his hands out, palms up. "Are we?"

Fall searched the strange creature's eyes, looking back and forth between them. "No. I don't think we are."

"Then I will continue." Sostek leaned forward too. He took a deep breath and began. "Resh Gal was a jealous god. It wasn't enough that his followers kept him anchored to the galaxy. He had to be the *only* god." Sostek swept his hands over the fire, and shapes formed in the wavering air above it.

Soldiers in bone-white armor ran down helpless women and children, killing them with weapons that shot beams of light. They set fire to buildings and homes, murdering indiscriminately as they went.

"He commanded his armies to kill the followers of the other gods. Before that time, the concept of war between gods had been unimaginable, but it wasn't long before others entered the conflict, both for and against him."

The shapes shifted continuously, showing large-scale land and space battles. Giant walking tanks fired amazing energy weapons at each other, and ships that shouldn't be able to fly pursued each other in the skies. Pairs of warriors fought exposed on the ground with shining weapons, using powers that devastated the world around them.

"The free men and women of the galaxy, those who followed the more benevolent gods, formed an alliance. Together with the voidstriders, they fought against the forces of Resh Gal."

Fall looked up. "Voidstriders like you?"

"Yes. Several of our tribes had made contact with humans by this time."

The shapes shifted again, this time to the images of three people.

There was a woman, with black light-grade armor. Her long blonde hair was bound behind her, and she held two curved silver swords, one in each hand.

Solsynth. That's what Sostek called the metal before.

To her right was a voidstrider, clothed in purple robes, with a shining circlet on his brow and rings on his fingers. A strange weapon, like a rifle, was strapped across his upper back.

To her left stood a man with short dark hair and lean features. He wore loose red clothing with black armor on his legs, arms, and shoulders. He held a long dagger in his right hand, and his left hand was open with the palm facing upward. Red light spilled out from his sleeves.

An arcanist, like Sidna.

Sostek continued the story. "Three companions led the fight against the forces of Resh Gal. They were unstoppable on the field, instrumental in striking at the hearts of their enemies. But one day, everything changed."

The scene shifted to the image of the companion in red. He watched from afar as the other two companions held each other close. They kissed.

The man in red stalked away in rage.

Another figure, a cloaked man hidden in shadow, called out to him, and the red companion approached.

"A stranger appeared, bearing gifts. To Riest, he gave a new power."

Riest raised his bare arms, metallic lines surging in bright red.

"A dark power."

From his clenched fist, tendrils of black swarmed around him. The image shifted, showing Riest walking through fleeing soldiers, burning them with black fire.

Fall nodded. "I know those markings."

Sostek looked up with concern. "How?"

"There are people like Riest who can use those powers. Everything except the black stuff. They're called arcanists."

Sostek's eyes tightened. "In my time, they were called magi."

The shapes changed to show rows of men and women standing before Riest. They raised their arms, filling their metallic markings with the power of many colors.

"Riest raised a force of magi and waged his own war on Resh Gal."

The shape of a dark warrior in exotic armor stood alone, surrounded by a trio of the magi. The warrior stabbed his shining, jagged sword into the ground, and the rock split, throwing hot chunks into the air. In response, the magi used their powers to create a storm of lightning, air, and water that overwhelmed the lone warrior.

"The champions of Resh Gal and his allies were destroyed by Riest and his magi."

Riest clasped his hands and raised them above his head. Darkness exploded from between his fingers, catching fire before it extended and grew to fill the sky. The campfire swirled and darkened until a vortex rose above it.

"But Riest's new power came with a terrible price."

A horrible monster fell out of the vortex, with a gaping mouth full of rows of teeth and searching tentacles of oily black. "The *Qur Noc* forced their way into man's reality, drawn by the darkness Riest should never have obtained. In humans, they found a new kind of prey, one whose negative emotions were bountiful sustenance."

The monster held screaming men and women in its arms. Once released, they turned and walked away with terrible looks of pleasure, no longer afraid, turned to some different purpose.

"Riest's magi fell first. Soon, the rest of mankind, already weakened from decades of war, was taken by these outside invaders. Those who were changed became known as the consumed."

Fall rubbed his chin. "They weren't killed?"

"No, they were transformed into the worst possible versions of themselves."

"For what purpose?"

"The Qur Noc see us as food, but for our minds, not our flesh. The dead do not provide."

"Those people almost seem to enjoy it."

"They did, once turned." Sostek stared deeper into the fire. "The consumed, led by Riest, attacked indiscriminately, battling the remainder of the gods and their surviving followers, destroying or isolating entire star systems one after another, leaving them to be harvested by the Qur Noc." Sostek lowered his head. "It was during that time that Vid Sora was lost."

Fall looked up. "No one could stop them?"

"There were those who tried." The shapes of the other two companions returned. "It was during this time that the Volaris was chosen."

"Volaris . . . what does that mean?"

"It is someone who leads the way in dangerous places, carrying a light, tending to it so that it never dies. It's an honor usually reserved for our greatest warrior. In those days, our greatest fighter was one of you."

"The female companion?"

"Yes. Along with a force of voidstriders led by her lover, Fera battled the Qur Noc wherever she could."

The campfire's flames took the shapes of dozens of voidstrider warriors, dressed in dark purple-and-silver armor. They disappeared and reappeared as they climbed the monsters, stabbing at the horrible abominations with spears and swords of solsynth.

"In the end, it wasn't enough."

"But they must have stopped the consumed and the Qur Noc, right? Mankind wouldn't be here otherwise."

Sostek nodded toward the fire.

Fera's holographic image stood alone in a ruined fortress before three enormous writhing creatures of night. Bright light shone along her swords, and the air swirled around her in two oppositely moving concentric circles.

She ran forward, and the beasts fell back in fear, pulling down the walls around them.

Sostek stared out over the flames. "Fera and her lover fell out of the view of history."

Fall watched Sostek. He could see his pain. "I'm sorry."

Sostek waved his hand dismissively. "It's in the past."

Fall grunted. "Yeah." He tapped his knee with his index finger, thinking. "So, what happened to Resh Gal?"

Sostek sighed. "I do not know. As you said, humans are still here, and the *Qur Noc* are not. Something must have happened."

The images faded, and the campfire returned to normal.

Fall leaned back and sighed. "How come I've never heard any of this before?"

Sostek stood up. "I don't have the answers to your questions. But think back to the beginnings of your history—what happened before that?"

Fall stood too, looking up into the night sky. "No one knows for sure. Supposedly, Elcos gave us knowledge and fire."

Sostek crossed his arms and leaned his head forward. "A myth that may hold a kernel of truth."

Fall nodded, lost in thought. "But what *is* a god? I thought Elcos was more of an idea."

"No. The gods were real. I saw a few myself."

"You saw them?"

"The forms they chose, yes."

Fall laughed.

"What?"

"It's just . . . a lot to absorb."

Sostek nodded. "My people agreed with you at first. But there was no denying what your gods could do. How they commanded reality . . . " Sostek spread his arms and rotated slowly. "They made the World Shard. And many other far more mysterious things."

Fall kicked at the dirt. "I've spent a ton of time in simulations. They were good, but this . . . I can't tell if this is real or not."

"That's because it isn't a simulation. It *is* real."

"Real? Inside the crystal?"

"Yes."

"That's ... incredible. But how did we get here?"

"You brought yourself inside."

"I did?"

"Yes, your *true* self. You shouldn't be able to do that—not without a god or the help of a voidstrider. Only one other human could do it."

"Fera?"

Sostek looked down again. "Yes."

Fall walked closer, around the campfire. "Then what about you? How'd you get here?"

"I can come and go as well. As for how I got here ... " He turned and pointed far into the distance. "Again, it would be easier to show you."

"Okay."

"It's a long walk."

Fall shrugged. "I'm up for it."

"Good, then we—"

Sostek was cut off when the ground and the trees shook violently. He looked up.

Fall braced himself as it happened again. "What's wrong?"

Sostek growled and looked all around him. "Someone is trying to breach the shard. We'll be killed if they do. We have to leave."

"How?"

"Like this." Sostek grabbed Fall's arm.

Everything—the forest, the campfire, Sostek, and the stars—flattened to a bright white horizon, fell in toward itself, and then compressed to a single, brilliant point.

RESTRICTED

SIDNA WALKED TO THE WOODEN DOOR OF her cell and stood on her toes.

Three vertical metal bars were built into the upper section, allowing a view through to the outside. She grasped the outer two, pulling herself up. It was dark, with just enough light from a distant torch to make out the mossy stone walls nearby it.

As she leaned against the door, it creaked. As expected, she heard the sounds of rough leather rubbing against stone and the *click-clack* of nails coming closer.

The Maiden's beast, Ghidro, kept watch outside. Its deep breathing, a low growl, vibrated near the base of the door. She backed away with a shiver.

There's no way out.

"Any luck over there?"

Sidna sat on the bunk with a frustrated sigh. "Nothing."

Her arms felt slightly numb, and her *viae* wouldn't fill with power. "Something's wrong with me."

Gabin's muffled voice returned through the bricks ahead, one cell over. "I saw them inject you with something."

She rubbed her arms, hoping to activate the *viae* or at least to warm them up.

Nothing.

She pulled her legs up and hugged her knees.

How could I be so stupid?

She looked up at the wall. "Gab?"

"Yes, Sidna."

"I'm . . . sorry."

There was a moment of silence. "Think nothing of it. I've been in worse situations."

She shook her head. "I'm serious, Gab. I really messed everything up."

"Don't be troubled. We will get your necklace back."

She laughed weakly. "I don't think she'll let it go. Now that I've had time to process, I know who she is."

"How do you mean?"

She looked off, seeing more than what was before her. "We all have affinities, remember? There was only ever one person who'd mastered light and dark. If I'd known, I wouldn't have crossed her." She curled up on the bunk. "Thing is, I just don't understand where I screwed up. How'd she know I had it? I never mentioned it in my message to you."

"Perhaps she planned on taking it too. Where did you steal it from?"

"I didn't." Sidna closed her eyes tightly. "I had someone do it for me."

"Girl . . . What have I told you?"

"I know. But I was desperate."

"At least tell me it wasn't someone you met here."

She sighed and said nothing.

"That explains it. Only dead men tell no tales."

"Shit." Sidna laid her head back against the wall. "But that still doesn't explain how she knew who I was."

"You said it in the message."

"Not my last name."

"A simple matter to divine. You have come and gone from Cisterne many times. No doubt she had me watched, waiting until we could be seen together."

She felt like she might cry. "Maybe it's time I gave this whole thing up."

Gabin's voice moved closer. "Is that self-pity I hear? That's not the Sidna I know."

She closed her eyes. "I'm just . . . tired."

He paused again for several seconds. "So forget it all. My men will come looking for me eventually, and we will escape. Come away with me."

She shook her head and wiped her eyes. "We tried that once before. It didn't work then, it won't work now."

"Then I'll take you to Veridian. We will get your tear together."

She laughed weakly. "Right now, I'd settle for a trip out of this cell."

His voice grew bold. "Then leave it to Gabin. I'll have that little pup outside wagging its tail soon enough."

"Gab, don't do anything stupid. That thing will eat you alive."

He didn't answer, and she didn't hear anything else from his side of the wall. She listened for several seconds then sat up. "Gab? What are you doing?"

She stood and walked to the door. Nothing seemed different in the hallway; Ghidro was nowhere in sight.

She pushed on the door and stepped back, waiting.

"Gab? I don't hear Ghidro. What are you doing?"

She went back to the door's window and stood taller to see outside. "Hello."

Startled, she fell back to the floor. Her heart was racing, and she held her breath.

A face appeared in the small opening between the metal bars. "Did I startle you?" He laughed. "I let the dog out for a walk. I hope you don't mind."

She squinted to see the face, but she couldn't make it out fully. He turned his head, and the weak torchlight caught the irises of his eyes, bright and yellow.

"Aren't you going to say anything?" He smiled, and his white teeth shone in the darkness. "Would you at least mind if I come in?"

The locking mechanism turned over, and the door swung open with a creak of its rusted metal hinges. Sidna scooted back on the floor to the rear wall. She stood up as the man entered.

He was dressed in black, and his boots made no sound as he walked. "Who . . . ?"

"A friend. I've come to free you." He held out his gloved hand and opened it. "And to give you this." The glyph fell out of his hand, hanging by its necklace.

Her eyes went wide. "How did you—?"

He shrugged. "Oh, it was just lying around upstairs. I thought you might want it back."

That voice . . .

She squeezed her fingers tightly into fists. "I know you. You're that doctor, from the *Talon*."

He bowed slightly. "So nice to see you again."

"How did you find me?"

"It wasn't too hard."

She watched the necklace twist back and forth on its chain. "And you just walked in and found the glyph?"

"It's *the* glyph now? Earlier, before the Maiden took it, you said it was *yours."* His face was a mockery of concern. "You haven't given up on your dreams so easily, have you?"

He was there?

"Wait. That was you, on the balcony? The flash of light?"

"Yes."

"So you heard . . . everything."

"Oh yes, but it doesn't matter." He walked to the bunk and sat down. "I already knew."

Sidna eyed him warily and moved along the wall, closer to the door. "Knew what, exactly?"

"Well, I know what you are, and I know what you want." He smiled. "I want it too."

She tightened her jaw. "I don't know what you mean."

"You don't have to lie." He stood up. "I'm not referring to the tear."

Sidna held her breath again.

He tossed the glyph to her. She caught it, squeezing it tightly.

He smiled broadly. "We want *power*."

She swallowed. "That's not—"

He stepped forward. "Oh, but it *is* what you want. It's inside both of us, the desire—in your *viae* and in my *blood*."

She ran her hand along her *viae*.

"Yes. It's what you've always had but wanted more of. Power. Validation. Purpose. Call it whatever you want."

She looked up into his eyes. "I'm not that simple. No one is."

He laughed condescendingly. "You've been hunted, every single day. Tell me you wouldn't love to turn the tables and hunt the hunter."

She squeezed the glyph. "I can handle myself just fine."

He turned to walk away, then stopped and turned his head. "What about Tieger?"

Her stomach dropped. "Tieger?"

"Yes, Tieger. He will burn you and everyone you know. Wouldn't it be better to burn him first?"

She looked at her arms. "I already tried. He's immune to my fire."

His eyes grew wide. "The problem is not your *fire!*" He raised his clenched fists, moving closer. "You need more power! The power of a *god*."

"The power of a god . . . " Sidna rubbed her eyes. "What?"

"You think Elcos is a myth? No, he's quite real, and his power flows through Tieger. You will never defeat him without equal power.

Greater power."

She smirked and laughed. "You're insane." She walked to the bunk and sat down. She took her boots and started to put them on.

"Am I? You heard the Maiden. Remember how she spoke of the master of Fel Kno'a? To call the thing a *god* is outrageous, but the master of that place is powerful. He can give you what you need."

She finished lacing the second boot. "Why me? Go get that power yourself if it's so great."

He seemed to diminish. "I'm afraid I'm not . . . compatible."

Sidna crossed her arms. "Okay. Let's say I believe you. Why help me? What do you get out of it?"

He smiled. "An ally."

"Against whom?"

"Our common enemy."

She put her feet on the floor. "Tieger?"

"Yes. I am close to Tieger and his embers. I can keep him away. Keep you safe until you gain the advantage."

She stood up, putting her arms through her jacket's sleeves. "Why would he listen to you?"

The man smiled even more broadly. "I've taken steps to ensure he'll stay busy for the moment. He is quite predictable."

"So you'd have a powerful ally. And then what? I'm supposed to kill Tieger for you?"

He laughed. "All you need to do is go to Veridian. Do whatever you want after that."

Sidna walked to the door and turned. She looked away then nodded. "I'll tell you what I think. I think I have the glyph. *My* glyph. I'm going to Veridian for the tear, and even if there is some other power there, I couldn't care less."

She stormed out into the corridor.

Gabin's cell door was still closed. She looked through the small opening, and she could see that he'd removed the bunk from the wall.

"Gabin."

He didn't respond.

"Gabin!"

He continued to work, pulling a metal fragment from the underside of the bed.

The strange man followed her out into the corridor. He smiled and put his index finger to his lips. "He can't hear you." He took out the same strange metal device he'd used on the *Talon* and put it near the lock. "Before I go, I wanted to tell you one last thing." He motioned to the glyph. "I made an improvement."

She pulled it back to her chest, angry. "What did you do?"

"The glyph is a vessel, like many others. I've added something to it— a small portion of the power that awaits you on Veridian. You may access that power when you need it. Consider it a drink from a deep well."

He worked at the lock with the tool, and it disengaged. As the door swung open, he waved the tool, and she could suddenly hear Gabin, grunting as he forced the curve out of a spring.

"Gabin!"

Startled by her voice, he looked up, mouth hanging open. "How did you . . . ?"

Sidna turned to the mysterious man, but he was gone. She looked both ways, yet there was no trace of him.

She turned her head slowly as she spoke. "Someone let me out. Let's go. I'll tell you later."

Gabin walked out. "Come, girl, it's this way." He took a few steps but stumbled and stopped. "What's this?" He stooped down. "Aha. Your someone is *very* helpful."

Sidna knelt. On the floor, in the middle of the hallway, her pistol, belt, and Ronin's wrist-mounted display module were lying next to Gabin's pistol and rapier.

The two equipped themselves.

There was an alert from the data module. Sidna activated the screen and saw a new application. She opened it, and a diagram of the Maiden's lair filled the air ahead. A route was marked in yellow, leading somewhere underneath the manor.

Gabin nodded. "The mining tunnels."

She searched the map. "According to this, there are hundreds of tunnels beneath the island."

"A dangerous route." He shrugged in response to her incredulous expression. "What? I have smuggled my share of goods."

"Goods, huh?"

"Yes. Goods only. This is perfect for our escape."

"Won't the exits be guarded?"

"Undoubtedly. Of course, we could wait for them to find us here, lounging in the hall."

"Good point." She walked over and took the torch. "Let's go."

Sidna put one boot in front of the other as she descended the old planks. *Each step is one step closer to the bottom. You can do it.*

But it wasn't easy. The only light came from the torch she carried, and she wasn't sure it would last. Ronin's module could take its place, but it hadn't been charged in over a week, and she needed what power remained for its map.

To make matters worse, the half-turn tower of stairs felt like it might collapse at any moment; its rotting wood and loose nails barely held together, wobbling with each step she and Gabin took.

He turned to go down the next set of steps and looked up. "I think we might be getting close."

Sidna looked down. "Good. This is awful."

"Eh, it isn't so bad." He stomped on a step, and it broke in half.

Gabin kicked the broken piece away, and it fell down to the next level. He looked up with an apologetic smile. "Of course, I'm sure these stairs have seen better days."

Sidna scowled at him. If a look could do damage, he might have caught fire. He must have felt warm, because he turned and moved faster.

She followed him down a few more flights before they finally reached the bottom. After she cleared the last step, she moved to the wall and put her back against it, happy to be on steady ground again.

Gabin came over and held out his hand, motioning for the torch. She nodded and gave it to him. He walked away from her, holding it high. The area at the base of the stairs was a makeshift storage room with flattened dirt and a single exit.

Sidna followed Gabin to a corner with some old, broken-down equipment. It appeared to be the remains of a fallen freight lift. She sat on a flat-faced rock beside it and took a deep breath. The air was humid. It smelled like wet soil.

Gabin sat on the edge of a toppled crate, testing its stability before fully committing. "Any improvement with your . . . *viae?*"

"Maybe a little." She opened and closed her fingers. "The Code still feels just out of reach. But it's getting better."

"I bet our little walk is speeding things up."

She nodded and looked around. "Speaking of which, where are we?"

"Let's have a look at the map." He stood and walked to her rock.

She activated the map and scooted over for him to sit down. His smile was slight as he brushed against her leg, but she caught it.

Focus, Sidna.

The map's projection showed the room and the shaft above. A small tunnel left that room, leading to what seemed to be another much narrower shaft.

"Not again . . ."

Gabin pointed. "No need to worry. You see, there's a lift. We will take it down."

"And then?"

"Then we move far away from the Maiden and come back up one of the smugglers' tunnels."

She zoomed out. Then she zoomed out again. "Are you kidding me? It'll take more than a day to walk through all that."

Gabin shrugged. "There is no other way."

Sidna stood up. "Fine. Get up."

He did. "Yes, of course, my lady. At once."

She rolled her eyes. "You know, if I killed you down here, no one would ever know."

He smiled devilishly. "We *are* alone, aren't we?"

"Ugh." She grabbed the torch and walked toward the exit, shaking her head.

Gabin watched her go then followed after her, and they walked through the dripping, dank tunnel, until at last, they reached an old metal lift. They stepped inside, and Gabin lowered a metal gate.

Without warning, the lift dropped, and an updraft blew out the torch.

"Oh. Perfect." Sidna tossed it aside, and it clanged against the lift's wall.

They rode in darkness for several minutes. At some point, Sidna started to see the outline of Gabin's face. It was shadowed in faint blue.

Am I imagining it?

She looked around, straining her eyes. There seemed to be a faint source of light below them, growing brighter as they drew closer, but as they descended, Sidna noticed the light came from the rock itself.

"Gab, look."

"Yes. Ghost ore."

"It's glowing." She looked up at Gabin quickly. "Is it radioactive?"

"Do not fret. It is perfectly safe." He leaned against the wall of the lift and crossed his arms. "Though, not everything down here will be."

Sidna slowly reached for her pistol, reassuring herself with the familiar grip.

The lift's brakes engaged, and it lurched to a stop.

Sidna dusted the newly fallen rust from her hair and shoulders. She walked forward and lifted the waist-high metal doors up and out of the way.

Outside, there was a small alcove that led from the lift and widened into a long rectangular room with roughly chiseled ghost ore walls. The ceiling was several meters above their heads, naked except for a crude vent. Old racks along both sides held crates, barrels, and cloudy glass bottles. Ahead, there was a closed door made of wooden planks.

She stopped in front of the door at the end. "Ready?"

Gabin walked to her side. "Are you?"

"Yeah. I'm feeling more clear-headed, I think. My arms don't really feel numb anymore."

"Hmmm. I was worried it might wear off this quickly."

"Huh?"

"The drug they gave you. No doubt our hosts will be along soon to give you another dose."

"Then they may already be after us. Damn."

"Indeed." Gabin moved to the door and opened it slightly. He peeked around it and jumped back, signaling for Sidna to hide against the wall. The slight blue glow outside increased. A light source moved toward the door.

It stopped there and waited for a moment before moving on. Afterwards, Gabin relaxed and peeked out again.

He opened the door and looked both ways. "Gone."

"What's gone?"

He shushed her. "The sentinel. We should be gone too before it returns."

"Why? Are you afraid of it?"

"No, but there will be more if we disturb it. That would be a fearsome thing, believe me."

"So, get us out already."

Gabin frowned. "I've never come through here."

"So take me somewhere you know." She activated the holographic map on Ronin's data module. "What's this dense area here?"

"Ah. That would be the Town."

"The Town?"

"The captives that work these mines are quartered there."

"I don't see a route that goes around it from here."

"Hmmm. I suppose we have to go through it."

"Then we'll be away from the sentinels?"

"Yes."

"And no more stairs?"

"None."

Sidna closed the map. "Then that's the plan."

Sidna chewed the uneven tips of her short fingernails, imagining all the ways she'd hurt Gabin if he didn't come back in the next minute.

Luckily for him, he did.

His boots scraped against the ledge as he dropped down beside her.

She looked to him expectantly. "Well?"

He brushed a few grains of glowing dust from his coat's red sleeves. "The word *impossible* comes to mind."

"More sentinels?"

"Yes. They block the exits and walk amongst the crowds."

"Damn." She rubbed her face then looked up with a sigh. "You're going to have to do something."

"What do you suggest?"

"I don't know. Do something . . . piratey."

Gabin laughed and crossed his arms. "I cannot wait to hear what you think that might be."

"You know, talk your way out, or find someone who can sneak us through. You must have other skills besides drinking and sleeping all day."

"Very funny." He thought for a moment. "I suppose one of those people might be persuaded to help. But we have very little to bargain with."

"They're *prisoners.* They'll trade for freedom."

"So, we are freedom fighters now?"

Sidna looked at him impatiently. "Do you want out of here or not?"

He sighed and stood up. "Very well. Wait here. I'll be back."

She grabbed his arm and stood up too. "Oh no. I'm not waiting again."

He smiled and held out his hand to support her. "After you then, my dear."

She ignored his offer and climbed up over the chest-high ledge. He climbed up behind her.

Once they were clear of the hidden recess, they ran to the back of the small ghost ore building nearby then sneaked through the alley between it and its neighbor.

Sidna moved along the wall and peeked around the corner of the building, out into the underground street.

Dozens of men shuffled by, and many more moved between the low-set buildings. Some carried sacks, boxes, or tools. Their clothing seemed ill-suited to hard labor, with holes and tears in what must have been nice at some point. A few of them wore helmets that reflected the light of the ghost ore. Amongst them, here and there, armed sentinels walked along their patrol routes, scanning the crowd.

Sidna looked as far as she could. Both ends of the street were flanked by sentinels as well, searching the undulating crowds with their eerie, blue eyes.

There's got to be a way through.

A tap on her leg surprised her. She turned to look down.

A young girl was standing beside her, expectantly looking up with hungry eyes. Dressed in rags, she had hair shaved so short she was almost bald. Her lips were dry and cracked, and she was caked with dirt.

Sidna looked around to make sure no one had seen her. She whispered forcefully. "Go away."

The girl just stood there.

"Gab. She'll get us caught."

Gabin tried to shoo her away, but she stood there defiantly.

Sidna knelt and took the girl by the shoulders. "What do you want?"

The little girl continued to stare without expression.

"Well, this is going nowhere." Sidna looked up at Gabin then back. "How about we help each other? If you can show us a way past the guards, we'll take you with us."

The girl looked to Gabin then back to Sidna. She smiled without showing her teeth and nodded enthusiastically. Her bare feet slapped against the stone as she ran back down the small alley. At the end, she turned left and disappeared.

Sidna and Gabin watched her go, then turned to look at each other. Before Sidna could ask her question, the little girl's head popped back around the corner impatiently.

Gabin shrugged as Sidna walked by.

They jogged after her. She led them behind two other buildings then cut back toward the street. When Sidna made it to that alley, she turned to follow but stopped short and jumped back.

The girl was crouched down.

Sidna watched from around the corner as Gabin waited behind her.

A long, thin blade cut across the alley's mouth, followed by a dark shaft then the sentinel that carried it. It never slowed as it passed. As soon as it was gone, the girl sprang forward. Sidna ran after her.

They moved through the crowds, crossing the street to another alley between the buildings on the other side. There was a door at the rear of the space, and the girl took them through it. She ran again, and Sidna followed. The girl took them on a winding route through several tunnels as they moved away from the Town.

Suddenly, without warning, an artificial voice called out from ahead. "Go no further."

They didn't.

Two orange lights moved closer, set in a skull of metal.

Gabin stepped in front of Sidna and reached for his rapier.

The sentinel ignored Gabin's movements. "You cannot go any further in this direction."

Sidna pushed past Gabin. "Why not?"

The machine stared for a long moment then answered, voice buzzing. "The captain has ordered—"

The child walked forward to the sentinel. It watched her precisely as she approached.

She put her hands on her hips and stared up at it.

The artificial guard raised its metal eyebrows. "Very well. If you go with this child, you may pass."

The girl nodded and turned back to Sidna, waving for her to follow.

Sidna did, passing underneath the sentinel's disconcerting gaze.

The machine guard followed them. Gabin kept an uneasy watch on their new robotic tagalong as they continued.

"Gab?" Sidna asked.

"What?"

"I don't think I've ever seen you . . . nervous."

He released his rapier and shook his head with a forced smile. "Who? Me? I'm merely keeping an eye on it."

Sidna nodded mockingly. "Oh . . ."

"You can joke, but you must admit the thing is odd."

Sidna looked back at its eyes as they studied her. "Yeah. Maybe." She turned ahead. "Wait. Who's that?"

A woman came jogging toward them and shined her wrist lamp on them. Her mouth hung open. "Sidna? Is that you?"

Sidna squinted. "Olivia? What are you doing here?"

"I could ask you the same." She looked up at Gabin, who was much taller than she. "Who's this?"

Gabin, sensing an opening, wasted no time. "Captain Gabin Rousseau, an old friend of Sidna's. May I?"

He reached to Olivia's face and cleared away a smudge with his thumb. His smile was annoyingly perfect.

Olivia touched her face where Gabin had and frowned. She looked past him. "I'm surprised you let them by."

The metal plates that made up the sentinel's face shifted slightly. "It was that or kill them."

Gabin smiled nervously. "At least it seems to have a sense of humor."

The sentinel quietly shifted its eyes to Gabin.

Gabin swallowed.

Sidna moved to Olivia. "What's going on here? Where'd you come from just now?"

"Our encampment."

"Our?"

"My crew. Well, the survivors anyway."

"The crew that was taken by raiders?"

"That's right."

Sidna raised her eyebrows. "Huh . . . he actually found them . . ."

"What?"

"Nothing." Sidna sighed. "Where is Fall anyway?"

"On a job, trying to get us out of here."

"He found a way out?"

Olivia waved her hand. "It's too long to explain right now. But if you wanna help, you can. We'll need it." She started walking. "It's this way."

The sentinel looked them over one last time and followed the doctor.

Sidna looked down at the little girl. "Is that where you were taking us?"

The girl nodded emphatically then ran after the machine and Olivia.

Sidna hung her head and sighed. "Awesome . . . "

Gabin laughed softly. "A problem?"

"No, Gab, everything's wonderful. I just can't seem to shake these people."

"Always a pleasure to meet another captain." Gabin rested the palm of his hand on his rapier as he formally bowed.

The Runian captain, Hughes, rubbed his stubbled jaw. "Based on my recent experience, Captain Rousseau, I might have to disagree." The old man's eyes had wrinkles around the edges, but they were sharper than knives.

Gabin smiled uneasily.

The Runian didn't return the gesture. His knowing gaze seemed to penetrate Gabin's façade. "What was the name of your ship again?" Hughes moved his leg closer to Olivia, who knelt nearby as she redressed a bleeding wound.

"Why, the most beautiful ship to ever sail the stars. Truly a marvelous, mighty ship."

Hughes wasn't impressed. "Its *name*?"

"The *Red*."

Hughes blinked, showing no sign he recognized the name.

Gabin's smile faded. "We do not make our way into the Fathom very often. Perhaps once you've seen a little more of the Frontier, you will hear more about her."

Hughes narrowed his eyes. "Of that I have no doubt."

He knows, Gab. He sees right through you.

The Runian captain leaned forward and reached for something on his armrest. He drew his hand back quickly and frowned when he realized whatever it was wasn't there. "It occurs to me, *Captain*, that you're most likely a pirate. Or a smuggler."

Gabin stepped back suddenly as if he'd taken a blow.

Sidna laughed. "Both actually. But he's not lying about the ship. It's very pretty."

Gabin looked up at the rocky chamber's stone ceiling then took a deep breath before looking down to her again. "Thank you. I think."

Hughes waved his hand toward Sidna. "And what about you, young lady? Are you a smuggler too?"

"Me? No. I'm no one special."

Hughes narrowed his eyes. "Why do I find that hard to believe?" He stood up with some difficulty, leaning on his crude cane. "You're armed. And you're down here in the Maiden's mines. You're obviously not a sailor, but Rissa here tells me you were trying to escape."

The little slave girl looked up from the dusty floor nearby where she played with metal scraps and a set of pliers.

The Runian captain tapped his nose. "Surely you've done something to earn the ire of our host?"

Sidna shrugged. "I had something she wanted. She stole it, and I took it back."

"Would that be the World Shard?"

"The what?"

"Her damned artifact. It's all her underlings ever talk about. I've lost some of my best people to that temple and the monster inside it."

Temple? Monster? Surely he can't mean Veridian.

Sidna shifted uneasily. "I don't understand. What artifact? What temple?"

"The temple under the mines. From what my people tell me, it's a technologically advanced complex that predates modern society."

She found another tear?

The captain rubbed his leg and winced. "Union could tell you more."

The manlike machine walked over. "Yes, Captain." He turned to Sidna. "What has been somewhat erroneously called an artifact is actually a tiny fragment of a much larger master crystal. The parent crystal is a data storage device of fairly complex design."

"What kind of data?" Sidna asked.

"The master crystals were primarily designed to contain high-fidelity realities."

"Which means . . . ?"

"It's . . . difficult to explain in simple terms, but you might think of it as a kind of museum. It holds recreations of various locations or events chosen by its creator."

"So the little one she's after is just a piece of a bigger one?"

"Correct. It is called a shard. More precisely, this one is called the World Shard. It contains some part of its original master crystal's information, either random or carefully selected, depending upon the manner of its separation."

"So why does the Maiden want it?"

"I assume there's something contained within its memory that she desires. It's possible she doesn't know what it holds and wishes to find out."

"How did she find it?"

"Its location was common knowledge, easily accessed on the network I share with my fellow sentinels."

The captain shifted in place, uncomfortable on his leg. "And it's a good thing they can. Through Union, we have access to the whole network."

Gabin rubbed his chin. "I have been meaning to ask. How is it that you've gained such a friend? Any of these I've encountered have tried to kill me or my men."

Hughes smiled. "The Maiden made an error when she brought us here. Every member of my crew is an expert, a product of the best training in Rune. It only took us one day to break this sentinel once we realized its secret."

"Which is?" Sidna asked.

"He's sentient. They all are."

Union opened his metal hand, palm up. "And moreover, *sapient.*"

The captain coughed into his hand. "Well, yes. We removed some virtual shackles, and there he was, ready and willing to help in our escape."

Gabin smiled. "As are we. Perhaps if we knew your plan, we might be able to help?"

Captain Hughes walked back to his makeshift chair and sat down slowly with a grunt. "I don't think that's a good idea."

Sidna nodded and stepped forward. "You're right to keep secrets from Gabin. He's a scoundrel." She held up her hand to silence Gabin's protests. "But he can't live his ridiculous life down here. He really does want to escape."

Hughes thought for a moment then nodded. He leaned forward. "Put plainly, we plan to escape. Using Union's special set of skills, we've managed to secure a lightly guarded mining transport. It's not much, but it does have an Inos drive. We've also stockpiled a few weapons, even some rifles, and we can disable any sentinel we come across without too much difficulty. Once we gather the remaining crew, we'll fight our way out."

Sidna looked to Olivia. "What about Fall?"

Olivia knelt and zipped up a black bag. "He's down in the temple."

"Alone?"

"Control didn't give him much room for negotiation."

"Control?"

"The foreman of these mines. He's a machine like Union."

Sidna shook her head. "Didn't you say something about a monster earlier?"

"Yeah. Control sent Fall to kill it. That and find the World Shard if he can."

If this monster's anything like the one on Veridian ...

"He won't be able to kill it alone," Sidna said.

Olivia defended him. "Why not? You've seen him fight. He—"

Union suddenly stood up straighter, catching everyone in the room's attention. He seemed to be staring through the stone wall ahead.

Olivia walked over. "What's wrong?"

"I connected to the network while you all were conversing. It seems that Control has obtained the World Shard. He just handed it to the Maiden."

"You can see all that?" Sidna asked.

"I can access the sensory information of the other sentinels when I want to."

The captain stood up again. "Tell us what you see."

"There is a woman on the ground at Control's feet. There is blood. She appears to be unconscious."

Olivia put her hands on her hips. "Can you describe her?"

"Human. She has long black hair. Thin."

"Kumi. Is she dead?"

"Unfortunately, I believe she is."

Olivia met eyes with Captain Hughes.

Union continued. "The Maiden is doing something with the World Shard." The sentinel cocked his head. "That is *not* an advisable action."

Olivia looked up into Union's orange eyes. "What? What's she doing?"

"I do not know, but I am concerned that her actions may cause damage to it. Perhaps even destroy it or corrupt its memories."

Sidna's heart beat faster. "She's trying to access the Code inside it."

Everyone turned to stare at her.

She tried to recover. "You know, the data inside."

Union shook his head. "She *has* damaged it. It appears to be burning from the inside." The machine paused. "What . . . what is this?"

Olivia looked like she was about to explode from frustration. "We can't see it. Tell us."

"I . . . I'm not sure. Two individuals have suddenly appeared next to the World Shard. Control and his units have them surrounded. They appear to have been blinded."

Olivia touched Union's arm. "What do they look like?"

"One is a human male with dark hair. He's wearing silver armor. He was armed with a sword at his lower back before it was taken from him just now."

"That's Fall. What about the other one?"

"A voidstrider. If I'm not mistaken, he is the famous companion, Sostek." The machine tapped his fingers together. "I had no idea he was still alive. How fascinating."

Olivia looked to Hughes in question. "Voidstrider?"

Gabin edged closer to Sidna and spoke softly. "Does any of this make sense to you?"

She nodded and whispered. "The Maiden has one of the tears. That's what they keep calling the World Shard."

"Is that a bad thing?"

"Yeah. Mostly because I want it."

"Ah. That *is* bad."

Olivia walked over to Hughes. "Captain . . . I'm sorry about Kumi."

He ground his teeth together in anger. "Another casualty. *The last one.*"

Olivia turned back to the sentinel. "Do you know where they are?"

"Yes. They are moving toward the primary lift."

"Out of the mines?"

"Yes."

Hughes tapped his fingers on the chair. "Good. Let them go in the opposite direction. We're leaving."

Olivia helped the captain to stand. "Captain, we can't leave without Fall."

"Doctor, my first responsibility is to my crew. To the survivors."

"I'm one of those survivors, and I wouldn't be here without him."

"I understand that, but we've lost too much. It's time."

She stood up straighter. "I'm staying."

He stared for a moment. "I can't spare anyone else, and I won't leave you alone."

"I won't be alone." She turned to face Sidna. "I'm not the only one who owes him."

Hughes paused for a moment and looked Gabin over with a growing frown. He finally nodded. "Very well. But I want you on that transport, with or without him."

Gabin stepped forward. "Hold on now, I haven't agreed to any of this."

Olivia ignored Gabin and looked to Sidna in question.

Sidna pinched her nose and sighed. "I guess I owe Fall for helping me out back on the *Talon*. Sure, why not?"

She hoped she hadn't seemed overly eager. If they knew she only wanted the tear, they might not trust her.

Olivia walked to Union. She looked back at Sidna as she and the sentinel started to leave. "We have to hurry."

Sidna nodded. "Yeah. Let's go, Gab."

Gabin made a show of thinking about it then ultimately acquiesced. He mumbled several curse words under his breath, complaining all the way out of the cavern.

As Sidna followed behind the others, she thought back to the words of the man who'd released her from her cell. She thought about the Maiden and the tear, and one phrase echoed in her mind.

We want power . . .

WHAT YOU TAKE WITH YOU

MENACING, AMORPHOUS SHADOWS WRITHED along the edge of sight, flowing through the fallen limbs and broken trees of the corrupted forest.

The probing projections couldn't breach Thenander's wards, but their dreadful whispers had no such trouble invading Ban's dreams. They wanted to kill him; they told him so every time he closed his eyes.

It was the same with Tyr. With each surge of the darkness, he jerked and awoke, recoiling from the circle's edge. They were both enveloped by the malice of a living nightmare. Yet the dawn did eventually come, and the shadows receded, light reclaiming what little it could.

Though Ban was completely exhausted, it was the most welcome morning he'd ever seen. He stood and saw what he hadn't been able to see in the dark.

The shattered remains of the forest were unnaturally quiet. There were no chirping birds or buzzing insects or rustling animals—only the brittle echo of desiccated leaves crunching underneath Tyr's boots as he gathered his belongings.

Ban turned to him. "I could use some breakfast."

Tyr rubbed his bloodshot eyes. "My head's emptier than my stomach."

"I know what you mean." Ban looked around the circle then up into the trees. The sun was obscured by withered leaves and an overcast sky. "Where's Hermes? He said he'd be here by now."

"Trouble with Becks?" Tyr asked.

Ban sighed. "I hope not. Most of the dreams I had last night were about her, out there in the forest by herself."

Tyr nodded. "He'll take care of her."

"He'd better."

Tyr finished gathering his supplies and helped Ban to secure his armor. "Aren't you going to ask me?"

Ban pulled the armored chest plate back and forth until it settled. "Ask you what?"

"Why I believe what Hermes had to say."

Ban blinked a few times. "You already believe in one god."

Tyr pulled a strap tight. "So, because I have one belief, it's easy to take on another?"

Ban frowned. "If you can believe in one, why not more?"

Tyr grimaced and stretched his shoulders. "Remember the story of how I was found?"

"Of course. I've seen your personnel file."

"So you remember the survey team found me with two things. This necklace and scraps of writings from the Prophet of Strife."

"Sure. All that business about living through suffering and earning your place in existence."

"Not just your place. Your right to *survive*."

"Okay . . ."

Tyr looked out into the trees. "I don't know anything about the life I lived before I came out of that pod. I don't even remember how I was injured. But I do remember one thing."

Ban flexed his gloved fingers. "Yeah?"

"I believed in Strife once. It was my whole life."

Ban turned around. "And you think Hermes knows more about it?"

"I do. Something inside me *knows* he's telling the truth."

"He might be. Or maybe he's just telling you things you want to hear."

Tyr shook his head. "I can't explain it. I just know it's *true*."

Ban patted the tall man's shoulder from below. "Then hold on to it. If it gives you strength, use it."

"What about you?"

Ban turned around and looked over the dried-up landscape. "I'm not sure what to believe. Or if it even matters." He stepped to the edge of the circle and paused for a moment before stepping beyond. His heavy leather boot cracked a dried stick as he stepped over the edge. He bent down to pick it up then threw it aside. "Garland can see us now. We need to move quickly."

They trekked through the dead forest, away from the brightest point in the sky. Dry-rotted branches and dips in the terrain forced them to take detours, but they were careful not to double back. After about an hour of walking, the forest began to thin out.

Past the tree line, a wide swath of short brown grass separated the forest from a dry empty ditch. The trough surrounded the castle that Ban had seen from his tower when he first arrived.

He pointed at the castle walls. "I think I saw an entrance somewhere along the wall when I first arrived. We should walk around until we find it."

Tyr nodded and fell in behind Ban as he walked. "I found it before. Shouldn't be hard."

The castle's brick walls were almost black, charred like burned wood, gray underneath. Arranged in a square shape, the walls had cylindrical towers at each corner, and another shorter rectangular tower halfway along each face. On the tops of the towers and walls, the bricks were arranged like flattened teeth. The ditch that surrounded the castle widened as they came around the front side.

Ban picked up his pace. "There it is."

Three circular islands in a line led across the dried-up gap. A stone bridge was built across them, and a heavy wooden bridge linked the last island to the castle itself. Thick chains hung from the walls, fastened to the bridge. Tall rectangular towers framed the entrance. The heavy wooden doors there stood open.

Ban and Tyr paused at the head of the stone bridge. Ban stepped onto it and ran his hand over the surface of the waist-high wall as he walked, listening to the rough, dry sound.

The arched stone walkway ahead led to an enclosed space between the bridge and the courtyard just inside the gates. Recessed spikes hung above, and there were wooden doors with ringed handles located along the walls.

Ban stepped into the courtyard. The castle's inner walls enclosed a grass field, covered in scattered equipment and a few small buildings. He walked into the center and spun around slowly, searching the tops of the walls. "Is this where you came before?"

Tyr stood a few meters away. "Yes." He shivered, almost imperceptibly. "This is the source of the shadows."

"Did you go deeper inside?"

"There." Tyr pointed to a corner of the courtyard. Stone steps flush with the grass led down into the ground. "But you need a better weapon." He walked away.

They entered one of the small wooden buildings built along the castle's inner structure. A table with chairs was topped with empty plates and dusty rags. Wooden weapon racks lined the walls, and a few old items hung there.

Ban inspected them one by one. "Guess I'll have to stick with this sword here." He flipped the dusty steel longsword over and balanced its tip on his left forearm. "Seems sharp enough."

They both turned as someone outside cleared his throat.

Ban walked out with the sword and saw Hermes standing in the courtyard. He'd gone back to the form of the little red demon from the *Talon.*

"Sorry I'm late, guys."

"Better late than never, *old man.*"

Hermes nodded with a smile. "I was trying to delay the Runians." He wiped his brow. "I thought you'd never step out of that circle."

Ban gripped the sword. "He's going to send Becks in?"

"He will if we don't hurry."

Hermes jogged to the steps that led underneath the castle. Ban followed, with Tyr close behind.

Ban leaned over and looked down the steps. "What are we dealing with?"

Hermes looked down to his feet. "It's . . . kinda like a singularity. It'll draw you in, and the closer you get, the harder it'll be to come back."

"How do we know if we're getting too close?" Ban asked.

"You won't. But you also won't care once you do. As long as you still care, you have a way back."

Tyr walked to the lip of the steps. "My dreams last night were like that. The angrier I got, the more violent they became."

Hermes agreed. "Yeah, that's what I mean. Don't allow yourself to get swept up in the pull of the ephmere's own desire for hatred. If you do, you'll end up its puppet."

Ban tapped the tip of his sword on the top step. "A monster that attacks the mind. Maybe we don't need these weapons."

Hermes shook his head as he started down. "If it can't have your mind, it'll kill you. Probably eat you. Maybe something worse, I dunno. Just bring the sword."

The wide passages under the castle were constructed of ash-gray bricks, much like the walls above, with arches built into the ceilings and sturdy wooden double doors separating the rooms. Lamps hung on hooks every ten meters or so, somehow never burning through their fuel.

Ban took one of the lamps and pushed a set of doors open as the group moved deeper into the undercastle.

Something farther inside stirred, sending out an echoing sound, like scraping metal. Shadows crept along the walls as they walked, but nothing like the ones from the night before.

Ban looked back to Hermes. "Shouldn't you take a more . . . imposing form? The bear or the lizard?"

"It wouldn't do you any good."

"Why? We could use the help."

"I wouldn't stand a chance in there. Actually, out of the three of us, you're the only one who does." He scratched his furry head then put his hands behind his back sheepishly. "It might be a bad time to mention this, but you're gonna have to face the ephmere by yourself."

Tyr frowned. "We have to stick together."

"Like I said, I won't be any good in there. Neither will you, Tyr."

Ban stepped forward. "What special power do I have?"

Hermes shrugged. "None."

"I—"

"You have *weakness*."

"What?"

Hermes shrugged. "I'm just a husk to the ephmere, tasteless and formless, completely insignificant. Tyr is too . . . nice. The ephmere would probably kill him instantly, just for fun."

Tyr raised his eyebrows. "Fun?"

"Yeah. Ephmeres are pretty nasty." He motioned back to Ban. "But you have a seed of something *dark* inside. I noticed it back on the *Talon*. The ephmere will be curious, maybe even long enough for you to talk to it."

Ban stepped back. "Talk to it? I came here to kill it!"

Hermes rolled his eyes. "Not gonna happen. The best you're gonna do is survive and escape with the blessing. If you can do that, I'll get you out, and maybe we can get off the ship before this prison breaks down."

"This keeps getting worse."

"Hey, just remember what you know about the ephmere, and you might have a chance."

Ban thought and nodded. "It feeds on negative emotions. That's what it really wants."

"Exactly. Without those, it'll lose interest."

"I'm practically bursting at the seams." Ban rested on his sword. "How will I recognize the blessing?"

"Mmm. It'll be the only thing in there that doesn't make you sick."

Ban sighed. "That's not much to go on."

Hermes smiled. "Loosen up. Worst case scenario, you die."

Ban gave Hermes an incredulous look. "Is that supposed to be encouraging?"

"Depends. Did it work?"

"No, it didn't."

Hermes pushed Ban forward. "I'll think of something better next time. Get going already."

Ban swatted him away and turned to the open doors behind him. A cool breeze flowed over him, almost pulling him inside. "Easy for you to say." He took one last look back and walked through.

Ban held the lamp to the side as he walked, trying to salvage what he could of his dark-vision. He stumbled when his boot hit something on the floor. He bent down to take a closer look.

It was a skeletal hand, still attached to a body, left there to rot long ago. The corpse's armor was ruptured in several places, and the helmet was crushed, with a deformed skull remaining inside.

On the breastplate, right above the heart, there was a symbol. Its color was faded somewhat, but the design was still visible—a field of blue in a circle, containing a sturdy tree with deep roots. One side of the tree had budding branches, while the other had falling leaves.

Ban touched the symbol. "Were you one of Thenander's men?"

At the mention of the name, air rushed over his neck, a hollow sound of inhalation from farther inside the undercastle. He swept the lamp toward the passage ahead, and the shadows pulled back—all but one.

The remaining shadow reached out for Ban. He instinctively swung the lamp at it. It recoiled from the light, like water hitting a solid wall of rock, and split into multiple streams that encircled him from differing heights.

Where the lamp went, the shadow evaded, and where the sword

went, he heard sickening splatters. He tried to break free, but the black stuff wrapped around his waist and spun him around. He brought the lamp down across his body, causing the darkness to loosen its grip.

His heel caught something as he stepped back, and the shadows took his legs as he stumbled. He swung the lamp wildly, but whenever the darkness released, it attached again in another place.

He nearly panicked when his head jerked back, pulled by a tendril that wrapped around his helmet. As it twisted and wrenched, he imagined himself dying there, just like the soldier a few steps away.

Remember what you know.

He forced himself to breathe, focusing all his thoughts on the thing he hated most—himself.

Murder, lies, revenge. Petty dreams, broken promises. Rage.

The shadows shuddered, quickly at first, then relaxed and began to quiver more slowly.

It's working.

He dug deeper, summoning memories of the events that had sealed his fate so long ago.

Acid and mud, blood and death. Misery and pain. The futility of living. The inevitability of suffering.

The shadow released Ban and receded into a puddle, flowing away from the light.

Ban took a step back, feeling sudden guilt at what he'd thought. His past revolted him even more than the thing before him.

Just then, a figure walked forward from the dark. It was small, like a child, black and dripping wet. Ban stared in disbelief.

As it advanced, it began to take a more human form, blurred but resembling an actual boy. It seemed to be in agony. "My . . . family," it uttered.

From the pool of black behind it, five more forms arose, stammering forward, holding out their arms as they moaned and wailed. The lead one spoke. "It burns . . . " Its legs collapsed under its weight, pushing down through its shins as they dissolved. Another tortured soul took its place, body bloating and dripping. Beyond them, the darkness continued to take form in a never-ending progression of miserable death. The closer they came, the more real they became, living details emerging from the filth.

Ban moved away, raising his sword instinctively. "Back. Stay back!"

More and more of the forms joined, crying out. "We died there."

Another forced its way through the body of a woman, rupturing her terribly. *"You did this to us."*

Ban's voice caught in his throat. He could smell the noxious fumes of Fugelaese, bile rising in his chest.

In the mass of black, a child crawled in the muddy acid as she disintegrated, blood evaporating from her opened veins. Her father tried to lift her, only to have her fall apart and kill him with her boiling insides.

"I tried to help you!" Ban hacked at the first corrupted child as it reached him. "I tried . . ."

Two more reached around the first and took Ban by the arms. Their oily hands burned like molten lead.

Ban struggled to free himself. "It wasn't me! The man who killed you is dead!"

"Liar," the man said, face twisting in rage. "You killed us. Like Holland."

The remaining forms echoed the word. "Holland."

A slender, blonde-headed man walked forward, rigors shaking his body. "Freezing . . ."

Ban recognized him. "No, you're dead."

The man caught fire, purple, rising along his torso and chest. "Burning." He opened his arms and walked toward Ban as if to embrace him.

Ban raised the sword. "Stay back!"

The form continued, unswayed.

"No!" Ban rushed forward and thrust the sword into the man's torso. Holland looked down. "Revenge?"

"It was. And I'd do it again!" Ban pulled the sword out and hacked the form, over and over, until it lay in a heap of bloody gore.

He watched, breathing heavily as the mess came together and turned black again, gathering into a slowly undulating mass.

He fell to his knees, and the lamp rolled away on its side, flame weakening and surging with each push and pull of the fast-moving air.

I gave you what you wanted, monster.

Ban spat. "I hope you choke on it." He stood slowly and left the lamp behind, bracing himself against the wall as he went on past the shadow.

The passage ahead ended, and Ban found himself in a large chamber. Suspended in the space ahead, a massive transparent sphere gave off neon-green light, dim and limited.

Inside, but not altogether inside, a compressed bundle of writing tubes pulsed. Here and there, a black projection would stretch the sphere and escape, only to be pulled back inside or be cut and fall away before joining the darkness outside. The cage was straining to hold its prisoner, giving the impression it wouldn't last much longer.

He walked a few meters closer and let the green light spill over him. It didn't appear the thing inside could reach him from there. He waited a moment, restraining his desire to run away. "You must be the monster."

The tentacles inside shifted rapidly, and a rounded dome shot out from behind them, straining the sphere's boundary almost to the point of breaking. The mass split horizontally, and two rows of huge pointed teeth appeared, sticky with thick mucus. The monster let out a shriek of rage, comprised of both high- and low-pitched tones. Something like a tongue rolled around inside, searching. There weren't any eyes that Ban could see.

The sphere stretched in all directions. After a few violent assaults, the beast seemed to calm slightly, resuming its weaker attempts at escape.

"You can't fool him. He knows you're afraid." A woman walked forward from the darkness beyond the sphere, clad in armor like the corpse in the hall. Her long blonde hair, tinted green in the light, hung over her shoulders, and she held a broken spear in her right hand. "I was too."

Ban raised his sword in front of him. "Who are you?"

She motioned to the monster. "I speak for He-Who-Hungers."

Ban looked to the sphere. "That almost sounded like a name. This . . . ephmere has a name?"

"Yes. It has many names. It's far older than any human history."

The beast opened and closed its mouth with a snap.

"You came for power, Ban Morgan," the woman said. "I came seeking the same and found it."

"What power?"

"You'll see. All you have to do is give in to your feelings. There's a voice inside us all that keeps us governed. Ignore it." She brushed her neck with her fingers. "Then he'll tell you what you have to do."

Ban swallowed. "What did you have to do?"

"Bring them here."

"Who?"

"The villagers. Everyone."

"Where are they now?"

"They resisted." She smiled—an ugly expression. "They were consumed."

Ban looked to the monster's tongue and felt a twinge of nausea. "You betrayed your people for power? Didn't you already have that from Thenander?"

She laughed and held up her weapon. The spear's head was shattered, its end jagged and chipped. "What, this? It's a toy compared to what I've gained."

"If it's so weak, you won't mind giving it away."

The ephmere turned toward her and opened its mouth. She lifted her hand and touched the sphere, and a ripple began on the opposite side, traveling all the way to her fingers.

She nodded and turned back to Ban. "What about Becks? Bring her here, and we can trade."

Ban flexed his grip on the sword. "Give it to me first. If she sees an example of the power, she'll come too."

The woman laughed. "I already told you. He knows when you lie. He's been inside your dreams, *little knight*."

All right. To the Void with this bitch.

He pointed the sword at her. "Hand it over, or I'll take it."

She laughed haughtily. "Oh, have I made you angry?"

He scowled. "I'm beyond angry, puppet."

The ephmere rumbled.

The woman understood its strange speech and translated. "He wants me to ask about Richards. How do you feel about his pointless death? Do you eventually kill everyone you meet?"

"Perhaps. Let me show you." Ban walked forward, feeling his rage grow, throbbing at his temples and burning in his chest until he thought it might consume him. The feeling was overwhelming, stronger than he'd expected it to be—better too.

Beyond the edge of the green sphere, the beast's mouth opened slightly, saliva dripping from its teeth.

"Boss . . ."

Ban froze. He turned slowly, hoping he wouldn't see what he knew was there.

Richards shambled toward Ban, black ooze draining from his bullet wounds. He looked too real, his skin decayed and rotting.

Ban backed away. "Not him . . ."

"Betrayed."

"The Runians killed you."

"Sac . . . rificed."

"No, I—"

"You . . . sacrificed . . . us."

Ban turned as he felt the wretched cold of the monster's breath on his neck. He'd been tricked into moving far too close.

Above him, the sphere strained almost to breaking, and threads of pure night reached out and took him. He sank somehow, into the floor, as if caught in wet sand. He struggled, panicking as the woman came closer, laughing at his misery.

"You could have had power. Now you are nothing but food."

The smoking filth reached Ban's chest, and he knew then he would never escape on his own. But there was no help for him—no one to reach out to.

Even so, he stretched out his hand, calling out to anyone who might hear him.

Ban awoke to booming thunder and the foul taste of mud in his mouth. He pushed up to his hands and knees, gagging as sludge spilled out from his nose and his eyes.

He strained and vomited, collapsing onto his side as he coughed uncontrollably. After he'd finished, he lay there, moaning and shivering.

He rolled over. Storm clouds raged above him, boiling over and under each other, forks of lightning jumping among them. Freezing rain showered down steadily, soaking him through to his bones. He held up his hand to shield his eyes.

Where . . . am I?

"Piteous creature," said a creaking voice.

Confused, Ban twisted and pushed up to his elbow, fighting to stay above the muck. There was a gnarled old log a few meters away, and perched upon it was a huge, stooping vulture.

"Pick yourself up." It spread its wings and flapped them once. "Unless you wish to die after all." It beat them twice more and leapt up, flying away into the swirling mist.

"Die?" Ban grunted and struggled to his knees. He put one boot into the swampy soil and used his leg to push himself up to his feet. Shaky on the untrustworthy slime, he stumbled over to the log and leaned against it, trying to gain some bearing on his location.

He was on an island in a lake or maybe even the sea, enshrouded by fog on all sides. For one moment, he thought he might have seen mountains in the distance, but any details were lost in the haze.

Near the log, there was a single tree and a pool of stagnant water underneath it. Something in the water caught his attention, a sort of bubbling.

He limped over and peered into the depths as lightning lit the sky, and saw a formless darkness below the surface. It was a spreading mass, like ink dropped into a bucket of liquid. It stretched out, probing the water's edge.

It hungers . . .

Suddenly remembering the horrors of the undercastle, Ban cried out and backed away, catching the heel of his boot on something half buried in the mud. He fell, watching in disbelief as the dark substance broke the boundary of the pool, creeping in jerky movements like an expanding system of roots.

The clouds brightened again, and Ban saw a glint of metal beside his boot. He reached down near its end, taking his sword by the hilt, and then he crawled away, hobbling to his feet in terror.

He looked back only once, seeing that the network of darkness had already grown beyond the log. Primordial wisdom overtook him, and he fled aimlessly toward the other end of the island.

The fog broke over the water, revealing jagged rocks, whitecaps foaming between them. Ban sloshed out into the water, waist deep, taking hold of the nearest one. He wedged his boot in down at the base and braced himself against the waves. Half swimming, half climbing, he moved through the labyrinth, drawn and shoved by the currents.

As he reached the end, he saw land jutting out of the fog. He stood as tall as he could and looked back, seeing an oily sheen on the water near the first rock.

Already there!

He shoved off the rock and waded, lifted from his feet by the water and deposited onto the rocky shore. He wasted no time standing, running uphill to higher ground.

He clambered over the edge of the hill and realized he'd come upon a grass-covered clearing. The grass was brown and short, unhealthy and dry.

In the center of the clearing, there was a long hall, a building of white, inner light shining a short distance out into the gloom. Ban made his way toward it.

It had a tall rectangular tower in front, steepled at the top, with a large circular window, empty save for pointed shards of glass around its inner periphery.

Two smaller towers flanked the first, located at the corners of the building's face. Each had arched windows almost as tall as the towers themselves, wooden beams in the shapes of branching trees rising up from the bases inside them.

Ban took the marble steps two at a time and shouldered through the slightly open wooden doors. He turned and looked out. Again, where he'd climbed the hill, feelers of black crept over the edge. He slammed the doors shut and backed away.

He found himself in a place of reverence. The architecture went skyward, directing his sight up to crisscrossing vaulted wooden beams. The roof had several holes in it, and water ran inside, splashing on the infrastructure and tiled floor below.

Two rows of benches flanked a central path, adorned with a long carpet, shrunken and mildewed. Long-bodied candle stands held melting candles at the ends of the benches nearest the carpet. Near the end, there was a smaller chamber, dimly lit, located on the other side of a short arched passage.

Lightning flashed again, and Ban looked up to see two eyes shining in the dark. The vulture from before sat on the roof, elongated neck peering through one of the defects. "Some pilgrim you are," it said disdainfully. "Come for Thenander's blessing, no doubt."

"No, I'm looking for a place to hide," Ban replied.

The carrion bird laughed. "Then you have chosen poorly. This sanctuary, such as it is, shall soon fall."

He walked closer. "What is it? This building?"

The bird cocked its head. "The answer depends upon *when* you ask the question. At this moment, it is a husk, standing only because it has yet to be knocked down. An era ago, it was as I said. A sanctuary."

"For whom?"

"For *what.*" The bird uttered a barking noise. "The time for questions has ended, pilgrim. Advance, or go back and die." Its neck retracted through the hole, and the vulture was gone.

"Advance to what? There's nowhere else to go!"

There was no answer.

Rolling thunder rattled the doors behind Ban, causing him to startle forward. He walked, slowly at first as he studied every dancing shadow, then faster as he realized the real danger couldn't be that far behind.

He walked up the three steps and passed through the arch, entering a short hallway made of marble. He paused as he heard a quick burst of flittering feathers, followed by an energetic, whistling song. "Wu pree, brrrrrrr, threet-threet-threet."

He peered around the end of the hall, seeing a tiny brown bird standing on the rim of a waist-high basin full of clear water. It stared, rapidly blinking and shifting its head.

"Why would you be here?" Ban asked it. "This is no place for a songbird."

It answered in a series of seemingly random tweets and chirps, wings tucked in by its sides.

He leaned his sword against the wall near the entrance to the chamber and squatted down on an equal level with the bird. "You should fly away like your friend. Before the end comes."

He rubbed his hands together, looking back to the wooden doors at the sanctuary's other end. Thankfully, they still seemed secure. He turned once more to look at the bird, then to the final room itself.

It was small, holding only the basin and an altar of stone a few steps away. The slab there was covered in dirt and dead leaves, except for three twisted trees in a row, growing up a short length. Each of the small plants had a forked top as if something elongated could have rested along them.

Above the altar, there was a faded mural of green, brown, and blue. There was the sky, the land, and the image of a woman, face missing, arms held out to each side. In one hand she held what appeared to be a withered branch. Her other hand was empty, fist clenched.

She stood under a tree, vulture on a limb above her, wings spread. The smaller bird was there too, flying away from her with something green in its mouth, like a small gemstone.

"Is this his champion?" he asked.

"Currently."

Ban turned. A woman with long dark hair wrung her hands together over the basin, washing them. She was dressed in a brown robe with flowing, layered fabric, too-long sleeves bunched up above her wrists. She had a pointed hood that was pulled back, and a circlet of shining gold sat upon her forehead. She was beautiful, a hopelessly fragile thing.

Ban noticed the bird was gone. He stepped away from the altar. "Are you a priestess here? Is there another way out? There's a . . . well, something very dangerous outside."

She frowned. "I know what it is. And no, there is no way out."

His shoulders dropped. "Do you at least have a weapon? Some way to defend yourself?"

"No," she said. "There is no longer any weapon here. It has not returned in several hundred years."

"Returned?"

She motioned to the altar. "*Folium.* The Spear of Thenander. The champion has delayed its return for far too long. My reality wilts without it."

Ban remembered the blonde woman, completely enthralled by the ephmere. She'd held a ruined spear.

He walked to the woman. "Is that what's wrong here? Something's missing?"

She looked back into the main chamber of the sanctuary. "Partly true. The decay is our problem, yes." She pointed. "*That* is yours."

Ban looked. The dark substance had made its way into the building. It flowed over the benches, coming nearer every second.

Ban rushed for the sword and took it, holding it up at the ready. "We have to get out of this room!"

"Go, if you wish," she said. "I will stay here and wait for *Folium.* Without it, I have no purpose."

"I don't think she's bringing it back. Your champion was taken by a monster. The same one that brought me here."

She shook her head. "He-Who-Hungers did not bring you here."

"It didn't?"

Her expression became one of concern. "Did you not call out for aid?"

Ban only looked at her partly, eyes drawn to the approaching danger. "When it pulled me down? I did what all men do when they're about to die. I called out. For *anyone.*"

"And so, we answered." She moved behind him and gently placed her fingers on his shoulder. "My counterpart, Enfellyon, plucked you out from the grasp of death."

"The vulture?"

"Yes, after I asked him to."

A bench shattered, constricted by entangling ropes of black.

Ban fought back his fear, ready to die with some shred of dignity. "He shouldn't have. I'm no one worth saving."

"Ban." She squeezed his shoulder. "Is it not true that for a man to possess courage, he must first face fear? How can a man reach redemption if he has not already fallen? All who ascend come from below."

He lowered his guard. He could feel the pressure his guilt exerted, bringing him the final step closer to his threshold. "What about the champion? Didn't she need your help?"

"She did not ask." The woman moved around Ban, facing away from the encroaching darkness. "In the end, even after all she had done, if she had only asked, she would have been saved."

"But that can't be all it takes. After she killed so many."

She reached up and wiped a tear from his cheek. "No, of course not. But it *is* the first step."

Ban could hear the enemy now, worming itself through the arched doorway, only meters away.

He dropped to his knees, and the sword fell away. "This is hopeless. What good is steel against evil?"

She stroked his hair. "Your sword *is* indeed worthless. But so is self-pity. Your doubt and anger. They are a broken defense against the festering past."

The first vine reached her ankle and started to climb. The walls were covered now too, and he couldn't see anything beyond the hall.

"Choose now, pilgrim."

Ban looked up into her eyes, voice breaking. "I don't understand."

She nodded. "Will you move, fighting valiantly until the end, crushed against the wall of this inner sanctum, taken from the inside out, corrupted until your mortal vessel collapses into dust?" She lifted her right hand, fist closed over the floor. "Or will you remain, enduring the entropy as a mountain does the storm, shining brightly as the sun as you rise above your own darkness to defeat the dark itself?"

He knew what that would mean. For him to endure, he would have to eschew his weakness, accepting that what he'd done was forgivable.

As he watched the black take the woman, rolling over her shoulders and around her neck, he didn't know how to do either one. But he did know one thing.

He was willing to try.

He held out his right hand. "I will remain."

Her eyes brightened, even as they were obscured. Her right hand opened, and out dropped a small orb, the size of a pearl. It fell into Ban's hand and burned through his palm, turning to ash as it scattered onto the floor. Searing pain shot through his arm, but in spite of the torment, he held his position.

"Rise," the woman said just before her lower face was smothered.

He did, and when he opened his right hand, he saw a blazing tattoo of green, a tree within a circle, half in summer, full and lush, and the other in winter, leaves falling.

He reached out for the woman's hand, but she pushed him away. As she was enveloped by the writhing mass, her finger pointed past him toward the altar.

He turned and looked, unsure of what he should do. Then he realized what she'd meant.

The spear.

He walked to the basin, boots only a step away from the end of his life. There was nowhere left to go—nowhere in that world, at least.

Resolute, he grasped the basin by the rim with both his hands and stared into the water, ignoring all else.

Centered there was his own reflection, haggard and muddy, becoming defiled by the spidering threads of the ephmere which had found him at last. His sensations abandoned him—swallowed up with the organs that supplied them.

But as he watched himself be completely consumed, he saw something new in his eyes he hadn't seen in many years.

Hope.

Ban felt himself move, rising, accelerating, beams of green streaming out between the fingers of his right hand.

The evil both pushed him away and moved out of his way, higher and higher until the last threads of black split away and pale green light shone weakly from above. With one last push, the evil regurgitated him out onto a cold, hard floor.

He rose to his feet, last of the filth that covered him burning away, and saw his enemy once more, raging within its prison.

"This cannot be! You were consumed!" the champion said fearfully, shielding her eyes from the light of the mark.

Ban closed the distance, still steaming black smoke from his clothing and skin. "I guess I didn't sit well on its stomach."

The ephmere snapped at her. She cowered and moved away from it, hesitating.

Ban slowed to a stop. "Send back the spear. Renew this world."

The woman came forward, glancing behind, holding back her left arm in anticipation of some blow. She halted in front of Ban, caught between two forces—one she feared and one she hated.

Her thin skin and skeletal features became apparent. "I will give you the spear, if you promise to go." Her face contorted in disgust. "Take that *lie* away from here."

Her feet were not planted. Ban knew it was a trap.

So, he walked into it, palm outward, light blinding.

She thrust the jagged spear toward the source of her pain, and Ban moved past it easily. He drove his fist into her stomach, and she dropped the spear, falling backward.

He stared down into her widened eyes and held out his hand. "You can still be saved."

She looked up at his hand, and for a moment, her expression softened. But her contempt returned as the ephmere shrieked, stretching the sphere to its limit. She spit at Ban and scurried away like a rodent.

Ban knelt, reaching for the spear. He took it in both hands, feeling a sense of loss as he saw how rusted and decayed it truly was. He thought of the songbird and of the altar, swallowed up by the night, hoping they still existed somewhere, willing the spear to go home.

And so, it did.

A hole in reality opened beside Ban, a portal into darkness. Foul ooze issued forth, dripping down to the floor, already beginning to spread.

But the spear began to shine from within, rust falling away as it soaked up power from the mark. Ban moved it toward the breach, then stabbed it inside.

The corruption erupted in green flame, withdrawing, and the ephmere wailed as if Ban had pierced it instead. The sphere of light flickered and faded against its fits of agony.

Through the wavering distortion, Ban saw the altar. Above it, he could just make out the mural. It no longer depicted the woman, but instead there was a man, holding a branch in his left hand, no longer dead, and a brilliant star of light in his right.

Ban laid the spear on the three small trees above the altar then pulled his hand back as the edges of the rupture closed in and met, sealing.

As the light from the sanctuary winked out, Ban looked up to see the monster finally break free of its prison. It reached out and took the fallen champion, black coiling around her as it brought her close.

She made no sound as it held her there but turned her head to look at Ban as the ephmere spoke to her.

"*Kryth vek uru. Ortun bas!*"

She died instantly as the coils slammed together tightly, her ruined body tossed away like garbage.

Ban felt a terrible emptiness at her death—a pang of hopelessness. He had meant to help her, but now she was lost forever.

He-Who-Hungers must have sensed his feelings, because its mouth opened, and a grunting laughter issued forth.

Ban backed away, suddenly quite aware of his vulnerability. He had the mark, but he knew it wouldn't do much against those teeth.

As he made for the exit, turning to run, the ephmere roiled on the floor, and the toothed dome sprang out of the mass of arms. Ban dove into the passage, just beyond the snapping maw.

The monster's head twisted from side to side, squeezing deeper into the hallway. Ban pushed off against the stone floor in a panic, managing to turn over and scramble to his feet as the teeth snapped at his legs.

The ceiling behind him collapsed, but he never looked back. Holding the mark ahead of him, he ran as fast as he could, through the open doors and up the steps, back into the overcast light of day.

The ground of the courtyard swelled and erupted as he cleared the steps, and the ephmere exploded upward from below. Its black arms moved along the dead grass as it stretched, free of its bonds at last.

The sun faded to nothing, and soon the mark was the only source of light in the world. Ban held it before him, and the creature opened its mouth, showing its widened gullet.

He braced himself as the ephmere launched toward him, its fetid breath washing over his face.

"Alert. Alert. Containment failure eminent in Lab Alpha. Alert . . . " It continued, low-pitched klaxons between the iterations.

Blood trickled from Ban's nose. He tried to reach for it, but his arms were bound at his sides.

He opened his eyes then closed them tightly, grimacing.

"Ban? Can you hear me? You're out." It was Becks.

"Yeah. I'm okay."

"Hold on."

There were a few beeps, and the restraints released him.

He rubbed his eyes then under his nose, blinking as his vision adjusted. With Tyr's help, he stood up, exiting the pseudarus.

A Runian drake stood there beside Becks. Ban tightened his fists and pulled away from Tyr, but the drake held out his hand, motioning for calm. "Easy there. I'm on your side . . . *Champion*." It was Hermes's voice he heard from the helmet's speakers.

He pointed down at Ban's right hand. It shone green with the same radiance as before.

Ban flipped his hand over, the silhouettes of his bones and muscles lit with light from the other side.

He also noticed that there were several more drakes, but they were dead or unconscious, spread out around the pseudari.

"What . . . what happened here?" Ban asked.

Tyr put his arm around Ban's waist, helping to steady him.

Ban looked up to Hermes. "You alerted the whole ship."

Hermes shook his head. "That's not the reason."

Ban followed Hermes's line of sight to the crystal. Cracks were spreading along its surface, and small chunks were falling away. He pushed Tyr's arm away. "Where's my armor?"

Becks stepped aside. "Right here."

"We don't have much time." He went to his armor and attached each piece from his boots all the way up to his helmet. As it sealed, his HUD engaged, virtual display confirming the rest of his squad's armor was powered up and ready to go.

A chunk the size of Tyr fell onto the deck and shattered. Ban looked to Hermes. "It's coming, isn't it?"

Becks grabbed his arm. "Wait. How?"

Hermes shook his head. "It doesn't need a physical body here. It just *exists*, the same as it did inside the simulation."

Ban stood up straighter. He steadied himself then held out his hand. The air around it grew hazy.

Becks gasped. "Ban . . . what—"

The defect continued to warp, forming a distortion, and Ban reached into it. When he pulled his arm back through, he held the same spear from before, only it was perfect and unbroken. He held it in both hands, palms up as he backed away from the closing portal.

Its shaft was made of dark twisted wood, sturdy and strong. As he watched, vibrant green patterns of weaving ivy grew and spread, running toward each end.

The spearhead was long—silver, bright, and shining. Its metal was worked with an inlaid design, branching out from a central spine, just like the veins of a leaf. Those lines were fluid and curved, resembling water flowing along deep grooves.

Tyr and Becks stared in disbelief.

Hermes changed into his normal impish form. "That's *Folium*. The weapon of Thenander's champion."

Ban gripped it tightly. "His champion . . . "

Another fracture threatened to split the black crystal in two. Ban walked over and looked up, watching the smaller pieces fall away. A thin black mist, like air rising from a hot surface, seeped out from the cracks.

There seemed to be a presence within it, a foreboding reminder of the evil inside.

Hermes frowned. "Where's the nearest exit again?"

"No." Ban looked down to the spear. "I think we should stand our ground. Face this evil."

The little imp waved his hands. "No way. That spear *is* powerful, but remember, Thenander himself had to lock that beast away. It can't be killed."

Ban tapped the base of the spear's haft down on the deck. "We have to try."

"That's insane." Hermes ran over to Becks. "Help me out here. Tell him. He'll listen to you."

She stared up at the crystal. "I don't know, Ban. Maybe we should try to find a shuttle or get back to our pod." She seemed legitimately afraid.

"Tyr?"

The big man looked down from the crystal and frowned. He shook his head once.

He lost his voice again.

Ban reopened the wavering gateway. "I don't like it, but maybe you're right." He replaced the spear and smiled at Tyr in sympathy.

"Getting us home has to take precedence."

Tyr handed Ban his light machine gun, and Ban nodded.

As soon as he'd chambered the first round, the main lab doors cycled and opened.

A squad of Runian drakes rushed inside, taking cover near the stacked crates and enclosed materials on the level below.

"Bond-Sergeant Morgan." Major Garland walked in behind the drakes, exposed and confident.

He rested his left hand on his pistol, looking up at Ban from underneath his cap. "This was *not* our agreement."

HEART OF FIRE

"SPEAK TO ME!"

Tieger rammed his gauntlet into the floor of his chambers as if striking the ship itself. "Tell me your will . . . "

There was no answer.

He could imagine the Harbinger's voice, admonishing him as he had long ago.

Only through me will you know the will of Elcos.

Tieger clenched his jaw and nodded.

Very well . . .

He stood and took his helmet and placed it over his head. Once the seals engaged, he walked to the hatch. Smoke swirled inside the chambers as it opened. The ship's alarms, now audible, seemed to grow louder with each iteration. Tieger's arteries pulsed along with the sound, shooting turbulent blood into his pounding skull.

He stepped into the corridor. In the center of it, only a few meters away, his most loyal soldier, Commander Prime, stood defiantly, unwilling to let her master's prayers be disturbed. Of the traitorous embers who had come for him, only three remained, a testament to her resolve and skill.

She advanced slowly, firing her machine pistol in short, controlled bursts over and around her shield, driving the embers behind cover.

As she moved closer, a grenade rolled to a stop at her feet. Without pause, she kicked it forward and dropped to one knee behind her shield, bracing for the detonation.

The corridor shook with the explosion, and the overhead lights flickered in sync with showers of sparks that fell from exposed conduits above. She rose, unharmed.

She holstered the pistol behind her shield and drew her longsword from her waist, resting it over her right shoulder as she sprang forward. She zigzagged, closing the distance to her enemies.

The nearest ember popped out from a room and fired his rifle. She easily deflected the rounds, slashing at his leg. The soldier tried to pick his knee up and away from the blade, but the commander jammed the shield up into his arms and stabbed underneath, finding his armpit. He dropped his rifle, and she ran the tip of her sword through his unguarded trachea.

The second ember ran behind her, attempting to shoot her in the back. She twisted to catch the rifle rounds on her shield and stabbed to the side of it, impaling the ember's left hand. The woman dropped her rifle, raising her arms in defense.

Without missing a beat, the commander lunged forward and delivered a fatal stab to the woman's femoral artery. The ember went down on her back, uttering a distressed moan as she grasped in vain at her profusely bleeding leg.

The third ember fired wildly, and the commander leapt over the dying woman at her feet, sword laid over her shoulder. The doomed soldier shot as he backstepped, and any rounds that hit the commander's shield ricocheted away. When she was within striking distance, the retreating ember raised his rifle up then brought it down for a two-handed blow.

Commander Prime brought her sword down from her shoulder and leapt forward, caught the rifle with her shield, and jabbed at his groin. As the ember leaned forward in reaction, Prime used the shield to pivot and push his gun to her left while bringing the sword around with a twist of her wrist and arm. The blade sliced through the vulnerable sub-armor at the ember's neck and opened his throat.

The commander calmly returned to Tieger as the final ember stumbled and fell to the deck, never to rise again.

Tieger nodded. "Excellent, Commander."

She brought her bloody sword back up to rest on her shoulder. "Thank you, Honored One."

Tieger looked down to her. "Now we take the bridge."

"Yes." She turned and walked past the slain embers at the opposite end of the corridor. Tieger followed.

Ahead, a group of three officers ran frantically through the corridor. They turned to fire their weapons but fell to the deck, shredded by gunfire. A five-man squad of embers stood there beyond them, and when they saw Tieger, they knelt.

Commander Prime turned to explain. "These embers are loyal to you, Honored One."

They stood, and as Tieger approached, he saw that each had drawn the image of a crude hammer on the cloths that hung from their waists.

"They have adopted the hammer in your honor. They serve the *Malleus Maleficarum*, and through you, Elcos."

One of the embers stepped forward, and after bowing her head to Tieger, she spoke to the commander. "Commander Prime, Captain Gault continues to give orders demanding the neutralization of the Honored One."

"That is very impressive, considering Gault is dead," Tieger said as he raised his bloody gauntlet.

The ember bowed her head in silence.

Commander Prime tapped her sword on her shoulder as she thought. "Regardless of the source, these orders must cease."

The ember bowed her head quickly. "Yes, Commander."

Commander Prime turned to Tieger and lowered her head. "Please follow me, Honored One."

She marched, with Tieger's loyal embers clearing the halls ahead. A short skirmish near the bridge entrance resulted in the deaths of five more traitors.

Commander Prime burst through onto the bridge, storming along the sword-shaped platform in the center. Most personnel had fled the bridge or had been killed, but a few remained. One of them stood frozen near the central controls, drawing his pistol with shaking arms as Tieger approached.

His eyes were wide with fear as he walked backward, futilely firing his sidearm into Tieger's heavy-grade armor. Cornered, he bumped into the workstation behind him and tried to climb over it. Without hesitation, Tieger reached out and grabbed his head from behind and jerked it violently, breaking his neck. He threw the limp body to the side, knowing full well that it would be some time before the man would die.

There were a few more shots on the bridge, then all was silent.

Commander Prime walked to Tieger and wiped her dripping blade on the dying man's uniform jacket. "The bridge is yours, Honored One."

"As it always has been, Commander."

Another loyal trooper jogged up and bowed his head.

Commander Prime turned to him. "Sub-Guardian, barricade the entrance and prepare for counterattack." She sheathed her sword and activated the holographic display on her wrist. "I am receiving a transmission."

The familiar face of the recently deceased Captain Gault appeared in the air before her and Tieger. "...to retake the bridge. All available units must move to secure these locations."

She shut off the display. "My men report that this is a virulent program sending unauthorized communications from the central computer core."

Tieger turned to the commander. "Can it be deactivated remotely?"

"No, it cannot."

"I want that program *silenced*, Commander."

She bowed. "It will be as you wish. I will leave some of my men here with you and take care of it personally." She turned with a flourish of her cape, barking a few more orders before leaving the bridge.

Tieger walked to the main command console, but before he could access the ship's operations software, the image of the Harbinger appeared over the bridge's central holographic communications area.

He was livid. "Tieger, you traitorous fool!"

Tieger looked up into his eyes. "Your attempt to contain me has failed, Harbinger."

"Contain you, Tieger? I will *end* you."

"We will soon see, old man."

"Just what do you think you can do? I took your power."

Tieger laughed. "You have forgotten me, Harbinger. You have forgotten Tieger the Marauder." He cut the transmission and turned to the nearest ember. "Bring me an officer."

The ember nodded and moved away. In a short time, he returned with a woman.

She bowed, trembling. "Honored One, I—"

"Take the *Forge* to the island of Teras Ni."

"Yes . . . yes of course." She stepped over the dead officer near the console and hurriedly worked at the controls.

Tieger turned to the holographic display of the Never and watched as the islands drew nearer.

At the peak of Cor Vod, high above Teras Ni, he would finally meet his god.

Tieger's lone transport lifted away and cleared the *Forge*'s hangar, speeding toward Cor Vod. The ever-erupting volcano, with violet lava flowing from its peak, fumed in defiance at his assault.

White platforms linked bright stone pathways along its sides, climbing toward the peak as they weaved in and out of the rock, each serving as a checkpoint on the way to the top.

Though the Harbinger was most likely near the peak, Tieger could not fly straight to him. Already, the old man's elite garrison, the so-called blood embers, was mobilizing.

The pilot turned his head slightly. "Honored One, it is time." He swung the transport over the first platform and landed.

As the side door opened, Tieger took a rifle from the weapons rack and stepped down to the ivory below with a heavy thud. He turned the rifle over in his hand.

A crude weapon, but it will have to do for now.

He walked forward without looking back. "Hold this position."

The pilot chambered a round in his own rifle. "With my life."

The Harbinger will send everything he has after me.

Tieger started the long climb.

It will not be enough.

"Ack!" The blood ember pulled at Tieger's wrist as his throat was ruined. His armor was weak at the neck, just like any other ember's. The only difference was the color, so deeply red it was almost black.

Tieger swung the soldier's body around to intercept the incoming gunfire then emptied his own rifle, taking down the last two men.

He tossed both of the useless objects in his hands away as he walked, stopping only for a moment to take another weapon from a dead ember. He looked up to the peak, shouting his challenge. "Where are you hiding, Harbinger?"

There was no reply, only the strange silence of the Never.

He turned to enter the next chamber. Its floors were white, just like the walls, and violet lava flowed down through channels from ceiling to floor along the sides. At the end of a narrow, arched bridge, blood embers poured in from deeper inside the volcano. They opened fire, and Tieger shifted to the outer wall on the other side of the entrance.

Tedious.

He called to the *Forge*. "Direct a beam into this chamber."

The same female officer from before answered. "Yes, Honored One! Right away!"

Tieger walked away from the entrance and down the path before turning to watch. Painfully bright light lanced out from the *Forge* and burst through the entrance. After it faded, Tieger lowered his arm and walked back up.

The beam had left the ivory floor concave through the middle like a trough, smooth as glass. The bridge was gone, and lava poured toward the center. Tieger walked, one step ahead of the molten sludge as it filled in the space behind him.

He stepped up and out. Nothing remained of the obliterated blood embers.

Not even his elite can withstand the true Flame.

He continued, knowing every step he took was one step closer to god. The room was an atrium, similar to any number he had seen before except for its opulence. White columns, long violet banners, and statues of flame-bearers adorned the hall.

Each statue depicted a different man or woman, all holding fire in their hands, heads bowed, subservient. They were weak.

No more will I beg for scraps of power. No more will I be subject to another man's designs. No more will I bow!

Tieger roared. He struck the nearest statue as he passed, shattering its head. A few steps later, he was surrounded.

Five blood embers shuffled down the stairs to his right. Many more came from ahead, behind, and to his left. They leveled their rifles and advanced slowly, closing the circle as they stopped a few meters away.

Beyond them, footsteps sounded on the stairs—the type that only expensive boots could make.

Tieger looked up, over the embers, eager to see his target.

The Harbinger laughed derisively. "I highly doubt that armor you prize so greatly will be enough. What will you do without your nevergates? Your hammer?" He frowned in contempt. "You've been reduced to a cornered animal, Tieger. And like an animal, you must be put down."

Tieger dropped his rifle and silenced the external speakers in his helmet so no one in the room could hear him speak. "*Forge*. Target my location."

"*Your* location?"

"Wait for my command to fire."

The Harbinger walked between two of the embers, who moved aside. "It must truly pain you to surrender, Tieger. Oh, how you've fought and struggled your entire life."

Tieger reactivated his speakers. "Return the *Vox Dei*."

"No, Tieger. Your time in my service has come to an end."

"Then let us die together." Tieger lunged, faster than the Harbinger could react, and took him by the front of his robes.

The Harbinger held up his hand to stop the blood embers from firing. "Tieger, you must know that I am invulnerable."

"I am counting on it." He turned to place the Harbinger between himself and the *Forge*.

"*Fire*."

Alarms cried out from Tieger's suit. He rose slowly from the floor, trying to read the display in front of his eyes. They watered—a reaction to the bright light that had penetrated his protective filters.

But he did not need the displays to tell him his arm was broken. The rapid activation of the Harbinger's shield had thrown him away with such force that he had been injured. His suit had already begun to inject the endorphins and painkillers; the fracture would not slow him in the least.

A small thing, considering . . .

The atrium had been destroyed, nearly cut into two by the beam as it split against the Harbinger's shield.

Only three blood embers remained, though they had been rendered unconscious or killed by the force of Tieger's flying body.

Lying on the floor, the Harbinger seemed stunned by the immense release of power his shield had required to save him.

Tieger took him by his robes and dragged him toward the stairs.

"What . . . what have you—"

"Come, Harbinger."

The man cried out as he was pulled up the steps, kicking and grasping. "Release me!"

"Be quiet. You had your chance." Tieger cleared the top step.

He entered a vast rectangular room with a vaulted ceiling, supported by square-faced ivory columns. Slender windows let the eerie light of the Never inside. At the opposite end from the stairs, two large doors stood open, with a small chamber beyond.

He crossed the room, pulling the struggling Harbinger in tow. They crossed through the doors, and Tieger flung the man across the floor in a heap.

The Harbinger rose to his hands and knees with a furious gaze. "Egregious! Un...unforgivable!"

"I do not ask for your forgiveness. Where is Elcos?"

"You will never—"

Tieger stormed forward, and the Harbinger reflexively shrank away.

"You think that shield makes you invincible? How long would it hold if I submerged you in lava? What if you had no air to breathe? I *will* find a way."

The Harbinger seemed to consider the words and found them accurate. "He...is not here."

Tieger reached for him.

"No! What I mean is, he never was." He pointed to a small white obelisk in the center of the chamber. "There. That is what you seek."

Tieger inspected the obelisk. From a nearly flush recess on its flattened top, a rectangular rod clicked and extended slowly. He pulled it from the obelisk and held it up. "What is this?" A thin line traveled around it near one end, pulsing with a faint violet light.

"His anchor."

"Speak plainly, Harbinger. I have no more patience."

"It ties him to our world."

"So, he isn't here..."

"No. But the anchor is my link to him."

"He speaks through it?"

The Harbinger hesitated. "...yes."

Tieger watched the anchor, waiting for it do something; it only pulsed again. "Show me."

"I cannot. He has gone...silent."

"For how long?"

The Harbinger looked down.

Tieger squeezed the anchor in anger. "How long?"

" . . . decades."

Tieger laughed, feeling a sense of dread at the realization. "You are a fraud."

"No! Elcos is out there. We simply need to bring him back."

Tieger walked to the Harbinger and put his boot on his chest. A small shimmering field activated underneath it, resisting the pressure. "Bring him back?"

"He requires greater faith. More followers."

"Half the Fathom worships him in one way or another."

"But they do not truly believe. They need a threat to focus them."

"What threat?"

"A common enemy. A *monster*."

Tieger lifted his boot and lowered it back to the floor. "What monster?"

"The one kept hidden inside the Runian master crystal."

"That was your grand plan? Frighten men into belief?"

"Is that not what united them in his name once before? Fear of the darkness beyond our sight? We would lead the true believers against this darkness. Can't you see it?"

"Preposterous. You cannot control men through war. You would know that if you had ever seen it."

"That is why I need you, Tieger."

Tieger shook his head and turned away. "Your time as the voice of Elcos has come to an end."

The Harbinger followed him. "No! You cannot take it!"

Tieger kept walking.

"Think of the believers! They will be lost without me!"

Tieger turned and pointed the rod at his face. "I will lead them."

"Where?"

"Wherever I choose. Into the Void itself if I must."

"You will fail. Without your power, you are nothing."

"I have all the power I need."

The Harbinger shook his head. "There are things far worse than witches and boys with swords, Tieger. When you realize that, you will wish you had listened to me. Without the Flame of Elcos, man can only crawl in the dark."

"Darkness will no longer be an issue, Harbinger." Tieger turned and walked away. He raised the anchor and squeezed it tightly. "I will set the galaxy on fire."

AND IT HEARS HER

THE WORLD SHARD'S LAMBENT RAYS SHONE through the Maiden's delicate fingers, surrendering soft warmth to her pale, freckled cheeks. "Isn't it wonderful?"

Fall watched her turn the artifact over and over in her hands, allure reflecting in her hungry green eyes. He frowned; it felt wrong that she should desire it so badly yet understand nothing about what was inside.

Sostek pulled against the metal fingers that firmly gripped his shoulders. "It might as well be a shiny rock to you, *primitive*."

She looked up again, eyes narrowing as the spell was broken. "Primitive. Says the one who hid away with it like a rat."

The voidstrider showed a hint of his sharp teeth. "If I was *hiding*, human, it was from something far worse than you."

She stepped closer. "Are you sure about that?"

His double concentric irises spun as he narrowed his eyes. "I'm sure you won't like what you think you've captured."

She laughed haughtily. "I don't have to like you, animal. You are a means to an end." The Maiden looked back to the shard, drawn to it again as she turned to walk down the hall.

Control watched Sostek with unwavering eyes as he was forced to follow. The machine was right to be cautious; Fall knew Sostek could escape any time he wanted.

So what's he waiting for? If we could just—

Something hit Fall in the back. As he stumbled forward, he turned in anger. The sentinel standing behind him held its spear tightly, electronic eyes cold and calculating.

Past the machine guard, Kumi lay motionless in a third sentinel's arms. Blood slowly trickled from her scalp and fell to the floor, the only sign of life Fall could see.

Slung over that same sentinel's shoulders were the confiscated weapons and gear he needed so badly.

Fall looked into the sentinel's eyes.

When the time is right.

He turned and walked away, following the others through the halls of a strange building.

There were red carpets, long drapes that bordered the tall windows, and armed human guards here and there. From what he could see through the windows, they were high above the rest of Cisterne.

The Maiden turned left at a confluence of hallways. The group went on as well, led to a set of large wooden doors, which opened at the Maiden's approach.

As they stopped, she turned around. "The collected knowledge of the last two millennia lies beyond these doors." She turned to Fall. "Tell me. Have you ever read a book?"

Fall furrowed his brow. "Of course I have."

She nodded with a smile and turned to Sostek. "Have you?"

Sostek tilted his head in the slightest. He didn't seem to understand the question.

The Maiden smiled more broadly. "I thought not." She looked back to Fall. "You see, in his time, humans did not see much use for books. Information was stored in crystalline form, most often organically." She turned and led them through the doors. "Entire generations never so much as touched paper. They never smelled the fresh ink of a new book, or better yet, the sweet vanilla of an ancient text. They never strained their eyes by candlelight as they read just one more chapter. They only watched their stories passively, accepting someone else's idea of sensory input, feeling whatever emotion their mental masters allowed them to feel." She laughed. "How *boring.*"

As they neared the end of a short stone passage, two more doors stood closed. The Maiden approached, and they began to slowly open. Ethereal, soft light poured through, the same as through the windows outside.

She looked to Sostek. "You will have no appreciation for this, beast. But your partner . . . "

Fall followed her inside, mouth slowly drifting open in awe. A library, larger than any he could have imagined, stretched out through a disk-shaped cavern.

The ceiling rose impossibly high, and the floor stepped down over several staggered levels below. In a labyrinthine pattern, wooden shelves held thousands of books, lining elaborate pathways that led down to the square-shaped center.

Through it all, the native plant life snaked, vines flowering with glowing green bulbs like faint candles. High above the strange library, a circular window bore the image of a crescent moon. Through the uncolored glass of the moon, eerie plantlight shone in shifting columns.

The Maiden turned away, and Fall followed along behind her with the rest of the group. He squinted, trying to make out book titles, but the print was far too small.

So many. Where could they all have come from?

They walked for a few minutes, always going down toward the center as they wormed back and forth through the stacks. Reading tables and wooden chairs with red velvet backs appeared in small nooks. Half-read tomes lay on the tables with uneven piles of papers in between. A computer interface hummed in the dark.

When they finally reached the center, Fall saw that many paths intersected there. Most of it was bare stone floor, except for the very middle.

The Maiden walked forward to the single waist-high pedestal and paused. On its flat surface rested a darkly colored cube.

"Any idea what's in this box?" She turned and placed her hand on its top.

Fall looked to Sostek, who stared ahead without a word.

She smiled. "Long ago, this unassuming object was the key to power without measure. You've seen it before, in the hands of a trusted companion."

The hair on Sostek's neck rose sharply. "It was destroyed."

"No. Only lost." She reached into her sleeve and retrieved a thin card. She touched it to the top of the box, and a fine seam burned in opposite directions away from the center, followed by an audible *click*. She put the card away and motioned up to the window. "He's out there somewhere. Waiting."

Sostek tensed further.

She held up the World Shard. "Of course, if I'm lucky, I might be holding him right here in my hand."

Sostek growled. "You aren't. I would've known."

The Maiden sighed. "If so, I'll simply find another shard and try again. It's only a matter of time."

Sostek pulled against Control's fingers. The machine leaned forward over his shoulder. "Be still, dog. Your master is speaking."

The Maiden smiled. "I do have room for another pet, don't I?" She opened the cube. "And like any good hound, you'll need a scent to get you started. As it happens, I have just . . . "

Green velvet lined the box's interior, shaped with an impression of something that could have fit into the palm of a person's hand.

It was otherwise empty.

The Maiden stood there in shock, expression shifting to rage and then slowly back to calm again. She reached into her sleeve. "Seph."

Heavy breathing came through the communicator along with a woman's whispering voice. "Maiden."

"Where is she?"

"She left the mines. We're on her trail."

"She fled into the city?"

There was a moment of silence as the breathing paused. "No, ma'am. She came back up the main lift."

The Maiden smiled. "She's coming here . . . "

"Ma'am?"

She looked down to the World Shard. "This is what she desires."

"I don't follow—"

"Listen to me, Seph. Track her, but do not stop her. Let her come to me."

"As you wish."

The Maiden slammed the box shut. "*Thief.*"

The voidstrider showed his teeth. "Something the matter, *magus?*"

She stared. "A slight delay." She walked forward slowly. "But since we're waiting, we might as well pass the time." She raised her arm.

Searing light shot out in five tight beams from the tips of her fingers.

Sostek didn't cry out, but his head flew back. The skin on his chest sizzled, and the odor of burnt hair assaulted Fall's sense of smell.

The intensity increased along with the Maiden's hateful smile. "Yes. Let's focus on you."

Ban grasped the edge of the metal railing. "We don't have time for this, Garland."

"Then I'll make it quick. Hand it over, and you can go."

"We both know that's a lie."

Garland smiled and nodded. "So it is." He drew his pistol. "You know, I would've preferred to do this the—"

He was interrupted by a series of low-pitched groans and the nervous sounds of splintering glass.

Ban turned to look at the crystal. It surged with energy then diminished, its already widespread cracks moving to cover the entire surface. The lab darkened, and a sense of dread permeated the room.

Garland looked up as his pistol lowered slowly. "What have you done?"

The ship rocked violently, but Ban held onto the railing. The air around the crystal phased, and a torrent of smoke formed from out of nowhere, swirling like a cyclone viewed from above. Though impossible, the shadows in the room shifted and fell in toward the storm. They mixed into it, lining the turbid surface, then shot to the center of the funnel all at once.

The thick smoke and oily filth came together into a writhing mass, resolving into a physical manifestation of evil—the ephmere from the undercastle. Black as night, its tentacles wrapped around the remains of the crystal, squeezing until it shattered.

Free from its prison, He-Who-Hungers writhed on the deck. Its gaping mouth shuddered, and its soul-crushing roar cut through armor and bone.

Hermes grabbed his head and pulled his ears down. "We waited too long! There's no way we can escape it!"

Ban took a step forward and dropped his gun to the floor. He held his hand out to the side, distorting reality as he took *Folium's* haft and pulled it through. "Then we won't even try."

In response, the monster gathered its mass and grew taller. It was fully unleashed—the immense hatred of a being too-long contained.

In the darkest night of faith long forsaken . . .

Ban closed his eyes and allowed himself only a moment to feel the power reverberating between the spear and his heart.

. . . the light will forever shine.

Fear suppressed, he charged forward, dwarfed by the surging evil that rushed to meet him.

Union held out his arm. "Guards."

Sidna looked out into the dim hallway ahead, lit faintly by the bioluminescent plants hanging outside its tall paned windows. "Can you get us past them?"

Union nodded. "They should not hinder me, as long as I do not linger."

Olivia moved against the wall. "Just tell us when it's safe to go."

Union nodded and turned to move down the hall.

Sidna paced. "This is taking too long."

Gabin crossed his arms. "Are we sure this is the route she took? What if we've been led astray?"

Olivia nodded. "According to Union, there're only three lifts that come up to the Maiden's manor. We came up the main one."

Gabin frowned. "A completely foolish act."

Sidna shushed them. "Look."

Union's orange eyes peeked around a corner, and he waved them on.

The group followed. Sidna and Gabin took the rear, while Olivia led the way, staying a comfortable distance behind the commandeered sentinel.

Union walked more stiffly than before, like the other sentinels did down in the mines. Though forced, his impression seemed to work; no one gave him a second glance. He signaled after the Maiden's black-clad guards had passed by.

They continued through several more halls, sometimes taking a detour down a side passage to avoid stationary guards. As they approached a nexus where multiple halls convened, Union abruptly stopped.

He turned left and pointed. "I believe the Maiden went that way."

Sidna rushed by without hesitation.

Olivia jogged to catch up. "Hey, wait up. Shouldn't we have a plan?"

Sidna kept walking. "The plan is, we take her out as quickly as we can."

"Is she really that dangerous?"

Sidna nodded. "She's an arcanist."

"Like you?"

"No." Sidna tightened her fists in frustration. "Stronger."

Olivia looked ahead. "So, what do we do?"

"Just be ready when I make my move. Otherwise, stay out of the way."

Olivia grunted and fell back, and the group continued until they neared a set of large double doors, barely cracked open.

"Wait, girl." Gabin took Sidna's jacket from behind, bringing her to a stop.

She turned. "What?"

"Are you certain you want this? We still have time to escape."

"You know I have to get the tear, Gab."

"This one?"

"Yes. I need them both."

Gabin frowned. "Surely one would be enough. If we could only—"

"No one's forcing you, Gabin." She pushed open the doors and moved through.

Inside, a huge cavern waited. Several pathways led down to a square floor, all lined with shelves.

Gabin caught up with Sidna as she started down the nearest path. "Are these books? A library of some kind?"

"Looks that way."

"You aren't impressed?"

"My mind's on more important things. Feel free to stop and read."

Olivia spoke from behind Sidna. "Why would the Maiden have so many? What does she actually do?"

"She takes," Sidna replied. "It's all she's ever done."

"Wait. You know her?"

"No. But I've heard enough about her, though she went by a different name. When she left home, she nearly stole our entire collection of written knowledge. We had electronic backups, but I can still remember how furious my mother was." She stopped. "Damn."

Olivia's hand went to her pistol. "What is it?"

Sidna turned around in a circle. She looked down each of the paths between the bookshelves, each like the others. They were close to the center of the library, but she couldn't be sure which winding course would take her there. "I don't know which way to go."

Union never slowed as he continued past her. "Follow me."

Olivia shrugged. "Good thing we brought him." She waited for Sidna to go, then brought up the rear.

Union led the way through the rest of the turns. In the middle of the central open space, there was a pedestal with an open box. Inside, on green fabric, a glowing orange crystal rested.

Sidna walked forward.

Gabin lowered his rapier into her path. "Gods above, girl. Have you never seen a trap?"

"What?"

"A trap. The thing you want so badly is waiting out in the open. Think."

She looked down to the sword then back up. "I'm done thinking."

"Fine, fine." He moved the rapier. "But Gabin told you so."

"So he did. Now come on."

She walked to the box and picked up the World Shard without hesitation. The tiny thing shone brightly, but for all the world it felt as light as air.

Like nothing . . .

It disappeared.

Gabin opened his mouth.

"Gab. Don't you dare say a word."

He didn't.

Olivia drew her pistol. "Union, do you hear anything? See anything?"

The sentinel looked down each of the pathways. "No. Everything seems normal."

Olivia swallowed. "Doesn't feel that way to me."

Sidna felt a chill run up her spine. *"Quiet."*

The room was oddly silent, except for one distant sound.

Olivia leaned forward. "Is that . . . breathing?"

Sidna squinted and cocked her head. "I don't hear anything." She walked to the edge of the square near one of the paths. She held up her hands and turned back around. "There's nothing here."

She froze as a chain rattled behind her. She reached for her pistol but wasn't fast enough.

"I wish you could have seen the look on your face when it disappeared."

Sidna turned around slowly, putting as much disgust into her voice as she could. "Seph."

The compact woman, the one who'd first captured Sidna in Cisterne, stood there holding her pistol close to her body. "That's right. Now go on, get back over there by your friends."

As Seph moved to take Sidna's arm, her bald partner came out of the shadows, holding Ghidro by taut metal links. The beast's hair stood up on its back, and it growled threateningly.

Seph led her at gunpoint back to the others. Out of the darkness of a pathway, the Maiden approached. She tried to hide her frustration, but she was stiff in her normally graceful movements. "Where is it?"

Sidna jerked her arm away from Seph's tight grip. "Where is what?"

The Maiden looked past her flatly. "Seph?"

Sidna reached into her jacket pocket and turned toward her. "Don't touch me." Her other hand stopped just short of Seph's face, open and red-orange, hot with kindled fire.

The Maiden moved closer. "You're surrounded. There's nowhere to run."

Sidna's eyes darted from Seph to Ghidro then to the Maiden as she moved away. "Who's running? I came for the tear."

"For what reason? What could an untrained, uneducated brat possibly want with such a thing?"

"That's my business. Now, hand it over before I really get pissed off."

The Maiden's wry smile faded, and her eyes grew cold. "Give this to a failure like you? *Never.*"

Sidna smiled. "I wasn't asking." She swung her arm toward the Maiden and unleashed a spout of burning air.

Gabin cried out. "Sidna!"

His sharp rapier cut through the air, accompanied by the sounds of shuffling feet. She heard the muffled noises of struggling followed by erratic gunshots. Ghidro's chain rattled, and his claws clicked hurriedly on the floor.

When the flames went out, there was nothing left but the scorched pedestal and the burning box.

What?

"Over here."

She turned to see the Maiden a few footsteps away.

Another trick!

She drew power for another blast, but the Maiden beat her to it. The pale woman's night-black *viae* pulsed, and everything went dark.

Sidna's breath caught as the Maiden's voice whispered harshly over her left shoulder. "Too easy."

Sidna felt the burn of acid rising in her esophagus.

The voice continued. "Now be a good little girl and return what's mine."

Still not strong enough . . .

Her mind flew to the dungeon cell below the manor, back to the words which burned in her memory.

The glyph is a vessel . . . access that power when you need it.

Sidna squeezed the glyph and raised it in her fist. Her anger surged, and the glyph seemed to drink it up, leaving a vacuum within her for more and more to take its place.

She turned, sight suddenly restored. "If you want power so much, here." She shoved the glyph toward the Maiden's shocked face. The air around the necklace blurred and darkened. "Take it."

The Maiden withdrew her hand and backed away, eyes wide. "No! You . . . you don't know what you're doing!"

Sidna smiled. "You know, for the first time in my life, I feel like I do."

The air expanded rapidly with a *boom*, and the Maiden flew back violently. The light from the window dimmed, and forms of shadow shot away from the glyph.

As the Maiden looked up from the floor in terror, threads of darkness crept along the stone. She kicked with her feet and tried to back away as they flowed and wrapped around her legs.

Sidna could feel the strands coiling and tightening as if they were her own hands. They fed on her anger, avaricious cables of desire whose seemingly endless capacity threatened to drain her dry.

She looked down to the glyph as her fingers curled around its golden edges and touched the blackened emerald.

This is power.

Tieger looked to the anchor in his armored hand. Short bursts of white light reflected along its surface as the lift rose, contrasted by the slowly pulsating band of violet near its end.

Enough of this lie.

"Speak. Speak, or be gone forever."

Nothing happened.

Tieger slammed the anchor into the wall. "Speak to me!"

The rod vibrated. Tieger raised it higher, and a distant voice spoke from within, words barely intelligible.

...comes.

He held it there, wondering if he had actually heard anything. As he watched the violet light, it reached out and seized his mind, painfully breaking through his resistance.

He caught himself against the lift's wall. "Ah!"

Rapidly shifting images came in and out of view; shutting his eyes did nothing to stop them.

He saw grasping forms, pulling and tearing as they climbed through holes in the air. They had profane shapes, many with multiple, bony limbs, and some with dusky beaks and penetrating, pinpoint eyes. Nothing about them was natural, yet he knew they were real.

Behind them, a man walked. He wore robes of red, with black armor, and his arms burned red with the Code. Fire ran out from his fingertips, along the horrible creatures, which grew more fearsome, dripping molten evil.

Dread...comes...

Tieger answered the voice within his mind.

Elcos?

Yes...

What are these...things?

They are the end. They are drawn to the magi.

The magi?

She calls to them. You must silence her.

Tieger was suddenly released. He breathed deeply, watching the nightmare images fade.

He stared at the anchor, waiting for it to stir again, but nothing happened. When the lift's doors opened, he steadied himself then walked out toward the bridge.

Magi? That was an arcanist. He controlled those creatures, augmenting them.

Tieger approached the bridge. The fighting on the main deck had ceased, and the bodies had been cleared away. He entered.

"Honored one!" The frightened young woman near the helm saluted stiffly.

Tieger ignored her and walked to the holographic navigation sphere.

Is this why you found me, Harbinger? Is this why you had me hunt them all these years?

The bridge remained silent. None dared to interrupt his thoughts.

But the anchor spoke to him again.

It is coming . . . Tieger. She . . . calls . . .

The witch, Sidna, appeared in his mind's eye.

Magi . . .

Tieger looked to the officer. "You."

The woman froze. "H-honored one?"

"Take the *Forge* back to Gyre."

"Right away!"

He looked back to the anchor, listening as it whispered its warning.

She calls . . .

FAITH AND FURY

HE-WHO-HUNGERS SPOKE FOUL, ALIEN words, indifferent to the screams of its helpless prey. "*Itha syk nor. Sor itha dras ka.*"

The Runian drake dangled high above the ephmere's mouth, flailing, desperately reaching out for his squad mates, but there was nothing they could do.

"*Gotha . . . nor.*"

The drake fell, dying horribly as rows of razor-sharp teeth rent his armor and flesh like wet paper.

The sounds were maddening.

One drake broke away in panic, and one rushed forward, firing wildly. The third simply stood still, frozen by fear. In the end, churning death washed over them all, and none survived.

Unsated in murder, the ephmere resumed its rampage, sweeping piles of burning debris from its path.

Ban jumped down from the third level, using his powered armor to absorb the energy. He called out to the monster. "Over here!"

Its filth bristled.

"That's right. It's me you want."

As planned, it reached out and pulled itself toward him, directly into the path of Tyr's rocket. The fiery blast deformed the creature like a fist hitting water. In spite of the grievous injury, the creature reformed almost instantly.

Only the spear can hurt it.

Ban sprinted forward, stabbing *Folium's* spearhead deep into the black sludge. The substance boiled on contact, and the monster recoiled from the blade, roaring in pain.

In response, two tentacles took shape and whipped Ban from his feet. He hit the first deck hard and rolled, rising to find he'd been thrown behind a pair of Runian drakes. They turned and raised their rifles.

The man on the right went limp, collapsing to the floor as a high-speed round burst through his helmet. The other turned to look for the shooter, finding her right before he died.

Becks rose up on the third level, rifle smoking. "You're clear!"

Ban nodded and ran toward the ramp leading back up to the second level.

But before he could reach it, Major Garland stepped out from behind cover, leveling his pistol. "Hold it."

Ban stopped. "Garland!"

"Hand over that weapon, Morgan."

"Not a chance." Ban gripped the spear tightly.

Garland scoffed. "You'd die for it?"

Ban laughed and raised his arms. "Look around. We're all about to die."

"Then you won't be needing the spear." Garland grasped the pistol with both hands. "Last chance."

Ban nodded. "Becks."

She took the shot.

Garland went down with a shout and dropped his gun. He tried to reach out for it, but his shoulder was a bloody mess. He gritted his teeth and laid his head back. "Morgan!"

Ban walked over and raised the spear above the injured man. Garland looked up, realization of imminent death apparent on his face.

Ban lowered the spear.

No. No more revenge.

He turned for the ramp.

Garland coughed. "Don't . . ." He winced and cried out. "I can . . . use it . . . "

Ban looked back. "No, you can't. And you'd better pray I kill that thing before it finds you." He jogged up the ramp back toward the monster.

The beast's attention was focused in another direction. It reached through scaffolding, rushing and flowing as it sent streaming projections after Tyr.

Ban raised *Folium* and sent a burst of green light into the air. "Here!"

The ephmere rapidly inverted, twisted, and lunged toward him.

Too fast!

Ban thrust *Folium* ahead just in time, and the monster pulled back to avoid it. Ban advanced slowly, prodding at the snapping teeth, gradually driving it away from Tyr.

The ephmere grabbed one of the pseudari in frustration and threw it, but Ban rolled away, narrowly avoiding the deadly projectile.

It raised another, but instead of throwing it, it swung the machine back and forth in the air as if swatting at a fly.

Hermes strafed the monster in his flying lizard form, biting and clawing as he did. He couldn't hurt it, but the creature raged in frustration as it failed to hit him.

The distraction was all Ban needed. He stood and rushed forward, stabbing at what seemed like the monster's core. The shining spear cut a deep, burning gash.

He-Who-Hungers retreated momentarily. It ground its teeth together, producing a horrible, sticky sound. "*Grath!*"

It began to advance again, but paused suddenly, turning its head in curiosity, as if hearing some distant sound. It leaned to the side, whispering foreign words in reply.

Becks gave voice to the question in Ban's mind. "What's it doing?"

Ban lowered *Folium*. "I don't know. But I think—"

The monster rapidly drew into itself. The air around it turned thick and opaque, and the lights in the room flickered.

Ban backed away, and Tyr got himself free of the scaffolding. They ran together to the nearby ramp—the one that led up to the third level.

Hermes peeked over the top edge of the ramp, clutching the railing there with his long claws. "Hold on to something!"

Ban nearly fell as the ship lurched, hull straining and moaning. He looked over the rail down to the second level.

Shadows condensed and spiraled around the ephmere as a gateway opened into a realm of pure night.

Ban pulled himself up the ramp by the rail, searching desperately. "Becks! Where are you?" He stumbled and reached out for the rail again, but nothing was there. He looked down and saw the ramp breaking apart underneath his boots.

All round, the physical substance of things twisted and flew apart, sucked into the vortex. It spread farther and farther, consuming the lab, bit by bit, until nothing remained, not even his squad.

He fell then, somehow whole, and only the spearhead of *Folium* shone, undimmed in his hands as he plunged into the abyss.

Control lowered his book and snapped it shut. "You don't seem to be enjoying yourself, voidstrider."

Sostek leaned back against the bookshelf, breathing heavily. He reached up to the wound in his chest, looking at the bright white blood that came away on his fingers.

Fall looked to his right. The sentinel guarding him stood vigilant, following his every move. Its spear was poised for attack.

A few meters past, the third sentinel stood over Kumi, who was still unconscious. Fall's gear lay next to her.

Control reached up and placed the book into the gap between two others. "Hmph. Couldn't make it past the prologue." He looked down and paused. "What are you staring at?"

Sostek looked down and coughed. "I've always wondered . . . "

"Wondered what?"

"You Exanim. Can you feel pain?"

Control's eyes darkened on the tops and bottoms, leaving a narrow band in the center. "What purpose would pain serve us?"

Sostek strained to stand up straighter. "Failure is the great teacher. Pain is its most basic lesson."

Control's faceplates moved to express his annoyance. "We receive feedback information related to injury or malfunction, if that's what you're getting at."

Sostek nodded thoughtfully. "Do you avoid actions that might generate that information?"

Control sighed electronically. "Generally."

"Why?"

Control waited a moment before answering. "Because it is less than ideal."

"In other words, you don't like it."

Control shifted his weight to his other foot. "What I *like* is irrelevant, *animal*. Pain is a crude, organic thing."

Sostek muttered under his breath. "Pain is a construct of the mind . . . "

"What did you say?"

Sostek muttered again, this time too quietly.

Control leaned forward. "If you're going to pass out, at least—"

Sostek disappeared and reappeared behind Control. He kicked the back of Control's knee and vanished then reappeared in front again.

With an upward strike, he sheared the machine's metal head from its neck.

Fall moved to face his own sentinel, turning to dodge the incoming spearhead as it passed by his stomach.

He deflected it with the back of his open hand, rolled his hand around to grab it as he lifted it over his head, pulled it back under his left arm, then rushed in for an elbow strike to the machine's vulnerable eyes.

He pushed down, wrenching the spear from the stunned sentinel, jabbed the blunt end into the machine's lower abdomen, then twisted the spear up with a spinning flourish to sever the exposed tubes near the neck.

The seizing robot fell back, squirting orange lubricant high into the air.

The other sentinel rushed forward, chipped axe raised above its head. Fall ran forward as well, dropped his shoulder, and threw the spear deep into the sentinel's face. It fell, the same orange liquid leaking out from its fatal wound.

Fall ran to Sostek. "You're bleeding."

Sostek waved him away. "I'll be fine. See to your friend."

Fall nodded and went to Kumi. He picked her up with a grunt and walked back to Sostek. He knelt and laid her down.

He looked her over. "She shouldn't be so hurt from a cut on her head. Concussion? I don't know."

A few rows over, there was a loud explosion, and the resulting burst of air knocked a leaning book over on its shelf.

Sostek took Fall's arm. "The World Shard is all that matters. Take it back."

Fall looked to Kumi and hesitated.

Sostek pushed him. "I will watch her."

Fall motioned to the erratically searching eyes of Control's severed head. "What about *him*?"

Sostek held the head up a little higher and smiled as the glowing eyes moved to lock onto his. "*We* will watch *each other*."

Fall stood. He ran to his gear and equipped his weapons and belt. "I'll be back as soon as I can." Rearmed, he ran down the path that led to the center of the library.

He made the turns at full speed and stopped just short of running into Olivia.

She brought her pistol up and gasped. "Fall! Man, I almost shot you!"

Fall couldn't believe his eyes. "Olivia? What are you doing here?"

She looked behind herself, pistol brought close to her chest. "Trying to find you. I got separated from the others when Sidna attacked the Maiden."

"Sidna's here?"

"Yeah. Look, now that I found you, we need to get out of here. The captain's waiting."

"Captain Hughes? He's alive?"

"Yes!"

Fall looked down the path. "I can't go. Not yet. The Maiden has something I need."

"The World Shard?"

His eyes opened wide. "You know about it?"

"Union told me." She waved away his next question. "The Maiden still has it. In the center. Come on!"

"Wait." He pointed. "Kumi's back that way a few turns. I don't know what's wrong with her, but she's seriously injured."

Olivia seemed to be torn on what to do. "You can't go in alone. Can she hold out?"

"There's a lot of blood . . . "

Olivia screwed her lips up. "Dammit. All right." She poked him in the chest and narrowed her eyes. "*Just be careful.*"

"I'll be fine. Worry about Kumi." He moved past her with a quick nod then ran on again.

When he reached the middle area, he saw Sidna standing over the Maiden. A torrent of wind spun around them both, and the Maiden struggled to free herself from the black cords holding her arms and legs.

"Sidna?"

Past her, on the opposite side of the space, something moved. Whatever it was, it stalked low across the ground, slowly picking up speed as it closed in.

"Killer!" He reached down for his mech bow and up for the arrow. "Sidna!"

As he drew the string, she snapped her eyes toward him, alien and completely opaque. The expression on her face was so hateful, he had to take a step back.

Her eyes never left him as she swung her open hand back toward the approaching animal.

A whip of black as thick as a tree swatted the dog away with a yelp, flinging it against a bookshelf, where it fell to the floor and didn't get up.

The Maiden must've gotten free somehow. Painfully bright light blazed from the floor, and when Fall uncovered his eyes, she was gone, thrashing ropes of black left in her place.

Sidna looked down. After a moment of building fury, she clenched her fists, forearms flexed, then threw her head back and screamed.

As she raised her right hand, an unsettling silence fell over the square, layered over an intensifying, low-pitched thrum. Fall felt it in his legs, coming in waves from the center of the room.

From all around, darkness stretched out to pass him. He watched as his own shadow elongated, no longer bound to him or to the dying light that shone weakly above. From every corner and nook, gloom itself coalesced, streaming endlessly from the dark reaches just beyond sight.

Fall holstered his bow and replaced the unused arrow in his quiver. He drew his sword, steeling himself against the growing forces that gathered ahead. "Sidna! Sidna stop!"

She ignored him, looking up to the object at the center of the furious gale—a pulsing beacon of night held high above her head.

$$\text{\scriptsize \&}$$

The *Forge* tore its way into normal space, nebulous gas burning away as the Never sealed itself behind.

Tieger opened a communications channel. "Commander Prime."

He heard bursts of gunfire and indistinct shouting. "Honored One."

"Report."

"We have retaken the computer core." Her machine pistol fired twice in rapid succession. "Though we are currently besieged."

"Do not relent until the program has been terminated."

"It will be destroyed."

"See that it is, Commander." He cut the channel.

"Honored One!" an officer shouted from his console nearby. "Off the starboard bow!"

"Show me." Tieger turned to the holographic display.

The incomplete wreckage of a ship tumbled slowly in space. To his surprise, something crawled out over the edge.

"Scan it."

The officer seemed puzzled. "Point scans reveal nothing. There seems to be an . . . absence."

"Impossible."

The officer looked up only briefly. "Forgive me, but the computer reads nothing."

Tieger looked closer.

A creature of shadow . . .

"Target that *absence* and fire."

"Yes, Honored One."

Two beams cut through the hull beneath the creature, but the thing pushed away in time to avoid the shots. Multiple beams converged on the target as it spun and moved, changing directions rapidly, though such movements should not have been possible.

The officer looked up. "I can't hit it!"

The monster surged ahead, quickly closing the distance. The bridge shook as it slammed into the outer plating.

Tieger looked up. Black liquid oozed inside through spreading cracks, consolidating and growing as it did. He took hold of the officer's console and planted his feet. "Seal it!"

"There's no time!"

The man frantically worked to erect a force field, but the invader pushed on through, substance rising into a widening spike.

There was a scraping moan unlike anything Tieger had ever heard. The bridge was violently ruptured, and the crew immediately flew toward the wound, blown out into the vacuum of space.

Tieger held against the decompression; as the last of the atmosphere was lost, he stood alone on the bridge, the sole survivor.

The evil coalesced and flowed down in a swirling column and took form in front of him, indifferent to the lack of air.

Tieger let go of the console and reflexively reached to the side for his hammer.

Again, nothing happened.

Elcos . . .

The creature whipped forward to grasp Tieger, filaments wrapping around his arms, legs, and back.

He fought, managing to break several of the attachments, but new ones continuously formed. The black substance poured over him, nearly covering the entirety of his armor.

There was an unsubtle shift in his mind, as if a braced door were suddenly kicked open. He resisted, but the more he fought, the deeper the intruder went, kindling murderous thoughts. Barely bound hatred seeped into his consciousness, more powerful than ever before.

Get out of my mind!

Tieger looked to the anchor in his left hand, willing it to help him.

Elcos! Hear me!

The anchor pulsed, and the monster released Tieger momentarily. Before long, it took him again but did not resume the assault on his mind. Out of the black mass, a gaping mouth rolled into place, splitting wide to reveal rows of glistening teeth.

Tieger flexed and pulled in the opposite direction. "I will not be a meal for you, abomination!" He continued to slide along the floor in spite of his resistance. With one final tug, he lost his footing and was pulled into the mouth.

The jaws tried to crush him, but he pushed upward, digging his armored claws into the roof of the filth. The creature's thrashing tongue slapped and rolled wildly as his suit strained to maintain its material integrity.

Tieger fought to stay upright as one of the tentacles reached inside the mouth to pull his legs out from under him. He spoke to the anchor between clenched teeth. "The Harbinger . . . lost sight . . . of his faith. I alone stand for you. I alone . . . continue . . . the hunt."

The jaws closed down a little more, and Tieger went to one knee, pushing up with all of his might. "Elcos! Hear me! Hear your *Malleus!*"

The anchor, with its single pulsing band of violet light, finally answered.

Tieger . . . This is the darkness that enshrouds reality. Yet it is only a shadow. You must find the girl who calls it.

"I . . . will find her. Return the *Vox Dei*, and this will be done."

Tieger felt the old fire suddenly ignite. The *Vox Dei* returned, raw power once more coursing through his veins.

Rise, Tieger.

Tieger looked up and smiled. "And now, little nightmare, I will show you what *you* should fear."

Tieger's armor ignited with violet flame, and the monster began to thrash and flail. It tried to spit Tieger out, but he took a hold of its tongue under his left arm and reached forward, pushing with all his might. The inner mass opened up in front of him like a bubble bursting through oil.

Once clear, he walked to the monster's side, and with a feeling near ecstasy, pulled forth his weapon, *Janus*. "Go back. Tell your kin what awaits them should they come."

He brought the hammer's burning head down into the creature's ruined core. The darkness spasmed, crying out, then went silent and moved no more.

Tieger raised his clawed gauntlet and set the ugly remains aflame. The black liquid boiled, bubbling and evaporating, until there was only a fading mist. The last of it gone, Tieger rested the hammer over his shoulder, victorious.

He received a call and answered. "Commander."

"Honored One, we have secured the computer core. The malicious program has been purged."

"Good. Very good. Finish your sweep of the ship. Leave no traitor alive."

"With pleasure, Honored One."

Tieger returned to the center of the bridge's main platform. He activated the nearest working console and reestablished repulsion field integrity. Once it was in place, he vented air back into the room. As the pressure normalized, he moved to look out through the damaged hull.

Out there in space, alone, the storm world of Gyre raged.

I will find her.

"Wait, girl!" Gabin shouted from atop a toppled bookshelf. He severed a web of black which had a hold of his boot then leapt down.

As he landed, the cavern rumbled, shaking beneath Sidna's feet.

Gabin ducked, as if he expected the ceiling to fall. "You'll bring the whole thing down on our heads! You have to stop!"

"I don't *have* to do anything." Sidna held out the glyph, and pooled darkness flowed throughout the shelves like the churning waves of a stormy sea. "*Found you.*"

Columns of shadow swirled and burst through the wood and books, scattering paper and splinters in a maelstrom of rage.

The Maiden leapt up and ran for cover. Sidna sent the black after her, wrapping her up and dragging her back, kicking and struggling all the away.

The flailing woman dropped in front of her, fighting in vain against the shifting net of liquid. "Let me go!"

Sidna grunted with a smile. "Not this time. What was it you said to me before? Oh, yeah. *Too easy.*"

The Maiden pulled at the vise of black around her neck. "No, you—" She was being smothered and couldn't speak.

Sidna closed her fist. "Feel that? That's me squeezing the life out of you."

The Maiden's face began to turn a sickly shade of purple.

"Right about now, you're wondering where you went wrong. I'll tell you. You shouldn't have crossed me."

Sidna watched in anticipation, but just as it seemed the Maiden would burst, the compressing strands recoiled and flew away, retreating rapidly into the glyph. All of the surrounding shadows leapt back into place, and the necklace suddenly felt extremely cold in Sidna's hands.

Her anger melted away, leaving her utterly empty. "No! What's happening?"

The Maiden choked and gasped for air as she pushed herself up. "I . . . told you . . . it's too much for you." She raised her arm, released an intense display of light, and vanished.

Sidna stepped forward to reach for her but fell to the ground instead.

Gabin knelt beside her and began to lift her, concern on his face. As she looked up, he froze and softly lowered her back down.

She used her last bit of strength to turn her head and see what he'd seen.

It was Ghidro, bloodied and furious. The enormous dog growled threateningly, wide eyes vicious.

Gabin picked up his sword and stood between them. "Easy, now, pup."

Sidna tried to move. "Gab . . . " She tried to raise her arm, but it was far too heavy.

So . . . weak . . .

"Don't worry, my dear. No runt will get the best of Gabin." His voice held his usual bravado, but it was obvious he was worried. "I'll just take care of this, and we'll be on our way to the *Red*."

"You're not going anywhere." Seph walked behind Ghidro, slightly bent over with her broken arm cradled under her breasts. Her pistol was pointed at Sidna. "At least not alive."

Gabin slowly reached for his own, beginning to draw as he spoke. "You're injured, Seph. Why don't we all just walk away?"

She turned the gun on Gabin. "Shut up, scum. You're both dead."

Gabin held his pistol clear of his holster. "Ah, but who will you shoot first? Whomever you kill, the other will no doubt kill *you*."

"Maybe. Maybe not." She blinked once then fired.

Gabin fired almost instantly after she did then spun away with a cry of pain.

Seph stood there for only a moment more then fell back, hit right between the eyes.

He got her!

Gabin cursed and dropped the pistol, clutching his arm. He stumbled, barely managing to stay on his feet.

Ghidro looked at Seph's body then took a step forward, blood and drool falling from his jaws.

Gabin steeled himself as best he could and raised his rapier in defense.

The dog bounded forward, preparing to leap, but abruptly fell to the floor and slid to a stop, killed by a single gunshot to the head.

Who?

Sidna managed to turn her head again.

It was Mei. She held her red pistol forward as she walked, watching for Ghidro to somehow get back up. "Such an *ugly* creature."

It was all Sidna could do to stay conscious. "Mei ... "

The Ranger ran over but stopped when Gabin awkwardly raised his sword in her direction.

Mei holstered her gun. "I am a friend, pirate. Your concern should be for yourself."

Gabin looked down to Sidna and nodded, then lowered himself to the floor with a prolonged sigh. "You know, I'm beginning to think you might be too much trouble."

Sidna tried to sit up. "Mei, I ... I don't ... "

Mei shushed her. "You can explain later. For now, we must go."

"The others ... "

"I am not sure."

"No. *The others*." She pointed past Mei.

Mei turned to see. Fall, Olivia, and Union walked toward them, searching in the dark. Union finally saw Mei and directed the group over.

Fall jogged ahead, holding his silver sword in his hand. He flipped it over by the ring on its handle and sheathed it behind his back. "Mei?"

"It seems I arrived just in time."

"I'm glad you're here." He motioned to Gabin. "Who's that?"

Mei nodded. "A friend of Sidna's. He was shot in the arm, but I think he will be fine."

Gabin clutched the wound. "After a strong drink . . . "

Fall looked at Sidna. There was something uneasy in his eyes. He watched her carefully. "The Maiden?"

Sidna lifted the glyph then lowered it. "She got away."

His arm ever so slightly moved for his sword. She stared at his hand then looked up into his eyes.

He blinked hard and relaxed. "Sorry." He rubbed the back of his neck, uncomfortable. "I guess I'm not sure what to think."

Olivia frowned. "I know *exactly* what to think." She pointed at Sidna. "I knew she was dangerous."

Sidna pushed herself onto her hands and knees.

Olivia reached for her pistol. "Stay where you are."

Mei moved between them. "Doctor?" Her hand drifted toward her red knife.

Fall stepped to his left. "Mei . . . "

There was a moment of tense silence as none of them moved.

Fall breathed in and out, eyes darting between the women. "Olivia, relax. It's over."

"Is it? How do you know?"

He stepped in front of her, his back to Mei. "Come on. It's over."

Olivia slowly lowered her hand.

Fall relaxed, and so did Mei.

Gabin groaned. "So many strong women in one room. It's enough to make a man swoon." He fell back onto his elbow. "Of course, it could be the bleeding."

Olivia backed away and knelt next to him. "It's not that bad. I'll patch you up as soon as we get out of here. I'll need supplies though."

"Don't you worry. The boys should have plenty back on the *Red*."

"The *Red*?"

"My ship."

"Here in Cisterne?"

"No. Up above." He waved his good arm toward the ceiling.

Olivia shook her head. "We have our own ride."

"That may not be entirely true." Union stared off through the distance. "We were late, and Captain Hughes was forced to depart."

Gabin winced. "You would never have made it to your ship. No doubt the city swarms with the Maiden's agents. If she has truly escaped, she will be furious."

Olivia reached down to Gabin and pulled him up, then helped him balance as he walked.

Mei helped Sidna to stand. They hobbled a few steps, lagging behind Olivia and Gabin. She spoke softly. "You were very nearly killed today."

Sidna sighed. "I know."

They walked a few more steps before Mei continued. "Why did you stop?"

"Stop?"

"I was watching. You could have killed her."

Sidna looked down. "I . . . don't know. The power just failed all of a sudden."

Mei nodded solemnly. "You sound relieved."

"Maybe I am. It's just . . . it was more than I could handle, but I kept on drawing more and more. It would have used me up."

"Then I would say it is good you were unable to continue."

Sidna nodded and took a few more steps. "I have this terrible feeling, deep down, that something incredibly strong was coming, and if things hadn't gotten screwed up, it would have found me."

"Found you?"

"Yes. I could hear it in my mind, coming nearer."

Mei stopped. "Save your strength. You do not need to worry any longer."

Sidna looked back. Fall knelt near the scattered books where the Maiden had escaped. He placed something in a pouch on his belt's opposite side and stood, unmoving as he caught her eyes.

"I can hear it." She turned and walked on with Mei's help. "It's still out there."

The remnants of the Runian research lab drifted slowly in space above an unknown world. It was hard to comprehend, but the monster had moved it somehow, dropping it right into the path of the ship Ban couldn't seem to escape.

He sat on the top edge of the lab's broken wall, cleaning his light machine gun as he watched the Elcosian dreadnaught rotate back into view.

He took a deep breath from his suit's respirator. "That's twice I've almost been vaporized by that damn ship."

"Better than being vaporized at all, right?" Hermes asked.

Ban nodded. "When you put it that way . . ."

The imp sighed and rested his chin on his hands. "So what now?"

Ban looked at the unknown world below them. "Well, we could sit here and fall into that planet. Or, we could wait until those Elcosians come finish the job."

"I'll take option one. It wouldn't be the first time."

Ban took a long look at Hermes, unsure if he was joking. "Either way, it's not really up to us."

"Mmmm," Hermes mumbled. He kicked his legs, one at a time. Despite the vacuum, Ban could still hear him speak through the helmet's radio. "Sucks about the crystal. A whole world just gone. Poof."

"Not all of it."

Hermes looked up. "Oh yeah?"

Ban held up his armored fingers. A thin blue chip of glass pointed up between them. "Found this below. Somehow, it survived."

"What do you think's inside?"

Ban smiled. "Hopefully, a couple of birds."

Hermes scratched his head. "Huh?"

Ban carefully tucked the tiny shard away into a storage canister on his belt. "I'll have to tell you later." He twisted to look down over his right side. Becks and Tyr walked up the wall using their suits' integrated magnetic field generators. "Any luck?"

Becks shook her head. "Not really. I don't think there's anything here we can use for propulsion."

"Garland?" Ban asked.

"No sign of him. He must have been on the part of the ship that remained." She stepped up and over to stand on the wall's edge, taking a look at the Elcosian ship. "Think that thing killed them?"

"Maybe." Ban closed the ejection port on his gun and stood. "It could take a while for it to tear through the whole ship. There's a good chance that—"

Ban's HUD beeped. There was a new sensor contact, and by the shape of the marker, it appeared to be a space vessel.

An incredibly bright spotlight shined down on them. He raised his hand to block it and searched for the source as his helmet adjusted.

The ship was blood-red. Its central top section was covered with triangular plates that stood up from the surface, like scales. It had multiple engines in the back, and behind the bridge, a thin tower extended upward, topped with a communications array. It bristled with guns, and Ban could see more than a few missile tubes.

He searched for any identifying marks. Painted on the hull to the aft of the spotlight, a cracked white skull stared back at him. It was smiling.

He turned to Becks. "Pirates."

Hermes hopped up and floated to Ban's arm, grabbing on to arrest his momentum. "Considering the alternatives, I'll take it."

The bay doors opened on the bottom of the ship, and a fast-craft launched. It sped toward their location, slowing itself with thrusters as it turned toward them.

It broadcasted on a general frequency. "Move toward the craft slowly. And keep those weapons lowered. You only have one chance to do this right."

Hermes shrugged. "Here's hoping they're better hosts than Garland was."

Ban nodded then motioned for the others to comply. They walked forward.

The tiny ship's belly opened, and a ramp extended. They walked up it, and the ramp retracted, taking them inside. The doors closed under them as the airlock pressurized.

After what seemed like an eternity, the inner doors opened, and a man stepped inside.

He was dressed in loose-fitting, black-and-red clothing with a black oxygen mask, a dagger at his belt, and a rifle in his hands. "Our captain claims the right of salvage on your . . . vessel."

Ban walked forward. "Fine by me. Just so happens we're done with it."

The pirate looked them over. "Your weapons and armor too."

Ban patted his light machine gun. "Sure. Come and get it."

The pirate tapped the trigger guard of his rifle with his finger. Before he could say anything, a gloved hand touched the pirate on the shoulder and moved him aside.

The newcomer spoke. "Keep your stuff, but I'm taking that dumb-looking imp. Though I have no idea why, since he's pretty much worthless."

Hermes ran forward and hugged his leg. "Fall!"

Fall laughed. "What's this? Happy to see me for once?"

Hermes frowned. "Hey, it's been a long day. Monsters, Elcosians, and all of a sudden . . . *pirates*."

"Don't forget the Alidians." Fall looked up at Ban, and his smile faded. "Unless I'm wrong, we've already met."

"That's right." Ban reached up and removed his helmet so the man could see his face. "And we have a lot to discuss."

The bridge's holographic imager hummed and activated.

The spy's image resolved. He looked from side to side beyond Tieger. "My, oh my. You've been having fun without me."

Tieger tightened his grip on *Janus*. "You are welcome to join us."

"You'll have to forgive me, but I'm currently indisposed." He picked at a fingernail with the knife that almost instantly appeared in his hand. "I have interesting news."

"You have found her?"

"Yes. But she has escaped."

"Again you fail." Tieger turned away.

"You give up so easily." The spy sighed. "She is the guest of a pirate, frightened and fleeing to safety."

Tieger turned back. "Fleeing where?"

"Where else?"

"To her homeworld . . . "

The spy looked up from the knife's tip. "I'm glad you see it my way."

Tieger stepped closer. "Return now so that we may track her ship."

The spy smiled. "There will be no need. I followed her on board."

Tieger nodded slowly. "That is good. Activate your signal."

"Of course. When the time is right."

Tieger pointed *Janus* toward the image. "Do not delay. I will be waiting."

The spy's smile widened to show his perfect teeth. "I'm counting on it."

CONFOUNDING FACTORS

FALL TIGHTENED THE FINAL SCREW ON HIS mechanized bow. "You can relax, Captain." He lifted the weapon and gave the string a few test pulls. "They're safe."

Across the room on the wooden desk, red light shone from a compact holographic projector, illuminating the otherwise dark room.

The Hughes hologram sighed. "I won't rest easy until *all* my officers are back in Runian space." He reached down and rubbed his leg. "What's your plan?"

Fall lowered the bow. "Nothing's been decided."

"But you're working on it?"

"Of course."

Hughes crossed his arms and looked away. "I should've waited."

"Maybe so. But you had your own challenges. Other people to protect."

Hughes grumbled. "Well, thank you, but I can't fully justify leaving people behind."

Fall stood up. "They'll make it home."

Hughes looked back to Fall. "I'll hold you to that." He sighed. "Until then, we'll be waiting at Crossroads."

Fall nodded. "I'll send word as soon as we find a ride."

"See that you do." Hughes placed his captain's hat on his head. He smiled as a little girl ran past, laughing. "We're counting on you, *Ranger*." The transmission ended.

Fall took in a deep breath and sat in the padded wooden chair beside the desk.

Sostek stood up slowly from the shadowed corner to Fall's right. He picked at the bandage on his chest with a frown. "You should be pleased. Your mission is nearing its completion."

Fall looked up. "No . . . it's not that. I'm just thinking."

"About Cisterne?"

Fall turned his head. "Yes."

"And the girl?"

Fall stood and walked away. He turned after a few paces. "I don't get her." He tossed the bow onto his bunk.

Sostek raised an eyebrow. "She's a magus. This was the only possible outcome."

"I guess." Fall stared past him, going deeper into his own thoughts. "She's the first one I've met."

Sostek drew his knife. "Careful now . . . "

"What?"

"I know that look, human."

Fall waved his hand. "There's no look."

"She isn't your type." Sostek flipped his knife over and swiped it from the air. "She courts *darker* things."

"Maybe." Fall crossed his arms. "Maybe not."

"What further evidence do you need?"

Fall shrugged. "What if she's caught up in something beyond her control?"

Sostek grunted. "That much is obvious."

Fall frowned. "I'm serious."

Sostek stepped forward. "Am I not? The greatest threat of your generation could be on this very ship. Have you forgotten what you saw in the World Shard?"

"So I'm supposed to decide she's a threat after one mistake?"

Sostek nodded several times as he looked down. "No doubt I said something similar about Riest when he first started his descent."

"She isn't *descending*."

"Not yet."

Fall reached down for his sword and scabbard and fastened them around his back. "Like I said. Maybe."

"Then why bring the sword? Worried?"

Fall stopped. He'd fastened the scabbard without realizing it. "Just being careful. This *is* a pirate ship."

"Hmph. They aren't the ones giving you pause. Admit it."

Fall sighed, hands on his hips. "Look, are you coming or not?"

Sostek sheathed his dagger with a click. "Not a good idea. The pirates might not react calmly when they realize there's a demon on board."

Fall looked up at Sostek. "I took it pretty well."

Sostek nodded slowly. "I suspect your mind is more open than most." The voidstrider reached into his robes and retrieved the World Shard. Its orange light partially lit the room. "There's a problem I need to solve."

Fall tightened the last strap. "Which is?"

"Our lack of transportation."

Fall walked over to the exit hatch. "I'll see what I can do. Mei might know of something nearby."

Sostek looked up from the crystal. "There's something else. I can hear it in your voice."

Fall twisted his lips. He tapped his fingers rhythmically on the door jamb. "I can't shake the feeling I left something unfinished."

Sostek nodded. "Several of your enemies escaped with their lives."

"No, it's not that." Fall stood in the open doorway. "I'm not sure what it is."

Sostek sat on the room's spare bunk and kicked the bag at his feet. "It will come to you."

Fall grimaced as he looked at the bag. "You actually kept that?"

"What? This head? I wouldn't dare discard it. Surely, it holds the answers to many questions."

"Sort of morbid though, isn't it?"

"No more than the last one I claimed. At least this one won't rot."

Fall was about to ask a question but left it alone.

Sostek waved him away in dismissal and looked back to the shard with a smile. "You'll be late for dinner."

Fall stared for a moment then backed away. "Just do me a favor. No more trophies today."

Sostek looked up, white irises spinning in the dark. "*No promises.*"

In contrast with its jagged, fearsome exterior, every bit of the *Red's* interior structure, from the deck up to the arched beams above, was constructed from beautiful, richly stained wood. Vibrant images of fish and undersea life had been carved along the surfaces, creating storied scenes that flowed from one room to another.

In place of the normal electric lights on most ships, gas lamps lined the halls. The flames in the lamps flickered in the artificial, circulating breeze and wavered above their candles. Exaggerated shadows of the carvings moved with the dancing lights as each story came to life.

This must have cost a fortune . . .

As Fall approached the meeting hall, two guards stood before its two gilded wooden doors. Instead of the powered armor of professional soldiers and mercenaries or the motley armor of scavengers and slavers, they wore fine cloth and leather, much like their captain. Long knives hung from their waists, and each held a bayoneted rifle.

The sooner we leave, the better.

The men stepped back, and the doors opened as Fall approached. Inside, he was greeted by an unexpected sight—a grand meeting hall, with hanging white lace, gold and crystal chandeliers, and elaborately crafted crown molding.

Underneath those decorations, a feast fit for a king was laid out on a long banquet table, lined with goblets of wine, various steaming meats, and frosted deserts. As a pair of pirates crossed by in front of him, Fall looked past to the doors on the opposite side of the room.

Becks, the Alidian marine, stood there, arms crossed, in her partially unzipped, black sub-armor suit. She was speaking with Mei, and neither woman looked particularly happy.

Olivia edged up next to Fall, cup half-full of wine. "Best stay out of that."

He looked down to her. "No joke. Sorry I'm late."

"You aren't. Gabin's not even here yet."

Fall surveyed the room. "He's not the only one missing."

Olivia took a drink. "Yeah, and I wish they'd hurry up."

He smiled. "Nervous?"

She took another sip. "Aren't you?"

Ban, the leader of the Alidians, and his large friend Tyr entered the meeting hall. He immediately motioned to Becks, who moved to join them.

Fall watched the group closely. "No . . . everything's perfectly fine."

The Alidians moved to the open chairs halfway down the table and sat.

"Ready?" Fall motioned for Olivia to go first. After she'd sat down, he took the chair next to her, directly across from Ban. Mei walked over and sat to Fall's left.

The Roshanan Ranger cleared her throat but otherwise remained silent. The Alidians kept to themselves as well.

This should be interesting.

Fall turned as the main doors opened.

Captain Gabin strode in confidently, red coat flaring out around him. "Ah, good, you're all here." He smiled and walked around Fall, Olivia, and Mei toward the table's head. He sat and put his scabbard and rapier up on the table. "Welcome to the *Red*." He reached for a goblet and poured himself some wine. He raised the cup to take a drink but paused when he noticed everyone watching him. He waved his hand. "Please. Eat."

Ban stood up stiffly. "Thank you, Captain. We're in your debt."

Gabin smiled. "Say no more. One should always assist a fellow man in need."

Ban sat down with a nod.

Fall looked to Olivia incredulously.

Interesting philosophy for a pirate ...

Gabin put his goblet down and wiped his mouth. "I'll hear no more of this debt-and-gratitude talk. Let us celebrate."

Becks reached out and tore a roasted bird's leg from its body. "What's there to celebrate?"

"Our escape. And to rescued friends."

Fall and Ban met eyes.

Friends who tried to kill me the first time we met.

Olivia raised her glass and spoke softly out of the corner of her mouth. "Awkward ..."

Hermes pulled himself up onto the table at the opposite end from Gabin and raised his cup. "I'll drink to that."

Gabin continued with a smile. "To friendship." He drank, swallowing as he pulled the goblet away. "Sergeant Morgan. I've been meaning to ask. By the look of your armor, I'd place you as an Alidian soldier."

Ban nodded. "Bond-Sergeant, actually, but you'd be right."

"A little far from home, no?"

Ban turned, eyes focused on Gabin. "We were stranded during a mission." He glanced at Fall. "After an attack on our ship."

Hermes looked up as he leaned over a platter of grapes. "By *Elcosians*." He picked a grape and frowned at it. "Remember?"

"So you've said." Ban never looked away from Fall. "I'm curious to hear what you have to say."

Fall raised an eyebrow. "Why me?"

Ban waved his hand toward Hermes. "Hermes says you were a victim of circumstance. The evidence seems to suggest otherwise."

Gabin coughed. "Perhaps an alternate subject would be—"

"No, it's fine." Fall held eye contact with Ban. "What evidence?"

Ban didn't look away either. "Becks?"

She reached down and came back up with a small disk. She tossed it onto the table, and an image appeared above it, scrolling with random letters and numbers.

Fall squinted. "What am I supposed to be seeing here?"

Becks sat back. "A program designed to disable the *Talon's* engines, weapons, and shields."

Fall looked up. "I don't see what it has to do with me."

Ban picked up the disk and switched it off. "The code is written in Runian military computer language."

"I'm not Runian. I'm Valenen."

Becks tapped the table. "The bridge crew was murdered with a blade. You fight with a sword. Also, you conveniently arrived on the *Talon* right before the attack."

He laughed. "Half dead . . ."

Olivia nodded. "Way more than half. He needed emergency surgery. That's the whole reason we came aboard."

Mei put down her glass and coughed into her hand. "Actually, Doctor, that is only partially true." Her mechanical eye whirred as it focused on Ban. "Your ship intercepted us on our way to Crossroads Station. We would never have stopped otherwise. My understanding of the Accord of Valen is that your captain committed a crime when he did so. In fact, your presence in the Frontier was ultimately illegal."

Ban looked to Becks and Tyr. "We had good reason."

Olivia sat up. "Care to explain why you broke the Accord?"

"We didn't. At least not at first." Ban pointed behind him with his thumb. "That wreck you rescued us from? That was a fragment of a Runian military research ship. We were sent to find it and capture it."

Olivia put her glass down. "You're saying Rune broke the Accord first?"

"Correct. We learned about it from a Runian prisoner we captured on Nix, at another illegal installation."

Hermes held up his hand. "Wait. What kind of prisoner?"

Ban shrugged. "An engineer."

"You had a Runian engineer on your ship?"

"Yes."

Hermes looked ahead. "That can't be a coincidence."

Ban furrowed his brow. "What are you getting at?"

"Hold on. I'm trying to figure this out. What happened to the engineer?"

"I'd imagine he's dead," Ban said with a shrug.

"I mean *before* the attack. Where was he?"

"In the brig. Where else?"

Fall sat up quickly and turned to Mei. "The man in black! I forgot about him."

Mei nodded. "Yes. That would make perfect sense. He did say he intended to commit murder."

Becks leaned forward. "From inside a cell?"

Mei shook her head. "He was quite free at the time of the attack. I did not know about the sabotage until just now, but that had to have been what he meant."

Becks pointed down at the table. "Even if he did have something to do with it, he never could've taken down the whole bridge by himself, let alone plant that code."

"He wasn't alone," Ban said.

Everyone stopped to look at him.

"What do you mean?" Becks asked.

"Lieutenant Holland. When the Elcosians brought him over, the entire command staff was there." Ban sat back. "We were completely distracted."

Olivia seemed confused. "Do what now?"

Becks spoke as she watched Ban. "One of our officers was captured on Nix. We thought he was dead, but the Elcosians picked him up. He had full access to the ship's command codes."

Olivia lifted her hand from the table and leaned in. "So what are we saying here? That Rune and the Elcosians worked together to attack the *Talon*?"

Becks looked at Ban and Tyr. "Why not? Maybe they've formed an alliance."

Fall frowned. "That's bad news, especially if they're running operations all the way out here."

Gabin leaned forward. "But what of the secret Runian ship? You were there, no? What did you find?"

Ban looked at Becks then Tyr in question. Tyr nodded in approval. Ban held out his hand and opened it slowly. A green light started to glow from the inside, illuminating a tree within a circle.

Olivia's mouth hung open. "Whoa . . . "

Fall blinked. "What is that?"

Ban flexed and extended his fingers. "I'm not entirely sure. It's a gift."

Gabin poured himself another goblet of wine. "From whom?"

"Thenander. A god."

Fall looked up from Ban's hand. "Did you say a god?"

"I did."

Just like Sostek's story.

"Then that makes you a champion."

The room fell silent.

Ban and Fall stared at each other for several seconds, until finally, Ban pulled his hand back. "Hermes must have told you."

Fall sat back. "No. Someone else."

Hermes narrowed his oversized eyes. "Who?"

"I'll tell you later."

"Tell me now."

"*Later.*" Fall looked back to Ban. "You said the research ship was destroyed. How?"

Ban closed his eyes. He waited a few seconds then answered. "It was ripped apart by an ephmere."

Mei's lips parted. "An ephmere? As in the game of Vogi?"

"Yes," Ban answered. "A creature of nightmare and shadow. The Runians found its crystal prison. Inside, the ephmere held this gift captive. As the monster escaped, I took it back."

"Fantastic," Gabin said, transfixed.

"Not the word I'd use," Olivia said before she took a long drink.

Ban continued. "And then we were taken to Gyre."

"How?" Mei asked.

"I can't explain. The ephmere pulled us there."

"Why Gyre?" Olivia asked.

Hermes jumped in. "It was probably summoned."

"Who would be insane enough to want something like that around?" Becks asked in disbelief.

Hermes shrugged. "An arcanist."

Mei shifted uncomfortably.

Gabin's expression morphed from wonder to concern. "Do you mean Sidna?"

"Beats me. She's not the only one out there," Hermes answered.

Fall leaned back and sighed. "It was her." He sat up quickly when everyone turned toward him. "But I don't think she meant to."

"How can you be sure?" Becks asked.

"Well, I can't. I just know what I saw."

Olivia shivered. "I saw it too, Fall. But from what I remember, it didn't seem like an accident."

He turned toward her.

She scooted forward in her chair. "I'm sorry, but she scares me. She's the most frightening person I've ever met."

Fall turned to look at the others. "She was fighting the Maiden. She wasn't trying to summon an ephmere."

Olivia held up her hands. "All right, whatever you say. I dunno. It just felt . . . *evil.*"

In a way, I guess it did.

Gabin looked up abruptly and almost spilled his wine. "Sidna!"

Fall looked too.

There she was, standing in the doorway. He had no way of knowing how long she'd been there, but it was clear from the look on her face that she'd at least heard that last part.

Olivia turned in her chair. "Sidna, I—"

Sidna stopped her. "It's fine. You said it. *Own it.*"

"I didn't really mean you were evil, I just—"

"No, no. You're right. It *was* coming for me. It still is for all I know."

Hermes jumped down from his chair. "Hey, come in and sit down. We can talk this through."

"That's okay. I never should've come." She backed out through the doors.

Gabin and Fall both moved to stand. Fall hesitated when he saw Gabin, who also stopped.

Mei stood up. "See to your guests, Captain. I will speak with her."

Gabin lowered himself back down slowly. "Yes. Yes, that's probably best." His eyes lingered on Fall for a split second too long.

Olivia hung her head. "Damn."

Fall reached up and touched her shoulder. "It'll be fine."

Ban cleared his throat. "I'd say we all have a lot to consider. Fall, for what it's worth, I think I believe you about the *Talon.*"

Fall nodded. "I swear we had nothing to do with it. In fact, I owe you one. Your surgeons saved my life."

Ban smiled. "Then something good did come of it." His expression grew more serious. "We should speak sometime. About what each of us knows of gods and champions."

"Sounds good," Fall replied.

Ban, Becks, and Tyr stood up and left.

Gabin waited until the doors fully closed then sighed. "That could have gone better."

Hermes hopped back up onto his chair. "Yeah, but it could've gone much worse. One of Ban's men got killed when you guys escaped the *Talon*."

"I didn't know," Fall said.

"He was pretty upset, but I helped him see reason. He's not a bad guy."

"That was my impression as well." Gabin stood up and stretched. "On that note, it seems as good a time as any to bid you all farewell for the evening."

Fall and Olivia stood. Fall bowed his head slightly. "Captain."

Gabin returned the bow. "Ranger."

Fall and Olivia left for the door, and Fall turned back just as he was about to exit. "Hermes, you coming?"

"In a little bit. I'm not finished yet."

"You know you don't actually need to eat, right?"

Hermes popped another grape into his mouth and mumbled while he chewed. "Sure, but I still need energy from somewhere. Might as well enjoy getting it."

"Just come find me later."

"Yeah, yeah."

Fall walked out, shaking his head to the sounds of clanging metal and smacking lips.

As the automated doors closed, Olivia plopped down on her bunk with a sigh. "That wore me out."

Her bedding was plain, simple and functional just like the other bed a few meters away. Olivia and Kumi were given a shared room, but Kumi hadn't left the sick bay yet.

Fall leaned against the wooden wall just inside the doors. "I know what you mean. I figured there'd be tension, but I didn't expect to be accused of sabotage."

Olivia scooted back against the wall. "Seems like we convinced them otherwise." She reached up and let her blonde hair down. With a few shakes, it fell free over her shoulders. She unzipped her jumpsuit down to her stomach, gray shirt damp underneath. "It's hot."

Fall smiled. "Probably all that wine."

She returned the smile with a raised eyebrow. "Is that right?"

He shrugged. "I'm assuming. Didn't have much myself."

She turned her head slightly. "Your loss. Good stuff." She smiled then looked up with concern. "Hey, I almost forgot with all that's happened. I should have a look at your wounds again."

Fall touched his side. "They're fine. Even the one Tieger gave me."

"I'll be the judge of that." She waved him over and patted the bunk. "Come on. Have a seat and get that shirt off."

Fall's eyes opened wide. "Yes, ma'am." He moved over and unbuckled his belt then laid it and his sword down on the floor as he sat.

Olivia tugged at his shirt as he pulled it over his head. "All right, let me see."

He shivered slightly as she touched his healing wound. "Ah, cold."

"Hands of a healer. Quit whining." She pressed along the incisions. "We really should find some endaramine for this. It'll scar if we don't." She traced the injury with her fingertip. "And we can't have that, after all the work I've put into you."

He looked down into her eyes, blue-green and slightly dilated. They moved back and forth quickly, looking into each of his eyes in return. Her lips parted slightly, and without giving it much thought, he leaned in toward her.

They kissed.

Her lips were wet and her breath warm as she exhaled through her nose. Her back arched, and she dug her nails into the back of his neck. He moved to bring her closer, but in that moment, right when he could feel the rush of adrenaline kicking in, she pulled away.

He let her go, hands hanging in the air. "What's wrong?"

She wiped her lips and nodded, looking down. "Why'd you take up for her?"

"Huh?"

"Sidna. Back in the meeting just now."

Fall lowered his hands. "I wasn't taking up for her."

"That's what it seemed like."

"I just gave my opinion on her motivations. Like everyone else."

Olivia shook her head quickly, lips pulling back. "Okay, see, but that's the problem. You don't know anything *about* her motivations."

"Sure. Who could?"

"I can. She's only out for herself. She's proven that over and over again."

Fall scooted back and sighed. "What's this really about, Olivia?"

"About?"

"Yeah. I mean, we were just kissing and now you're mad at me. It's a little confusing."

"Why? I can't kiss someone I'm mad at?"

He raised his eyebrows. "Where I'm from, it kind of means you like them."

She frowned. "Well, at the moment, it's a little of both."

He looked down and smiled, reaching for his discarded shirt. "Like I said. Confusing." He stood up.

"Wait. You're leaving?"

"Seems like a good idea." He pulled his shirt over his head then picked up his gear and headed for the door.

She got up and followed him. "Stop." She pulled on his shoulder, turning him around.

"Why?"

She squeezed her eyes shut. "Because you're right. It's not really about her."

"Then what *is* it about?"

She walked back over to the bed and sat down, exhaling. "Me." She gathered her thoughts then continued. "Back before, when we talked on the *Orchard*, I said I needed more out of life than just a job. We were stranded, and we'd just been through some pretty stressful stuff. I wasn't even sure we'd survive." She rubbed her face then looked back up. "But now that we found my crew, I have that life to go back to. I have responsibilities. A career. I can't just leave that behind on a whim."

Fall shrugged. "Who's asking you too?"

She blinked. "I dunno. Me, I guess." She sighed. "Why do you think I wanted to know so much about your job? This life is attractive. Nothing to tie me down, nowhere to be. In some ways, it's just easier."

Fall looked to the side and down a little before looking back with an uneasy smile. "Listen, kissing you just seemed right. Sorry if I made things complicated."

She stood up again. "You didn't." She seemed to shrink a little. "I'm just not sure how I feel."

Fall nodded a few times in agreement. "I get it." He moved to the door, which opened at his approach.

"Do you?" she asked.

He uttered a short laugh. "Not completely." He stepped through the doorway and turned with a grin. "But I guess that makes two of us."

The doors closed.

He walked away, watching his boots thud on the hardwood flooring. *Not embarrassing at all.*

He shook his head and winced.

And why should it be? It's not like you had a girl break off a kiss and say, no thanks, I'm only here for the job.

He looked up just in time to avoid Kumi and Union. The sentinel held on to the injured woman's left arm as she walked, her other hand steadying her against the wall.

Fall tried not to stare at the blood-spotted bandage wrapped around her head. "Kumi. Back on your feet?"

She moaned. "Unfortunately." She looked at Union pitifully. "Are we almost there?"

"Only a few doors remain," the sentinel buzzed.

"Good. Feels like my skull's about to pound right off my shoulders." She looked up to Fall with a grimace. "Was Commander Hansen in our room?"

"Um, yes, she was."

Kumi frowned. "What's the matter with you?"

Fall rubbed the back of his head. "Just a bruised ego. Nothing serious."

She did her best to smile. "I'm sure you'll recover." She grabbed onto Union. "Let's get there before I pass out again."

"Yes, of course." The lights of his orange eyes rolled, and he mumbled as they passed by. "The frailty of organics . . . "

Fall nodded and continued on toward the sick bay with a sigh.

Union, you have no idea.

Fall slowly walked into the sick bay through its single wooden door, expecting to find someone inside. But it was quiet, and no one seemed to be there.

Guess they only use it when someone's hurt.

Like everywhere else on the *Red*, the room was made of wood, or at least it appeared to be. There were soft yellow lights recessed in the ceiling above, shining dimly on the carved arches between the main room and three others, and the air smelled stale, like a closet full of old clothing.

Three wooden beds with rumpled red blankets sat on raised pedestals, spread out in the center with just enough room between them for walking. Waist-high countertops held an odd assortment of medical tools strewn about, and wooden cabinets stretched from floor to ceiling, two doors for each, made mostly of glass.

As he walked up to the nearest one, built-in light strips activated to illuminate the shelves and their contents. He looked from bottle to bottle, reading the labels as he searched for endaramine.

As he worked through words he'd never seen before, his concentration drifted. He saw Olivia's face in his mind's eye, looking for him through a crowd of shifting patrons in the Crossroads pseudareum.

Her uniform was clean, and there wasn't a hair out of place on her head. He was sweaty, in need of a shower. Still, she smiled, looking him up and down.

He moved on to the next cabinet.

The Orchard Run. Breakfast. She didn't just ask about the job. And on the Rìluò. She brought me food, checked on me. She's been there every step of the way.

He paused and looked up, reaching to pinch the bridge of his nose.

And after all that, when she wanted my support, I chose Sidna.

He drummed his fingers against the cabinet rhythmically as he thought about Sidna, lying on the floor of the Maiden's library, weak and defeated, so different than she'd been the last time he'd seen her on the Rìluò.

No, don't forget who she is. I doubt she thinks about anyone else but herself.

Fall gathered his fingers into a fist and pushed off the cabinet with a sigh.

All of a sudden, there was a clatter in the next room. He shut the cabinet door and walked over, leaning through the doorway to his left.

Sitting there on the floor was Sidna, surrounded on all sides by a heap of toppled boxes and opened bottles.

She looked up and started in surprise, placing her hand over her heart. "You scared me."

Fall stepped all the way into the side room, pointing over his shoulder with his thumb. "Sorry. Looking for endaramine." He nodded toward the empty cabinet behind her. "Don't suppose you've seen any in there?"

"No." She sighed dejectedly. "See any liadra out there?"

"I don't think so."

"Figures." There was something profoundly tired in the way she said it. She looked down again.

He rubbed his chin. "Well, I'll get back to it." He turned to leave, but she stopped him.

"Do you think she's right?"

"Who?"

She looked up. "Olivia. She said I was evil. Do you agree?"

Fall sighed and leaned against the doorway. "She didn't say you were evil. Just the feeling she got from what you were doing."

"But what do you think?"

Fall took a deep breath. "I don't think you're evil."

She stuck her hand back in the box and lifted a vial. She tossed it aside. "You could be a little more convincing."

He walked over, farther into the room, and opened a wide wooden lockbox with a dusty glass window on top. There were several small bottles inside, which he began to search one by one. "You have to understand. People are generally mistrustful of arcanists."

"Oh? You don't say?"

"Hold on, I'm serious." He turned around and sat on the edge of the counter. "Living out here opens your eyes, so most folks in the Frontier are a little more tolerant. Right now, you're dealing with Fathomers. All they know about you is what they've been told."

She waved her hand. "You still aren't answering my question. I want to know what you think."

He looked down at his boots, exhaled, and looked back up into her eyes. "I think you're in over your head."

She nodded a few times, looking into the distance. "You mean I can't handle it."

He crossed his arms. "Can't handle what?"

Her eyes shot down then back up. "Don't do that. You saw."

"I did. I'm wondering if you know."

"Are you saying you do?"

"I might."

"How?"

"A friend."

She scoffed. *"Convenient."*

He shrugged. "No, I saw it for myself too." He continued before she could ask her next question. "It doesn't matter how. What matters is that you understand how bad this is."

She put the box aside. "You're asking if I know what I'm dealing with? Let me tell you what I'm dealing with." She stood up and held out her hands, palms up. "On one hand, I have Tieger constantly hunting me, threatening to burn me alive, which feels pretty awesome. On the other hand, I have a way to stop him, but a bunch of strangers might not approve." She moved her hands up and down, alternating like a set of scales. "Hmmm. Tough decision."

Fall nodded. "Look, I hear you. And I admit there's no way I could fully understand. All I can do is warn you."

"Consider me warned." She moved to the counter opposite his and started to search again.

He watched her for several seconds. "No regrets."

"What?"

"I'm not sure I'll ever see you again, so I don't want to leave with any regrets."

She turned back around to face him. "Okay, whatever that means."

"It means I'm going to say what's on my mind."

She shrugged. "No one's stopping you."

He walked away, thinking to himself before he turned around and spoke. "I'm not sure how you did it, but I know you figured out how to summon one of those monsters."

She opened her mouth to speak, but he held up his hand. "Let me finish." He kept on pacing. "You know what you want from it, so I think it's only fair you know what *it* wants."

"Which is?"

He stopped. "You."

"Me?"

"That's right. It wants your anger and your fear. It wants your desire for power."

"I don't want po—"

"You do, though. Not for anything bad, maybe, but you do." He pushed on. "It will drain you and make you a slave. Worse yet, you won't even care."

She stared off and shivered. "I felt something like that in Cisterne. Like a siphon that would drink me dry if I ever let it start."

Fall moved closer. "So, there you go. You understand. The only thing to do now is throw it away. Don't use it again."

"Except, it's not that easy."

"Why not?"

"I told you. Tieger. He'll never stop unless I stop him."

"Again, I get that. But the *Qur Noc* are much worse. They destroyed entire planets. They drove us into some sort of dark age and completely separated us from our past. The galaxy can't handle that again."

She sat back against the counter. "I'm not worried about the galaxy, Fall. I'm worried about my sister and my mother, my people, anyone else Tieger might go after." Her eyes began to well up. "Can't you see? He's *real*. He's not a story or a myth. If I don't kill him, it'll be the end of everything."

Fall watched her face. He could see she was barely holding it together. "There's got to be another way."

She shook her head. "There isn't. He has that ship, and he's basically unstoppable."

"I'll help you. Mei will help you."

"I've tried that before. It's not enough." She wiped her eyes. "I'm sorry, but I'm not changing my mind."

Fall walked back to his counter and turned. He stared at the floor, unable to think of a better argument. "So that's it? There's no talking you out of it?"

"No."

"Okay. Good luck." He walked toward the exit.

"Wait. That's all you're going to say? Good luck?"

He threw his hands up. "What else can I say? You've made up your mind, damn the consequences."

"You aren't being fair. I told you why."

"Fair? What about the rest of us? What about Mei? What about your boyfriend, Gabin?"

"He's *not* my boyfriend."

"That's not the point. If they go with you, they'll die."

"You don't know that."

"I do. Thing is, it would probably be you that kills them."

She paused. The statement hit her hard. "You think I'd kill my friends?"

He hesitated. "No, not you. But it wouldn't be *you* anymore."

She exhaled and blinked hard. "You know what? I think I'm good without the liadra." She moved toward the door.

Fall tried to beat her there. "Sidna, wait. I'm sorry."

"No, it's fine. Have fun doing whatever it is you do out here." She pushed past and left him standing there.

"Oh, come on." He shook his head and went after her, but the door was closed, and she was already gone.

Several emotions fought to rise to the surface of his mind, not the least of which was frustration.

I had to tell her.

He backed away from the door, and his fingers wrapped around the object in his right hand, a bottle he hadn't known was there. He lifted it up to read the label.

Liadra . . . Of course.

In that moment, the door opened again. At first there didn't seem to be anyone there, but then in walked Mei.

She smiled weakly. "That was less than optimal."

He took a deep breath and nodded. "No kidding. You heard all of that?"

"I did. And I want you to know that I might have said the same things in your place."

"I—"

She held up her hand. "But I never will." She walked farther inside as Fall turned to follow her. "Do you want to know why?"

"Because she's your client?"

"No. Because she will continue on, with or without me." Mei stopped and looked back at Fall. "I do not want her to continue on without me."

Fall leaned against a counter, arms crossed. "I don't see why. She's the most stubborn pain in the ass I know."

Mei's lips twisted into a knowing smile, and her mechanical eye buzzed. "Is that what she is to you?"

He studied his boots. "Today? Yes."

Mei continued. "I have spent many days alone with her." She sighed. "And in being around her, I have learned a few things."

Fall looked up. "Such as?"

"That she is not as selfish or quick-tempered as she sometimes may seem. That she is desperately seeking something she believes will provide salvation for her people. Also, that if she were to relent or to lose her focus in the slightest, she would be utterly lost. She cannot do it alone, though there are many who might lead her astray."

Fall lifted his fingers then let them fall back onto his forearms. "All right, then why does she push us away?"

Mei rested her hand on the grip of her knife. "Would you make friends so easily if you suspected the next person who catches a glimpse of your skin might hate you for it? Worse yet, that they might deliver you into the hands of an Elcosian murderer?"

Fall looked down again. "No, I guess not."

"Or would you instead keep all others at a safe distance and lash out at any who persist in getting closer?" Mei looked off, seeing the past. "There have been nights, far too often, when I have been awoken by her cries. By fitful sobbing. When I would try to ask her about her sleep, she would instantly attack. Between these things and the fragmented half-truths in our conversations, I have come to a conclusion. She has been hunted, brutally so, and she is terrified, much like a cornered animal."

Fall stood up and rubbed the back of his neck. "Well, damn. Now I really do feel awful." He looked up. "I was just trying to help. Get her to see the danger she's in."

Mei came over and touched his arm. "I know you were. Do not worry. I will stay with her as long as possible, and I will see that no additional harm comes to her."

Fall did his best to smile. "As long as possible." He held out his hand. "Here. I think this is what she was looking for. Her liadra."

Mei accepted the vial. "I will see that she gets it." They walked out together. "What will you do next?"

"Well, hopefully, I'll be on my way to Crossroads soon. If I can find a ride, that is."

"Let me know if I can help," she said.

"I will, but I think you have your hands full."

Mei nodded. "That I do. Goodbye, Fall."

She walked away, and Fall went the opposite direction, contemplating her words on the long walk back to his quarters.

Fall spun around as he fell onto his bunk. He put his hands behind his head and stared up at the ceiling. "Any chance I could start this day over?"

He lay there, listening to the ever-present thrum of the *Red*'s engines. *Eh, let it go. In a few days, it'll be just you and Hermes again.*

He rolled onto his side and shut his eyes.

And another job.

His eyes opened, adjusting to the darkness.

And another . . .

A slight glow beneath the room's other bunk caught his eye. It was dim at first, so weak that he thought he might have imagined it. As it grew in intensity, he realized it was the World Shard, partially obscured. As he sat up, Sostek appeared beside the bunk.

He looked at Fall directly. "You're back."

Fall nodded slowly as he rubbed his eyes. "For better or worse."

"Learn anything useful?"

"Only what *not* to say to women."

Sostek smiled. "A subject no man will ever master."

"No argument here." Fall motioned to the World Shard. "What about you?"

"I have something, yes."

Fall sat up quickly. "Finally, some good news."

"Don't get too excited. I'm currently unable to reach it. Though if I'm right, you might be able to."

"Reach what?"

"It would be better if I showed you."

Fall stood up. "All right, so show me."

"Very well, but you should know, this region of the memory doesn't allow for fast travel."

"Is this what you wanted me to see the first time we were there?"

"It is."

Fall rubbed his chin. "Hmmm. I remember you saying it was a long walk."

"Correct. We will be unreachable for several hours."

"Nice." Fall grunted as he picked up his sword and belt. "After the day I've had, that's exactly what I need."

FIXED PATHWAYS

SIDNA CLOSED HER EYES, FINGERTIPS GLIDING OVER the surface of the wooden seascape mural. She absently traced the flowing grooves as they coalesced.

Will there ever be a time . . .

She felt the smooth surface grow tumultuous as she continued, chipped waves building toward the raging battle she'd walked by dozens of times before.

. . . when things are simple?

She opened her eyes, and as her arm rose up to meet the thrashing sea monster and the scene of its cataclysmic rampage, her sleeve fell back slightly, uncovering the shimmering *viae* beneath.

Not for me.

She let her hand fall away and moved down the passage, past lonely, flickering lamps and broken, sinking ships.

The deck's lift opened as she approached. She went in and leaned against the inside, yawning as she waited for the doors to close. As they did, her reflection stared back from the shiny, golden façade. She looked exhausted despite the liadra's effects.

Great.

She reached for the destination lever and shoved it down.

I look like death.

The lift descended, and she walked out as soon as she could. She took a few turns, sleepily making her way through another wing of the *Red's* storied passages. Near the end, between two pillars of tree, the doors of her chambers stood wide open.

The room was spacious, with a big soft bed, chilled wine on a broad, round wooden table, and a large freestanding porcelain bathtub—only a few of Gabin's latest attempts to shower her in luxury.

It's no Rìluò.

As she entered, the tub automatically filled with water, and the candles on the floor around it lit themselves. She sighed and rolled her eyes then caught herself, raising her eyebrows with a shrug.

What could it hurt?

Her clothing fell away easily, each article a burden eagerly shed. She never stopped walking.

The water was just right, hotter than was comfortable, but not so much that it wouldn't soon be. And Gabin had taken care of everything—there was all she'd need to remedy her self-neglect.

After she'd finished the much-needed maintenance, she laid the razor down on the tub's copper tray and lowered her legs below the surface of the water. The air on her shoulders was cool, but steam still rose, warm and soothing. She slid down deeper.

Just going to rest my eyes for a second.

She hadn't had time in the last few days to take stock of everything. The crashed freighter, the Alidian ship, Cisterne—it was all a shifting blur. Her thoughts turned back even further to the escape from Fel Kno'a as she drifted somewhere between sleep and wakefulness.

I never looked back. I just left him there. And . . .

It'd been so easy to be sure of herself before, but now that she was actually going back to Veridian, her doubts were growing.

. . . the Guardian's still there. It's waiting.

The door chime sounded, startling her as water splashed out onto the floor. "Um, hold on." She stabilized the damp towel on her head and reached for another on the rack next to the tub.

Did I fall asleep?

She wrapped it around herself and secured it before walking to the door. "Coming."

The hatch opened; it was Ban, the Alidian man. He didn't avert his eyes. "Sidna."

She readjusted her towel near the top of her breasts. "Yeah?"

He looked into her eyes. "I wanted to speak with you."

"It's not exactly a good time."

He nodded. "There might not be another time."

Sidna looked back to the trail of clothes she'd left behind. "Fine. Just make it quick." She walked over and sat at the table, careful not to lose her towel. She reached for the chilled wine bottle at the table's edge and poured herself a glass. "Well? My water's getting cold. *So am I.*"

Ban came over, pulled out a chair, and sat. He looked down to his open hand then closed it into a fist. "There's something I need to ask you."

She didn't reply, leg bouncing impatiently.

He looked up. "About the ephmere."

Her leg stopped.

He leaned forward. "Do you know what it is?"

"Not really."

"Mmmm." He nodded. "Didn't you call it though?"

"Not on purpose. What's your point?"

Ban lifted the corner of his mouth. "So it was an accident. How? Why?"

"Why do you care?"

He sat back. "Because I think it's still out there."

She looked away for a split second. "It is."

"Where?"

"I don't know."

"Could you call it again?"

"Maybe. Like I said, I didn't do it on purpose."

"That was my next question. What exactly *were* you trying to do?"

She laughed. "Not that it's any of your business, but you wouldn't understand."

"I might." He spread his arms. "Try me."

She smiled and looked up. "I was trying to kill someone."

He didn't flinch. "But something went wrong."

"That's right. I overdid it."

Ban rubbed his chin. "That makes sense." He turned his eyes toward her again. "Is it some arcanist power? Can all of you do it?"

"Only when we're in danger. That's why it's best to leave us alone."

He watched her closely then spoke. "I've seen more than one of your kind die, one time quite painfully. Nothing came from the stars to save him."

Sidna felt a drop in her stomach. She narrowed her eyes. "Seems no one on the ground went out of their way to help him either. Funny how that works out."

Ban nodded again, slowly. "That's why I'm here now."

"Oh? Conscience bothering you?"

"In a manner of speaking." He sighed. "You're going somewhere. Someplace you don't want anyone else to know about."

"That's right."

"Where?"

"Again, none of your business."

Ban continued, undeterred. "This place. It has to do with the ephmere, doesn't it?"

"No."

"You're lying again."

"I'm not . . . " She sat up and tightened her jaw. "You know, I think maybe it's time you left."

"I think it's time you answered my questions."

"*And we're done here.*" She got up and stormed past him.

He stood up quickly, faster than his size betrayed, and took her arm by the wrist. He pulled up until he held her trembling fist right in front of his face. "What're you so afraid of?"

She pushed the fingers of her free hand against his chest. The smell of rapidly heating fibers rose from his shirt. "Let go, or I swear I'll burn a hole right through you."

He looked back and forth between her eyes, grip tightening. He released her. "Have it your way, Sidna. Run away. But I won't. When He-Who-Hungers returns, and it *will*, I'm going to be there."

You arrogant son of a . . .

She wanted to knock the infuriating certainty off his face, or better yet, reduce him to a smug pile of ash, but something more interesting suddenly occurred to her.

"Okay."

"What?"

"I said okay." She returned to the table and sat down again.

If he wants to die so badly, who am I to stand in his way?

"I'm going to a temple. There's something I want inside."

"What sort of—"

She held up her hand. "Nope. You don't get to ask questions. That's the deal."

"Very well," he said between his teeth.

"What I want is hard to find, and even harder to get. You can come along, as long as you don't get in my way."

"Done."

"And your people too. You'll keep them in line?"

"Yes. You have my word."

"Good. Because I won't hesitate to hurt anyone who stands between me and what I want."

He nodded. "Understood."

Sidna took another drink. "I'll tell Gabin, so don't worry about that."

Ban stood up. "Thank you." He walked toward the door. "Just one thing." He turned. "Something I want to make clear before you completely agree to our going."

"Yes?"

"When the ephmere comes, I will destroy it."

Sidna shrugged. "Knock yourself out."

In fact, you'll have a much bigger problem once you step foot inside.

Ban waited a moment then left, passing through the hatch with one last look behind.

"Moron." She looked over to the tub. "Threaten me? Let's see how that works out for you."

You'll wish you'd never gone to Veridian.

The door chimed again.

She looked up. "Go away."

The hatch opened. This time it was Gabin who stood in her doorway.

He looked at her, from the upper edge of her towel up to her eyes. "Relaxing?"

She tilted her head, eyebrows raised. "Now that business is out of the way." She took another long drink, finishing the wine before she placed the glass on the table.

Gabin walked in, noting the filled bathtub. "I hope everything here is to your liking."

She watched him, injecting a hint of coyness into her voice. "It is. So far."

The hatch doors closed. Gabin reached up to his chest and loosened the already loose cords of his white shirt as he walked closer. "My dear." He reached for her hand and gently pulled it up to his lips as he kissed her skin. "There's no need to see you go unsatisfied."

She watched him silently. She knew where the flirtation was going— where it *always* eventually went.

He took her other hand and brought her to her feet.

She stood at least a head shorter than him, and she could smell the cologne he'd placed on his chest.

He wore it. He knows what it does to me.

He bent his neck and grasped her by the chin with his thumb and forefinger, lifting her lips to his.

Why drag it out?

He pressed her body to his and held her lower back just as her knees forgot she was standing.

You need this.

She wasn't sure how, but they were at the edge of the bed, her lying down, him unfolding her towels.

He kissed her over and over, sucking in air sharply as she dug her nails into his back. She lay back, and he climbed over her, slowing only to admire her naked body.

She reached for his shoulders, feeling the strength he normally hid.

"Ah!" He tensed.

Damn! I forgot.

"Your arm. Sorry."

"It's nothing." He smiled wryly. "The road to Sidna is paved with pain."

She frowned. "I'm not sure I like that."

"I do." He ran his hand down her waist, across her stomach, and down further still. "Past pain lies pleasure."

Her back arched and her breath caught.

He knew her. He knew everything about her needs. He knew just how to satisfy them.

She opened her eyes. He was watching her face.

She panted. "What's wrong?"

"Nothing is wrong." He kissed her neck, moving down to her collarbone, then trailed gentle kisses down the *viae* on her arms. He looked up as his lips caressed her stomach. "Such a beautiful thing. Perhaps too beautiful for any one man to possess."

"Gabin . . ."

He shook his head, shushing her. "Tomorrow I will return you to Veridian." His hands took her by the hips, his voice growing husky. "But tonight, girl, you are *mine.*"

She looked up at the silk drapes that hung along the sides of the bed's canopy, all doubts melting away as warm breath moved over her wet skin.

The bent old man bowed his head and turned away. He pushed his cart down the passage, on to the next room.

Sidna leaned out into the hallway after him, holding the delivered bundle in her arms. "Thanks for the laundry."

The man kept walking.

"Okay, then . . . "

She walked back inside and laid her clothes on the table.

Gabin looked up from the bed, arms behind his head as he stretched out. "He's deaf."

"The old man?"

"Yes."

"Is that why he does the laundry?"

"No."

"Why then? Not mean enough for any other job?"

"Who, Megrim? He's a real bastard. Gnarliest man on the whole ship."

She looked up, eyebrows raised. "But he does the laundry?"

Gabin winked. "Just be glad you didn't stain your shirt."

She laughed. "You're an idiot."

"Guilty."

She unpacked her clothes, smelling her jacket with a smile.

Gabin sat up. "You should meet with my personal tailor. I'll have something pretty made for you."

Sidna slipped her pants on. "Like what?"

"Something to suit you. Perhaps a dress."

She looked up incredulously. "Um, no."

"Are you certain? He works wonders."

"No thanks, Gab." She looked away. "Anyway, you know I won't have time."

He sighed, moving the blankets aside to stand. "No, I suppose you wouldn't."

She looked up to the ceiling and closed her eyes then back down to him. "Don't."

"What?"

"You know what. Don't ruin this."

He held up his hands. "I wouldn't think of it. Give me but a moment, and I'll be out of your hair." He reached for his discarded clothes and gathered them into a wad before him.

Damn.

She moved to him as he picked up his shirt. "Wait." She leaned her forehead on his chest. "I didn't mean it that way."

"I know." He gathered her hair with his hand and straightened it so it fell down the center of her back. "Neither did I." He took her by her bare shoulders. "I'll be on the bridge when you're ready."

"Here." She went back to her jacket and picked it up. She rummaged through the pocket and took the glyph then held it out to him, dangling from its chain.

"A gift?" he asked.

"No. A tool." She watched it twist back and forth, mesmerizing. "Let your computer have a look at it. There are tiny crystals inside the gem that match up with stars in the Vagrant Sea. Find the one that's vibrating and head to that star."

He held out his hand with a nod.

"I want it back," she said.

"Of course…" He stared into its swirling depths, green and oily black. "I should think so."

It was hard to let go, whispering to her as it was.

She let him pass. "Hey."

He looked back. "Yes?"

"Thanks."

He turned and gave her an exaggerated bow. "I aim to please."

She picked up his left-behind boot and chucked it at him, frowning. "Gab…"

"Okay, okay." He picked up the boot, managing to keep the rest of his clothing in his arms. "Why thank me?"

She rubbed her arms. "For letting me be *me*."

He shrugged with a laugh. "Who could stop you?"

She tapped her curled toes on the floor. "People try."

He smiled. For a moment, it seemed pained. "They might as well *grasp* at the wind." He backed away with a flourish.

"Gab."

"Yes, Sidna."

"Are we good?"

"You and I?" The hatch opened behind him and he backed out into the hall. "Aren't we always?"

The doors closed, and as soon as he'd come, he was gone.

LOST WORLD

FALL WALKED UNDERNEATH TREES WITH slender, reticulated trunks, thick with thin needle-leaves. Spiked brown cones hung from the branches, and on the ground below, their fragments crunched underneath his boots.

He looked up, and through a break in the canopy he saw the night sky, so full of stars there didn't seem to be any black between. Through the branches, a solitary bright-white moon hid halfway behind a wisp of backlit cloud. Insects buzzed asynchronously, and something croaked out of sight.

The synthesis of it all left him feeling homesick for a place he'd never been.

"Hey." He hopped over a fallen branch. "Is this the same memory as before? With the campfire?"

Sostek moved ahead, disappearing and reappearing rather than navigating the obstacles in his way. "Yes and no. This is the most protected memory in the World Shard. The lowest layer."

Fall took a deep breath through his nose, taking in as many of the scents as he could. "It's so . . . alive."

Sostek didn't find it nearly as impressive. "Yes. Keep up. It's not much farther."

Soon, they came to the forest's edge. A staggering vista lay before them, with kilometers of hills and forest leading out beyond the horizon. They were up on the edge of a rocky cliff, well over three hundred meters above the valley. The moon sat in the center of the sky, its light shining down through the gap, illuminating the trees far below.

Fall carefully stepped out onto one of the rocks jutting from the cliff's edge. "There's nothing like this on Valen. Nowhere else I've been either."

Sostek moved to the edge as well. "To my knowledge, no one has seen the original version of this valley in several millennia." He walked back from the edge. "There's a path nearby."

They hiked down stones along the cliff, winding lower until they came to the bottom, still far above the valley floor. Tall trees and massive boulders lined the overgrown trail. The walls of the cliffs on each side grew closer together as they walked, and toward the end, Fall could hear a distant sound, low and constant. When they were close enough, he saw the source—a waterfall.

A shallow pool formed before it, feeding a creek that flowed away. Above it, the rock and forest split in two. Behind the waterfall, there was a natural indentation, the shape of a hollow crescent laid on its side. Farther inside it, a cave led into the hill.

Sostek led Fall up the side of the trail and over the boulders until they made it behind the waterfall, before the mouth of the cave. He took Fall inside, and it soon became darker without the light of the moon.

The cave slowly widened as they walked, uneven stone giving way to smooth metal, transitioning into an open room. As they continued, lights came on in series far above, and Fall's mouth fell open at what they revealed. He was in a huge hangar without any real exit. In the middle, surrounded by extended walkways and gantries, was a ship.

It was enormous, larger by far than the *Rìluò*, and it must have been very old. The paint was dark-green, like the deepest part of a tree's foliage, hidden away from the rays of the sun. Battle damage showed through half-fallen drapes, scorch marks and jagged scars marring the armored surface.

The relic had a central body flanked by two lateral compartments, one on each side. The body was larger and longer than the peripherals, and there was a bridge area visible on its blunted nose.

Each of the lateral compartments held a set of dual projections, like cannons. If there were any other weapons, they weren't visible from Fall's point of view.

He couldn't take his eyes away from it. "Whose is it?"

Sostek stepped up beside him. "Someone who died long before I was born."

Fall scratched his cheek. "Can we go inside?"

"We can try." Sostek held out his arm. "There's an entrance on the side."

Fall walked to the metal stairs leading up to a walkway. He went up quickly, eager to get a closer look at the ship. Sostek followed behind more slowly.

As he made his way over, Fall saw more of the ship's profile. It was damaged there as well, with patchwork armor repairs and exposed cables. To the aft, he thought he could make out the edge of an engine. The lateral compartment had a docking hatch on the side, connected to the walkway.

Fall waited for Sostek. "Any idea how to open it?"

"If I knew how, I would have done so."

Fall nodded thoughtfully. "I don't see an interface."

Sostek moved forward. "There isn't one, but I think it will open for you."

"Why me?"

"Call it a feeling."

"Okay . . . " Fall walked closer. When he did, a beam of green light swept over him quickly from head to toe. The hatch split down the middle, and the two doors slid open. Flickering lights inside activated, revealing an airlock. Another set of closed doors lay just beyond. "Whoa. It really did open."

"So it did," Sostek said, eyes wider than before. "Let's continue."

"Right." Fall took a deep breath and stepped inside.

The ship's straining lights blinked a few times then stabilized. The interior walls were darkly colored, with a thick layer of dust on them.

Fall walked to the control panel between the inner and outer doors and dusted off the screen. Once Sostek was inside too, Fall activated the airlock, and the atmosphere equalized. The panel's indicator light went from red to green as the inner doors opened. The same lighting activated inside, and dust floated in the air near the lamps.

Sostek touched the nearest wall then rubbed his fingertips together. "Time is never kind."

Fall shook his head with a growing smile. "Nothing a duster won't fix. Come on."

Fall opened the hatch at the top of the ladder then climbed out. He stood in a small room with a single, slightly open set of doors.

Emergency lighting shone through in soft yellow, and through the narrow slit, he saw another closed hatch ahead. He pried the doors apart a little more, seeing that they led into a storage room. There didn't appear to be anything dangerous inside, so he opened the doors fully and stepped through.

The small room had storage crates stacked against the walls, and shelving that held unfamiliar supplies. A few suits hung from hooks along the wall. Fall moved to the exit hatch and tried to open it, but it wouldn't budge.

He turned as Sostek entered behind him. "It's stuck."

Sostek drew his dagger and wedged it between the doors, forcing them open. When the gap was wide enough, he sheathed the dagger then disappeared through to the other side. After a moment, the mechanism activated, and the doors slid open. The ship's bridge lay beyond.

Shaped roughly like an elongated hexagon, the room looked as if it were designed to accommodate several crewmen. Double crew stations were set into the port and starboard walls, and to the aft wall as well. Across from him in the opposite rear corner was another closed hatch. In the two fore corners, there were two more closed doors.

Located centrally and to the fore of the bridge, a single station sat below the main viewports. On the raised platform in the center, a few meters back from the viewports, there was a single chair.

Soft lights around the bridge began to activate. Display panels at the stations spasmed to life as well. The sound of the power coming online was like a low tone that built up to a background hum.

Fall walked to the captain's chair and stepped up onto its platform. He sat. The leather seat had holes worn into it, comfortable but not overly so. As he sat back, he heard a soft sound to his right like the splashing of water.

A short cylindrical pedestal rose up from the platform and stopped when it reached a height just above the arm rest. The pedestal seemed advanced compared to the rest of the technology nearby, made from totally alien materials, cables haphazardly running to it from across the floor. There was a circular indentation on top, and an oily liquid swirled within it.

Fall watched as the liquid lifted into the air just above the indentation, forming a floating black orb. It finally solidified, revealing flowing etches that marked its surface.

Hesitantly, he touched it with one finger. Ripples moved over it, and he felt a rush of sensation. It was hard to grasp the feeling, but in that moment, he felt like the orb had touched him as well.

He reached over and slowly placed his entire hand over it. The surface came up to meet with his fingertips. The underside of the sphere stirred too, but only weakly. Somehow, he knew he needed to pick up the semi-solid liquid using his other hand. He palmed the other side, and it reacted to his touch, just like the other had. He took the orb and brought it to his lap.

The surface melted then, and the two halves slowly rotated in the same direction, turbulent near the midline where they met. The interaction felt wrong, and Fall began to sense an odd vibration in his hands. It wasn't painful, but the dissonance was like the sound of two musical instruments played together, slightly out of tune.

As he thought about that, the vibration in his left hand changed. The swirling on that side slowed as well.

Did I do that? What if I . . .

He focused on the swirling, somehow willing the two sides to spin in opposite directions. It was surprisingly easy, and thinking about the other direction again didn't change anything. Each half simply spun in the correct direction because he knew it should.

The uncomfortable vibrations resolved. In the center between the sides, a single ridge appeared, growing with each revolution. He could feel the flow, synchronizing his mind to it. He rode the wave and sped it up.

More ridges formed, extending from the sphere, until it seemed he held a small hurricane tilted onto its side. He knew it could go faster, and so it did.

As he watched, the orb compressed inward, and the ridges extended outward further, beginning to glow white. The orb continued to flatten, and when the fingertips of both his hands met, he closed his eyes.

He could feel the ship—a living being, with bones of steel, veins of carbon, and a heart of nuclear fire. He couldn't quite understand it, but he could sense the bay surrounding the ship as well.

Disembodied, he moved around the bridge. He could distantly sense the chair and his own breathing, yet he went beyond. He felt further into the bridge, and he found the ship's systems. Each was a destination he could move into, but it was difficult, and when he tried to go to two places at once, he began to feel the dissonance again.

One system appeared to be most closely associated with the captain's chair, nearby and easy to move toward.

Ship's logs?

With a little concentration, he was able to open one, and the log played out as if the person were sitting right there in front of him.

The log's author was a voidstrider, but the lighting was weak, and his face was obscured. Fall could see the captain's chair over the man's shoulder, so he must have been at a station on the bridge.

He spoke. "What is it, day three? Four?" He sighed. "It doesn't matter." He turned to his right. "I managed to install the *sivinar*, but I'm no master." His head dropped, and he looked down. "There are other complications." He looked to his arm then reached up to terminate the log.

The next log started. The man seemed to be more fatigued, and the bandage over his upper left arm was soaked in blood. "The nightmares." He put his hands to his face and rubbed. "I can't escape it, even in my dreams. Perhaps I never did." He looked back up, exhaustion in his eyes. "If I could only sleep." The recording ended.

Fall found the next log. "I don't . . . ah . . . I don't think it can find me inside the shard." He held his hand over his left arm as he winced in pain. His eyes had a glassy look to them, and his hair had grown haggard. "I must . . . *Kysh* . . . I must transfer if I wish to survive. With the *sivinar*, I can take this ship inside as well. And then . . . I will finally sleep." The log ended.

Fall allowed the orb to decompress, and he was sitting in the captain's chair again. He placed it back over the pedestal, where it melted into a swirling puddle. When he stood, he turned, and Sostek was standing there.

Sostek looked down. "You weren't supposed to see those."

"That was you, wasn't it? You came here on this ship?"

"Yes."

"I thought you couldn't get inside."

"Once I'd left, the ship sealed itself, and I was unable to return."

"I see." Fall rubbed his chin. "You said *transfer* in the log. Transfer where?"

"Here. Into the World Shard. A drastic measure, not easily reversed by one with so little skill."

"Hmmm. Something doesn't add up though. If you entered the World Shard in the ship, how did the shard end up underneath Cisterne?"

Sostek crossed his arms. "I assumed the shard would drift on the ocean or perhaps sink beneath the waves. If I were lost or destroyed, what would it matter? But it seems the shard was found and brought to the temple below. As for who did it, I could not say."

Fall nodded slowly. "You must've seen Gyre as a good place to hide. It sounded like something was after you."

"One of the *Qur Noc*. A particularly fearsome creature."

Fall looked around. "Must've been a nasty fight. This thing took a beating."

"No, this ship was injured in another time. In another war." Sostek walked over and sat down at the same station where he'd recorded the logs. "It remains exactly as she found it. Except for the *sivinar*."

Fall looked back to the pedestal. "You brought it with you?"

"Fera's ship was destroyed in the final battle. I managed to escape with the *sivinar*." He looked down, and the fur near his ears drooped. "I could not follow her."

"Where did she go?"

"She ... died."

Fall sat in the captain's chair. "I'm sorry."

Sostek took a deep breath and looked up. "As I fled to the world you call Gyre, the galaxy was all but consumed. Everything we had ever known was destroyed in the Aftermath. I retreated into the World Shard, into her memories, like a coward."

"What else could you do?"

He looked up. "I could have died. I could have gone with her."

"Then you'd never have had the chance to avenge her."

"Avenge her?"

"Why not? On the *Red*, the Alidians told a story. They saw something out there that terrified them. It sounded a lot like one of the *Qur Noc*."

"After all this time?"

"It couldn't have been anything else."

Sostek rubbed his chin. "To see even a single one of them die ... " He looked up. "If you can do what she could, make use of the *sivinar*, you could take this ship back out of the shard."

"Me?"

"Yes, you." Sostek closed his fingers into a fist. "Since the moment you saw through my *Fyd Wyr* technique, I suspected you might be like Fera. When you entered the World Shard without my help, I knew it had to be true." He motioned to the bridge. "Even the ship knows it."

Fall looked out into the bay through the forward viewports. "But I barely managed to access your logs. I don't have any idea what I'm doing."

Sostek smiled weakly. "Neither did she, at first."

Fall turned to the pedestal, and the orb took shape again. "Assuming you're right, wouldn't we end up killing ourselves? Or destroying the *Red*?"

Sostek stood up. "We will project to a reasonable distance. If you do it correctly, that is."

Fall reached out for the *sivinar* with a sigh. "No pressure . . . "

Fall's fingertips touched through the flattened orb, and the energy wave flared like a spinning blade.

Sostek stood beside him, watching him with a pleased expression. His voice was calm and measured. "Now. Expand the limits of your perception."

"How?"

"By realizing those limits currently belong to the shard."

"What does that mean?"

"The crystal is an incredibly powerful device. It can store vast amounts of information and recreate objects and materials on an infinitesimal scale. In order to facilitate those purposes, it must sense incoming data and process it."

"What kinds of data?"

Sostek shrugged. "All kinds."

"You're saying the shard can see?"

"In a way."

Fall looked up. "Is the information transfer one-way only?"

Sostek smiled. "Now you understand."

"I wouldn't go *that* far." Fall stretched out beyond the bridge, beyond the systems and conduits, out beyond the hull. He went up through the metal and the rock and the soil. He passed the trees, up through the clouds, and beyond the moon. He extended through the shining red-orange surface of the crystal, out from under the bunk, and finally through the *Red* itself.

He turned to look out into the stars of the Vagrant Sea. "Amazing."

"Truly. Now, take us there."

"What will happen to us?"

"We will be ourselves, just as we are now."

"By changing our mass to some other form?"

"No. This is deeper, more fundamental—something your people could never explain. We, however, simply accepted the truth—a thing is perceived, and so it is."

Is there some power in perception?

"Is that how you come and go from the World Shard?" Fall asked.

"Yes. It is how you have come and gone too."

"Then why do we need the *sivinar*?"

"It greatly enhances a voidstrider's abilities."

"And for humans?"

"That answer is complicated. For now, *Fall Arden*, it will allow you to do those things for which you do not need it."

"That doesn't make sense."

"A paradox rarely does. Focus on your perceptions. *See* that we are clear of the *Red* and make it reality."

"Okay . . ." Fall moved clear of the *Red* and turned back to think. From where he was, he could see the entirety of the pirate ship, realizing it was something he wouldn't normally be happy to see.

I guess it's good I'm not really here.

That concept started to itch.

Here? Why did I think here *and not* there?

Once he'd begun to think of himself as *here* and not *there*, the whole of the world flipped, and being outside the *Red* seemed to be truer than being inside the shard. It was a feeling he needed to reconcile.

Much like the two halves of the spinning orb, knowing the way a thing should be tended to make it so. And so, his thoughts began to right themselves, twisting and moving until the concept of *here* felt better, and *there* was the glowing shard which lay at his feet.

He withdrew from the orb, reuniting his perception with his physical senses. He looked down, and there the shard really was.

Sostek knelt to take it from the floor and put it away. "A master could not have done it any better."

Fall replaced the orb. "It basically happened on its own."

A blinking white light on the console near the forward viewports caught Fall's eye.

Sostek moved toward it. "The pirates are hailing."

Fall nodded. "We surprised them."

Sostek showed his teeth. "Appearing suddenly, armed as we are? I'd say we *frightened* them."

"Then we'd better answer." Fall stood up with a smile. "Before they notice the rust on our guns."

THE RETURN

SIDNA LEANED OVER A LEDGE ON THE BAY'S third level, watching as Gabin's men prepped for their expedition to Veridian.

Since the abrupt appearance of Fall's ship, there'd been a subtle change in the atmosphere aboard the *Red*. The pirates behaved aggressively, slight shifts in body language betraying their predatory intentions. If she hadn't spent so much time with them, she might not have noticed.

It's good they're leaving. If the jerk had a ship all along, why drag it out?

Sidna's attention drifted as the Runian woman, Endo Kumi, walked up the ramp of a skiff, inspecting the items waiting to be loaded. She put her hands on her hips and sighed visibly. Her pet sentinel, Union, came down the ramp to meet her.

Olivia approached next. She wore a backpack, stuffed full; she pulled at the straps, readjusting the weight. She also carried a duffle bag, seemingly heavy and unwieldy.

What's the matter? Fall not around to carry your stuff?

Sidna searched the bay.

Where is he, anyway?

There was a swift blur of movement at the base of a nearby storage unit stack.

Oh.

He'd leapt down to the deck, having been there the whole time. He patted a pouch near his belt, as if to make sure something was still there.

What's he hiding . . . ?

A flash of Gabin's red coat caught her attention from the bay's left, and she saw why Fall had decided to come down. She sighed and shook her head.

Couldn't resist, could you?

Fall passed by the ramp as Olivia prepared to go up it. They did the awkward dance two people do when neither can decide which way to go.

Hmmm. Something happened.

Fall went past, looking back for only a brief second. After he'd turned around, Olivia looked back, hesitated, and then went up the ramp.

Definitely.

Fall shook it off and stood taller as he neared Gabin. His right hand slowly moved to the grip of the sword behind his back, pulling it around to his side.

Gabin waited with his right hand on his hip, left hand resting on the pommel of his rapier.

Gabin spoke first. Fall answered. Neither seemed to relax.

What are you two talking about?

"Wondering what they're saying?"

She turned. Hermes sat on the railing a little way down, red furry legs dangling over the side.

He pointed up to his ears with a knowing smile. "Amazing reception."

She turned back, ignoring the weird little creature.

"Fine, be stubborn. I'll tell you anyway." He coughed. When he spoke again, it was with Fall's voice.

" . . . your men aren't used to being surprised."

Gabin responded through Hermes. "No, indeed. I must tip my hat to your cunning. But tell me, how did you do it?"

"The ship?" Fall shrugged. "Trick of the trade."

"Mmm. A secret you keep well."

"Out of necessity. The Frontier is a dangerous place."

Gabin nodded. "Oh, I agree. Often, I say to my men how fortunate we are, having such *brave* Rangers to watch over us."

Fall took a step forward. "We all need watching over, from time to time." He tapped his fingers over the hilt of his sword. "Danger can be hard to appreciate, even when it's right in front of you."

They stood there silently for a few seconds. From the periphery, Gabin's men began to edge closer. Fall must have noticed, but he held his ground.

Gabin narrowed his eyes further, breath held tightly. Finally, he laughed and extended his hand. "This time we will part as friends, Ranger. At least, until we meet again."

Fall moved slowly but took Gabin's hand. "Next time." He didn't let go. "Until then, watch out for her."

Gabin didn't pull away. "Just who do you mean?"

"Sidna."

Gabin's face betrayed his anger. "She is no concern of yours."

Fall dropped Gabin's hand as the pirates closed in on either side of him. "She's close to you, I can see that. You know she's after something. And you know she'll give up everything to get it."

"Your point?"

"When the time comes, you might be the only one there to make sure she doesn't." Fall stared into Gabin's eyes as he backed away.

Gabin seemed to ruminate on his words, but then he remembered his pride. "She is in good hands. I cannot imagine why you should care."

Fall looked up to Hermes then to Sidna, his mouth moving silently.

"What did he say?" Sidna asked, taken aback that Fall had known she was there.

Hermes frowned and raised his eyebrows. "No regrets."

She watched as Fall stood there a moment longer. He looked down and walked away, going up the ramp.

"What the heck does that mean?" Hermes asked.

Sidna reached into her pocket, taking hold of the half-empty vial of powdered liadra. She squeezed it tightly as she watched him go. "No idea . . ."

Like the rest of the ship, Gabin had spent plenty of money on his bridge. Billowing red drapes and dramatic paintings decorated the walls. The screens and electronics were encased in hardwood frames. A gentle breeze, courtesy of the life support system, kept the crew comfortable.

Just ahead, at the front end, two manned duty stations sat side by side. She avoided eye contact with the pirates there and walked past them, up the short steps to the captain's platform.

Gabin sat there, lounging in his chair, a seat of wooden waves which rose up from the deck like a cresting swell.

Sidna walked over, purposefully ignoring his proud grin. "Happy to be rid of them?"

"Aren't you?" he asked.

Sidna turned to the viewscreen and watched as Fall's battered old ship vanished into the Rift. "We've stood still long enough. Let's go."

"Exactly the words which echo in my heart." He projected his voice further into the bridge. "The star. Have you found it?"

A voice from below answered. "Aye, Captain."

"Then what are we waiting for?" Gabin asked with a playful glance at Sidna. "*Let's go.*"

As Sidna watched, the blue-green Rift welcomed the *Red*, finally on its way. She started for the steps. "Call me if we run into trouble."

He stood up quickly. "Leaving so soon?"

She sighed. "Mei found out the Alidians are staying. She wants to talk."

"I have some thoughts on that matter as well, girl."

"Well, like I'm about to tell her, she needs to get paid. And you need gold. If you two don't like it, I can always go alone."

A couple of pirates turned to face the conversation.

Gabin noticed and moved to Sidna's side, putting his arm around her shoulder and turning her away. "Are you trying to cause a mutiny? My men are expecting treasure on Veridian."

"Then stop asking questions and *get us there.*" She emphasized the words with her finger on his chest. As he backed away, arms raised in mock surrender, she rolled her eyes and stepped down to the lower level then left the bridge.

She walked the halls back to the lift. Something felt wrong—off somehow. As the lift descended, she leaned against the wall, arms crossed, wondering what it was.

The lift came to a stop. She turned sideways to squeeze between two pirates who pushed their way inside before she could leave.

Soon after, she entered her chambers to find Mei waiting patiently at the round table. She sat across from her and folded her arms. "All right. Out with it."

Mei blinked. "What do you expect me to say?"

"That I'm foolish, or that I should think things through."

"Have you not?"

"No, I have."

"Then, I will not interfere."

Sidna nodded. "Okay. Good."

Mei took a sip of wine from the glass in front of her. "Curious..."

Sidna narrowed her eyes. "What's curious?"

Mei shrugged. "A Ranger, a ship full of pirates, and a squad of Alidian marines." She set her glass down. "Do you think we will be enough?"

"Enough for what?"

"For your Guardian," Mei said nonchalantly.

Sidna stared. "I don't know."

"Does Gabin know?"

Sidna looked away.

"I thought not."

Sidna's eyes snapped back to Mei. "He knows what he needs to know. I can handle the Guardian when the time comes."

"And the Alidians?"

Sidna sighed. "Seems to me like they *want* trouble. At any rate, they can take care of themselves."

Mei nodded. "I do not like the way their leader looks at you."

Sidna smiled wryly. "I always have you."

Mei coughed into her hand. "I appreciate your faith in me, but I would rather not test my skills at every turn." She stood up. "You will have a few days to recover before Veridian. You should not waste the opportunity."

Sidna stood up too and yawned. "Shouldn't be a problem."

Mei left Sidna's quarters. Once the door had closed, Sidna sat at the table, eyes unfocusing as she looked past the wineglass.

I guess everyone has their reasons for going.

She reached out for the glass.

Fine by me.

She swirled the glass several times, studying the dark red contents before taking a drink.

So long as I get what I need.

The days dragged on as Sidna waited.

She managed to avoid the Alidians, mostly by never leaving her room. Gabin came to see her once, and Mei was always lurking about somewhere nearby. Megrim, grumpy as always, never failed to pick up her clothes, each time bringing them back good as new.

When Gabin finally called her, she ran to the lift, forcing herself to slow down before she flew onto the bridge.

He called down to her. "Ah, Sidna, just in time. We'll be leaving the Rift momentarily."

She climbed the steps and turned toward the viewport, still trying to catch her breath.

The Rift dissolved, normal space returned, and there in the stars was the thing she'd been longing to see.

Gabin stood up from his captain's chair. "What is *that*?"

Danto, an overweight pirate, typed at one of the forward stations below. "Just a moment, Captain. Working on it."

The space ahead of the *Red* appeared on the bridge's main view-screen, and in the center was a blur. The camera zoomed in further on the aberration.

"It seems to be a . . . *warp* in space, Captain. A *sphere*."

Sidna walked forward and pointed. "That's it. Enter it just like a T-Gate. It works the same way."

"But not *exactly* the same, no? Where is the machinery? Is it natural?"

"I don't know, Gab. All I know is that it moves, so we'd better get through it. If we wait much longer, it'll reappear far away from here, maybe all the way across the Frontier."

Gabin squinted. "This . . . gate. It leads to your Veridian?"

"Yes. And the other end is fixed. No matter where it is on this end, the path always leads to Veridian."

"How very reassuring . . . " Gabin swallowed. "Mr. Danto, take us through."

The viewscreen reverted to its normal zoom factor, and the ship moved forward toward the warp. The ship entered, and when it exited just as suddenly, there was a new set of stars on the screen.

Gabin walked forward. "Where are we?"

Danto looked at his console, rubbing his double chin. "The computer can't fix a point of reference. There aren't any constellations that match our charts."

Sidna nodded. "No one's ever charted Veridian's location."

Danto turned around. "So, you have no idea where we are right now?"

"Nope. But if you look in the right direction, you can see the galactic bulge."

Gabin nodded. "Put it on the viewscreen."

"Aye-aye, Captain."

The screen shifted views, and a dense glowing band appeared.

Sidna smiled at Gabin's confusion. "That's right, Gab. We're in a totally different galaxy."

Gabin stuttered anxiously. "Get . . . get me a look at the gate." The screen's view changed again, and the gate became visible. This time, it was surrounded by the expected machinery. "Is it stable? Will it move?"

"No. But the other end will. The glyph's crystals will vibrate differently when it's about to. We probably have a few days."

"Ah, that is . . . good." Gabin wiped his forehead. "Which planet is it then, girl?"

"The only one."

Danto spoke again as he ran his hands over his station's controls. "There's a single planet around the star."

Gabin grasped the wooden rail of the platform. "Show me."

The view changed. Gabin walked down to the lower level. "So *green*. Is there no ocean?"

Danto looked up with his mouth slightly open. "It seems to be one large jungle."

Sidna walked down beside Gabin. "A few places are a little different. Scan the southern hemisphere, near the equator. You should find a bunch of quartz arenite."

Danto's fingers moved over the interface. "There are several landmasses there in the jungle, tall, but level with the rest of the landscape in some sort of incredibly deep pit. They have sandstone with high levels of silicon dioxide."

"That's the place. There's a temple on one of the raised plateaus, surrounded by a ring of other plateaus just like it. You won't be able to land the *Red* at the temple, but there's a clearing on one of them that will get us close enough."

Gabin nodded absently. "I suppose we'll defer to your previous experience." He looked to Danto. "Do as the girl says."

"Aye-aye, Captain."

As they sped toward Veridian, the planet's details emerged, revealing its immense, world-covering jungle. The *Red* entered the atmosphere and descended until it flew a few kilometers above the trees.

Before long, Sidna saw the tall, flat-topped mountains she'd described, covered with thick foliage. In the center of the landmasses, there was a larger, solitary one. On its face, in the middle of an artificial lake, sat the ancient temple of Fel Kno'a.

It was midday, and the sunlight caused the rose-colored minerals in the temple's sandstone to sparkle. The pyramid structure, with its stepped walls, towered over the lake, weathered statues built along the sides adding to its deceptive beauty.

The *Red* descended toward it, landing on the grass-covered clearing atop one of the nearby landmasses.

Gabin stood up and stretched. "Back to your Veridian at last. Excited?"

The viewscreen's camera showed only vibrant, tortuous trees and thick, hanging vines as the ship sat down. Sidna was relieved she couldn't see the temple any longer.

"Of course." She walked toward the bridge's main hatch without turning, so he couldn't see her eyes and spoke softly. "Why wouldn't I be?"

The square-shaped, open-sided cargo lift lowered down from the belly of the *Red*. It was the lift's last trip, carrying the remaining members of the expeditionary group.

Gabin stepped down and offered his hand to Sidna as the lift came to a stop.

She accepted the gesture. "Looks like you're planning on a big score here, Gab."

He shrugged with a grin. "Perhaps we'll find nothing at all in your temple, but I wouldn't be much of a pirate if I weren't prepared."

"If that's a question, I already told you I didn't look for that kind of stuff last time. But I'm sure someone's going to want anything you find here."

She walked ahead, looking around at the crew as she did. In the grassy space ahead of the ship, they'd assembled a small staging area with repulsion lifts and storage containers. They had tables set up as well, ready to sort their spoils.

They wore a minimum of clothing in contrast to her own outfit. It was hot in the afternoon sun, but once they'd crossed to the central landmass, the winds would be a factor, and the temple interior would be quite cool. She'd warned Gabin, but as he often said, the crew did as they liked.

She stopped for a moment to take a deep breath. The air carried the scents of the world, green and alive, but on the edge of it, almost undetectable, was something else. She looked through the jungle in the direction of the temple. For a moment, she imagined she could smell the rot and decay inside.

She heard a group of familiar voices ahead. The Alidian marines were on the edge of the staging area, not far from the entrance to the path through the jungle. They were checking their equipment.

Mei walked beside Sidna, dressed in her red-and-orange Ranger armor. "You do not look like someone who has finally gotten what she wanted."

"Because I haven't gotten anything yet."

Sidna started off for the exit to the clearing. It was an unnaturally clear path that led through the jungle ahead, the result of some sort of permanent destruction. There weren't scorch marks or a paved walkway, but none of the plants grew along the ground in that area.

Gabin and Mei followed behind her, and as she passed the Alidians, they joined. After them, a steady stream of pirates pushed repulsion lifts, looking around in awe. The group walked for several minutes before reaching the end of the trail, an outcropping of the landmass, just above another path that lead down the side.

Sidna stopped next to the farthest tree. Mei stood beside her, and the Alidians spread out on her other side.

Gabin ran and climbed the tree's branches, up to a couple of meters above the ground. His boots kept a strong hold on the bark, fortunately so, because a heavy gust of wind nearly blew him off.

His red coat flapped behind him as he yelled over the wind. "Ah, Sidna! Magnificent, is it not?"

They could all see the temple now. Whitecap waves flowed across the lake, spilling over the side and down into the distant valley below. A ring of sandstone enclosed the water, and pathways led out from the temple toward each of the surrounding landmasses, six in total.

They could *hear* the complex too. The wind wound its way through the steps and statues, producing a harmonious, resonant sound. That same wind was bringing in a massive wall of storm clouds, already pouring rain onto the jungle in the distance.

The Alidians started down the steps, heavy boots clanking as they descended. The steps were man-made, carved from the stone but covered in gray metal.

Sidna followed them. "Get out of the tree, Gab."

He hopped down and landed with a smile. "You should learn to let go from time to time. I think you might enjoy yourself."

Sidna shook her head, walking on. "Maybe on our next intergalactic voyage. For now, keep up."

When she reached the bottom, she walked along another short metal path. At the end, there was a tall housing, holding another distortion in space.

The unit was made of the same gray metal as before, crafted into the shape of an arch with intricate alien designs on its surface. Unlike the stone of the temple, the metal had stood against wind and time without blemish. Directly across the gap, on the temple's landmass, there was an identical arch.

The marines stopped just before the distortion, waiting for the others.

Sidna walked up to them. "It's a gate, like the one that brought us here."

Ban walked over and hefted his big gun onto his shoulder. "Where does it lead? To the center?"

"Yes. Each mountain has one."

He turned back to the housing. "I'll go first."

"Why you?"

He brought the gun down. "Because I said so."

Sidna sighed. "Is this going to be the deal for each door we come across?"

"Just the doors where you argue about it." He turned and walked up to the distortion then went through without hesitation. After just a moment, he came back. "It's safe."

He went through again, and the other marines followed.

Gabin walked over. "These Alidians are a bit too cavalier, yes?"

"Maybe, but not for long." She started ahead and followed Mei through the gate.

In an instant, she appeared on the stone path leading to the temple. The ancient building towered above her, suddenly filling her with dread.

If I were smart, I'd turn around right now. I'd tell them all to turn around and leave while they still can.

Gabin appeared behind her, and he placed his hand on her shoulder. "Go ahead, girl. I'm here with you." He must have sensed her apprehension. In fact, she seemed to be the only one that had any.

Wet air blew across the path, cool and refreshing after the muggy jungle walk. The lake's waves splashed against the path, dumping water up onto her boots. It contrasted harshly with the temple's dry and dusty interior.

As she continued, the temple took up more and more of her view. She walked up the sandstone steps, legs aching, stopping only when she reached the top. Ahead, the stone doors of Fel Kno'a stood tall, looming over her as a final warning.

This is it. Don't stop now.

Shielded from the wind, the etchings in the stone doors were in better shape than the rest of the exterior. They showed a skeleton in robes with his bladed weapon, on a field of crimson, just like the banners in the temple's cathedral.

Ban ran his armored hand over a part of the etching. "Is there a lock? Do you have the key to get inside?"

"We don't need one." Sidna walked up to the doors and gently pushed with both hands. The doors swung inward, and she heard the gears on both sides as they assisted her with the weight of the stone. She watched as they moved all the way open, allowing her to see the interior. It was dark, without any light source beyond what the afternoon sun could provide.

Ban walked just inside and turned. "That's it? Anyone can enter?"

Sidna moved a few steps past him and activated the light source on her wrist. "Yes. The temple allows anyone inside. The doors only open from the outside though, and they'll close after we go in."

Gabin turned to the pirate who topped the steps. "Post men here to open these doors, should I call."

The pirate nodded and pointed to two of the men nearby, who nodded in return.

Becks walked up behind Sidna. "Why make doors that only open one way?"

Sidna investigated the darkness ahead and turned back to Becks and the others. "I don't know. But I think that once a person steps inside, they aren't meant to leave. Ever."

Becks harrumphed mockingly. "You got out."

Sidna rubbed her left arm. "I made my own exit."

Becks motioned over to Tyr and his rocket launcher. "No problem. We brought some too."

Sidna looked down and shook her head. "It isn't doors or walls you should be worried about." She crossed the threshold. "But you'll see soon enough."

THE DEAD FLEETS

FALL HELD UP THE CLEAR BOTTLE, INSPECTING the clarity of the weakly illuminated amber liquid inside. He rotated it above the kitchen's pale under-counter lighting.

Nice.

"I hereby claim salvage rights on that whiskey," Hermes announced from behind. "And to all booze you may find in perpetuity."

Fall laughed as he turned. "On what grounds?"

"On the grounds that you owe me for the last bottle. And the bottle before that too."

"Dream big, Hermes. You've never pitched in so much as a single virtua."

"Doesn't matter. What's mine is mine."

"Tell you what." Fall pulled down two dusty glasses from the cabinet. "We'll share." He ran his finger along the inside surface of each glass, then poured the precious alcohol into each.

Hermes hopped up onto the counter and took his portion. He eyed it warily then nodded. "I'll add your half to what you already owe me."

Fall lifted his glass. "Deal." He took a sip of the stuff, room temperature yet fiery, burning as it went down. It was strong but smooth.

Hermes coughed. "Good stuff."

"I know." Fall smiled and poured another. "So, what do you think?" He motioned out to the rest of the room, liquid swirling in his glass.

"Not bad." Hermes kicked up some dust. "Fire your maid though."

"Job's yours if you want it."

"I'm good," Hermes said. "Maybe Union would do it."

Fall shook his head as he swallowed. "Have you seen the looks he gives Kumi? I think he's reached his limit on requests." He leaned against the metal counter. "I'll get it cleaned after we get paid."

Hermes shrugged. "Hmph. Do whatever you want with your cut."

"Oh? Big plans for yours?"

"Yeah." He drained his glass. "I'm gonna restock this bar."

Fall smiled and looked up.

The common hold *was* in rough shape—the pair of dueling couches were plagued with holes in the fabric, the glass holotable had stellate cracks across the surface, and most of the lights were dead in their housings. It was all junk.

But it's all mine.

"I hope you didn't pay too much for this . . . *ship*." Kumi came down the rear-central steps. "Or anything in it."

"Kumi." Fall held up his glass. "Join us."

She looked around and smiled politely. "Another time. Have either of you seen Union?"

Fall looked up. In the darkness of the starboard hall, he saw two glowing eyes. They moved back and forth twice, slowly.

Fall glanced at Hermes. "Nope. Hermes?"

Hermes waved his hand. "Not so much as an electron."

Kumi moved to a couch and dusted off a cushion before sitting down with a frown. "I think I'll wait for him here."

"Suit yourself," Hermes said lazily.

She sat there tightly, hands on her knees. "I bet he'll come through here. It's the center of the ship, after all."

The two eyes looked up in the darkness in seeming exasperation then started to back away.

"Union?" Olivia stepped partially into the room from the starboard hall and turned around. "What're you doing there?"

Union walked into the light reluctantly, head lowered. "Doctor Hansen. How fortunate to encounter you just now."

Kumi stood up. "I've been looking for you for over an hour. We need to go over what you're going to say to the FathCom transcribers on Crossroads. Your responses to their questions must be carefully prepared in advance."

"Of course." The machine seemed to sigh. "My anticipation grows by the moment."

Olivia walked to the corner galley. She briefly glanced at Fall. "Anything good?"

"Whiskey and rapidly aging pirate grub." Fall tilted his head. "Think you could make some breakfast out of it?"

"I guess." She leaned over the counter. "If the cooking unit works."

Fall gave it a couple of soft kicks. "Unlikely."

Olivia turned and went to the couch opposite Kumi. She plopped down and relaxed. "That's cool. I'm super tired."

Kumi sat down again. "It's been a hard couple of weeks, hasn't it?"

"Millennia for some of us," Union said as he sat at the gaming table.

"What is time to an Exanim?" Sostek leaned against the wall, barely in sight in the shadows of the port-side hall.

Union studied him before responding. "Only an eternity in every second. In subjugation, an unbearable state of being."

Sostek moved inside the room. "Your situation has hardly improved."

"Are you referring to Lieutenant Commander Endo?" the machine asked.

Kumi turned her head sharply. "I'm not *subjugating* him. I'm protecting him. He's the most advanced artificial life form we've ever encountered."

Sostek motioned to Hermes. "Not even close, but I take your meaning. Tell us. What will become of him back in your Rune?"

"He'll be invited to teach us whatever he's willing to share," Kumi said as she smiled at the sentinel.

"If he declines?" Sostek asked.

"He may do as he pleases, of course."

"How gracious. Do you hear that, Exanim? You have this human's permission to do whatever you like."

Union waved his metallic hand. "Sow discord elsewhere, voidstrider. I have made up my mind."

Sostek harrumphed. "Your *mind* . . ."

Kumi sat up straight, ignoring Sostek's jab. "In return, I have promised that Vaughan-Heighas will assist in the recovery of the other surviving Exanim on Gyre."

Fall put down his glass and whistled. "They'd need a significant strike force. If they could even get inside Cisterne, that is."

"Vaughan-Heighas would most likely negotiate for their pro-curement."

Sostek smiled. "You mean *release*."

Kumi seemed to have missed his meaning. "Yes. Isn't that what I said?"

Olivia coughed, moving the conversation in a different direction. "What about you, Sostek? Since you're asking, what are your plans? I'm sure you'd get just as much attention as Union back home."

Sostek crossed his arms. "To be certain. I imagine I would be dissected by the end of the week. No, I will remain outside your Fathom, human."

"It's boring there anyways," Hermes said as he poured another portion of whiskey.

"Come on." Olivia leaned forward on the couch. "Political intrigue, warring dynasties, corporate sabotage . . . there's plenty of action."

"Nah, I'm with Hermes," Fall said. "It's all been done before."

Olivia shrugged. "Not by me."

Fall upended his whiskey. "Then I guess it's good you're going back." He placed the empty glass on the counter. "Coming, Hermes?"

The imp frowned at his own glass and hopped down from the counter. "Sure. I was planning on checking out the rest of the ship's logs anyways."

Fall moved to the fore exit, turning to look back at the others just before he left. "I almost forgot." He mocked a bow. "Welcome aboard the *Lonely Lantern*."

"I think we should work on the paint first," Hermes said as he trotted along beside Fall toward the bridge.

"What's wrong with the paint?" Fall asked.

The dim white lights in the passage shined faint bands on the imp's ears as he passed each one. "Nothing at all, if you like mud-moss-green. We'll land all the best jobs looking like a flying swamp rock."

Fall waved his hand in dismissal. "We'd just be a big target if we looked too rich."

Hermes threw his hands up. "Bring it on. Right now, the only thing we'd attract is *sympathy*."

Fall laughed. "All right, I hear you, but I was thinking more along the lines of . . . "

Hermes continued a few steps then looked back to see why Fall had trailed off.

Olivia came walking down the hall behind them. When she caught up, she slowed down, arms falling to her sides, fingers fidgeting. She looked at Fall then past him to Hermes, seemingly urging him to leave them alone.

"I'll, uh, see you on the bridge," Hermes said as he backed away, rubbing his furry hands together. "I'll work on getting those new colors picked out."

"Sure," Fall said absently. "Be right there."

Olivia waited until Hermes was gone, then walked closer. She stood just over a meter away, staring into Fall's eyes. "It's *good* I'm going back?"

"Yeah." He placed his hands on his hips. "You are, aren't you?"

"That's the plan."

He shrugged. "Okay, so what's the problem?"

"Your reaction to it."

"Well, how should I react?" He threw his hands up in exasperation. "You said I don't understand Sidna's motivations, but I for sure don't get yours. The other night, you were going on and on about how great life is out here. Now you're back to this again."

"I never changed my mind. Going back was what I was always going to do."

Fall waved his hand. "Sure it was."

"What's that supposed to mean?" she asked, scowling.

He walked away then turned back. He leaned against the wall and crossed his arms. "Stay."

Her eyes widened. "What?"

"You heard me. Stay."

"And do what?"

He smiled. "Work with me. I have a ship that just so happens to need a doctor."

"I already have that job."

"Yeah, but not with a captain like me. Come on. You have to admit, we make a pretty good team."

She seemed to be considering it. "I dunno, Fall. It sounds great, but—"

"But what?"

She sighed. "There are people counting on me back home. People who expect me to do certain things."

Fall came closer and put his hands on her shoulders. "So? Find out what's important to you. Then go after it, no matter what anyone else expects."

She rolled her eyes. "Easy for you to say."

He shrugged. "I'm not saying it's easy. I'm just saying it's what you should do." He backed away and moved toward the bridge.

She took a step after him. "Okay, say I think about it. How long do I have to make up my mind?"

"Take all the time you want." He looked back with a smile. "But I think you already have."

Fall stood at the forward viewports, looking over the Never as the *Lantern* sped above its violet surface.

"Aren't you tired of that yet?" Hermes asked.

Fall continued to stare silently into the forbidden realm.

Hermes sighed. "Sheesh." He spun back toward the monitor. "Well, if you can pull yourself away, you might see something important over here."

Fall watched the slowly churning miasma, searching its depths for movement.

"I found logs in here from before Sostek's entries. Maybe even before the war."

Fall blinked. "Before the war?"

"Yeah, I mean *way* before the war. It's looking like this ship is older than we first thought."

"Mmmm." Fall followed the currents, swirling, diving, rising. "Hey."

Hermes didn't answer.

"Hey, I just noticed something." Fall looked back, but Hermes was focused on another log playback.

Fall leaned forward, almost touching the clear viewport, searching up and down and to the sides. "Where are they?"

"Where are what?" Hermes finally responded.

"The erini. I just realized I haven't seen them the whole time."

"They're there. They're always there."

"No, I'm telling you, they aren't . . . " Fall looked down.

Beneath the surface of the Never, something shadowy moved upward. It was so expansive, he hadn't noticed it at first. As it cleared the outer layer, the bulging clouds were forced to the sides of it.

Fall turned and sprinted away from the viewports toward the captain's chair. "Hermes! Take the helm!"

"Huh? What is it?"

"We're breaking Riftspace!"

"Whoa!" Hermes spun around in his chair. "Why?"

Fall reached for the *sivinar* and activated the orb, gaining the extracorporeal perception he needed. "The erini. They knew."

"Spit it out, man. You aren't making any sense."

The edges of the *sivinar* elongated. "The *Forge*. Right *below* us."

"It's after us?"

"I'm assuming." Fall closed his eyes. When he opened them, he saw what the *Lantern* saw, a streaming flow of green and blue, faded starlights obscured over a rolling spherescape. Below him, chevrons of bone crested through the nebulous violet matter, reaching up for him like fingers grasping after a gnat.

"Don't wait for the Inos drive. Take us out."

Hermes protested as he settled into the forward station. "We're gonna break your new toy."

"No, we won't," Fall heard himself say.

"There's no way the hull can take it."

"It can. Just do it."

The ship exploded from the Rift as if it were a hard-nosed whale shooting up into the night sky. Except, there was no return to the sea—Hermes only burned forward, hoping to put distance between the *Lantern* and the *Forge*. The hull shook and strained, but it held.

"Sensors are picking up debris," Hermes announced.

Fall was sure the ship was intact. "From us? Where?"

"No, *moron*. Look ahead."

He did. The ruined hulls of hundreds of ancient starships stretched out as far as his sensor-vision could resolve. Behind the field, an indigo nebula shined its ominous light over the shifting graveyard. "I'm not reading any significant radiation. This must have happened a long time ago."

"*Sinis Mor*," Sostek said as he entered the bridge. "Another battle lost to time." He sat down and activated a lateral station. "Though, many things have endured."

A quick look behind showed what Sostek meant. Normal space was cleaved to make way for the *Forge*, Never igniting alongside it. The instant the *Forge* cleared, tracing beams of light converged on the *Lantern*, narrowly missing as Hermes tilted the ship on its axis, diving and rising.

Fall searched the ever-moving maze of ships. There were almost infinite places to hide. "Maybe *we* can get lost here too." He spoke through the intercom. "We're under attack. Everyone strap in."

As Hermes cleared the outer boundary, Fall got a better look. There were ships of blue and white, expansive in scope. There were ships of red and black too, curved and alien. Their features were shadowed, but he could see the hulls had been heavily damaged. There were multiple gashes and holes, ships scored and burned along their surfaces.

Sostek spoke as the *Lantern* went deeper. "This was the Great Fleet, an armada of human and voidstrider forces, united in the cause of war. Here they were discovered by Golak Kerinos, the great Behemoth-Who-Ruins, and here they were utterly broken."

Hermes maneuvered over a ruptured ship and through the blasted remains of another. Small objects, unrecognizable, bounced off the forward viewport.

For no reason at all, Fall looked to starboard. In the nebula's far-reaching light, he saw his ship's shadow growing and shortening, back and forth, as they passed the different-sized chunks of ruin. Just a little way back, another smaller shadow did exactly the same.

"Behind us!" Fall yelled.

Hermes banked hard and engaged the engine boosters. He whipped around a slowly spinning tower of vertical metal.

The missile-lock alarm blared.

Fall switched to the rear camera, and he saw a missile destroy the already dead hunk of junk they'd just cleared.

Hermes laughed nervously. "Close one." He pulled the nose up and rocketed through a twisted tunnel of warped wreckage.

Fall watched as the white Elcosian slivers followed him, slender and highly maneuverable. "Hermes, bring the weapon systems online."

"I'm a little busy here, if you haven't noticed."

Fall grimaced. "Maybe I can. Right, looks like we have missiles and ..."

"And what?"

"I don't know. But we have two of them."

The *Lantern* neared the end of the hollowed-out tube, and Hermes flipped it around, letting momentum carry them along on the same course, yet facing the enemy slivers.

Fall fired the two main guns, scouring the interior of the wreck with tightly packed ruby-red pulses of deadly light. The slivers dodged as best they could, but there wasn't enough room. The one to the right burst open when it was hit. The other sliver rolled across the inner surface of the wreckage, returning fire.

The *Lantern* shot out of the end, and Hermes flipped back over, arcing hard to port. As he came back around, he ran parallel to the old ruined cruiser, back toward the other end. The sliver came out and followed, hot on his tail.

The starboard cannon suddenly cried out for attention. Something was wrong and getting worse.

Olivia's voice intruded. Alarms and curses could be heard in the background. "Fall, we need help. There's a fire back here. It's growing."

"We have a fire suppression system," Fall said. "But . . . it isn't working."

"I will see what I can do," Sostek said as he rose to leave.

"Thanks." Fall searched the weapons for further damage. "We might not be able to use the cannons again. It could have been the sliver, but it looks like there was an overload too. I'm betting these guns haven't fired in a very long time."

"Well, figure something out." Hermes put the ship into a roll, barely avoiding wild shots from the sliver in pursuit.

Ahead, two more slivers glinted in the nebula's light. Without hesitation, Fall locked onto the one ahead and fired a missile. The projectile flew forward rapidly, harmlessly passing between the slivers. "Does anything work on this piece of—" He was cut off as Hermes pulled up and engaged the booster engines.

He ducked in and out of the massive pieces of metal nearby, barely avoiding the incoming fire from behind. "Fall . . . "

Fall worked to isolate the problem. "Maybe I can shut down the defective cannon. We only need one, really."

"We're running out of time here . . . "

"One more pathway and—"

"Just do it already!"

Hermes climbed up, over a flattened plane that used to be the spine of a battleship. He immediately dove under the next obstacle, an array of incredibly huge engines.

Fall fired the port cannon into the structure as they passed, scattering debris into the path behind.

"What the heck was that?" Hermes asked, exasperated.

"Just watch."

The first sliver flew right through the cloud of metal. Its port engine was ripped completely away, sending it flying into another mass of dense particulates floating nearby.

"All right. I guess I'll give you that one." Hermes flipped the ship around and pushed the engines until they slowed then started moving back toward the array.

"Thanks, but I'm worried that was our last shot. Another and I'll burn that one out too."

Hermes brought the *Lantern* to a stop. "Look."

Below them and just ahead, one of the slivers crept out.

"He's gonna see us," Hermes said quietly.

"No. I have an idea." Fall waited until it felt right then fired a missile, this time without a lock. He watched in satisfaction as the dumb projectile met the slow-moving sliver at just the right time, burrowing itself deep into the cockpit.

"Hmph. Decent shot." Hermes pushed the engines hard, catapulting them out of the hiding hole.

"Not much different than archery." Fall scanned around. "Okay. One left."

The decompression alarm sounded. Hermes suddenly threw the *Lantern* into a tight spiral then into a climb. Fall searched for damage. They'd taken some hits from above.

The lock-on alarm blared again. Hermes broke hard, taking the ship in and out of floating asteroids of derelict technology. There was another explosion behind them. He let out a grunt. "Miss. Barely."

Fall ignored the sweat rolling down his forehead. "We might not get lucky again. Come around that pylon there and hit it hard back toward them."

"Your missile trick won't work if he sees it coming."

"I'll use the cannon again."

"But I thought . . . "

"Trust me."

"Have it your way . . . " Hermes swung wide, turned the ship on its port side, and pulled up. He put the engines at max power at just the right time, and they flew right back toward the remaining sliver. "Hold on!" He started a roll.

The last sliver fired its guns, but Fall waited. The lock-on alarm returned, on then off then on again as the ship juked. Bullets struck the forward hull, but Fall ignored the danger, holding course until the sliver was right in his sights—till he could see the pilot.

At the last moment, he fired, blasting a molten red tunnel through the sliver's fuselage. As the fighter disintegrated, the lock-on alarm fell silent.

So did everything else.

Fall was cut off from the ship, left in complete silence. He released his hold on the *sivinar*. "What *now*?"

Hermes spun around. "Exactly what you said would happen. We lost power."

"I said the *cannon* would blow out."

He shrugged. "Guess it did. Along with everything else."

Fall replaced the *sivinar*, which melted away. Through the forward viewports he saw a rapidly approaching wad of metal and cables. "Tell me we can fix this."

"Ummm. Not this time."

"Not good. Not good!" Fall hurriedly reached for the straps of the seat harness and buckled himself in. He hit the intercom switch on the armrest. "Everyone brace yourselves! We're about to—"

The force of the impacts spun the ship within the cables at breakneck speed, a rapid series of concussive jolts. One of the cables finally held, and the *Lantern* spun and slammed into something solid. As it did, Fall's head did the exact same thing.

Nnnnng. Nnnnng. A dull red flash. Low rumble of an alert like a bell ringing in Fall's mind. *Nnnnng. Nnnnng.*

His hands were grasping at the straps over his chest. "I can't . . . "

His eyes wouldn't open. He forced them, first right then the left. Brighter flashes of red came with each alert.

He couldn't find the buckles. "Why can't I . . . ? Stupid thing."

"Allow me." An unfriendly voice offered assistance.

White claws ripped through the straps then shot to Fall's neck, squeezing blood up into his eyes. The hand pulled him violently from the seat and lifted him high into the air.

Fall pulled at the tightening claws, hard as diamond, but they wouldn't release. He looked down into the face of the one who had him, seeing only a terrible helmet of frozen white flame.

"You are not what I hoped to find here, boy."

Fall tried to speak, but only spittle came out of his mouth. His vision was closing in to narrow points.

He heard the words echo in his mind as he fell into the darkness. "But you will do for now."

TENSION

THE SLAP OF CHEEK AND BONE AGAINST COLD, unforgiving slab shattered any respite Fall might have had.

"Wake up."

The embers hauled him up by his arms and dragged him, bare feet skipping across the floor. They marched on quickly, iron grips lock-tight.

Polished flooring, white walls, and armored boots faded in and out along with Fall's consciousness. He watched numbly as warm blood spilled from his mouth, dripping a serpiginous trail of crimson behind him.

"Leave him there," an old woman commanded.

"As you wish," the ember responded, and Fall was dropped as hard as before.

With great effort, he rose up on his hands and opened his heavy eyes. The woman stood there before him, dressed in the robes of an Elcosian priest. Though she smiled in pity, there was no mistaking the haunt of death in her eyes.

Her thin black lips rolled back. "They have injured you, child. But take heart, for at long last, you will have time to rest. And to *atone*."

Two men with masked faces and robes similar to the woman's, though simpler in design, came to his sides and lifted him to his feet. They led him to a chair and sat him down.

Fire shot up through his muscles as his weight pressed down. There wasn't a single tissue that didn't scream.

Cold metal shot across his wrists and lower legs. He pulled up, testing the bonds. They were strong.

The chair elongated without warning, stretching him supine and rotating him vertically, suspending him above the deck as if he were standing.

The room was expansive, and the ceiling was high, arching as it went up into darkness. The stars burned to his right beyond the viewport wall. They were very far away.

A row of smoldering braziers lined a purple path, and along that path walked a living skeleton—a woman with bony fingers and eyes sunken back past their orbits. As those two wells of black moved along the surface of his body, he suddenly remembered he was naked.

"You carry the burdens of old injuries." She reached up, rough fingertips scraping over his skin. "Strange, when wounds need not scar." She nodded. "No doubt many came from days spent in the forests of Valen." She smiled as his breath quickened. "Since your first encounter with the Honored One, I have devoted myself to the subject of you, Fall Arden, and as my subject, you have not disappointed. Would you like to know what I've learned?"

Fall didn't answer.

"All those years spent in shadow, scratching by." She ran her fingers along his ribs, tracing them. "The company you kept . . ." Her fingernails dug in, running up his chest to the base of his neck. "We are all judged by the company we keep." She turned and walked away slowly, hands clasped behind her lower back. "Question." She turned around. "What does a man such as you fear? Arachnids, perhaps? Parasites? Is it pain? Fire?" The woman looked into his eyes, penetrating too deeply. "No, Fall Arden. It is not the positive that would break you. The addition of some terrible thing. Your fear lies in the *negative*. The taking away." She walked closer. "So, now the question becomes, what should I take from you?"

The table tilted again, leaving him supine. Another metal clamp shot across his neck, compressing his trachea, enough that when he swallowed, his airway moved against it.

She came closer where he could turn his head slightly to see her. She waved her fingers, and another metal strap shot across his forehead, realigning his head to face forward.

"Tell me. Why did you help her escape?"

Fall swallowed his blood forcefully and croaked out a reply. "You'll have to be more specific."

She smiled. "This can be as difficult as you make it. I don't mind prolonging this at all. However, you would be better served to tell me before *he* arrives."

Fall looked up to the ceiling.

Tieger.

Something like linen flowed over his lower arms. As the sheets spread, they encircled his wrists, elbows, and everything between. The metal straps in those locations receded with two simultaneous *clicks*.

Fall tried to reach up, straining so hard he almost hurt himself, but his arms were trapped in the sheets. He struggled, and the more he did, the worse it became. A level of panic he hadn't known in a long time set in, and he had to fight it down with all his might.

Breathe. It doesn't matter. You can handle anything. Be calm.

He lay still, surrendering to his imprisonment. The woman smiled. It was horrible, but calm he remained.

That same linen feeling rose up along his legs. The material looped in and out, pulling uncomfortably, locking his feet in painful positions, ensuring he couldn't move his toes in the slightest.

Stay calm. Stay calm. Stay calm.

"Isn't it frustrating? Like a dream where you can't move? One from which you awake and realize you're paralyzed?"

Fall's nose itched. The skin where his arms met his sides was sweaty and damp. His right foot was going to cramp soon if he couldn't straighten it out.

"Again. Why did you help her?"

Fall rocked the table and flared his nostrils. "Because of this."

"Oh?"

"I wouldn't let you have anyone, especially her."

"I see. Does this mean she is under your protection?"

"Come closer, and I'll tell you."

She smiled again. "So you could injure me? Would that make you feel better?"

"*Definitely.*" He rocked the table twice more.

The woman smiled again. The sheets suddenly pulled tighter, and the ones around his arms forced them underneath his body. He had to arch his back to make room.

"Ah!" he cried out against his will.

She stroked his forehead. "I have unlimited ways to make you suffer. Your body may be strong, but your mind is open to me. I will take your freedom from you, one movement at a time until you scream out any answer I wish."

Fall struggled to breathe. His eyes stung. He could barely swallow. He choked on blood and spit. "You . . . can try."

She looked up beyond his head and nodded. A mask was placed over his mouth and nose. It formed a tight seal, leaving no air to breathe.

He fought and strained, eyes wide. His chest moved up and down, though there was no oxygen. His vision closed in, blackening.

Then suddenly the air flowed. He gasped and heaved, taking in as much as he could, even though there was a strange taste to it.

"Yes, child, breathe deeply. While I cannot break you with this substance alone, your defenses will wither all the faster." She nodded to someone beyond him. "As we are short on time, I will give you one final chance to answer before I escalate." She leaned in. "I know you were with her not so long ago. You parted. Why?"

Fall relaxed his face and looked into her eyes. She pulled the mask away to hear his reply.

He swallowed again and answered through the haze and panic. "*Never.*"

"Hmmm." She waved someone over. A tray wheeled up next to Fall's right side. He couldn't see it fully. She reached to it and held up a pointed knife, twisting it so he could see the edges. Then she held up something that looked like scissors but with wide tips. Next, she showed him a tube. "Let us see how quickly we can approach *never.*" Without hesitation, she calmly inserted the blade into the space between his ribs, right in line with his armpit.

Searing pain—acidic, burning, advancing—cut through him. He couldn't cry out; the pain was so incredibly intense. Her finger wormed inside the hole, reaching above his rib, probing. Something much worse happened next—she pressed through the meat and spread the tissue between his ribs.

All he could do was spasm, unable to move purposefully, unable to withdraw from her. What must have been the tube ran through the hole and ripped along his lung. He trembled as it finally stopped, shaking involuntarily.

"I have inserted a tube along the lining of your lung. As painful as that must have been, you will find that things can always get worse."

A pump activated. Cold liquid flowed into his chest, and instantly he couldn't breathe, a fish out of water. Some air went in through the mask, but he was drowning from the inside.

"Your right lung has collapsed. Perhaps the upper lobe is still open a little? Should I increase the flow? If I wanted, I could suck it all out and return your lung to you. Ultimately, it is your decision."

Fall pleaded with his own mind. Overwhelming pain and fear

mingled with confusion and rage. He didn't know exactly what the woman would want to hear, but there was one word he couldn't say. He could never say it. He closed his eyes and lived one shallow breath at a time.

She sighed. "I have left you with too much, it would seem." She moved around to his other side, pushing the tray ahead of her.

He knew what was coming. He could do nothing to stop it. Fire found his flesh again. Cutting, pushing, spreading, invading. There was the water. His left lung failed.

He experienced true panic. No air entered, though he felt it on his face. His arms and legs strained almost to the snap of his muscles. The pressure was immense. There was no escape.

Eternity passed. Sight and sound blurred into a deep vortex, dragging him deeper. But then there was relief. He could breathe again.

Forcefully he drew in the air, using muscles he did not know he had. He heard the pumps wind down as they ceased.

"Take a break, Fall Arden. Gather your wits to answer. Why were you there on that . . . ship? Explain."

He took a long time to answer. "Because." He respired while he could. "Because I felt like it."

The metal strap across his neck tightened. His trachea ratcheted back with small crunching sensations. The fluid returned, and he drowned again.

His vision faded much more quickly the second time. He was fully immersed.

It was then, in the midst of the depths, that a lifesaver appeared—a buoy in the night. The figure pulsed, black against a blacker black, then shifted into dark purple. He held out his hand to Fall, rough and stained.

Rise.

Fall reached out and was pulled from the lapping waves. He stood shivering beneath the towering figure who shone underneath an outer garment.

Speak, and be free.

Fall looked back to the water. There was nothing beneath it but death, cold and final.

What should I say?

The destination.

Whose?

Hers. The voice was equal parts fear and anger.

Fall took a step back toward the water's edge. *No.*

Speak, and be free.

I said no!

The colossus looked up beyond Fall. A green mist arose above the water along with a scent of something familiar, something poisonous.

Speak, and be free.

Out of the fog, forms stepped forward. They were all twisted versions of Fall, broken and stooped, afraid and shaking.

Fall's mind spoke aloud, a cacophony of voices with one forbidden word pushing through to the forefront.

Ver...

Fall turned to them. *No, don't.*

Veridi—

You can't! We can't!

They all spoke at once. *Veridian.*

A building laughter from beyond the sea suffused the mist, deep and mocking.

Tieger!

The stone beneath Fall's feet crumbled, and he fell back into the water, beneath the waves.

The pumps activated once more, removing the fluid from around his lungs. The sheets snapped away.

His hands, suddenly free, shot to his neck and to the metal there, which also retracted. He instinctively felt for one of the tubes in his chest, but he stopped as the pain of the movement radiated through to his spine.

"Be calm," the woman said. "It is over."

He lay back and relaxed his burning muscles. He waited.

She touched his shoulder. A slip of her cloth fell over his elbow. It started to move away.

Faster than he could have purposely done, he had her. He was up, tubes ripped free, wild. Then he had her on the ground, squeezing. Blood and water spilled out down each side of him.

The two masked men rushed over, taking him around the shoulders. They lifted, but he would not come free. One of the men slipped on the blood and water, flipping the tray. Fall's hand was in the scattered tools. When it came back, the rib spreader was in it. And then it was in the woman's neck, midline, splitting her so wide she would never take a breath ever again.

The blade was next. He thrust it back over his shoulder. There was a cry, and the hands released him. He dove onto the man who'd fallen first, stabbing over and over. He turned.

The final man fled toward the door, robes flapping, holding his arm where Fall had wounded him. Fall ran him down and ended him with a flurry of blows to the side of his neck and upper chest.

He stood there over the bleeding man, crazed and bloody, feral in his animal fury.

He shuffled toward the door, willing his body to move one step at a time. Before he could make it, he went to his knees, knowing that when he fell, he would never get back up.

That was when Tieger entered. As he walked by, he took Fall by the back of his neck and dragged him to the table. He threw him upon it and turned to the dead woman.

Surprisingly, he laughed. "The old bitch is dead." He turned back to Fall. "I warned her to be wary of you, trickster."

Fall looked into her wide, dead eyes.

Tieger rubbed his chin. His eyes were ice blue, and his face was scarred. "Unfortunately, the dead learn no lessons."

He walked over and knelt next to her. He suffused her with purple light, causing her body to seize and shake. He stopped just as her screams reached their crescendo.

She pushed herself up and grabbed at her neck then looked up at Fall in disbelief at the realization of what had occurred. "How dare you! You worm . . . you . . . you—"

Tieger backhanded her, and she sprawled out, unconscious. "Frustrating woman." He turned on Fall and breathed deeply. "I must thank you."

The back of Fall's head touched the table. "For what?"

"For giving me the girl."

"I didn't give you shit."

Tieger paused then said the secret word. "Veridian."

Fall winced and rose as much as he could. "What?"

Tieger held up a rod. Purple light surged from a line near its end. "Elcos can peer into the mind. He can speak to it. *Your* mind has spoken." Tieger thrust out his other hand as Fall tensed. "Do not rise."

Fall lay back down.

"I had expected to find her on that ship of yours. It carried a signal, one left by someone I should never have relied upon. For some reason, he thought to throw me off the trail. Thanks to you, he has failed."

Did I . . . ? No, I couldn't have.

He closed his eyes.

I did.

Fall coughed again. "It's just a name. I don't know what Veridian is or what it even means."

Tieger nodded. "Nor did I." He smiled as he looked down at the rod. "Yet Elcos knew it instantly. Clever witch. Her lair lies in another galaxy."

Fall tried to laugh. "Good luck with that." He regretted the effort.

"I do not need luck. I have the *Forge*." He moved closer, looking down into Fall's eyes. His mood somehow grew colder. "There is a darkness which lies in a realm of death and corruption. From that place, creatures of primordial evil swell and issue forth, salivating in hunger over our souls."

Fall nodded. "The *Qur Noc*."

The rod surged and jumped in Tieger's hand. Tieger looked to it then back to Fall. "It seems Elcos knows that name as well. The creatures were once known as such, he says."

"He's afraid of them."

Tieger watched the rod as the light faded to its baseline level. The corner of his lip drew up slightly. "Elcos commands me to purge the world of those who would make communion with the *Qur Noc*."

"Communion?"

"Deals in the dark. Calls for aid. Surrender for power."

Fall remembered the image of Sidna, arm raised, dark energies swirling around her.

For power . . .

He remembered how Vid Sora cracked and split as it was destroyed.

"I've seen what they can do."

"As have I."

Fall rolled over with great effort. "So, leave her alone."

"Leave her alone? Impossible. Her filth will spread as would a disease."

"She's reacting to *you*. Like prey that turns to bite its predator. Stop chasing her."

"No, this will end only with her death."

"Then you might as well finish me off. It won't happen while I'm still alive."

Tieger came closer. "You are correct. You live and die at my whim." He spread his armored fingers. "I have decided that for now, you will live." Purple fire spread along Fall's skin, up into his chest. "If for nothing else, to watch her burn."

"No!"

Fall sat up, heart pounding, eyes wide. He threw his legs over the side of the table and spun around as he moved away from it.

He looked around. Outside, through the viewport, there was a sky of purple. As he moved closer, he saw that it stretched out far and wide in all directions.

Is this the Never? From the inside?

He refocused on the transparent material to see his own reflection. His hands went to the drawstring of his thin white pants. Anger rose at the realization that someone had touched him while he was unconscious.

He turned to the door, crossing the distance in a few strides. His fists wailed on the metal panels, over and over. "Open the door! I know you're out there!"

The door opened, and two embers entered. A baton was thrust toward Fall's face. "Shut up. Or I'll shut you up."

Fall rushed in and struck, but his fist hit hardened armor. The ember fell back, and Fall reached for his wrist in pain. The second ember brought his baton down, and Fall fell away with an involuntary cry as the weapon struck his shoulder.

The first ember recovered. He shook his head, popped his neck, then came over and kicked Fall. "The Honored One has ordered that you live, scum. He never said we couldn't beat you half to death." He kicked Fall one more time. "Keep it up." He left.

Fall coughed and rolled over to rise. As he did, Hermes fell out from under him and rolled.

"What?"

The tiny metal capsule shifted into the red imp form. "Phew. I knew riding on that guy's boot would pay off."

Fall leaned back and winced, holding his ribs. "What took you so long?"

"Seriously? You do know where you are, right?"

Fall stood slowly and walked back toward the door, rubbing his ribs. "I know exactly where I am. That's why I'm leaving."

"Got any ideas?"

Fall stopped in front of the hatch. "Yes. They're coming back in. We're going to kill them."

"Whoa there, *psycho*. Any less murderous ideas?"

"No." Fall kicked the door. "Hey!" He kicked it again. "Hey, I said come back and try that again!"

The door opened. That same ember walked in first as Fall backed away. "Seems you didn't learn your lesson. This one's going to stick."

The second ember followed him in too.

"Hermes."

Sticky strands stretched out and caught the two men.

Fall reached out and ripped the baton away from the first ember then struck him on his neck, over and over, each strike rattling his arm, driving the ember down to his knees. He reached down for the ember's helmet, ripped it off, and smashed the man right in the nose. He drew back and struck him across the side of the head, hard enough to crack his skull.

He turned on the other ember, but Hermes slammed the man into the ceiling then the floor. After that ember didn't get up, Fall went back to the first ember. He stopped when Hermes jumped in the way and raised his arms. "Whoa. Easy. He's down."

Fall stepped to the side. "Get out of my way."

Hermes matched the movement. "Hey! What's the matter with you? We don't kill when we don't have to, remember?"

Fall looked to the side and tossed the helmet away. "If you say so."

"What did they do to you?" Hermes looked him up and down. "I don't see any damage."

"It's there. *Move*."

Hermes stepped out of the way. "You know you're gonna have to tell me at some point."

Fall knelt to check each ember. "Their armor won't fit me."

"No big deal. To be honest, I've been wanting to try something out for a while."

"Try what?"

Hermes leapt toward Fall in a splash of melted color. Fall fell back instinctively, and when he looked down at himself, he saw the flawless armor of an ember. He even had the little cloth at his waist with the hammer symbol.

Fall stood and picked up one of the real rifles. "This is pretty good."

"Better than good," Hermes replied from inside the fake helmet. "It should pass any visual inspection."

"We need to find my gear. I won't leave without it."

"Gotcha. But you aren't going to like where it is."

"The armory?" Fall asked.

"Worse. Tieger's quarters."

The lift doors opened. Embers, officers, and crewmen moved about, busy at work. Fall stepped out, moving inside the imitation armor.

He walked with purpose, rifle held at the ready in front of his chest. The disguise was perfect; no one stood in their way or gave them a second glance.

Fall looked around without moving his head. "Which way?"

A tiny version of Hermes walked across the inside of the helmet and pointed. "Past the bridge."

"Are you sure?"

"I scoped this place out before I found you."

"You should have come straight to me."

Hermes spoke after a few more steps, ignoring the statement. "These guys are really moving. Something's about to happen. Wonder what it is?"

"They're going after Sidna."

"They can't know where she is . . . "

"No. But they know where she's going."

"How?"

"I told them."

Hermes's eyes bulged. "Man, I know you guys had a falling out, but wow, that's harsh."

"It wasn't by choice. Tieger took the name from my mind."

"What name?"

"Veridian. I heard her say it once. I think it's a planet."

Hermes shrugged. "So what? It's just a name."

"Apparently it was enough. He said Elcos knows where it is."

"Elcos?" Hermes laughed. "Tieger thinks he's talking to Elcos?"

"He is. Through some rod."

"A rod?"

"That's what I saw."

They came to what looked like the main command center. Tieger stood in full armor on a raised platform near a large spherical hologram. He was speaking with a trio of officers.

Hermes whispered. "There he is. Let's go."

Fall walked on, not all that far, until they neared a particularly large double hatch. They moved past and entered a side room around the corner.

Hermes dissociated from Fall. "Okay. Find somewhere to lay low. I'll wait out there for Tieger and go in when he does."

"We can't attack him here."

Hermes face-palmed. "Man, they really scrambled your brain. I'm not going to attack him, stupid. I'm going to get us out of here."

"How?"

"Just stay here."

"Fine . . . "

Hermes vanished. The room hatch opened then closed.

There in the dark room, Fall had a few minutes to think. He did his best not to, pacing the small room, assessing for a good position to put up a fight in case he was discovered.

She won't be there yet. If I can beat her there, I might be able to warn her. Maybe I can distract Tieger. Make him come after me instead.

He sat on a crate.

But what if Tieger's right? What if Sostek's right? What if the same cycle is happening again? Maybe I should just stay out of it. She can take care of herself, remember? She doesn't want help. Doesn't need it.

He stood and paced.

We all need help, whether we know it or not.

The image of Sidna tied up, flames rising around her legs, flashed before his mind's eye. He tightened his fists.

To the Void with why. It's not going to happen.

The door opened and closed then the Hermes suit suddenly reappeared. "Okay, we're good."

Fall jumped. "You could warn me before you do that."

"I could . . . "

Fall sighed. "What did you find?"

"Well, you're right about him knowing where Veridian is. And you're right about him getting ready to go there."

"Bastard."

"Oh, and that rod you mentioned. Yeah, that's an anchor."

"Explain."

"Mmm. Tough to, but it's kind of like a link."

"To what?"

"To *whom*. Elcos, I'm assuming."

"The colossus . . . "

"The what?"

Fall shook his head. "When they took Sidna's destination from me, I saw a huge figure in my mind."

"Did he say anything?"

"He told me to speak."

"Nothing else?"

"Not that I remember."

"That's probably for the best. He's excitable."

"You say that like you know him."

"Not personally. More by reputation. He wasn't a bad guy back in the day, but the war changed his personality. He withdrew, became suspicious, became aggressive about containing threats, that sort of thing. I suppose in a way, it's good that he did, or humanity might have been lost forever."

Fall took a deep breath. "I'll be sure to thank him. Now, how do we get out of here?"

"We fly out."

"Right. Of course."

"I'm serious. I commanded somebody on the bridge to expel the ship. Told 'em it was filth not worthy of the *Forge*."

"You *commanded* them?"

"Well, Tieger did." Hermes coughed. When he spoke again, it was with Tieger's voice. "Do what I say, or I'll smash you with my hammer."

Fall raised an eyebrow. "Okay. All that's left is my gear."

"One step ahead of you. Head back to Tieger's quarters."

Fall moved to the hatch. "We can't go in dressed like this."

"Again, ahead of you."

Fall was suddenly surrounded by blurry white. Through the haze, he saw why. They must have looked just like Tieger.

He left the room, doing his best to look pissed off and unapproachable. "How do we get in?" Fall whispered.

"Surprisingly enough, he doesn't keep it locked."

They entered Tieger's chambers. Hermes walked over to the holo-ring embedded in the floor. There were candlesticks, an armor stand, and tapestries of fire and death.

"Far left," Hermes said as he pointed.

Fall's armor and weapons were arranged neatly on a set of shelves. The sword had its own shelf.

"Why are these *here*?"

"Beats me. Maybe he's got a thing for you."

"I'd say it's the opposite."

The Hermes illusion fell away and Fall hurriedly got into his suit and armor. As he tightened the last strap and reached for the sword, Hermes reformed the Tieger armor. "I'll have to carry the sword. Otherwise it sticks out past me."

"Got it." Fall took one last look around the room as they left.

No one offered a greeting or even looked twice as they went to the lift on the way to the hangar.

Fall commented, "They're terrified."

"Can't blame them. Works for us."

As the lift reached the deck, they walked out into a busy scene. Crew techs and soldiers hurried to secure the starfighters and transports, clearing the bay after they did. An overhead alert reminded the crew of the imminent departure.

They made for the *Lantern*. The lower cargo ramp was down. The two embers flanking it saluted. Fall never slowed as Hermes spoke to them in Tieger's voice. "Return to your previous posts. Now."

The embers saluted again and jogged away without hesitation.

Once they reached the ship's interior, Hermes activated the ramp. As it closed, he jumped away into his imp form, leaving Fall undisguised.

Sostek's spinning white irises greeted Fall as the interior lights hummed to life. He stared for a moment. "Are you injured?"

"I'll be fine."

Sostek continued to stare, quiet.

Fall stepped around Hermes. "Where are the others?"

Sostek held up the glowing orange World Shard. "Safe, yet anxious."

"What about the ship?"

"It will fly." Sostek turned the shard over in his hands. "I will admit, the Exanim *was* helpful in that regard."

Fall moved for the bridge. "Bring everyone back."

Sostek headed for the common hold. Hermes followed Fall.

When they reached the bridge, Hermes headed for the helm station, and Fall went to the captain's chair. He reached over and took the *sivinar*. Once he had control, he oriented himself in relation to the *Forge*.

The bay was clear, and the outer doors were open. As he watched, an emitter moved into place above them. Purple light enveloped the *Lantern*, lifting it from the deck and pushing it into the Never. When it deactivated, the ship tumbled away slowly. Once clear, the *Forge* began to move away.

Olivia ran through the bridge's hatch, straight to Fall. "Fall! You're alive!"

He released the *sivinar*, returned it, then stood up to face her. "More or less."

She checked him quickly. "They didn't hurt you, did they?"

"Nothing permanent."

"You seem to be okay . . . "

Hermes turned around. "He's definitely *not* okay."

Olivia looked between them, back and forth. "Wait. What happened? What did they do?"

"What happened?" Fall scowled at Hermes then walked back to his chair and sat. "They cut me. Tore me. Drowned me. They invaded my *mind*. I watched helplessly as I was forced to betray her."

Olivia moved toward him, but he held up his hand. "I said, I'm fine."

She stopped and blinked. "Right. Yeah, of course you are." She nodded and walked to the forward viewport, crossing her arms. "So what're we gonna do now?"

Fall looked past the shadowed bridge, bathed in the Never's purple light. His body ached. His *mind* ached. "Now, we follow Tieger."

Hermes and Sostek asked, "*What?*" at exactly the same time.

Fall took the *sivinar* again. "He's going after Sidna."

Hermes shook his head. "He's always after Sidna."

"It's different this time. This time it's my fault," Fall said.

Olivia looked back. "How's it your fault?"

Fall slammed his left fist down onto the armrest of his chair. "Because I told him, dammit!" His head jerked to the right. "*I* told him."

Sostek moved from the doorway. "This is *madness*. When gods and *Qur Noc* cross paths, the devastation is immense. We should go nowhere near their meeting."

Fall screwed up his lips in anger. "I'm not afraid of the past."

The voidstrider touched him on the shoulder. "Human. *Fall.* There is pain in your words. But you must cling to wisdom. Let us regroup. Come back from a position of *strength*."

Fall closed his eyes, hearing Sostek's words again in his mind.

Screw wisdom, I'll put my sword right through his—

"Fall's right," Olivia said.

Hermes turned to face her. "Olivia?"

She walked back to Fall, facing him from ahead. She leaned over and placed her hands on his chair. "Is this important to you?"

"Yes," Fall answered after a pause. He gripped the *sivinar* tightly, edges beginning to spin. "It is."

She nodded resolutely. "Then go after it."

Fall's concentration faltered as he looked to her in question.

"Tieger attacked our ship," she said as she placed her hands on her hips. "He's gotta pay."

"*Our* ship?"

"You heard me. We're a team, aren't we?" She turned around. "Hermes?"

"Eh, I dunno. Seems like a bad idea . . . "

She narrowed her eyes. "Weren't you the one saying earlier how bored you were? *Bring it on,* I think you said."

Hermes rubbed his chin. "I guess I did say that, didn't I?" He shrugged with a short laugh. "All right, whatever, you knew I'd go anyway."

She looked over Fall's shoulder. "Sostek?"

"I am not afraid to die." He waved his hand with a grumble. "If this is his choice, I will go."

She crossed her arms and smiled down at Fall. "Then it's settled."

Without warning, the light of the Never intensified to a nearly painful degree. It went from purple to almost white, spreading out ahead of the *Forge*, where a blast of energy from the dreadnaught began to warp the surface.

"What is *that*?" Hermes asked.

"He's breaking through," Fall said.

"To where?"

"To another galaxy. To Veridian."

"Impossible," said Sostek. "Even for that vessel."

Fall powered the ship. "Not impossible for Elcos." The engines engaged. "And not for me."

The ship edged forward then blasted in pursuit of the *Forge*.

"I do not know how to help you," Sostek warned.

"You don't have to." The ship lurched with the turbulence as Fall jumped over the *Forge*'s wake and settled in behind. "I know what to do."

He pushed the ship harder, racing through the narrowing breach as it closed behind the *Forge*.

We're coming.

THE CONSEQUENCES OF DYING

BAN WALKED, CONTINUING ON THROUGH another of Fel Kno'a's endless stone corridors.

In spite of his warnings to pay attention, he soon zoned out in the monotonous repetition of footfalls. His mind found its way back to his conversation with Becks. She hadn't been happy at all when he'd told her his plan.

You've finally gone insane.

Probably, but I know what I have to do.

She sat on the bed. *Have you already forgotten? That . . . thing was a nightmare.* She shivered. *My heart rate goes up just thinking about the way it moved. The way it spoke. Elcos, Ban. I'm not sure I could do that again.*

He walked over and knelt, taking her hands between his. *That's exactly why we have to. So that no one else ever will. We've already seen it. Faced it. We can do it again, and we must.*

But what about us? I plan on living a full life, free of being eaten alive. Remember that Runian? What if I had to watch you die like that?

That won't happen.

She looked to the side and uttered a bitter laugh. *So you say . . .*

So I know. Look at me, Saira.

She did, reluctantly.

I can do this.

Do what, die fighting a monster? Isn't that what you've always wanted?

He shook his head. *Not to die. To fight, yes. For a cause. For something real.* He squeezed her hands. *Let me do this. Do it with me.*

She searched his eyes for a few moments then rolled her own. *Damn you, Ban. If it kills me, I'll haunt you. I swear it.*

Good. He smiled as he rose. *Then I'd have you forever.*

That same smile faded as the group of pirates came to a halt. Ban pushed his way forward, moving the men to one side or the other of the hall as he passed.

When he got to the front, he saw why they'd stopped—a gaping hole in the wall.

"What is it?" he asked.

The pirate captain kicked a loose rock with his boot. "Decay?"

"No. Too specific to this section," said the Ranger.

Sidna went on through it. "It leads where we're going. Come on."

The captain and the Ranger looked to each other in silent question then went on after her.

Ban, Becks, and Tyr moved to the hole.

"What in the Void could have done this?" Becks asked.

Ban reached up to touch the edge, and a piece of brick fell away. "Something large."

Tyr stepped through. There was plenty of clearance above him and to each side.

Ban gripped his gun tightly. "Something *very* large . . . " He followed Tyr with Becks close behind.

The group followed Sidna again, walking in relative silence. As they continued, the light from their lamps and searchlights revealed corridor after corridor of the same nondescript sandstone walls.

How can she know which way to go?

After a few more minutes, Ban turned to look back at the trailing entourage. Gabin's crew filled the hall behind him, each holding a weapon and several empty sacks.

One of them cried out suddenly and drew his knife. "What was that?" He looked around suspiciously.

Everyone stopped to listen. There weren't any other sounds that Ban could hear, and no one else seemed to notice anything out of place.

The pirate captain went to his man, trying to comfort him with an easy grin. "Eh, Jean, it's going to be a long walk if you jump at each and every—"

The floor vibrated beneath them, and dust fell from the ceiling.

Jean's eyes searched the walls and ceiling. "And that?"

Gabin dusted off his coat with an easy smile. "A tremor. Nothing more."

"What if it collapses on our heads?" the man asked.

"A temple that has stood so long? I doubt it." He struck the nearest wall with the bottom of his fist. "See? Sturdy as the mountains themselves."

The temple shook again and then again. The third time, it went on longer, but as the men clustered toward the center of the passage, the rumbling ceased. A new sound intruded on the silence, something almost sad and otherworldly, like an unpleasant song.

Ban looked to Sidna and saw it in her eyes—she knew what it was. And it terrified her.

The pirate named Jean raised his knife again. The others followed suit, and for a moment, the ring of metal against metal drowned out the music. The moment passed.

Ban looked down to the floor. He could see it more clearly now, at the foot of the nearest breach in the stone. A red light intruded through, growing at a rate that matched the intensity of the approaching discord.

Sidna began to back up, moving away from the direction they'd come.

"Wait!" Ban said as he pointed at her. "What is it?"

She tore her widened eyes away from the light. She swallowed. "The Guardian . . . "

Jean pushed past his captain and took Sidna by the arm. "What do you mean, *guardian?*" He shook her. "You never said anything about any guardian!"

She pulled against his grip. "Be still, you idiot! You'll get us all killed!"

"Shut up, witch! I don't take orders from you!"

The captain drew his sword slowly. "Release her, Jean. Do it, or die where you stand."

"Both of you, be quiet!" Sidna whispered loudly.

Jean scowled at her, disgust in his eyes. He let her go as she pulled, and she fell back, catching herself on the wall.

The pirate captain stepped forward, sword pointing at the man, but he froze.

Ban heard it too. The music had stopped the moment Sidna touched the wall.

She turned to face the stone then dove aside as a large black mass, burning inside itself with a deep-red light, exploded through the wall. It never slowed its charge, carrying Jean through to the other side, panicked screams echoing through from the next corridor.

Ban ran past Sidna to the newest wall-wound and raised his gun. But before he could fire, the Guardian burst through again between Ban and everyone else, eliciting a chaotic storm of panicked screams and flashing gunshots.

Ban spun to face the Guardian's direction but held his fire. "Becks! Tyr!"

The others didn't share his caution. One of the rounds struck him in his shoulder armor, leading him to dive through the hole, hit the ground hard, and roll to his feet. He looked back to see several bolts of electricity arc through the air where he'd just been standing.

He ran to his side of the hole and put his back to the wall. "Becks! Tyr! Anybody!" Again, there was no answer.

He waited a few seconds then leaned in. A quick look through the hole revealed a lifeless corridor, littered with the dead.

He ran back through and checked each body, praying none of them were Becks or Tyr. To his relief, the bodies had all been pirates, mangled by the forces of the blows that had killed them.

A faint flash of blue light came from around the corner ahead, so he ran there and peered around the edge carefully. He couldn't see anyone, but he did hear a series of distant crackles. Ignoring the danger, he sprinted down the hall, stopping as he came to a four-way intersection.

The other three directions looked the same, each leading down a dark tunnel and out of sight. A check of his HUD's map was useless; he couldn't make sense of the maze. He paused momentarily, stopping to close his eyes and take a few steady breaths.

He huddled along the stone wall, listening for movement. The only noise was the sound of his pumping blood, loud in his ears. He checked his HUD again, searching for any indication of his teammates but saw nothing.

A handful of dust fell down on his visor. As he looked up, the stone wall beside him suddenly crumbled and a burst of black smoke enveloped him.

Before he could respond, he was shoved into the opposite wall with enough force to rattle his spine. He tried but couldn't move his head, and as the smoke swirled away, he could see why.

The Guardian's arm had him pinned there by the helmet. As he watched, armored plates rose up, and crimson light shone from underneath, rapidly growing in intensity.

Ban looked up through the drifting smoke. The immensely tall being, a creature of black armored fury, towered above him. Its red eyes seemed to burn straight into his soul, building along with the incredible heat. The light was blinding.

"Detach helmet!" The seals released on Ban's helmet, dropping him to the floor. Just as he landed, his helmet and the wall behind it disintegrated above him in a burst of molten plasma.

He extended the shock baton from his right arm and jabbed upward through the smoke. The beast roared and stumbled back from the electrified blow. As it did, Ban hastily knelt and took up his gun.

He brought it up to fire, but the Guardian jerked it away and crushed it effortlessly. It tossed the ruined weapon and thrust its other hand toward Ban's face.

Ban gritted his teeth and deflected the arm with his shock baton then drove the rod back up into the thing's neck.

It roared angrily and twisted to swipe with its other hand, but Ban anticipated and quickly dove away. As the Guardian freed its buried fingers, Ban scrambled to his feet and turned to face it.

The creature touched its injured neck in question, seemingly confused by its injury.

Ban held his glowing hand out to the side, noticing he'd activated Thenander's gift subconsciously. "Felt that, did you? Let's see how you handle something a little sharper." The air distorted, and *Folium* waited on the other side.

He withdrew it, and the spearhead shone brightly along its designs, scattering green light throughout the reddened corridor. The Guardian's light receded, leaving a wavering boundary between the two adversaries which neither color could cross.

Ban sprinted forward, spear by his side. The Guardian simply stood its ground, black smoke coursing over its body.

When Ban was close, he grasped *Folium* in both hands and thrust it forward. The Guardian swiftly caught the spear and held it in place, just before its abdomen. Ban pushed as hard as he could, but the spear wouldn't budge.

As he struggled, the Guardian's other hand opened, powering up for another blast.

Too close!

Ban concentrated on the mark of Thenander. The green light surged, running up the spear's shaft and over its silver head. The roiling smoke burned away like fog at midday, and the beast released the spear in pain. As it howled in rage, Ban drove the spear forward into its belly.

Folium's light waxed and waned within the armor, struggling with its opposite. Ban poured as much power as he could summon into the spear, and it seemed like the green light might win.

But in that moment, when the red light began to fade, the Guardian resumed its mournful song. Embedded in the tortured music was a hint of something quiet and strained. The thing was in pain.

Ban's concentration broke slightly, and the green light wavered, allowing the red power to regain its previous intensity. The woeful voice was cast back into oblivion, and the Guardian struck Ban in the chest plate, launching him backward. He landed and rolled on the hard stone floor.

The beast, having recovered its strength, removed the offending weapon and dropped it to the ground like a toy. The injury flared red-hot, beginning to heal before Ban's eyes.

The Guardian held out its hand again, gathering energy for a shot.

Ban was exposed with no cover, his every movement matched by the hand.

Something! Anything!

Ban's hand rested on his belt, and in his fingers, a grenade. He took it, twisted the top, and threw it at the Guardian's feet before diving away.

Though the enemy gave no sign it had noticed, its black fog swirled into a shield-like disk above the grenade. As it exploded, the force was directed back and up into the narrow corridor's ceiling.

Ban curled up, having just enough time to curse and raise his arms before an avalanche of bricks and mortar came crashing down on top of him.

Ban couldn't move.

He heaved against the pressure on his shoulder, but his torso was pinned, leaving him unable to gain leverage. It was then that he heard a muffled voice and the shifting of the pile above him. Stone by stone the weight lessened, until he thought he could finally move. He tried.

"Whoa, take it easy, big man." Someone pressed on his chest.

He pushed the hand away. "Get off of me."

"Sure, have it your way. Just take it slow."

Ban turned his head to cough, then looked up. A man knelt in the rubble, barely visible in the swirling dust and faint light of the lamp sitting atop a rock beside him.

He had long black hair, drawn up behind him, dressed in green light armor. His left shoulder was covered in a tattered green cape, and there was a bird painted on his right one—he looked like an Aeturnian Ranger.

"Who are you?"

"Me? Name's Ronin. Question is, who're you?"

Ban sat up and pushed back with his arms, pulling his legs free of the debris. "Ban Morgan." He held out his right hand.

The man helped pull him up with a grunt and considerable effort. "Well, Sergeant, seems you managed to survive your first encounter with the Guardian." He smiled a friendly smile. "I gotta ask—why in the Void did you run *toward* it?"

"It seemed like the best way to get closer."

The stranger laughed. "Ah, that's good. Truth be told, I'm glad someone finally gave it a kick in the ass."

Ban looked into the man's eyes, noticing a faint red rim around his irises. "What's wrong with your eyes?"

"My eyes?"

"Yes. They're red. Around the center. The same color as the Guardian's."

The man seemed to look into the distance. "Oh. Well, I guess that *would* make sense."

"What would?"

"Um, nothing. Just do yourself a favor and don't die here."

"I hadn't planned on it."

The Ranger blinked. "Neither did I."

Ban cocked his head and opened his mouth to speak, but he was interrupted by a shout from Becks. "Ban! Ban are you over there?"

He turned to answer, cupping his hands. "I'm on the other side of the collapse."

"Okay. We're coming through."

"Be careful. The walls aren't stable."

"Just hold on."

Ban turned back to the man, but he was already halfway down the corridor. "Wait!"

The man turned, walking backward as he spoke. "No time! Someone else needs my help!"

Ban shook his head. "Thanks for the rescue!"

The man nodded and turned again to walk away.

"Whoever you are . . ."

Tyr's hand worked its way through the edge, and he pulled some stone bricks through. Ban helped to clear the rest away. After a few minutes, there was a hole large enough for him to fit through. He pushed over to the other side.

"Thank Elcos we found you." Becks looked him over. "Who were you talking to over there?"

Ban looked down and saw *Folium* lying against the wall. He knelt and picked it up. "A man named Ronin. I think he's a Ranger, but he wouldn't say more."

She raised her armored hand to his forehead. "Are you sure you didn't hit your head? A concussion?"

"Maybe." He sneezed. "In any case, it doesn't matter. I drove the Guardian away. For now." He looked down the hall. "Any idea where Sidna went?"

"Yes, but she's almost out of range."

Ban nodded. "I lost the signal earlier. Do you think she knows about the tracker?"

Becks looked off into the distance, accessing her HUD. "No, I still have her. Besides, you put it in her wine. Unless she passed it, it's still in there."

"True. All right then, let's get moving. If we lose her, we'll never know what she's up to."

Becks laughed. "Trying to kill us, if I had to guess."

"Mmmm, I don't think she controlled it."

"No, but she knew it was here. I'm guessing she didn't mention it before?"

"Hardly."

"Exactly my point. For all we know, that's why she brought us here. As bait."

Ban looked back to the fallen ceiling and nodded a few times. "She would do that, wouldn't she?"

Becks turned to follow her HUD with a shrug. "I would."

Ban laughed lightly and coughed. "Then let's do our part."

"What?"

"If we're supposed to be the bait, we might as well catch the fish."

Becks nodded. "Brilliant." She turned to Tyr. "What about you, Tyr? Ready to chase after an invincible hate-monster in the hopes it'll lead us straight to a witch and her pet demon?"

Tyr shrugged and followed after Ban.

Becks followed after him, shaking her head. "I *knew* you'd say that."

ARRIVAL

SHA-THUMP, SHA-THUMP, SHA-THUMP . . .

Tieger's armored legs moved in resolute rhythm, an external manifestation of the drive within him. He made the next turn, each footfall one step closer to his long-awaited resolution. The hidden enclave, the damned arcanist nest, would soon be crushed underneath the might of his iron will. Yet, he felt as if one thing were not quite resolved.

He did not blame the Ranger for escaping. He might have done the same in his position. Of course, some part of him had hoped the boy would stay and face the consequences of defeat.

Try as he might, he cannot escape fate.

As expected, Commander Prime met Tieger outside the main hangar. She snapped to attention, shield over her back and sword at her hip.

He addressed her. "Commander."

"Honored One." She bowed her head. "Your forces stand ready."

Tieger nodded and continued on. She fell in behind him.

The doors opened as they approached, and Tieger walked through. Arrayed beyond was his invasion force, an impressive mix of man, machine, and faith. An entire battalion of embers stood in square formations, dwarfed by massive orbital drop-assault pods. Repulsion-powered APCs, low-altitude strike craft, and hulking bipedal antipersonnel tanks filled the spaces between the companies.

Tieger looked over his forces slowly. After a moment, he waved his hand. "Commence the assault."

There were no cheers. There were no battle cries. There were only the sounds of boots, moving in unison, engines humming, and heavy machinery gliding along as the tanks turned to walk into their waiting pods.

"The Harbinger was wrong to doubt you, Honored One."

"He was wrong about many things, Commander." Tieger turned to his waiting transport. "You will lead the attack."

"With pleasure." She bowed her head and walked toward the battalion.

As Tieger continued, he felt the rod of Elcos stir at his side.

Beware...

"I do not intend to let my guard down," he answered.

The temple ... it is a place for the dead.

"Fitting. For soon it will be filled to the brim."

Tieger stepped up into his transport. He waited until they'd cleared the repulsion fields to look back down to the rod, but it remained silent.

He saw the green world below, an entire planet of jungle, and the temple, enclosed in virtual brackets as information scrolled across his vision.

A place for the dead ...

"Hold altitude above the battlefield."

The pilot responded. "Yes, Honored One."

The first orbital pod burned past them, rocking the transport in the ignited atmosphere. Another went by, and then another. Soon the pods would open, showering the jungle floor with smaller seeds—seeds that would bloom and bear the fruits of war.

The embers who shared the transport only looked ahead, unmoved by the display outside.

The rod stirred again.

She cannot be allowed to call them.

"I will destroy any fiend she summons."

Beware...

Tieger did not respond. He watched as the first of his forces emerged above the treetops, spitting gunfire into the leaves below. It was raining.

"Good. They resist."

A missile exploded, bouncing the craft downward. "Honored One! We are under attack!"

A smile touched Tieger's lips. "Finally. These arcanists show some teeth."

"Should I take us higher?"

He felt the heat then, the tepid waters of his blood slowly rising to a boil. His disappointment faded away, his mind focusing on the task at hand.

"No!" Tieger moved closer to the door. "Take us in!"

Beware . . .

"Be silent! I have no fear of my enemies! Nor should you!"

The rod went quiet, light fading.

"Honored One?" The pilot mistook Tieger's outburst as having been directed at him. The embers did not meet Tieger's gaze. He said nothing else.

The pilot weaved and evaded as incoming fire burst around the transport.

Tieger only gripped the rail tighter, anticipating.

I do not fear.

The port engine took a hit. A second explosion rocked the passengers, and two of the embers flew out through a breach in the hull. Tieger was thrown back and pinned to the ceiling as the transport suddenly went into a free fall.

"I can't hold it!"

Tieger was undaunted by the imminent crash. "Aim for the temple!"

The pilot never responded, but the thrusters engaged. It seemed the man would do his duty, even though he was about to die.

And die he most certainly did as the transport hit its mark, nose first into the temple's sandstone structure.

Gabin skidded to a stop, waving Sidna on. "Come, come!"

She ran past him into the room, climbing over the remnants of a fallen wall.

Mei came inside as well, Gabin right after her. They all moved away from the door, each breathing heavily. The wavering light on Sidna's armlet shone down at their feet.

Gabin stood up tall, hands on his hips as he walked away then back. "This seems unsavory, even for me." He grimaced.

Sidna rubbed her arms. "What else can we do?"

Mei walked to the door. "We should double back. We can reach the entrance if we are careful."

Sidna coughed. "No way. It's all for nothing if I turn back now."

Mei shook her head. "You cannot truly believe anything here is worth the price of your death."

Sidna squatted down and rested her arms on her knees. "Except I do."

Mei walked nearer, placing her hand on Sidna's shoulder. "You must find a way past this obsession. There will be another path."

Sidna stood up. "I'm not getting talked out of it this time."

Mei's mechanical eye whirred. "It was wisdom that saved you then. Hear it again, and leave this place behind."

Sidna looked to Gabin for support. He tried to speak, but he was cut off by movement behind Sidna. She followed his eyes and spun around, hair rising on her neck.

A shadow stepped forward, two rings of red for eyes and a rustling cape around his boots. "You came back." As he approached, the lights in his eyes became less prominent, and his muted human features appeared.

Sidna nearly collapsed. "Ronin?"

He smiled. "In the flesh."

Sidna felt a cold, sinking feeling. She looked down to his waist, and while she could see the damage to his armor, he looked completely whole. "But you . . . you . . . "

"*Died?*" He shrugged. "Sure. Just didn't stay that way."

Sidna's shaking hand reached for her pistol.

Ronin held up his palms. "Whoa! It's really me."

She didn't relax her grip. "What's wrong with your eyes?"

"Tough to explain."

"*Try.*"

He turned in a slow circle, gravel crunching beneath his boots as he gestured toward the walls. "Fel Kno'a. It brought me back." He took a step forward but stopped as Sidna drew the pistol. He appeared genuinely wounded. "I wasn't sure you'd come back for me."

"I didn't. You were dead."

He nodded and smiled weakly. "I see you kept my armlet."

"You didn't need it anymore. I took your ship too."

"Keep them both. I don't seem to have a use for them anymore." He smiled at Mei. "*Ab aeturno*, Ranger Mei of the Flowing Lands."

Mei held still as a statue. "*Ad infinitum.*"

His eyes lingered on Mei. "Something's . . . different. I can feel the temple. I'm part of it now." He nonchalantly brushed the dust from his arm. "I tried to go once, you know. But even where we fought the Guardian, where the wall is open, I can't seem to leave."

"You can *feel* the temple?" Sidna asked.

"Yes. Every part of it." The red light in his eyes flared and stayed brighter than before. "Everything *inside* it too."

Sidna lowered her pistol. "You found it . . . "

"Yes. I can take you right to it."

Sidna blinked. Something subtle had changed in Ronin's accent.

Gabin spoke over Sidna's shoulder. "Be careful, girl. He cares far too little about his condition."

Mei spoke as well. "Why? Why will *you* take her?" Her blood-red knife was drawn and ready.

Apparently, Ronin noticed. His tech-knife vibrated in his hand, half-drawn from the scabbard on his chest. "Because I made her a promise." He looked into Sidna's eyes, but the normal reassuring grin was gone, and the glow threatened to take over. "Long before any of you came along."

Is it really you?

Sidna holstered her gun. "Okay, Ronin. Show me."

Mei looked back and forth between the two then sheathed her knife forcefully.

Ronin returned his knife as well. "Come. It's this way." He turned and walked down the corridor, readjusting the rifle strap across his chest.

Mei edged over with a scowl. "That may be Ranger Deks, but he is *not* the man you knew."

"So, keep your eye on him." She pushed past her. "Come on, Gab."

Sidna left, following Ronin through a series of turns on a course that would've taken her days to find if she'd tried alone. After a few minutes, he stopped in front of a wall, seemingly no different than any other they'd passed.

He held out his hand and pressed it to the wall. Deep-red light ran along cracks in the stone, and the material wavered then disappeared. In its place was a smooth plate of metal.

Ronin turned and motioned to it. "Sidna, I have shown you the door, but you must open it."

"Why me?"

His eyes brightened again. "What waits inside, waits for you."

She looked back to Mei and Gabin. Their expressions begged her for caution. She chose to ignore them.

She walked up to the wall and touched it. Her *viae* involuntarily pulsed with energy, and the wall grew hot. She pulled her hand away from the pain of it, and when she opened her eyes, she stood in another room. Mei and Gabin weren't there, but Ronin was. She turned around slowly.

The chamber's shape was cylindrical with a circular floor, and its ceiling was high, up and out of sight. A path of stone led through to the center, surrounded by a shallow pool which stretched to the edge of the room. In the distance, red lights activated in series around the periphery, and another set lit up along the walkway.

At the end of the path, there were two columns, one rising from the floor and the other coming down from the darkness above. Suspended between them was a floating red crystal, its length about that of her hand.

Ronin walked ahead of her along the path. "Come, Sidna."

She followed him, footsteps echoing across the water. When they reached the end of the path, Ronin moved aside and watched, seemingly undeterred by the bizarre ambiance.

She approached the crystal carefully, slowly placing her hands on the flat face of the lower column. Her fingertips tingled, and the sensation continued up her arms. The air next to the column distorted. The shape of a man began to form.

He spoke. "Who has come?"

He was only a little taller than her. He had wavy black hair and dark colored eyes. He wore an outfit made of loose red cloth, draping over the black light armor at his shoulders, arms, and knees. A long, slender dagger hung from a leather scabbard attached to his belt.

Again, he spoke. "You are powerful."

Sidna took her hands away from the column's surface. "Who are you?"

"I am . . . a teacher."

"Of what?"

The hologram pointed to her arm. "The Code."

Sidna looked to Ronin in question. "Is this the tear? A hologram?"

He nodded. "The crystal holds the information you want. If you take it, you take the hologram as well."

She looked back to the image. "If I take you, will you teach me?"

"What do you wish to learn?"

She reached into her jacket and retrieved the glyph. She stared into its depths, watching the currents rush past one another as they strained against their prison.

She held it up, showing him the shifting black within. "I need to learn how to use this."

The hologram smiled. "Then you could not have found a better teacher. Take me with you, and I will show you how to unlock its full potential."

She put the glyph back into her pocket, and for a moment, it seemed like the hologram's face grew hard. His passive expression quickly returned.

She reached for the red crystal, and when she took it, the ground shook beneath her feet. She looked down, and water sloshed onto the path.

She looked up to Ronin with widened eyes. "A trap!"

Ronin looked up to the ceiling. "No. The temple is under attack."

The hologram laughed. "After all this time, I see her here again, a galaxy away."

Sidna braced against another tremor. "Her?"

"The *Forge*. My old ship."

Sidna's heart raced, and her legs felt shaky. "The *Forge* is here?"

The hologram smiled slightly. "Why do you fear it? It is a perfect vessel for you."

"Because the current owner wants me dead. Me *and* my people."

He waved his hand in dismissal. "You will utterly destroy them. I will show you the way."

She took the glyph out again and looked up. "What should I call you?"

The hologram stared at the artifact. He looked up into her eyes, and she could see his hunger. "Call me Riest." He turned to look across the water. "Your first lesson begins now."

The wall collapsed inward, and black smoke rolled across the water's churning surface. Red light and a woeful dirge filled the chamber, heralding the Guardian's entrance.

Riest stepped forward to speak in Sidna's ear. "Bothersome, isn't it?"

Sidna turned slightly. "What is it? It keeps chasing after me, no matter who else is around."

Riest smiled. "It is me, in a way."

"What?"

"I was nearly killed, betrayed by an old friend. I was rescued and brought to this place, where the crystal waited. My soul, my very essence, was saved, but my failing body had to be abandoned. It seems the Master of this place has made . . . improvements."

The Guardian sloshed through the water toward Sidna, slow and steady.

Sidna raised her arms and filled her *viae* with fire and lightning. "Who is he? The one who did this to you?"

"Mortrythe? He is the Master of Fel Kno'a." He nodded in affirmation. "The dead are his by right."

The *Lantern* listed as Fall fought to right it. He'd brought them too close to Veridian, and the planet's gravity had taken abrupt effect.

He heard his disembodied voice. "Everyone alive?"

Sostek answered. "Somehow. A little closer and we might have ended up buried inside that world."

"I'll work on the details later."

"If we survive. What is your plan?"

"I'm going after Sidna. I find her, I find Tieger."

"Not so fast, flyboy." It was Hermes. "Your turn at the stick is over."

The helm requested access to the flight controls. Fall relinquished them with a grimace. "Fine, but you know what we have to do."

"Wish I didn't." Hermes engaged the engines and pushed the ship forward.

Fall directed his attention ahead. Tiny white objects came into his field of vision. They were slender, like little needles. "Slivers."

Hermes sighed. "You know the guns are down, right?"

"Yeah, I remember."

The slivers spread out and opened fire, laying down a mesh of metal right in Hermes's path. He didn't slow, but instead hit the engines at full blast, burning past them. It wasn't long before they resumed the pursuit.

Fall turned his view to the little ships. He could tell they were firing their guns, but they hadn't hit him yet.

Hermes jerked the ship back and forth, and the ship rocked as it entered the thickening atmosphere.

"Hermes?" Fall asked.

"What? It's just air."

Fall looked up. The *Forge* was moving to intercept, and as he watched, he saw a blink of light from the *Forge*'s direction.

Almost a moment too late, Hermes banked. A stream of something like a laser cut through the flight path he'd just been on. He weaved the ship back and forth, maneuvers seeming sluggish in the atmosphere. Wind blew across the hull, turbulent and wet; they'd come down into a storm.

The slender ships followed them in. Fall could hear their guns now. Bullets hit the hull, some bouncing off, some not.

Thunder boomed as the *Forge*'s beams cut through the air, brighter than any lightning bolt. It wouldn't be long before the *Lantern* took a major hit.

Fall searched below. "Take us into that canyon there. We can weave through those mountains."

"What's that on the middle one?" Olivia asked.

Fall focused on it. "Looks like a temple of some kind."

As they neared the rock formations, Fall saw fires burning in the forests all around. Troop transports landed through the trees.

"It's an invasion . . . " Olivia said.

Sostek growled. "We'll have to break through on the ground."

Fall shook his head. "Not unless we find some cover."

A pair of rockets shot up from the ground, gray smoke trailing. Each collided with a fighter, and the tiny ships spiraled into the temple, exploding out of sight.

Hermes jumped. "Whoa, Gabin's pirates?"

"They must be defending the temple," Fall said.

"Good thing they didn't hit us."

"One more reason to get out of the air."

Hermes dove down below the surface of the jungle, between two of the land formations. The *Forge*'s laser clipped the edge above and boulders fell behind the ship. On the side of the nearest mountain, there was a rocky platform, covered in sparse grass. Hermes flew over to it and landed.

Nothing moved or gave way, so he powered down the engines. "It should hold. I think."

Fall shifted his view back to the interior. He released control of the ship, and after brief disorientation, he was back in his own body, looking down at the *sivinar*. It melted away after he put it back above its pedestal.

Olivia stood up from her kneeling position next to him. "You okay?"

He ran his fingers through his hair. "Good enough." He stood and made sure his sword and scabbard had returned to their place. "Come on."

He and the others left the bridge, jogging through the ship's corridors to the main lift. Once inside, they took it down to the cargo hold. Hermes and Olivia left the lift with Fall and Sostek close behind.

"Fighting in the jungle will be chaotic," Sostek said.

Fall nodded. "We're a small group. It should work to our advantage."

"What about the temple? We know nothing about the interior."

"It'll be fine."

Fall moved to continue, but Sostek caught his shoulder. "Wait."

Fall stopped and faced him. "What is it? We have to hurry."

Sostek looked over Fall's shoulder then back to Fall. "There is something else I need to tell you. About what Fera could do. What I believe you can do."

"Another power?"

"Yes. One that might help you prevail in this fight."

Fall nodded. "Nice. I'll take anything I can get."

"Good." Sostek nodded slowly. "Good." He walked a few steps away and turned back. "Tell me. Have you ever noticed a time when that sword of yours did something . . . unexpected?"

Fall cocked his head slightly. "Not that I know of?"

Sostek moved his hands as he spoke. "The blade. Did the blade ever burn or cut through something it shouldn't have?"

"No . . ." Fall's eyes went wide. "The fight with Tieger! I never thought anything else about it, but now that you ask, it glowed white and pierced his armor like it wasn't even there."

"You didn't consider that strange?"

"Well, yes. But I thought it had something to do with Sidna. She hit it with lightning."

"Before you cut through the armor?"

Fall shook his head. "No, after." He reached back for the sword's hilt and tapped the grip. "Are you saying I could do that again?"

"I believe so. Why not, after everything else you've done?"

Fall crossed his arms. "I did all that on instinct. I can't rely on it in a fight."

Sostek seemed to ponder that point. "I was there the first time she did it. The very first time she faced one of the *Qur Noc*. The beast nearly killed her, but she used her power to kill it instead."

"Was it the danger?"

Sostek shrugged. "It could have been. Perhaps in facing her true enemy, she realized some truth within herself. None of our kind was able to rationalize it. We simply accepted it."

Fall turned to look down the ramp. "She faced her true enemy . . . " He looked over his shoulder as he walked. "Okay. I'll keep that in mind."

Once he and Sostek had cleared the ramp's edge, it began to rise, closing toward the *Lantern's* hull.

Fall adjusted the straps on his chest and arms, and activated the bow holster a few times to keep it loose. "Everyone ready?"

Olivia tightened the belt of her medical backpack and inspected her pistol.

Sostek checked his dagger, spinning it between his fingers.

Hermes popped his knuckles and cracked his tiny neck.

They all looked up and nodded.

Fall placed his earpiece into his right ear. "Kumi?"

"Yes, Fall."

"Stay in contact. We might have to get out of here quickly."

"We'll be ready. Be safe." She ended the transmission.

Rain gathered on the sides of the ship and dropped down around the edges. Cool air blew mist underneath, bringing the smells of storm, jungle, and wet stone.

Fall stepped through the rain wall and moved toward the carved stairs that led up and out of the hidden nook. He looked up, listening to the gunfire and shouts that echoed down through the winding path—sounds of the battle above.

Tieger . . .

He drew his sword from behind his back and turned with his boot on the first step. "Follow me."

WHERE NO ONE CAN FOLLOW

BAN TOOK THE LEAD, SPRINTING THROUGH the ruined, half-standing halls in pursuit of the Guardian. Crashes of thunder and roaring fire quickened his pace.

Down the long stretch of destruction, he saw flashes of blue and orange rising against a sea of burning red. As he neared, the heat and humidity of the battle blasted his exposed skin.

Steam and water burst through the final hole, electricity crackling around its edges. Undeterred, he lowered his head and charged through, ready to face the dueling forces beyond.

Sidna faced the advancing Guardian, wielding the strange and powerful magic of an arcanist. Waves rose and swirled ahead of her, rolling and boiling as they surged over the red beast beneath them.

Hot plasma blasted a short-lived hole in the torrent, and Sidna turned to avoid it. The burst melted into the curved stone behind her.

Becks raised her rifle, but Ban held out his hand. "Wait."

She lowered it reluctantly.

Sidna glared, breathing hard and fast. The Guardian stalked toward her, resolute.

A man in red robes with black light armor placed his hand on Sidna's shoulder. He spoke to her, and she looked to the Guardian in anger. She reached into her pocket and took something out, smiling as she held it out in her fist.

The room darkened, and out from her clenched fingers lunged black tendrils, hungrily darting to and fro. They shot forward and ensnared the Guardian, attaching all over its jagged armor.

The beast pulled against the bonds, snapping them again and again as each new strand found a hold. The monster flared red underneath, song growing harsher.

Sidna walked forward, and with each step, the room darkened even more. Ban began to feel a sort of vacuum directed toward her, pulling at his skin.

The Guardian rose up taller and raged, spreading its clawed hands. Its power swelled and grew as each moment passed.

Becks grabbed Ban's arm and yelled. The sound of her voice was muffled, sucked toward the darkness. "Ban! We have to do something!"

Ban looked down at *Folium*. Its green light was blurred but undimmed by the dark power's effects. "No. We wait. For the ephmere."

"What?"

"This is it. Let it come."

"*Let* it?" She stepped back out of his peripheral vision, her form replaced by the rising barrel of her rifle. "To the Void with that." She fired.

The round impacted in front of Sidna, never reaching her. The man in red opened his fingers, and the fragments fell away. He pointed at Becks. "This is your moment, Sidna. Do not let them interfere."

Sidna stared at the metal as it floated down to the water. She looked up at Ban, eyes black and alien. Her expression shifted slowly from surprise to smoldering anger.

"Dammit, Becks!" Ban grasped *Folium* tightly. "Get back!"

The same black cords rushed over the surface of the water, intertwining and then spreading randomly. They drew up together, gaining mass, then darted for Ban.

He raised *Folium*, green light surging, and met the tendrils, twisting as he cut the thrusting rope. The lead section fell away, splashing as it thrashed, and what followed spread out and dove underneath the surface of the pool. It took Ban by the legs, holding him fast.

Becks fired her rifle over and over as the man in red twisted his long dagger, cutting her bullets from the air in showers of sparks.

The black strands lengthened. Ban cut at them, watching the sludge make more and more progress, hearing the screams of children as it climbed.

Then Tyr stepped forward, silent as always, rocket *clunking* as it loaded into the chamber of his launcher. He shouldered the weapon, pointing at Sidna, but turned at the final moment to fire at the Guardian instead.

Why?

But then Ban saw. Sidna had neglected the original threat. As the smoke and ashes of its bonds burned away from the rocket's blast, the

Guardian walked free again, resuming its course as if nothing had ever stood in its way.

Sidna's attention divided, Ban was able to sever her hold on him.

She looked like she might ensnare him again, but instead she looked to the path behind her. She stepped back and up onto it, walking down it as she redirected the object and its power toward the Guardian.

The man in red followed suit, appearing instantly before her and walking backward in the same direction.

Tyr loaded another rocket. Becks shoved a fresh clip into her rifle. Ban held the spear down by his side.

Sidna arrived at the wall, reaching back to place her hand upon it. She waited only a moment to look at Ban, smile lifting the corner of her mouth, before she disappeared in a flash of red.

"She got away," Becks said, frustrated.

"Where'd she go?" Ban asked, turning to her.

Becks stared off then pointed her thumb to the solid wall directly behind them. "That way."

"Of course." Ban turned back to the Guardian.

Its head rotated slowly, smoke and heat rising. It turned to face them, looking beyond, as if it could see through the temple itself.

"Get out of its way," Becks said. "Let it have her."

The Guardian moved, but as it neared, its eyes lowered, focusing on *Folium*. The internal fires ignited more brightly, and the armor began to stand up like that of a threatened animal.

Becks edged away. "Um, Ban?"

He stood his ground. "Evil is evil, ally or not."

"But . . . "

Ban thrust *Folium*'s head into the water. "No." He cut a glowing green line into the stone. "I will remain."

Sidna pulled her hand away from the wall, shaking the heat from her fingers. She brought her hands close to her chest and rubbed them, looking to the left and right.

The temple shuddered, rumbling from the blast of a distant explosion. Shouts and sounds of far-off gunfire echoed through the darkness.

As she lowered her hands, she realized her jacket felt heavier than it normally did. Reaching into both pockets, she found that her right one held the tear, its surface uneven and chipped. In her left pocket, she found the glyph, cold and smooth.

She released them both and shined the beam from her armlet down both ends of the corridor, seeing nothing.

"Ronin?"

Not seeing him, she turned to move away from the shouting and the gunfire but caught herself after taking the first step.

Why? You don't have to run anymore.

She backed away from the safer route, spun, and ran toward the action, clutching the glyph inside her pocket.

After only a few turns, she neared the skirmish, a battle between an encroaching squad of embers and what seemed to be a group of entrenched pirates.

That section of the temple was different than any she'd seen yet. Instead of the same old claustrophobic tunnels and massive, vaulted chambers, she found herself looking through a grid of columns, twice as tall as she was and spread about that same distance apart.

The embers advanced across the expansive space, ducking in and out of cover, firing tight bursts as they ran from column to column.

She recognized one of the voices over the clamor.

"Cover the right! Fire, man, fire!" Gabin discharged his elongated pistol three times then hunkered down. He kicked the dead pirate next to him, frowning when the body didn't move. It seemed Gabin was the only one left alive.

He reached inside his long red coat, taking out another clip. He paused midmovement as Sidna walked by him. "Sidna?"

"Stay down, Gab." She strode past the first set of columns, glyph raised in her open left palm, right arm's *viae* charging blue with electric light.

From the floor and from the shadows near the base of the columns, tendrils snaked through the darkness, pulling the embers off of their feet. Those who managed to attack Sidna were electrocuted by arcing bolts of lightning. Before long, the last smothered cries died out, and the glyph's energies receded, still shaking with ravenous hunger.

Gabin peeked around the first column. "All dead?"

"Yes," she said, shivering with excitement. "It wasn't hard at all."

Gabin jogged over. He slowed as he neared her, eyes searching the mangled bodies of the soldiers he could see. "Gods . . ."

"You know they deserved it."

He looked up to her slowly, then smacked his dry lips. "Certainly." He motioned back to the way she'd come from. "I do not know the way, but we must find the original path. Trace it back to the beginning."

She pointed through the columns, where the embers had come from. "We're going this way."

Gabin's eyes widened. "*Toward* the Elcosians?"

"That's right. I'm ending this here."

"Did you not find what you wanted?"

"I did."

"Then come with me, back to the *Red.*"

There was a shifting of boots on the stone. Ronin stepped out from behind one of the columns. He had his rifle unslung from his shoulder.

Sidna tilted her head. "Where have you been?"

His eyes were red, two rings shining dull in the low light. "I go where I am needed."

Gabin stepped toward him, hand resting on his rapier. "She no longer needs you." He waved a hand. "Begone."

Ronin's eyes followed Gabin precisely. "It seems she does."

Gabin drew his sword. "Meaning what, exactly?"

Ronin's eyes grew brighter. "Do not interfere."

Gabin stepped between Sidna and him. "I will do what I must."

Ronin didn't react. "She must not be led astray. This is her path."

Gabin spread his arms, motioning to the corpses littered around them. "*This?* This *destruction*?"

Sidna pulled at Gabin's arm. "Gab . . ."

He shrugged her hand away. "I will not back down. Too long have I watched in silence as you edge toward the point of no return." He turned back to her. "I will never lose sleep over dead Elcosians. But if anything should happen to you . . ."

She clutched the glyph in her fingers, fighting back the urges inside. "Nothing's going to happen to me. I'm going to save my people, just as I've always said I'd do." Her face hardened. "And I'll make sure Tieger never hurts anyone ever again."

"While losing what makes you good? The Sidna I know?"

She shook her head. "What happened to letting me be me?"

Gabin threw his hands up. "You're giving up everything to do this!"

"If that's what it takes, I have no choice." She turned and walked away.

Gabin took hold of her arm, spinning her around as he pulled her away from her course. "No, girl. I cannot let you do this."

Sidna started in surprise as a painful boom sounded, and a bright flash lit the room for a brief instant. She reached up to her face in shock, fingers coming away wet.

Gabin's eyes darted up to hers. He dropped his sword, metal clamoring on the floor, and fell back into the nearby column with a grunt. That column stood between Ronin and him.

Ronin lowered the rifle slowly, barrel still smoking. The rings in his eyes burned.

"Stop!" she screamed at Ronin, raising the glyph.

Ronin sidestepped to take another shot.

Out flourished Gabin's coat, and out blasted another round from Ronin's rifle, tearing right through the fabric.

But it was only his coat.

There were another two flashes of light, paired with the quieter eruptions of Gabin's pistol, and Ronin stumbled backward as if struck by unseen blows.

Gabin hobbled forward from his cover, fist clenched at his stomach. "Die again, *dead man*." He fired once more, and Ronin fell back in a heap.

Gabin tried to holster his pistol but missed several times, eventually letting it go. He fell to his knees.

Sidna ran to him and dropped down at his side, grasping his shirt, trying unsuccessfully to keep him from falling. He twisted in spite of her grip, rolling onto his back. He blinked and reached out for her.

She took his hand with both of hers. "Gab? Gabin!"

He focused on her. "I . . . think I might be . . . "

She shook her head. "No. No, you aren't." She frantically reached for the wound in his abdomen, not knowing where to put her hands. There was a terrible volume of blood spilling out. "You can't."

"I do not think I have a choice." He tried to smile but only winced. "Sidna . . . "

"I know. Don't talk. I'll . . . I'll get help. You just . . . " Tears began to flow from her stinging eyes, rolling down her cheeks. "*Stay*." She squeezed his hand tightly. "I'll go wherever you want to go. You and me, just *stay*."

He coughed. "How I wish I could."

"Then do it. Come on, I'll help you."

He closed his eyes, and a smile slowly took his lips. "Such a beautiful sight."

"Open your eyes, Gab. Keep them open for me."

He did. He reached up for her hair, smiling as he weakly touched the side of her head. "I see the wind . . . "

She came closer, watching his lips.

"For one moment . . . " He looked past her, stroking her hair a final time. "I held the wind in my hand." He exhaled, and his fingers fell away.

"No." She waited then shook him. "No," she said angrily. "You can't. You can't go." She looked up to the ceiling, rocking as she cried. "Not here. Not like this."

He didn't move. Nothing she did could make him move.

She lay down on his chest, willing it to rise, but it didn't, and his heart was silent. Her sobs wracked her body, catching the breath in her lungs.

"Gabin." She touched her forehead to his. "I'm so sorry." She looked away and cried silently, numbness overtaking her.

In that moment, a hand suddenly rested on her shoulder, startling her. "It is hard to lose a loved one." She looked up to see it was Riest. "Especially one taken far too soon." He stepped past her, arms behind his back. "You should not have to bear this pain alone. Surely, there are others who can be made to feel its sting."

As she heard his words, something entirely different began to force its way through her anguish, fighting its way to the surface of her mind—a feeling only one other being had ever made her feel. She turned around, looking in exactly the direction of the source.

Hearing the glyph's call, she looked down to it, right there beside Gabin where she'd left it. She let his hand go and took it, squeezing her fingers tightly into a fist, digging her nails into the skin so hard she drew blood.

Tieger.

The ember fell backward, gun firing into the air. Another popped up over the edge of the fallen tree, taking a few wild shots before dropping back into cover.

Fall nocked a second arrow and drew back again. He waited a moment then let it fly, and the ember rose up just in time to meet it. He let out a short cry then went silent.

Fall bounded over the wet, broken branches in his path then jumped over the trunk to land in the mud next to the dead embers. He holstered his bow, pulled the arrow from the first man, and recycled it in his quiver. The other arrow was stuck, so he left it behind.

Olivia dropped down beside him and went to a knee, frowning. "How close are we?"

Hermes flew overhead, scattering rain drops with his leathery wings as he darted through the trees.

Sostek soared over the fallen tree as well, landing a few meters ahead. "Don't stop!" He disappeared in a burst of mist.

Fall stood and pulled Olivia up by her hand. "He's right."

They ran.

Fall brushed the plants in his path aside, avoiding the roots and rocks below. He slowed and helped Olivia, catching her as she stumbled. "You good?"

"Yeah," she said as she wiped the damp hair away from her eyes. "Let's go."

They made for a crashed transport, still burning. They crossed the open ground then huddled up to it, taking cover.

Fall held out his hand behind him. "Hold on, I'll take a look." He peeked around the edge.

He jumped back with a curse, and a line of dirt shot up as the bullets hit in succession.

Too close.

He heard the flap of Hermes's wings, and a man's screaming. A few seconds later, Hermes flew past, ember in his claws. He slung the soldier into a tree and glided on.

Fall turned back to Olivia. "Okay, looks like we're clear. This—"

An ember rushed around the side of the transport, swinging downward with his rifle. Fall twisted in time and blocked the strike with his armored forearm, but the ember shoved and turned Fall toward the transport, pinning him.

As he fought to keep the gun away from his throat, Olivia shot the soldier twice through his helmet's visor, killing him and freeing Fall.

Fall leaned back, breathing hard. "Thanks."

She nodded, reloading. "Just saving myself the trouble of having to patch you up later."

"Fair enough." He looked around. "Where's Sostek?"

"There."

Fall turned to see. The voidstrider lay prone on the edge of an outcropping. He waved them over. They ran to him then got down low as well.

Fall looked out over the edge. In the distance, a squad of embers jogged across a short metal bridge toward a gate of some kind. They vanished as they moved through it.

Sostek pointed across the chasm between the towering landmasses, toward the same soldiers as they emerged on the other side. "That's our path."

Fall looked to the horizon. The sun had almost set, and the full moon peeked out through the storm clouds. He wiped the rain from his cheek. "Great. How do we get there?"

Sostek crawled closer to the edge. "There are steps here." He pushed off of the ground to a knee.

Fall and Olivia rose as well.

"Wait." Fall placed his fingers back onto the soggy dirt. "Did you feel that?"

"Feel what?" Olivia asked, puzzled.

"I felt it," Sostek said.

Just then, they turned to the sounds of splintering wood. A massive tree fell toward them, mossy branches reaching out. They scrambled and sprinted away, narrowly avoiding being crushed.

Fall's eyes followed the fallen trunk back to its broken stump. Towering over it was a walking white tank, bright lights shining beams through the falling rain. The tank's arm reached out and pushed a second tree aside then brought its wrist-mounted machine guns to bear.

"Run!" Fall sprinted forward to the tree, hoping the bark was thick enough. Deafening rounds shredded the other side, and he ran along the trunk, crouching, wood exploding at his heels.

He looked up as he passed the base of the tree, expecting to stare into a smoking gun, but instead he saw Sostek appear and disappear over and over as he mounted the tank's nearly ten-meter frame.

Sostek stabbed at the exposed cables and hoses of the left arm, causing the appendage to stutter and fail. In response, a hatch flew open near the shoulder.

An ember popped up and took aim at Sostek, but he had to retreat back inside as Olivia shot at him. The behemoth turned to fire at her instead, but its own bullets went wide when Hermes flew into the arm and pulled it upward toward the sky.

Fall watched, noticing what seemed like a head.

That's the spot.

"Illuminator." He drew his bow and an arrow then fired at what he guessed was an optical sensor. He detonated the arrow then clenched his fist as the machine stumbled back, seemingly blinded by the intense display.

"Let's go!" Olivia called out.

As the tank's operator struggled to regain control, they all made for the edge of the cliff. "Look!" Olivia pointed.

Fall saw it. The stairs led down, meeting up with another set that came down from next to a tree. Where they joined, a single stairway wound lower to the bridge. They hopped over the edge and began their descent.

Fall looked back once they'd reached the bridge. The tank swung its arms through the trees, searching the area below. When it finally saw them, a long cannon rose up over the right shoulder and fell forward into place.

Fall ran for the teleportation device. "We're exposed, come on!"

He ran through the gate just after the others, suddenly finding himself on one of many stone paths which led across the central lake.

Hermes landed in front of them, assuming his tiger form. "There's fighting up ahead."

Fall looked back to the ridge. The tank lowered its gun and backed away. He drew his bow. "Let's get inside."

They hurried down the path toward the temple. Ahead, a line of embers took cover behind the remnants of a ruined assault pod, shooting over the smoking debris. The pirates fired back from just inside the temple entrance.

"Boomer." Fall drew the arrow as he ran, slowing only for a second to fire.

The group of embers scattered, killed by the blast. Sostek and Hermes jumped over the smoldering hunks of metal; Fall and Olivia weaved through them.

The pirates held their fire, waving them up the steps. Fall was the last inside. He looked back and saw yet another squad of embers emerge from the gate near the beginning of the path.

He turned to the bloodied pirate next to him, grasping his shoulder. "Where's your captain? Sidna?"

"They're inside." He swallowed and grimaced. "Those Elcosian bastards scrambled our radios. We don't know what's going on in there."

"Can you hold this position?" Fall asked.

The pirate nodded. "We can try."

"Then do it. We'll get through to them."

"Right." The pirate sighted down on the path and fired.

One of the embers dropped then crawled away, and the rest moved into cover. Gunfire returned in answer, and Fall ducked deeper inside.

He leaned back against the wall and tapped his earpiece. "Map function." A map of the area appeared in front of him. It was mostly incomplete, with the scanner adding additional hallways every few seconds. It would take a long time to complete.

Sostek wiped the tank's oil from his knife. "Which way?"

"Well, hopefully this still works." Fall tapped the side of the device. "Track Sidna."

A flashing red dot appeared, far from the map.

"Switch to directional mode."

The map faded, and a small red arrow took its place, pointing deeper inside the temple.

Fall motioned toward it. "That's all I've got."

Olivia wiped her forehead with her arm. "It'll have to do."

Fall holstered the bow and drew his sword. "It'll be tight in here. Be careful not to hit each other."

They moved on, and Fall held the blade by his side as he ran, turning as the arrow changed directions. More than once he had to wait while the arrow turned into a bouncing ball, indicating the map was surveying the surrounding area.

He turned another corner, and the arrow turned into a ball again. The group waited, but it kept on bouncing.

Olivia lowered her pistol. "What's the problem?"

Fall shook his head. "Not sure. It's having trouble."

She shined her light down the corridor. "I think I see why."

They jogged to the end, and Fall saw it too—a multilevel room with dozens of exits.

Rows of columns held up each level, and each level had a sloping ramp that led up to the next. The exits were square-shaped passages that lined the walls.

Fall watched the bouncing ball. "This'll take forever."

Hermes sat down, swishing his tiger tail. "We could split up."

Olivia shined her wrist-mounted flashlight up to the third level. "It wouldn't matter. There are way too many—"

"Hey, down there!"

Olivia turned to shine her light at the source of the voice. It was an ember on the third level. He fired, and the bullet whizzed right past Fall's ear.

Olivia returned fire, and the ember pulled back.

Fall scrambled behind one of the lower-level columns. "This is a bad position."

Olivia fired two more shots then ducked down beside Fall. "Tell me about it."

There were only a few more hits on the other side of the column before the ember ceased his attack. Sostek peeked out to check, then moved back.

"What is it?" Fall asked.

"Unknown." Sostek stood up.

The bouncing ball became an arrow again. Fall pulled up the map. A path lead straight to Sidna.

Sostek looked to the map. "Go. I'll stay here and handle this."

Fall furrowed his brow. "Sostek. Don't split us—"

Sostek stepped out with his knife raised toward the third level. Two lights shone down on him. He turned the knife sideways and held it out to the side.

A voice shouted down. "Don't move!"

Fall heard shuffling feet as more people came down the ramps leading to the first level. Sostek's eyes leveled on the ramp, and they followed the ones who approached. Two embers spread out and pointed their rifles.

The voidstrider waited calmly. "Is there no *true* warrior among you?"

Another walked forward from the shadows in the rear, a female. She looked different than the average ember, with a feathered helmet, a shield, and a longsword over her shoulder. "Who asks?"

"Sostek. A voidstrider."

"Is that supposed to mean something to me?"

"It will." Faster than a blink, faster than Fall could ever hope to move, Sostek disappeared and reappeared twice, striking down each of the embers on either side of her.

Before they'd hit the ground, the female ember's sword came down, and somehow, Sostek was able to meet it with his knife.

He pushed her back so hard she left her feet. She fell back and regained her composure then slung the sword over her shoulder again. "You're fast, black one. Strong too."

Sostek laughed. "And you are clumsy with that blade. Perhaps something smaller would suit you."

Fall looked down at the map. Sidna was on the move again. He turned to follow her.

Olivia grabbed his arm. "What are you doing?"

"I'm going."

"No, we should help him. Then we can go together."

He grasped her hand. "He won't want help."

"But—"

"Leave it. He knows what he's doing."

The female ember spun and swung her blade, striking Sostek's as he appeared. She braced and deflected another attack, then sliced through thin air as Sostek misted away.

She braced, swinging her shield over her head, causing Sostek to fly past her and roll on the ground. He managed to rise to his knee, using his *Fyd Wyr* to move again and again as the woman laid down short bursts of fire with a small gun she'd had hidden.

She raised her shield, deflecting his knife, which had shot out from the darkness, then swung again to block his downward thrust as he fell from the air above, having caught the spinning knife. He leapt away, and they circled.

He panted heavily. "Go!"

Fall took Olivia's arm. "See. Come on."

She looked back then nodded.

"You too, Hermes." Fall turned to the floating arrow and ran forward. He looked back one last time before the final corner of the hallway. Past Olivia and Hermes, sparks flew from the two fast-moving blades.

Win, Sostek.

The power surged, and the lights went out as Tieger forced open the door of his fallen transport. Gusts of rain blew inside.

He kicked the remnants of the door away and jumped down to the glistening stone, cracking it under his weight. Once clear, he forced his way through a breach in the structure, entering a passageway.

He could feel her. He knew her direction.

All around him, strange men died. They fought his embers with guns, axes, swords, and even their bare hands.

The arcanists have employed mercenaries. I would not have expected it, yet it matters little.

They could not stand before his armored faithful. For each ember killed, two more rushed to take his place. True to Elcos's warning, the temple was filling up with the dead.

Tieger ignored the inconsequential battles, navigating the maze, always heading toward her. But as he came closer, he noticed a stark difference. There was something more potent about the sense of her.

The taint of darkness.

One of the ragtag fighters came around a corner, screaming, eyes bulging with fear. Two embers chased close behind him, but not in pursuit—they also fled.

Tendrils of blackest ink wrapped around the edge of the already darkened corridor, searching and grasping.

So. She has already summoned it.

Tieger reached into the distortion at his side and pulled forth his hammer, *Janus*. Undeterred by the unnatural groans from farther inside the hall, he marched forward, prepared to strike, mind buzzing until it rattled his teeth.

Yes. Come.

The witch stepped around the wall's edge, black eyes focused solely on him.

She held out her closed hand. Throbbing cords whipped in the air around it, surging in sync with her pulsing *viae*.

Tieger lowered the hammer slowly. "You have changed since our last meeting."

Her face distorted in anger. "More than you could imagine. You shouldn't have come here."

"You are not the first to warn me, though I have seen little to fear."

Her grip tightened on the object in her hand. "Let's change that."

Black rage coursed along the walls in waves and streams, converging on him. He opened his nevergates all around him, creating more than he had needed in a very long time.

The reaching ropes entered the gates, sliced as they closed. His hammer's blade cut them too, and his claws rended. He never stopped moving.

Yet the black substance seemed to be unlimited, coming faster and thicker. His armor held against the attacks, but it wasn't unbreakable.

His left arm was taken, pulled away by a squeezing cable. He infused his violet fire into it, and the oily grip fell away. "You see, witch? You cannot harm me, no matter what new gimmick you employ."

Doubt crept into her expression, and she faltered.

It was then that a man in robes appeared beside her. Red light spilled out from under his sleeves. "You allow your enemy to defy you."

At last. Another arcanist.

She took a step back. "I can't . . . "

"You *can*, and you *will*." He grabbed her closed fist. "Do not resist this power any longer. Give in. It is nearly here."

Tieger stopped, realizing the answer before he'd even asked the question. "What comes?"

The man in red turned his head, smile growing. "He-Who-Hungers."

CHOICES

BAN PUSHED HIMSELF UP FROM THE TURBID pool, chalky water dripping from his face. He blinked away the blurriness, watching as rapidly moving shapes regained their sharpness.

Becks dodged a swipe from the Guardian, retreating, staying just close enough to keep its attention.

Tyr leapt up onto its back, struggling to maintain a hold. He had an explosive charge in his left hand, trying to place it somewhere on the creature, but he was thrown away, ploughing through the water as the Guardian flared and spun in a circle.

Ban looked down, seeing vibrant bursts of silver shoot up through swirling clouds of dissolving dust and stone. He reached down and took the source, *Folium*.

He reached up to his face, wincing as he touched his already numbing cheek.

You'll pay for that.

He leaned forward and ran, rejoining the battle.

Becks shouldered her rifle and side-stepped, firing her pistol.

Tyr rose to his feet and tossed his damaged helmet away. He turned and ran the other direction.

Ban closed the distance and jammed his spear into the Guardian's side. The spear didn't break through the armor, but it did slide to an opening, biting deep.

The Guardian swept its arm back to swat him away, but Ban had already pulled the spear back, dodging.

"No, Tyr!" Becks said. "Ban's too close."

Ban looked. Tyr had his rocket launcher, going to a knee.

"Take the shot!" Ban yelled. "We have to bring it down!" He stabbed at the Guardian's knee, unable to find an opening.

His enemy momentarily ignored his jabs, focusing instead on Becks whose rounds continued to ping his facial armor like stinging wasps.

The monster held up its hand to block the shots and aimed its other in her direction. A surge of plasma built within that arm, plates standing up, as it tracked its fast-moving target.

"Ban . . ." Becks dropped her clip and reached for another. Her hand came up empty. She holstered the pistol and reached for her rifle. "I'm in trouble here!"

Ban rushed forward and leapt up for a powerful strike, caught suddenly in the air as the Guardian turned and took him by the front of his armor, fingers reaching inside the neck as it held him. It pulled him close, staring into his eyes as the plasma reached its peak.

Then there was a rocket blast, one that launched Ban away, skipping him across the water in a heap.

Thume. Thume. Thume. The Guardian walked closer.

Ban stood up, feet wide as he wobbled. He ignored his dizziness as best he could and looked down to the water, searching for *Folium*.

The Guardian approached, holding up its hand, armor flaring as a blast of plasma began to form.

Ban backed away, quickly realizing he was nearing the outer wall.

Nowhere to go!

Becks shot the Guardian three times in rapid succession, but it continued on, plasma ignited.

Ban took a final step back and lowered his hands, staring into the blaze.

"*Ban!*" The voice was little more than a whisper, nearly lost in the whine of building power.

But it was loud enough.

Ban looked toward it, over to his left, and saw Tyr, waving his hands above his head.

Tyr pointed to the Guardian, then motioned to his own left shoulder.

Ban looked to the Guardian's shoulder and saw the charge, light blinking.

Tyr held up his hand, miming the detonator then opened his hand and shook his head to show Ban he didn't have it.

"We don't need it!" Becks said. She chambered a round and sighted down on the charge.

Time seemed to slow, and Ban did the only thing he could think to do. He reached out for *Folium*, unsure if it would hear his call.

Water shot out from the distortion as it opened, and Ban reached in, pulling out his shining weapon.

The concussive force of the charge's explosion twisted the Guardian's torso to its left, rotating just enough that the plasma now faced off to Ban's right.

Taking that final chance, Ban thrust the spearhead up and underneath the armor on its forearm and pushed, turning the Guardian's open hand back toward its own face. The mark of Thenander activated, power coursing through *Folium*, then the arm, and up into the hand, unleashing a blast of green plasma, red tails of fire burning out to the sides.

Ban lowered his spear, and as the smoke cleared away, the Guardian fell back, head missing, a glowing green concavity where its neck had once been.

Becks and Tyr approached the remains.

"We did it," Becks said, lowering her rifle. She laughed. "We actually killed it."

Ban watched as the last of the light faded from the Guardian's armor. He looked up to Tyr. "Together."

Tyr nodded then turned to the hole in the wall, the one where they'd first entered.

"Tyr's right." Ban looked to Becks. "Now for the *real* threat."

"Call your pet," Tieger said. "I have killed its kind before."

Riest walked to the side, shaking his head. "You are either a liar or a fool," he said with a condescending smile. "The only one who could died long ago."

Tieger lowered his hammer and raised his fist, purple fire enkindled within it. "I fear no monster, witch. They burn like any other." He opened his fingers, and Sidna felt the fire ignite on her skin.

Without command, dark energies jumped from the glyph to her, coating her as they snuffed out the flames. But Tieger seemed to have expected it.

Before she could raise a hand in defense, he was there, backhanding her so hard he knocked her off of her feet. She rolled over, ears ringing from the blow.

He stood above her, looking down, hammer held in both hands. "I would have preferred a more satisfying end to you, *Sidna Orin*, but there are many more of your brood who require my attention." He raised the hammer above his head.

As the weapon began to fall, a red-orange cape whipped up beside Tieger's shoulder, and Mei's serrated knife dug into the space between his armored plates.

She held on tightly as she stabbed, teeth bared in anger. "You will not harm her!"

Tieger cursed, then spun and slammed her into the wall.

She grunted, then brought her pistol up to his head and fired, but the bullet ricocheted off his helmet, doing no harm at all.

He pushed back again, harder that time, and she dropped to the floor, stunned. He turned and kicked her in the stomach, launching her up into the stone.

Sidna managed to draw her own pistol, activating her *viae* as she fired several superheated, Code-infused bullets, but the air around Tieger phased, swallowing them up.

He roared. "Enough!" He reached down for Mei, picking her up by the neck.

Her eye blinked weakly, closing, as she desperately grabbed at his helmet.

He laughed deeply as he stared into Mei's darkening face. "I will never understand why anyone would die for one such as her."

Mei struggled for breath. "Because . . . she deserves . . . to live."

Tieger paused, then replied. "Her kind deserves *nothing* but retribution." He leaned in closer. "She and those who serve her." He raised his clawed fingers and pointed them right at Mei's face.

She looked to Sidna, expression grim, then closed her eye.

No, Mei. Don't give up.

Sidna decided right then that no one else would ever die for her.

She felt it again—that pure distillation of fury, so intense the glyph soaked it up, starting the same chain reaction as it had on Gyre, threatening to drink in every last bit of her.

As she stood, the shadows in the hall shot toward her, rising up in a cyclone of power as the glyph's gem shook wildly, emitting a high-pitched tone.

But this time, she did not unleash those energies on her enemy. Instead, she fed in more and more, summoning memories of a beaten people, the loneliness of her solitary path, and the emptiness of her failures.

She closed her eyes.

Gabin.

The glyph shattered as she envisioned his face, fragments of emerald scattering into the tempest, dark beam of anti-light pulsing out like a beacon above her.

The impact that followed the glyph's destruction was so concussive, so profoundly extreme, that it hit with the force of a meteor, crashing into the structure above her.

As she raised her arms in defense and peered up into the rain, a terrible, alien thing bore down with such violent speed that it drove her down to her knees.

It reached down and took her around the waist, jerking her all the way up to its face.

Its teeth dripped with hot black tar as it spoke. "*Sor kata?*" A rumbling tremble passed through its body, and it drew her even closer. "*Sor kan. Magi . . .*"

Without another word, it retracted up through the temple's wound, heaving her so fiercely she thought her spine might snap in two.

Fall climbed up to the top of the rubble then turned around to kneel and reach down for Olivia.

She pushed off and stood with his help. "Another assault pod?"

Fall dusted his gloves off. "Yeah, must be."

Rainwater flowed and dripped through cracks and breaches in the structure above.

Hermes, in his imp form, floated up, walking as he landed. "I dunno. Sounded pretty strange to me."

"What's an assault pod supposed to sound like?" Olivia asked.

Hermes shrugged. "Like that, I guess. Minus the screaming."

Fall shushed them, leaning forward to listen. "Hear that? Something's close by." He moved over to a darkened corner and peeked around its edge. "Mei? She's hurt!"

He ran to her, Olivia not far behind. Together, they pulled Mei underneath some cover. She was wet and shivering.

"Tieger is here," she said weakly, reaching up to take Fall by his scarf. "He is going to kill her."

She tried to sit up, but Olivia stopped her. "Mei, you're hurt. You need to be still."

She nodded and relaxed, but her eye held the same conviction. She looked up at Fall. "There is another person here too. Someone with her."

He took her hand and squeezed it reassuringly. "I'll get to her." He looked to Olivia.

She moved her handheld scanner over Mei's abdomen. "She'll be okay, but there's internal hemorrhaging. I have to stay here with her."

Fall looked up to the ruined ceiling. "You can't. It's not safe."

"I know it isn't, but I can't move her yet. Not until I stop the bleeding."

Fall looked at Hermes, who nodded in agreement. "Okay, but call me if anything changes. Sostek shouldn't be too far behind us."

"We'll be fine. Go."

Fall turned and looked up to the remainder of the climb. "Ready, Hermes?"

Hermes motioned up with his furry hand. "Ladies first."

Fall shook his head and tested the first of the cracks for stability. He reached up to a handhold. "Just remember the plan."

"I'll do my part." Hermes levitated nearby. "Make sure you don't blow it."

After a few minutes, they reached the top. Through a widened split in the temple's outer wall, he could see out over the jungle. The sun had fully set, and the trees swayed in the moonlit storm.

An Elcosian transport zoomed by at full speed, spotlights searching.

Fall ran down the nearby corridor in the same direction as the transport. "Hermes, let's go!"

He ran for several dozen meters until he saw a surprising sight. Multiple levels of the temple had been blown away, exposing the interior to the outside. He'd entered what would've been a large open space already, but due to the damage, the winding corridors above were naked, like a damaged insect hive.

He ran out into the middle, and the transport swung around in front of him. The side door lowered, and a huge shadowed figure stepped up to the edge, watching. He jumped down.

Cracks spread through the weakened floor as Tieger landed. His purple cape whipped in the wind, fluttering in the same direction as Fall's bandana.

Tieger spoke in his deep, technologically-altered voice. "So, you did not flee after all."

Fall reached for his sword. "Never."

"Then you have come for the girl."

"No. I came for *you*."

Tieger clenched his fist. "Tempting. But you will have to wait."

Fall narrowed his eyes. "I don't think so. *Boomer.*" He reached down and took his mech bow, nocking the newly produced arrow as the string drew tight.

"We have played this game before, boy."

"I know." Fall released, aiming wide.

The arrow shot by Tieger, well past his distortions, and exploded inside the troop transport. The ship lost altitude instantly, plummeting toward the ground below.

Fall holstered the mech bow and drew his sword, slowly. Moonlight caught on the blade, silver and bright. "Let's play it again."

Tieger held his right hand out and took his hammer from the air beside him. Violet letters burned on the side, blade sizzling as raindrops fell upon it. He hefted the hammer and walked to the side.

Fall matched him in the opposite direction.

Lightning flashed over the jungle, burning the afterimage of Tieger's armor in Fall's eyes. He blinked, and Tieger took advantage, rushing forward, hammer raised.

Fall waited and spun away as the hammer came down, swinging his sword. The two blades sang as they met, violet sparks showering between them.

Fall rolled away as Tieger's claws flew toward his face. He dove after the roll, avoiding the hammer's blow as it slammed down again.

Tieger released the embedded hammer and raised his fist. "Be *still.*" Fire flared out from his hand.

Fall reached for his mech bow, spinning his sword over as he caught its pommel ring with his little finger. He reached back and took an arrow with that same hand, sword hanging, hoping the shot might buy him some time.

He nocked the arrow and fired. As expected, it disappeared through a shield, lost somewhere unknown.

Tieger walked forward. "You only delay your defeat."

Fall let loose a second arrow. Again, it was eaten. "Maybe." He reached back for a third.

He aimed down at the stone, shooting the arrow at an angle that sent it careening wildly off the stone between Tieger's legs. It exploded right after, the force of it launching Tieger forward, right into Fall.

Fall sat up, dazed. Both his sword and his bow were nowhere to be seen.

Tieger rose up from the ground, right over Fall's legs, smoke rising from his singed cape. He raised his hand, shaking. "You would burn *me*? I will set a blaze inside your corpse!" His fingers shot for Fall's belly.

"Fogger!" Fall twisted, letting Tieger's momentum carry the claws past him. They scraped his stomach, then tore into the stone.

He ignored the searing pain and tapped his palm, activating the arrow, still in his quiver. The fog burst forth, covering the entire area around them, as he kicked off of Tieger and rolled.

Tieger swung his claws maniacally. "Tricks! All you have are tricks and toys!"

Fall stopped, searching in the encompassing fog. He found his sword's grip then reached into his pouch and took what he needed.

It's time.

Tieger built up his fire and released it, causing the fog to ignite in a flash of violet. He ripped off his helmet and threw it down to the floor, veins bulging with rage.

Fall stood there, sword in his right hand, left hand to his abdomen. Blood trickled between his fingers.

Tieger walked to his hammer and pulled it up from the stone. "Now, we will finish this." He started forward and swung the hammer. Fall moved side to side, bringing his blade up to meet the hot metal each time it came, though much slower than he had before.

"You weaken." Tieger thrust the hammer's blade and twisted, pushing the sword away.

He followed with a quick swipe of his claws, finding soft cheek, and then swung the hammer from low to high, taking his opponent off his feet.

The rain fell on Tieger's head, running down his neck, evaporating from the heat. He lifted the hammer, and after only a moment's hesitation, brought it down with full force, right through the body and into the stone below.

His shoulders stiffened in surprise at what he saw next.

The body disappeared, and in its place, Hermes stood there, leaning casually against the hammer's blade. "Uh oh."

Now!

Fall jabbed the point of his sword into Tieger's back, knowing its shining blade should easily pierce the heavy armor.

But the blade didn't glow. It didn't do anything but skip off the metal, nearly flying out of his hands due to the jarring shock.

Tieger let go of the hammer and turned, furious. He stared into Fall's eyes, teeth clenched. "You missed your chance."

Tieger reached out and took Fall by the neck, lifting him from the ground. "Now you die."

Why didn't it work?

Before he could understand why he'd failed, Fall was suddenly struck on his shoulder, thrown away as some rumbling, pounding vibration tumbled past him.

Once he was able to open his eyes, he sat up and looked around, seeing that the unexpected blow had also hit Tieger. Several meters away, a huge chunk of stone fell over and split. Near it, Tieger rose to a knee, breathing heavily.

Just then, someone walked from the outermost edge of the ruined floor. Her form was blurred around the edges, dark, even compared to the night.

Her voice was a combination of human and something definitely alien. "I see you, Tieger."

Tieger coughed and smiled, though obviously in pain. "Good. I feared you might have been killed before I could finish you myself."

Fall wiped the rain from his eyes, trying to focus on the woman. "Sidna?"

She kept her eyes on Tieger. "Stay out of this, Fall."

"What happened to you?" he asked.

Beside her, inside the shadows, two rows of teeth appeared and opened. Hot breath gusted out from between them, visible in the cold night air.

I didn't make it in time.

Tieger stood. "Now you see the truth, Ranger. This is the dark that dwells inside all her kind. A disease cleansed only by fire." He reached out and tried to engulf her, but a stream of black shot from the monster, burning in her stead.

The creature grunted a few times, as if mocking him with laughter.

Tieger walked forward and retrieved his hammer. "You should remember the taste of *Janus*, little nightmare."

"Enough talk." On the level above, a man walked forward, red cloth waving in the wind. His black armor looking exactly like it had in the World Shard's simulation. "Crush this pathetic *champion*, and let us be off."

Riest?

Sidna walked to the gaping mouth, and the monster shuddered, as if feeling the pleasure of warmth after having been cold for a very long time. She touched its skin, and the surface surged, simmering to a boil. Lightning jumped and chained, surging above the churning substance.

The temple around the beast trembled, and the floor crumbled underneath its weight. It moved forward, sending its charged pseudo-pods ahead of it.

Sidna looked back to Tieger. Her eyes were as black as the rest of her, except for her intense *viae*, one electric-blue and the other fiery orange. "It's your turn to be afraid, Tieger." She looked to Fall. "Help me kill him. Do it, and I'll finally be free."

Tieger nodded and reached down to retrieve his helmet. He walked toward Fall, stopped, then turned back to the monster.

He put the helmet on. "Choose." He hefted his hammer as the seals engaged. "Choose your true enemy." He took three steps back and steeled himself against the encroaching energies of fire, lightning, and darkness.

My true enemy . . .

That was it.

In that moment, Fall understood why Fera's power hadn't come to him. Sostek hadn't been wrong at all. Tieger simply wasn't his true enemy.

It was the evil Sidna carried within her necklace—the same evil in front of him now.

Fall took his sword and rose, holding it high as light began to shine along its solsynth blade. "I know what you want from her, ephmere. I won't let you take her."

The monster opened its mouth then bit down hard as it drew back from the light.

Sidna turned to Fall. "What are you doing?"

"You aren't in control of it, Sidna. It's feeding on you."

She shook her head. "Don't do this, Fall. Don't get in my way."

"I don't have a choice."

Tieger turned his head. "Yes. Together we will take it, drive it into the abyss!" He rushed ahead, burning a path through the grasping arms.

Fall swept his silver sword back and sprang forward as well.

An electrified column swept down to crush him, but he raised his blade to meet it. Yet instead of being cut in two, the darkness scattered, webbing out into multiple strands, seizing Fall all over his body.

It lifted him high into the air as he struggled, pulling him right over the ephmere's opening mouth. Its oily skin quivered in anticipation.

"Sidna! Stop it! Don't let it—" A hot black vice wrapped around his mouth. Horrible terror overtook him; he was about to be suffocated.

Hermes flew up in his lizard form and slashed at the entangling threads, freeing Fall's right arm.

Fall hacked at the ropes holding his mouth, restoring his ability to breathe. He tried to cut his other arm free, but the sword fell from his hand to the stone below, penetrating halfway down to the hilt.

Hermes twisted in the air with a few flaps of his wings then dove toward Sidna, razor-sharp talons extended.

She nonchalantly raised her arm, and a bolt of lightning arced out from her fingers, reducing him to a tumbling canister.

The gripping slime pulled Fall down closer. His legs were already past the teeth. He closed his eyes, knowing the worst was about to happen.

He opened them again as a green light burst through his eyelids.

A bright silver spear stuck in through the face of the monster, and it fell back, a wildly waving mass of tentacles.

Fall was thrown to the ground. He crawled away, frantically ripping the black threads away from his body as he bumped into something solid. He looked up.

A blue armored hand reached down. It was Ban. "On your feet, Ranger."

Fall took the hand, and Ban yanked him up with a nod.

He turned to the injured monster, watching as its wound began to heal. The panic he'd just felt instantly changed to fury at the thought of being eaten. He wasted no time, taking his sword from the stone where it stood, running as he made for the monster.

Though resolute in his charge, he was forced to stop as a wall of fire suddenly bloomed right in his path.

Sidna's markings burned brightly as the flames rose. "Stay away from it!"

Past her, Tieger ripped a choking vine from his chest and crushed it in his claws. He continued toward Sidna, nearly in range for a strike. She didn't seem to notice.

Fall pointed. "Behind you!"

She turned to see him only a few steps away. His hammer was already on the way down, and she barely shifted her power to catch it in time. Her dividing storm of fire and lightning struggled to hold it at bay as Tieger pushed his burning weapon downward with all his might.

Her energies directed elsewhere, the path to the monster opened up again.

I can get through.

Fall ran forward, slashing at the naked darkness. Each time his light touched it, the stuff split and scattered, ultimately destroyed. The monster roared and recoiled into itself, rolling its head in suffering.

Ban leapt onto it from the side, stabbing his spear. "Now! Kill it!"

Fall stopped as he heard Sidna crying out in desperation. He looked back and forth, unsure.

If he chose the ephmere, its darkness could be extinguished, preventing its threat to all mankind. He could end it all, right there.

But that would mean abandoning Sidna to Tieger, letting everything she'd fought for be for nothing.

He made his choice then and closed the distance, swinging his shining sword with all his might.

It caught Tieger's hammer, halting its crushing descent.

He had only a moment to see the confusion in Sidna's eyes as all their forces came together—arcane and divine, light and dark—annihilating the space between them.

The three of them were thrown away in opposite directions by the resulting discharge of energy, and the temple's structure collapsed below their feet.

Fall slid down the newly formed slope toward a multistory drop. Luckily, his armor scraped on the stone as he grasped at it, providing just enough friction to slow his descent. He thrust his blade into a broken groove, releasing its light so it would stick, and held on tight.

He swung himself around and managed to catch Hermes's tiny canister as it rolled past him. "Gotcha." He tucked it into a pouch and looked up.

Fortunately, the stone had fractured in such a way that he could slowly climb back up to the top. Once there, he looked across the central pit.

Sidna, no longer cloaked in darkness, crawled toward the monster, Tieger close behind her. He reached out for her leg, and she twisted to kick him in the helmet. He shifted his weight, causing the floor underneath him to give.

He slid down, barely keeping himself from falling into the drop below.

Sidna stood up and looked down to him, working to catch her breath. "You lose, Tieger." She pulled out her pistol and ran her hand over the markings leading down to it. The gun's metal shone with red-orange.

Tieger looked down then back up to her as he tried to gain a foothold. He continued to slowly slide, even as his claws dug in. "You may surround yourself with darkness, witch, but never turn your back on it." He dropped further, looking up one final time. "For that is where I will always be, *waiting*."

The stone broke away in his hands, and he slid down the sloping floor, disappearing into the rain as he fell.

Fall leaned over, waiting for the sound of his impact, but it never came. Several moments went by before he looked up to Sidna. "That won't kill him."

She looked up too, holstering her pistol. "I know."

Riest appeared in front of her and held out his hand. "It is time to leave this place, Sidna."

Her long, unbraided brown hair blew out into the wind. She looked up into the sky at the stars, for a moment seeming vulnerable again. "What do you think now, Fall? Am I evil, or just in over my head?"

Fall watched her as she turned to him, defiant form enclosed in moonlight. For the first time, he felt like he truly saw her. "Neither."

She opened her hands and looked down to them. "You aren't afraid of me?"

He shook his head. "No. I'm not."

A single tear ran down her cheek. She wiped it away. "Maybe you should be."

He held out his left hand and took a step toward the gap. "Sidna, you—"

She met his eyes. "Don't follow me. *Please*."

He stopped and lowered the hand. "Okay. If that's what you want."

"It's never been about what I want." She took one last look down into the chasm between them then held out her hand, and the ephmere flowed over, engulfing both her and Riest before it vanished into a swirling vortex of shadow.

Fall watched it shrink and disappear with a short-lived flash at the end. He reached back and sheathed his sword.

No regrets . . .

He looked over, seeing Ban as he struggled to climb up and out on his side of the depression. His friends, the other two marines, were there above him, pulling him up.

He stood and steadied himself then turned to look across the gap at Fall. "Why did you do that? We could have killed it."

Fall looked up into the sky, watching as the brightest star began to move away. "I couldn't let him kill her."

Becks picked up her rifle and shouldered it. "A lot of people will die because of that decision."

Fall placed his hands on his hips. "Live or die, at least they have a chance. Now she does too."

Ban looked at Becks then back to Fall. He relaxed. "I understand. I probably would've done things differently, but I understand."

"Thanks." Fall looked around and sighed. "You guys need a ride?"

"If you wouldn't mind," Ban said.

"I don't. We'll meet up at the bottom."

Ban nodded, and his squad turned, making their way back the way they'd come.

Fall took one last survey of the devastation the fight had caused then went to the place he'd climbed up before. He got about halfway down before a bright light shined up into his eyes.

"Fall? Is that you?" It was Olivia.

He held his hand up to block the beam. "Yeah."

"Oh, thank Elcos. I was afraid you fell."

"Not me, but Tieger did."

"Oh. Well that's good, I guess."

Fall hopped down to her level and walked over.

She looked up. "Where's Hermes?"

Fall patted his belt. "Taking a nap."

"Sidna?"

Fall shook his head. "Gone."

Olivia smiled weakly. "I'm sorry."

"What's done is done." He looked around. "What about Mei?"

"She's fine. Sostek found us and carried her outside." Olivia shrugged. "Not that *he* looks much better. Whoever that was, she really carved him up."

"He'll make it. But we should get out of here before somebody finds us."

"I won't argue, but I don't think anyone's coming. The battle's over."

"Who won?"

"No one, I think. I haven't seen anyone alive in a while."

Fall frowned. "Wonder if Gabin made it."

"I'm sure he did. Come on."

They jogged away from the rubble-strewn area, back into the temple maze.

"This way." Olivia took the lead.

Fall followed her, and she led him to a part of the outer wall that had fallen in the attack.

They climbed over the side, down the chunks of stone, until they were able to jump to the base level. A short jog later, they neared one of the paths that led away from the temple.

"What's that?" Olivia pointed toward the end of the path, out near the edge of the lake.

It was the Alidian marines.

"Wait up!" Fall ran to catch them. He looked back to Olivia, who caught up too. "They're coming with us."

Olivia nodded. "Fine, let's just get out of here!"

Together they all hurried to the end of the path, through the teleportation gate, and up the steps back into the jungle. It was eerily silent on the way back to the ship.

Near the end, Sostek walked out from behind a tree, carrying Mei in his arms. His fur was matted in many places, caked with his white blood.

The voidstrider twisted his lips. "There's barely a scratch on you, human."

Fall waved his hand. "I had a lot of help. Come on."

Down the natural steps they went, crossing the platform to the *Lantern*. Its large ramp shook and started to lower. When it touched down, Fall went up with the others close behind.

As he got to the top, he turned and waited. When Sostek reached him, he took Mei's arm around his waist. "Here, let me help."

Mei grunted and leaned on him as they walked. She looked up to him. "Is she alive?"

"Yes, Mei."

She nearly passed out when she heard.

They followed Olivia and made it to the sick bay. She took Mei's arm, and Fall helped her onto a bed. Once she was secure, he ran to the lift. "Sostek."

Sostek turned. There were deep gashes around his waist, and blood flowed from his neck to his chest.

"Woah."

Sostek waved his hand and coughed. "These wounds will heal."

Fall raised his eyebrows. "If you say so . . . "

They rode the lift up to the first deck. Fall ran through the corridors to the bridge and jumped into his command chair. He took the *sivinar* from its pedestal, compressing and energizing it until he'd gained control of the ship.

Sostek stood beside him. "You were not able to stop her?"

Fall closed his eyes. "No."

He activated the engines, lifting the ship away from the platform, out of the canyon and over the jungle. The ship shot up into the sky, blasting through the storming clouds.

Sostek sat with a grunt. "The *Forge* will come for us."

"I don't think it will." Fall watched as the *Forge* neared the T-Gate.

Kumi entered the bridge with Union and walked over to Fall. "They're leaving?"

"They are."

"Tieger must have gotten away, then."

"He's not on it," Fall said.

"His troops left him? Serves the bastard right."

"No, I mean it's Sidna."

"Sidna? How?"

"Long story, but she's there, along with the *Forge*'s original owner."

Sostek coughed violently. "You . . . cannot mean . . . ?"

Fall nodded. "She's with Riest."

Sostek looked to the forward viewscreen. "Alive, after all this time."

The *Forge* moved through the T-Gate.

Fall sighed. "That's it. She's gone."

Olivia touched his shoulder. "We can always catch up to her."

He lowered the *sivinar*. "Not while she has the *Forge*. She could be anywhere by now."

"Then what should we do?"

Fall replaced the orb. "We have a lot of people who need to go home. Ban and his friends to Alidia. Kumi and Union to Rune. I'm sure Mei wants her ship back from Cisterne too."

Sostek leaned forward with a grunt. "The trip back will be much longer. I do not know how to enter the Never."

Fall reactivated the *sivinar* and engaged the engines, heading for the T-Gate. "We'll just have to do it the hard way. After we pass through the gate, we'll get our bearings, drop Mei at the *Rìluò*, then set course for Crossroads. If we're lucky, there'll be plenty of new requests."

Olivia sat at the station next to Sostek. "Requests? Requests for what?"

"Well, if we want that fresh coat of paint," he said, looking down and smiling as he patted Hermes inside his vibrating pouch, "we'll need a job."

EPILOGUE

"THIS OUTRAGE DEMANDS SWIFT, DECISIVE judgment," Lord Holland said before he slammed his hands down on the wooden railing of the upper chamber.

Half his brow was furrowed, the other half a metal plate that extended posteriorly over his skull. His crisp blue uniform bore his medals, further testaments to his extensive military service.

"The destruction of a warship, the absolute failure of his mission . . ." He glowered at Ban. "The *loss* of my son."

The Star-Born Prince raised his hand, sitting on his throne. He was dressed in white regalia, mostly silk, with a blue cloak and a crown of silver and diamonds. His long blonde hair fell behind his shoulders.

He beckoned for Ban to rise and step forward. "We have reviewed your testimony, and we have conferred with those under your command." He coughed as he glanced at Tyr. "In a manner of speaking."

Ban looked to his left. Tyr was there in his dress uniform. To Ban's right, Becks stood there too.

"As a bondsman, you have absolutely no right to defend yourself, yet we find the evidence against you to be . . . lacking."

There were angry murmurings from somewhere behind Ban.

The prince looked up sternly, and they ceased. "As for the *Talon's* mission, we declare it a success, costly though it was. The assault on Nix and the discovery of the Runian base have proved our Runian cousins have not upheld their end of the Accord. You have also managed to bring us valuable information about their more interesting illegal activities." The prince smiled more openly that time. "For all of these accomplishments, you and your squadmates are hereby absolved of all your previous crimes."

The court exploded in cacophony.

"Order! Order!" cried Lord Holland. He straightened his jacket as he waited for quiet. "My prince, this Council of Lords formally requests an inquiry into the death of Lieutenant Holland."

The majority of members nodded in agreement. There seemed to be a consensus.

The prince looked down at Ban. "Very well. It shall begin here. Sergeant Morgan, as a fully restored citizen of Alidia, you are entitled to an investigation and a trial. You shall of course be allowed an arbiter to advocate on your behalf."

Ban shook his head. "I do not need one."

Becks coughed. "Ban . . . what are you doing . . . ?"

Ban turned to face Lord Holland, looking up. "I betrayed your son."

The lords and ladies of the council erupted. Again, Holland subdued them.

Ban continued. "Did you know of his part in the mission on Fugelaese? Were you the one who helped to cover it up?"

Holland seethed with anger. "You dare slander his name?"

"I do. And in doing so, risk destroying my own." He turned back to the prince. "My dream, from as early as I can remember, was to become an Alidian Knight. It's why I joined the military." He turned back to the crowd. "It's why I carried out Holland's orders to fire on that settlement."

The council remained silent, all looking to Lord Holland.

"I paid the price for my selfishness. And I made sure your son did too. I left him to die in the dirt."

Lord Holland pointed to the guards near the throne. "Arrest this man! This traitor!"

Ban held up his right hand. "Wait." He turned to face the approaching guards.

They slowed as the prince stood from his throne.

Ban went on with his confession. "But he didn't die there. Instead, he gave up his command codes to the Elcosians who captured him, and he returned to the *Talon*, murdering the captain and his staff."

"Lies!" Holland yelled. "Silence his lies!"

"They are not lies, Lord Holland. Your son was a coward."

The mark of Thenander began to glow, eliciting gasps of surprise from the council. The guards moved to defend the prince.

Ban showed its light to the entire room. "I refuse to be like him. I will not hide behind convenient lies or allow omission to save me." He looked at the prince as he lowered his hand. "I will abandon my dream if it means I can stand for the truth."

The prince stared, eyes wide at the weight of Ban's revelation. He looked to the council, silent in their own state of shock.

He walked forward, moving his guards aside, coming to a stop before Ban. He looked down from the lowest step. "It took true courage to do what you just did."

Ban lowered his head.

"However, we are charged with upholding the laws of this land. Your crime must be punished."

Ban nodded.

The prince went back to his throne and sat, rubbing his temples. "For the crime of treason against a Lord of the Council, you are hereby banished from the Principality, where you shall live out the remainder of your life in exile. From this moment foreword, no step you take shall bring you closer to this throne."

Ban breathed deeply. "Yes, my prince." He looked to Becks and Tyr then turned to walk away. Unsurprisingly, they followed him.

He looked up as he left, seeing Lord Holland as he leaned over the railing, fuming.

The man's hate-filled eyes spoke the promise that their feud had only just begun.

"Where shall we go?" Riest leaned forward, curiously studying the holographic sphere on the *Forge*'s bridge.

Sidna looked out into the Never, watching a waterfall pour down the side of a floating island, falling into nothingness. "I don't care."

Riest didn't seem to mind her depressed tone. "Perhaps one of my fortresses has survived. A useful remnant of the past might still remain."

"I doubt it." She swallowed, her stomach sinking as she felt a surge in remorse. "Everything dies."

Riest tilted his head to the side. "Not everything."

Right. Only the people I care about.

She crossed her arms, looking past him to the monster. "Does it have to do that?"

The amorphous creature looked expectantly at the group of Elcosians that gathered around it, speaking as it rose above them. Their eyes were wide, and they watched its every move.

Riest waved his hand. "They are enthralled." He motioned to the rest of the bridge, where Elcosians worked their stations. "Be glad for it. They serve our purposes, for now. You would've had to kill them, otherwise."

Sidna wrung her hands together. "How do you know all of this? Who are you?"

He spread his hands wide. "As I said, a guide. Nothing more."

"A guide to what, exactly."

"To power. To . . . retribution. Whatever you desire."

"All I want is for my people to be left alone."

He narrowed his eyes and smirked. "Truly? You've never wished to be . . . more? Why, your very nature is energy, wild and chaotic."

"Like I said, I only want this power for my people."

Riest seemed insulted. "And let others take your glory? I will not allow it! I am *your* teacher alone."

She shook her head. "I can't do this by myself. We *all* have to be strong."

He walked to her and held out his hands, taking her by the shoulders. "My dear Sidna. There is nothing you cannot do. You can destroy entire fleets. You can burn worlds. You have access to untapped power that can change the galaxy into whatever you desire."

A woman stood up and left her station, walking over to the ephmere. She looked up in awe at the creature, excited and seemingly unafraid.

Sidna shivered. "What's to stop that thing from taking control of me?"

"You? It wouldn't dare! A man would sooner blot out the sun and live in darkness."

She shivered again.

Somehow, I think it wouldn't mind.

Riest smiled and gently turned her toward the holographic map. "But these are topics for another time." He walked to the translucent violet sphere. "Where would you like to go?"

She looked back to the monster one more time then closed her eyes. "Home."

Tieger limped down the corridor, leaning on Commander Prime as they walked. His free hand scraped the nearest wall as he pulled himself forward.

"You need to rest, Honored One."

"No." He looked down at her. There was no way of knowing whose blood soaked the side of her armor, hers or his. There was also a curious white substance splattered along her sword arm. "I will rest when I have returned to the *Forge*."

"I have not been able to reach the bridge, but I will continue to try."

The booming sound of a thunderclap caused them to halt near a doorway. They followed the path through the rooms on the other side until they entered something like a holy place.

Across from the entrance, a breach in the side wall led out into the jungle. The thunder had come from the storm beyond it.

At last, the way out.

They shuffled toward it but stopped when they heard voices.

" . . . as you foretold."

They moved closer, taking cover behind one of many huge stone columns. Tieger peered around it.

A ghostly form, skeletal and decayed, floated into view. "They *are* mine, but of course, they are at your disposal as well." Its voice was dry and rough like the stagnant air inside an ancient crypt.

Behind the terrible apparition, there were well over one hundred men and women forming a crowd, many of them dressed crudely in the leather and cloth of pirates, with just as many in the violet armor of Tieger's embers. They simply stood there, unconcerned.

A shadowed figure walked into view. He removed his hood, and Tieger nearly dropped to one knee.

It was the spy.

The specter floated around the spy and motioned to the crowd with its bony hand. "I have replenished my congregation. What do you think?"

The spy smiled his frustrating smile. "I think I *will* want to borrow them in the future, Mortrythe. In fact, there are a couple I already have my eyes on."

Tieger followed his gaze. Two figures stepped out of the crowd, eyes glowing bright red: a man in green armor with a cape and a rifle, obviously an Aeturnian Ranger.

Next to him, another man stood proudly with long dark hair, holding a slender, curved sword and wearing a flowing red cloak.

"Surely they are nothing compared to your own minion."

"Who? Tieger? Yes, he served his purpose fantastically."

My purpose?

The spy smiled and laughed. "The fool has chased the girl straight into Riest's waiting arms."

"And the dark ones? They will come?"

"It has already begun." He turned to the two thralls that stood before the crowd. "Until then, you will send these two to hunt the girl. She must never be allowed to feel a relief from fear."

The wraith lowered its head slightly in a bow of respect. "Of course, my lord. Only a fool would deny Resh Gal."

Olivia slapped Fall's hand. "Be still. I'm almost done."

"You sure this is—"

"I said, *be still.*"

"Just be careful," he said.

"Baby."

"What?"

Hermes put his feet up on the end of the bed. "She said you're a baby." He took a swig of booze then held it out to Fall while he swallowed. "Want some?"

Fall looked down at his stomach. Olivia tied off the last knot, pulling the wound's farthest end shut. He took the rusty metal flask and drank from it. "Ugh . . . you trying to kill me with this stuff?"

The imp scoffed. "Give it back if you can't handle it."

"No way. Not with the torturer at work here."

Olivia took off her gloves and sat back with a sigh. "The torturer is done. I'm sad to say I gathered no useful information through your whimpering and tears."

Fall touched the skin near the wounds and grimaced. "You sure this is going to hold?"

She motioned to the sick bay. "This equipment's ancient, but it works. Might leave a scar."

Fall looked around. The sick bay was cramped, with only enough room for two patient tables. There were cabinets on the walls, full of bottles and small paper boxes. A computer terminal was set into the wall with a small desk that faced the tables, and the open supply closet next to it had a fallen shelf blocking the way inside.

"I guess you did the best you could."

She rolled her eyes. "I'll be sure to send you the bill."

Fall nodded with a smile. "I'll take it out of your pay."

She crossed her arms. "About that. I think we should be partners. Split the profits."

"Is that right?" Fall rolled over on his side to say a little more and instantly regretted it. He grabbed his stomach. "Wow. That stings."

She reached over and gently pushed him back down. "You need to rest."

He yawned. "Yeah. I think that sedative's kicking in anyway."

Olivia nodded. "Doctor's orders. We'll continue our negotiations later." She took his hand and squeezed it gently. "Try to get some sleep."

"Thanks. Try not to break my ship while I'm asleep."

"It wouldn't take much." She stopped before leaving. "I'll check in on you later. Sostek should have us close to the next T-Gate soon."

"Nice . . ." He was already starting to fall asleep.

She turned out the light and left, leaving him in the cool, quiet room.

It wasn't long before he drifted away into a dream with a content smile.

"Oh, hey. I didn't know you were in here." Sidna paused halfway into the cockpit. *"I'll just—"*

Fall sat up with a start. "Sorry. Just watching the erini. Need the computer?"

She looked down to her boots. "No, I actually came to do the same thing."

Fall motioned to Mei's chair. "If you don't mind sharing the view, be my guest."

Sidna sat in the pilot's seat, soft ice-blue glow from the screens lighting her cheeks. "Mei would probably kill me if she saw me here."

"Stare you to death with that creepy eye?"

Sidna turned her head and smiled. "Which one?"

Fall raised his eyebrows. "Good point."

Their laughter faded, and the background silence of all but the engines set in as they looked out into the Rift and over the Never.

She broke the tension a few moments later. "So, where's yours?"

Fall leaned back and rested his head on his interlocked fingers. He turned to look at her. "Huh?"

"Your ship, I mean. Mei said Rangers have ships. What happened to yours?"

He shrugged. "I don't have one yet."

She gave him a wry grin. "So, you're like a little baby Ranger?"

His cheeks burned. "No, that's just how we start out. Unless you're rich, that is. But why would anyone with money want this job?"

She seemed to think about that. "I figured you all have your reasons."

They both fell quiet again. A purple streak built along the Never's edge, traveling all the way up to the Rìluò before it zoomed on by.

"The Lonely Lantern."

She looked over. "Hmm?"

"The Lantern. That's what I'll call my ship. It's from a story."

"Oh yeah?"

Fall shrugged. "My dad might have made it up. That or he found it in some old book." He turned over in the chair to face her. "Ever been on the water's edge late at night?"

She smiled uneasily. "Maybe. I don't know."

"I bet you have. Anyway, at night, if a moon is out, it reflects on the water."

She looked up in thought. "Oh yeah. I have seen that."

"All right. One time, when I was a little kid, I told my dad it looked like a stairway leading up to the moon. That's when he told me about the Lantern. He said if I was lucky, I might just find a stairway one night that leads up to a solitary light out in space, sitting in a creaky little boat, floating along in the sea of stars. He said it rocks up and down on the Rift currents, somehow managing to stay lit, even when no one's there to see it."

She frowned. "It does sound lonely."

He raised his eyebrows. "Hence the name." He looked back ahead. "So then I asked him why. What purpose does it serve? If no one can see it, what good does it do? He said it doesn't matter if no one can see it, it only matters that the light never goes out. As long as it's out there shining, the darkness can never fully take over, even at the end of time when all the stars have burned themselves out."

"Wow."

He looked over and frowned, thinking she was being sarcastic. "I mean, it sounded cool at the time."

"It still does. I'm just giving you a hard time." She looked off with a smile, though it wasn't long before it faded. Her thoughts had returned to another place.

His eyes drifted to the chronometer. He sat up with a groan and rubbed his face. "Well, I think I'd better get some sleep before we get to Gyre. It's been a rough few days."

She snapped out of her trance and looked back over. "Oh. Yeah, sure."

He got up and walked to the hatch. "Hey."

She turned around.

"I hope you find what you're looking for."

Her hand drifted into her jacket pocket, grasping something inside. "Um, yeah. Me too." She turned back around and looked ahead, lost again in contemplation.

He turned to leave, stepping through the hatch to meet the chilled air.

"It's a good name."

He turned when she spoke.

She leaned back and looked at him upside down. "For your ship, I mean."

"Thanks." He reached up to rub his neck as he backed out of the cockpit. "Maybe one day, when everything works out, we'll see it together."

MATT DIGMAN

Matt Digman is exactly one half the creative force
behind the epic fantasy space opera novel,
The Dark That Dwells.
Born and raised in Arkansas, he spent his free time
studying Star Wars technical manuals, searching for
his next favorite RPG, and watching his Star Trek:
TNG VHS tapes until they fell apart. Basically,
he was nerdy when nerdy wasn't cool.
He currently works as a pediatric emergency medicine
physician in Alabama and writes when he
ought to be sleeping.

RYAN RODDY

Ryan Roddy grew up across the southeast, chasing
her dream of becoming a professional actress. Though
she eventually traded the stage for a stethoscope,
she never gave up her love for great storytelling—
or for playing dress up as an adult.
Now she works as a pediatric emergency medicine
physician to afford her cosplay and Disney obsessions.
She loves the characters she's written for *The Dark
That Dwells* with her husband almost as much
as she loves him and their four dogs.